THE BEST SHORT STORIES of the MODERN AGE

Premier Books are designed to bring to a larger reading public outstanding books at small cost

THE BEST SHORT STORIES of the MODERN AGE

Edited by

Douglas Angus

A Premier Book

FAWCETT PUBLICATIONS, INC., GREENWICH, CONN.

MEMBER OF AMERICAN BOOK PUBLISHERS COUNCIL, INC.

The editor and publisher wish to thank all those who have contributed to this volume:

GOOSEBERRIES, reprinted from **The Portable Chekhov,** translated by Avrahm Yarmolinsky, by permission of The Viking Press, Inc. Copyright 1947 by The Viking Press, Inc.
THE TREE OF KNOWLEDGE, reprinted from **The Soft Side** by Henry James, copyright 1900 by Henry James, by permission of Paul R. Reynolds & Son, 599 Fifth Avenue, New York 17, New York.
THE CAT, A GOLDFINCH AND THE STARS, reprinted from **Horse in the Moon** by Luigi Pirandello, translated by Samuel Putnam, by permission of E. P. Dutton & Co., Inc. Copyright, 1932 and renewed 1960 by E. P. Dutton & Co., Inc.
YOUTH, reprinted from **Youth: A Narrative and Two Other Stories** by Joseph Conrad, by permission of J. M. Dent and Sons, Ltd., London. Copyright, 1903, by Doubleday & Co., Inc., New York, and J. H. Dent and Sons, Ltd., Messrs. William Blackwood and the Trustees of the Conrad Estate, London.
THE ROCKING-HORSE WINNER reprinted from **The Lovely Lady** by D. H. Lawrence. Included in **The Portable D. H. Lawrence,** Copyright 1933 by the Estate of D. H. Lawrence, by permission of The Viking Press, Inc.
BLISS, reprinted from **The Short Stories of Katherine Mansfield** by Katherine Mansfield, by permission of Alfred A. Knopf, Inc. Copyright 1920, 1937 by Alfred A. Knopf, Inc. Canada with permission of The Society of Authors as the literary representative of the Estate of the late Miss Katherine Mansfield.
THE DEAD, reprinted from **The Dubliners** by James Joyce, by permission of The Viking Press, Inc. All rights reserved.
LITTLE HERR FRIEDEMANN, reprinted from **Stories of Three Decades** by Thomas Mann by permission of Alfred A. Knopf, Inc. Copyright 1936 by Alfred A. Knopf, Inc.
SOPHISTICATION, reprinted from **Winesburg, Ohio** by Sherwood Anderson by permission of The Viking Press, Inc. Copyright 1919 by B. W. Huebsch, 1947 by Eleanor Copenhaver Anderson.
THE STORY OF MY DOVECOT, reprinted from **The Collected Stories of Isaac Babel.** Copyright 1955 by Criterion Books, Inc., by permission of the publishers.
THE DEVIL AND DANIEL WEBSTER, reprinted from **The Selected Works of Stephen Vincent Benét,** Holt, Rinehart and Winston, Inc.; Copyright, 1936, by The Curtis Publishing Company; Copyright, 1936, by Stephen Vincent Benét; by permission of Brandt & Brandt.
A ROSE FOR EMILY, reprinted from **Collected Stories of William Faulkner** by permission of Random House, Inc. Copyright 1930 and renewed 1957 by William Faulkner.
THE METAMORPHOSIS, Part One, reprinted from **The Metamorphosis** by Franz Kafka, published by The Vanguard Press, Inc.
THE WALL, reprinted from **Intimacy** by Jean-Paul Sartre, translated by Lloyd Alexander by permission of New Directions. Copyright 1948 by New Directions.
JUDAS, reprinted from **More Stories by Frank O'Connor** by Frank O'Connor by permission of Alfred A. Knopf, Inc. Copyright 1948, 1954 by Frank O'Connor. Canada with permission of Harold Matson Company.
OF THIS TIME, OF THAT PLACE, reprinted by permission of Lionel Trilling; Copyright 1943 by Lionel Trilling.
THE LOTTERY, reprinted from **The Lottery** by Shirley Jackson, by permission of Farrar, Straus and Cudahy, Inc. Copyright 1949 by Shirley Jackson, 1948 by The New Yorker Magazine, Inc. Originally published by **The New Yorker.**
THE LEDGE, reprinted by permission of Lawrence S. Hall. Copyright 1959 by Lawrence S. Hall. Originally published by **The Hudson Review.**

Third Premier printing, March 1964

Premier Books are published by Fawcett World Library, 67 West 44th Street, New York 36, New York.
Printed in the United States of America.

CONTENTS

INTRODUCTION

Perhaps it is some kinship between the short-story form and the urgency of the modern age that explains why, with hardly any marketing outlets, with little reward to the author in either fame or money, the short story continues to be a rich and fertile strain of literary expression. At its best, it achieves a degree of perfection rarely attained by the novel. Indeed, the distinctive power and beauty of the short story are involved in its very brevity, the discipline of its strict limits challenging the writer to ever more brilliant inventiveness in such areas as symbolism, suggestiveness and plotting.

By far the most remarkable era in the long history of the short story is the modern period. This astonishing flowering of the form, which has already lasted over a century and shows no sign of waning, originated in the works of three nineteenth-century masters—Poe, Maupassant, and Chekhov. The literary renaissance which they inaugurated is represented, in all its richness and diversity, by the stories in this book.

From Poe came the idea that power and unity could best be achieved within the brief limits of short works of fiction. His best stories, as typified by "The Tell-Tale Heart," are as moving today as when they were written. But Poe's art lay in the direction of fantasy, symbolism and surrealism, and it remained for Maupassant to reveal how the short story could be shaped into a crisp and penetrating interpretation of everyday reality. The careful construction, the selective eye, and the ever-dominant intelligence, now savagely ironical, now gently humorous, all contribute to making Maupassant's short stories equal in quality to the finest nineteenth-century novels. However, before the short story could attain its distinctive modern form, it had to enter one more important phase—impressionism.

Impressionism is the gateway to modernism for all the arts. It is the phase in art that corresponds to the refinement of analysis in science that has so enlarged man's knowledge and altered his way of life during the past one hundred years. It is distinguished by a greatly increased subtlety, complexity and fluidity in the treatment of light in painting, of tone and atmosphere in music, and of character in literature. It entered literature chiefly through the creative genius of a writer of short stories—Anton Chekhov, whose sympathetic little story "Gooseberries" remains today a masterpiece of the impressionistic technique.

The impact of Chekhov's art may be seen in the works of a variety of twentieth-century European writers, ranging from Katherine Mansfield's brilliant satire "Bliss," for example, to the exotic sea stories of Joseph Conrad. The new method was introduced into America after World War I by Hemingway and by Sherwood Anderson, whose story "Sophistication" is one of the finest examples of early impressionism in America. There followed in this country, partly at least due to the stimulus of this new mode of writing, a development of the short story unequalled by any other country. A few names taken at random of writers of impressionistic stories of high quality are Kay Boyle, Katherine Anne Porter, John Cheever, Dorothy Canfield Fisher, Peter Taylor, John Updike, Irwin Shaw, Lionel Trilling, Truman Capote, and Flannery O'Connor. It is possible, however, that this mode of writing reached its apex in the best work of William Faulkner, as represented by his unforgettable impressionistic analysis of the decay of the South in "A Rose for Emily."

Impressionism has not been an unmixed blessing. It has led to a proliferation of brief "slice of life" stories of facile, undisciplined, and superficial brilliance, lacking memorability and breadth of view. Even though many of these stories generate considerable dramatic tension, a vital part of the reader is not touched or committed. Consequently, the effort has been made in the present collection to select only stories of enduring value, in which the writer has commented with arresting earnestness and penetration upon contemporary society.

The term *impressionism* does not, of course, cover the

wide range of the modern short story. It does not include entirely the poetic insight of Pirandello, nor the stylistic achievement of Henry James, nor the important contribution of such an original genius as D. H. Lawrence. Lawrence's famous story "The Rocking-Horse Winner" shows how tragedy may result from the hidden workings of the unconscious. That limitless sea of nodal swirls, inner conflicts, of dark and guilt-laden secrets and uncontrollable storms of passion which, for Lawrence, is the human soul represents in art the major shift in modern man's comprehension of his own psyche, and makes Lawrence a writer of great historical significance.

With the story "The Dead" we come in contact with the writer whom many consider to be the greatest literary genius of the twentieth century—James Joyce. If such an estimate is correct, it is because Joyce has assimilated for purposes of his art the widest and deepest awareness of the significant social, religious, psychological and metaphysical insights of his time. Gabriel, the hero of "The Dead," like Leopold Bloom, the hero of *Ulysses,* is the literary prototype of the new mass man, the white-collar worker, an individual without roots, beliefs, loyalties, or idealism. In truth, he is a cubistic figure—the modern relativity man, sliced and segmented by innumerable social pressures, surviving myths, and hidden complexes. In Joyce's great story we see this new type of hero almost overwhelmed by the multitudinous anxieties, frustrations, and endlessly accumulating fragments of knowledge that fill his large, restless intelligence. His compulsion to analyze everything, even love, undermines the old simplicities of passion, and so he cannot awaken desire in his pretty country wife.

Some writers have reacted to the complexity of modern civilization by turning to violence and more primitive rules of conduct. Thomas Mann, on the other hand, endeavors to capture the multi-hued subtlety of a decaying society by the use of symbols and the repetition of motifs after the manner of music. These qualities are brilliantly developed in his moving story, "Little Herr Friedemann."

All in all, the short story of the age of analysis and anxiety does not depict man in an heroic guise or reflect any deep, abiding faith in his destiny. In the works of those European writers of the thirties and forties who came under the influence of existentialism, the most important philosophical influence upon fiction during these years, the devaluation of man plumbed new depths of despair. Finding the outer aims of life meaningless in an absurd universe, the existentialist turned inward in search of the essence of man. This reversal of the natural outward orientation of the mind only heightened his sense of disillusionment. Thus Sartre finds at the center of man a nothing, a "Not" as he puts it. This is what happens to the hero of Sartre's most important story, "The Wall," a hero with no future since he is going to be executed in the morning. With no future, and therefore with no outer purpose, it is his tragic discovery that he himself has become no more than a thing of flesh and bones, a badly functioning organism.

In the works of Kafka, existentialism and surrealism combine to produce the strangest and most original short stories of the twentieth century. Here a personal symbolism is so poignant that it fairly bursts through the barriers of such a private art to communicate to the reader Kafka's terrible vision of existence. In his amazing story, "The Metamorphosis," we follow a dream which appears to recreate symbolically Kafka's own oppressive inferiority complex, its origin in an unfortunate father-son relationship, and his crushing sense of exclusion and futility. His symbol of modern man—a great black beetle lying on its back with its many legs threshing ineffectually—marks perhaps the highest point of horror attained by expressionistic symbolism in modern fiction.

It would seem impossible to go beyond the "Not" of Sartre and the "Black beetle" of Kafka in man's self-devaluation, and one should look for a counteraction to the intensely somber tone that has prevailed in literature from the last quarter of the nineteenth century to the present. In this connection, the undermining of scientific determinism by the uncertainty principle of quantum physics, and the new evolutionary synthesis broadened to cover the entire range of natural and social phenomena now offer the metaphysical basis for a more positive evaluation of man and a more meaningful conception of the universe than prevailed during the age of analysis. Metaphysically, existentialism is outdated. Man is no longer an insignificant accident in an immense and indifferent universe, but the very center and foreshoot of the vast evolutionary process. This is not to say that an easy optimism prevails among contemporary writers in the presence of the momentous crisis now facing all mankind. Yet the broadest view of man's destiny perceives human consciousness involved in a dramatic and heroic race against catastrophe; it is essentially a tragic-heroic view. Evidence of such a shift may already be seen in the increased dignity and symbolic power of the tragic hero in such works as Pierre Boulle's *The Bridge on the River Kwai,* Romain Gary's *Roots of Heaven* and a number of other novels. It is also interesting to note that in 1960, for the first time in its long history, the O. Henry Memorial first prize was given to a story in which the hero is tragic in the uncompromising, stark classical tradition. The story is "The Ledge" by Lawrence Sargent Hall, and it is because of its possible special significance that it has been selected to close this anthology.

There remain a few stories of unusual interest in this collection that are outside of the main contemporary developments. One of these is Isaac Babel's "The Story of My Dovecot." Babel has only recently been discovered, but he is already recognized to be the most significant short-story writer yet to appear in Communist Russia. Somehow this essentially non-Communist artist managed, through an irony too subtle for his Bolshevik masters to detect, to produce a few vital masterpieces before he was finally destroyed by the Soviet system.

Stephen Vincent Benét's American classic "The Devil and Daniel Webster" also belongs in a special class. In this story Benét, through sheer wit and invention, has raised the primitive American tall story to a high level of sophisticated art. Again, in Shirley Jackson's remarkable story "The Lottery," which caused such a sensation when it first appeared in *The New Yorker,* still another important, special type of story is illustrated. This story reveals the influence of modern sociology and historical analysis upon contemporary fiction. It may well be a type of story of increasing significance, a type that invents special kinds of society to delineate important artistic truths.

Finally, Frank O'Connor's story "Judas" was included, not because it is a story of unusual profundity but because of the rarity, and therefore special value, of its warmth and humor in an age of anxiety and disillusionment.

The reader will find this collection unusually comprehensive, although inevitably a few familiar names had to be omitted. Every effort has been made not only to select stories highly entertaining and teachable, but also to select wh-

possible the most historically significant work of each major writer, so that the main trends of the modern short story would be truly represented. The result is that within the brief limits of this book will be found a remarkably inclusive record of the odyssey of man's soul during the past eventful hundred years.

DOUGLAS ANGUS

THE TELL-TALE HEART

Edgar Allan Poe

Born in Boston in 1809 of actor parents, Poe was left an orphan at the age of three and was brought up by John Allan of Richmond, Virginia. He attended school in England, the University of Virginia for one year, and West Point for a short time. Poet, editor, literary critic and short-story writer, he, as much as any other writer, deserves the name of father of the modern short story. His story "The Murders in the Rue Morgue" (1841) is considered to be the first detective story. "The Tell-Tale Heart" (1843) is one of his finest tales of psychological horror.

True!—nervous—very, very dreadfully nervous I had been and am! but why *will* you say that I am mad? The disease had sharpened my senses—not destroyed—not dulled them. Above all was the sense of hearing acute. I heard all things in the heaven and in the earth. I heard many things in hell. How, then, am I mad? Hearken! and observe how healthily—how calmly I can tell you the whole story.

It is impossible to tell how first the idea entered my brain; but once conceived, it haunted me day and night. Object there was none. Passion there was none. I loved the old man. He had never wronged me. He had never given me insult. For his gold I had no desire. I think it was his eye! Yes, it was this! One of his eyes resembled that of a vulture—a pale blue eye, with a film over it. Whenever it fell upon me, my blood ran cold; and so by degrees—very gradually—I made up my mind to take the life of the old man, and thus rid myself of the eye forever.

Now this is the point. You fancy me mad. Madmen know nothing. But you should have seen *me*. You should have seen how wisely I proceeded—with what caution—with what foresight—with what dissimulation I went to work!

I was never kinder to the old man than during the whole week before I killed him. And every night, about midnight, I turned the latch of his door and opened it—oh, so gently! And then, when I had made an opening sufficient for my head, I put in a dark lantern, all closed, closed, so that no light shone out, and then I thrust in my head. Oh, you would have laughed to see how cunningly I thrust it in! I moved it slowly—very, very slowly, so that I might not disturb the old man's sleep. It took me an hour to place my whole head within the opening so far that I could see him as he lay upon his bed. Ha!—would a madman have been so wise as this? And then, when my head was well in the room, I undid the lantern cautiously—oh, so cautiously—cautiously (for the hinges creaked)—I undid it just so much that a single thin ray fell upon the vulture eye. And this I did for seven long nights—every night just at midnight—but I found the eye always closed; and so it was impossible to do the work; for it was not the old man who vexed me, but his Evil Eye. And every morning, when the day broke, I went boldly into the chamber, and spoke courageously to him, calling him by name in a hearty tone, and inquiring how he had passed the night. So you see he would have been a very profound old man, indeed, to suspect that every night, just at twelve, I looked in upon him while he slept.

Upon the eighth night I was more than usually cautious in opening the door. A watch's minute hand moves more quickly than did mine. Never before that night had I *felt* the extent of my own powers—of my sagacity. I could scarcely contain my feelings of triumph. To think that there I was, opening the door, little by little, and he not even to dream of my secret deeds or thoughts. I fairly chuckled at the idea; and perhaps he heard me; for he moved on the bed suddenly, as if startled. Now you may think that I drew back—but no. His room was as black as pitch with the thick darkness (for the shutters were close fastened, through fear of robbers), and so I knew that he could not see the opening of the door, and I kept pushing it on steadily, steadily.

I had my head in, and was about to open the lantern, when

my thumb slipped upon the tin fastening, and the old man sprang up in bed, crying out: "Who's there?"

I kept quite still and said nothing. For a whole hour I did not move a muscle, and in the meantime I did not hear him lie down. He was still sitting up in the bed listening;—just as I have done, night after night, hearkening to the death watches in the wall.

Presently I heard a slight groan, and I knew it was the groan of mortal terror. It was not a groan of pain or grief—oh no!—it was the low stifled sound that arises from the bottom of the soul when overcharged with awe. I knew the sound well. Many a night, just at midnight, when all the world slept, it has welled up from my own bosom, deepening, with its dreadful echo, the terrors that distracted me. I say I knew it well. I knew what the old man felt, and pitied him, although I chuckled at heart. I knew that he had been lying awake ever since the first slight noise, when he had turned in the bed. His fears had been ever since growing upon him. He had been trying to fancy them causeless, but could not. He had been saying to himself: "It is nothing but the wind in the chimney—it is only a mouse crossing the floor," or "it is merely a cricket which has made a single chirp." Yes, he had been trying to comfort himself with these suppositions; but he had found all in vain. *All in vain;* because Death, in approaching him, had stalked with his black shadow before him, and enveloped the victim. And it was the mournful influence of the unperceived shadow that caused him to feel—although he neither saw nor heard—to *feel* the presence of my head within the room.

When I had waited a long time, very patiently, without hearing him lie down, I resolved to open a little—a very, very little crevice in the lantern. So I opened it—you cannot imagine how stealthily, stealthily—until, at length, a single dim ray, like the thread of the spider, shot from out the crevice and full upon the vulture eye.

It was open—wide, wide open—and I grew furious as I gazed upon it. I saw it with perfect distinctness—all a dull blue, with a hideous veil over it that chilled the very marrow in my bones; but I could see nothing else of the old man's face or person: for I had directed the ray, as if by instinct, precisely upon the damned spot.

And now—have I not told you that what you mistake for madness is but over-acuteness of the senses?—now, I say, there came to my ears a low, dull, quick sound, such as a watch makes when enveloped in cotton. I knew *that* sound well too. It was the beating of the old man's heart. It increased my fury, as the beating of a drum stimulates the soldier into courage.

But even yet I refrained and kept still. I scarcely breathed. I held the lantern motionless. I tried how steadily I could maintain the ray upon the eye. Meantime the hellish tattoo of the heart increased. It grew quicker and quicker, and louder and louder every instant. The old man's terror *must* have been extreme! It grew louder, I say, louder every moment!—do you mark me well? I have told you that I am nervous: so I am. And now at the dead hour of night, amid the dreadful silence of that old house, so strange a noise as this excited me to uncontrollable terror. Yet, for some minutes longer I refrained and stood still. But the beating grew louder, louder! I thought the heart must burst. And now a new anxiety seized me—the sound would be heard by a neighbor! The old man's hour had come! With a loud yell, I threw open the lantern and leaped into the room. He shrieked once —once only. In an instant I dragged him to the floor, and pulled the heavy bed over him. I then smiled gaily, to find the deed so far done. But, for many minutes, the heart beat on with a muffled sound. This, however, did not vex me; it would not be heard through the wall. At length it ceased. The old man was dead. I removed the bed and examined the corpse. Yes, he was stone, stone dead. I placed my hand upon the heart and held it there many minutes. There was no pulsation. He was stone dead. His eye would trouble me no more.

If still you think me mad, you will think so no longer when I describe the wise precautions I took for the concealment of the body. The night waned, and I worked hastily, but in silence. First of all I dismembered the corpse. I cut off the head and the arms and the legs.

I then took up three planks from the flooring of the chamber, and deposited all between the scantlings. I then replaced the boards so cleverly, so cunningly, that no human eye—not even *his*—could have detected anything wrong. There was nothing to wash out—no stain of any kind—no blood-spot whatever. I had been too wary for that. A tub had caught all—ha! ha!

When I had made an end of these labors, it was four o'clock —still dark as midnight. As the bell sounded the hour, there came a knocking at the street door. I went down to open it with a light heart—for what had I *now* to fear? There entered three men, who introduced themselves, with perfect suavity, as officers of the police. A shriek had been heard by a neighbor during the night: suspicion of foul play had been aroused; information had been lodged at the police office, and they (the officers) had been deputed to search the premises.

I smiled—for *what* had I to fear? I bade the gentlemen welcome. The shriek, I said, was my own in a dream. The old man, I mentioned, was absent in the country. I took my visitors all over the house. I bade them search—search *well*. I led them, at length, to *his* chamber. I showed them his treasures, secure, undisturbed. In the enthusiasm of my confidence, I brought chairs into the room, and desired them *here* to rest from their fatigues, while I myself, in the wild audacity of my perfect triumph, placed my own seat upon the very spot beneath which reposed the corpse of the victim.

The officers were satisfied. My *manner* had convinced them. I was singularly at ease. They sat, and while I answered cheerily, they chatted familiar things. But, ere long, I felt myself getting pale and wished them gone. My head ached, and I fancied a ringing in my ears: but still they sat and still chatted. The ringing became more distinct:—it continued and became more distinct: I talked more freely to get rid of the feeling: but it continued and gained definiteness—until, at length, I found that the noise was *not* within my ears.

No doubt I now grew *very* pale;—but I talked more fluently, and with a heightened voice. Yet the sound increased —and what could I do? It was *a low, dull, quick sound—much such a sound as a watch makes when enveloped in cotton*. I gasped for breath—and yet the officers heard it not. I talked more quickly—more vehemently; but the noise steadily increased. Why *would* they not be gone? I paced the floor to and fro with heavy strides, as if excited to fury by the observation of the men—but the noise steadily increased. Oh, God; what *could* I do? I foamed—I raved—I swore! I swung the chair upon which I had been sitting, and grated it upon the boards, but the noise arose over all and continually increased. It grew louder—louder—*louder!* And still the men chatted pleasantly, and smiled. Was it possible they heard not? Almighty God!—no, no! They heard!—they suspected—they *knew!*—they were making a *mockery* of my horror!—this

I thought, and this I think. But anything was better than this agony! Anything was more tolerable than this derision! I could bear those hypocritical smiles no longer! I felt that I must scream or die!—and now again!—hark! louder! louder! *louder!*—

"Villains!" I shrieked, "dissemble no more! I admit the deed!—tear up the planks!—here, here!—it is the beating of his hideous heart!"

THE JEWELS

Guy de Maupassant

Guy de Maupassant is one of the handful of great short-story writers of the nineteenth century. Born in 1850, he became a protégé of Flaubert, and an important influence upon the development of the modern short story. He died in 1893. Maupassant is considered a "naturalist," writing about ordinary people without sentimentalism or romantic idealism. "The Jewels" is not so well known as his other great story about jewels and women, "The Necklace," but its irony is more complex and more profound. Little in fiction is quite so coolly sardonic as the subtle conclusion to this memorable story.

Having met the young girl at a party at the home of the under-secretary of his office, M. Lantin was caught in the web of love.

She was the daughter of a provincial tax collector who had been dead several years. She had then come to Paris with her mother, who made friends with some middle-class families in the neighborhood in hopes of marrying off the young lady. They were poor and respectable, gentle and sweet. The young girl seemed the perfect type of upright young woman to whom the wise young man dreams of entrusting his future. Her simple beauty had the charm of an angelic modesty, and the faint smile which never left her lips seemed a reflection of her heart.

Translated by Sylvia Angus.

Everybody sang her praises; all those who knew her repeated endlessly: "Ah happy man who will get her. One could not find a better." M. Lantin, then chief book keeper to the Minister of the Interior, making thirty-five hundred francs a year, proposed to her and married her.

He was incredibly happy with her. She ran her home with such adroit economy that they seemed to live in luxury. There were no attentions, delicacies, or bits of playfulness that she did not provide for her husband; and the seductiveness of her person was so great that six years after their meeting he loved her more than in the first days.

He criticized her for only two tastes, her passion for the theatre and her love for imitation jewels.

Her friends (she knew several wives of minor officials) were always getting her tickets for plays which were the rage, even for first nights; and she dragged her husband, with or without his consent, to these diversions which tired him horribly after his day's work. He eventually begged her to go with some lady of her acquaintance who would bring her back afterward. She was slow to agree to this, since she thought it improper. Finally, however, she complied and he was immensely grateful.

However, this taste for the theatre soon made her want to adorn herself. Her clothes remained simple, to be sure, always in good taste, but modest; and her sweet grace, her irresistible grace, meek and smiling, seemed to acquire a new charm from this simplicity of dress, but she had the habit of hanging from her ears two large rhinestone earrings which were like imitation diamonds and she wore a necklace of false pearls, bracelets of an alloy like gold, and combs ornamented with various glass imitations of fine stones.

Her husband, who was a bit shocked by this love of glitter, often said, "My dear, when one hasn't the money to pay for real jewels, one should show off only one's beauty and charm. Those are the rarest jewels."

But she smiled sweetly and answered: "What can I do? It is my vice. I know you are right, but I can't change my character. I just adore jewels!"

And she would roll in her fingers the pearl necklaces, making the cut crystal facets flash, and saying again: "But look how well it is made. One would think it was genuine."

He smiled, saying, "You have the tastes of a gypsy."

Sometimes in the evening when they sat together near the fire, she would bring out on the table where they took their tea the morocco box in which she kept her collection of "junk," as M. Lantin called it; and she would examine these imitation jewels with passionate attention, as if she savored some deep secret joy; and she would insist on putting a necklace around her husband's neck, laughing heartily and crying "How funny you are!" Then she would throw herself in his arms and embrace him feverishly.

When she had been to the opera one evening in the winter, she returned home shivering with cold. The next day she began to cough. Eight days later she died from an inflammation of the lungs.

Lantin almost followed her into the grave. His despair was so terrible that his hair turned white in a month. He wept from morning to night, his heart torn by intolerable suffering, haunted by the memory, the smile, the voice, all the charms of the dead girl.

Time did not soften his grief. Often during his hours at work, when his colleagues were chatting of everyday events, one would see his cheeks swell, his nose pucker, his eyes fill with tears; he would make a dreadful face and begin to sob.

He had kept his wife's room untouched, and every day he shut himself up in it to think of her; all the furniture, even her clothes remained where they had been on her last day.

But life was now hard for him. His salary, which in his wife's hands, was sufficient for all the household needs, was now inadequate for him alone. And he asked himself with amazement how she had always been able to get for him fine wines and delicacies which he was no longer able to afford with his modest resources.

He contracted several debts and chased after money in the manner of men reduced in the world. At last one morning when he found himself without a cent a whole week before the end of the month, he thought of selling something; and at once the thought came to him of disposing of his wife's box of junk, because he still held in his heart a sort of rancor against the fakeries which had formerly irritated him. Even the sight of them every day had spoiled a little the memory of his beloved.

He searched for a long time in the heap of cheap jewelry

which she had left, for until the last days of her life she had bought them obstinately, bringing home almost every evening a new trinket, and he decided on a large necklace she had seemed to like especially, and which should be worth, he thought, six or eight francs because it was really very well made for an imitation.

He put it in his pocket and went to his office by way of the main boulevards, looking for a jeweler's shop which inspired confidence.

He saw one at last and entered, a little ashamed of displaying his poverty thus by attempting to sell something of so little value.

"Sir," he said to the merchant, "I would like very much to know your evaluation of this trifle."

The man took the thing, examined it, turned it about, tried its weight, looked at it through a magnifying glass, called his assistant, talked to him in whispers, put the necklace down again on the counter and looked at it from a distance so as to better judge the effect.

M. Lantin, annoyed by all these ceremonies, was about to open his mouth to say: "Oh, I know it has no value," when the jeweler said: "Sir, this is worth from twelve to fifteen thousand francs; but I would not be able to buy it unless you can tell me the owner."

The widower opened his eyes wide and stood gaping, not understanding. At last he stuttered: "What? . . . You are sure?"

The other misunderstood his astonishment and said in a dry tone: "You may search further if you think anyone will give you more. To me, it is worth, at the most, fifteen thousand francs. You can come back to me if you don't do better."

M. Lantin, like an idiot, took back his necklace and went out, obeying a confused need to be alone to think.

But as soon as he was in the street, the need to laugh seized him, and he thought: "The imbecile! Oh, the imbecile! If I had only taken him at his word. That's a jeweler for you; he can't tell the real from the fake!"

And he went into another jeweler's at the head of the Rue de La Paix. As soon as he saw the jewel, the jeweler cried:

"Ah, yes! I know this necklace well. It comes from my shop."

M. Lantin, much troubled, demanded: "What is it worth?"

"Sir, I sold it for twenty-five thousand. I am ready to buy it back for eighteen thousand, when you have told me, according to police regulations, where you got it."

This time M. Lantin sat down, paralyzed with astonishment. He replied: "But . . . But examine it carefully, Sir. I have thought until just now that it was . . . false."

The jeweler said: "Will you tell me your name, sir?"

"Certainly. My name is Lantin, I am employed at the Ministry of the Interior, and I live at 16, rue des Martyrs."

The merchant opened his registers, looked, and announced: "This necklace was sent to the address of Mme. Lantin, 16, rue des Martyrs, on July 20th, 1876."

And the two men looked each other in the eye, the government employee aghast with surprise, the jeweler suspecting a thief.

The latter said: "Will you leave me this article for just twenty-four hours if I give you a receipt?"

M. Lantin stammered: "Yes, certainly." And he left, folding the paper to put it in his pocket.

Then he crossed the street, went up it, saw that he had lost his way, went down again to the Tuileries, crossed the Seine, again realized his error, and returned to the Champs Elysées without a clear idea in his head. He forced himself to reason, to understand. His wife could not have bought an object of such value. No, surely not. But then, it was a gift! A gift from whom? Why?

He stopped and he stood there in the middle of the street. A horrible doubt plucked at him. She? But then, all the other jewels were also gifts! It seemed to him that the earth turned, that the tree before him was falling; he stretched out his arms and fell down unconscious.

He regained his consciousness in a drug store where passers-by had brought him. He got someone to take him home and shut himself in. Until nightfall he wept distractedly, biting a handkerchief to keep from crying out. Then he went to bed, overcome with fatigue and grief and slept heavily.

A ray of sun awakened him and he got up to go to his office. It was hard to work after such a shock. Then he thought he would have to excuse himself to his chief and he wrote to him. Then he thought he would return to the jeweler's shop; and shame stopped him. He stayed thinking for a long time. He could not, after all, leave the necklace with that man; he dressed and went out.

It was a beautiful day, the blue sky spread over a city which seemed to smile. Idlers strolled about, hands in their pockets.

Lantin said to himself as he watched them pass by: "How happy one is when one is rich! With money you can save yourself from all miseries, you go where you wish, you travel, you amuse yourself! Oh, if I were only rich!"

He realized that he was hungry, not having eaten since before his vigil. But his purse was empty and he remembered the necklace. Eighteen thousand francs! Eighteen thousand francs! *That* was certainly a sum!

He arrived at the rue de la Paix and began to walk back and forth on the pavement across from the shop. Eighteen thousand francs! Twenty times he started to enter; but shame always stopped him.

He was hungry, however, very hungry, and hadn't a cent. He decided abruptly, crossed the street at a run so as not to have time to think and burst through the door of the jeweler.

When he saw him, the merchant hurried over, offered him a seat with smiling courtesy. The assistants also came, looking sideways at Lantin with laughter in their eyes and on their lips.

The jeweler declared: "I have my information, sir, and if you are in agreement, I am ready to pay you the sum that I named."

The official stammered: "But, certainly!"

The jeweler took out of a drawer eighteen large bills, counted them and gave them to Lantin, who signed a little receipt and with a trembling hand, put the money in his purse.

Then, as he was going out, he turned to the merchant, who was still smiling, and dropping his eyes, said: "I have . . . I have other jewels . . . which came to me . . . from the same inheritance. Would it suit you to buy those too?"

The merchant bowed. "But certainly, sir."

One of the assistants went out to laugh at his ease; another blew his nose with vigor.

Lantin, impassive, red-faced and solemn, said: "I will bring them to you."

And he took a cab to go look for the jewels.

When he returned to the merchant an hour later, he had not yet eaten lunch. They began to examine the pieces one by one, assessing each. Almost all had come from that shop.

Lantin now showed a tendency to argue over the estimations, grew angry, demanded that they show him the books of sale, and talked louder and louder as the sum went up.

The big diamond earrings were worth twenty thousand francs, the bracelets thirty-five thousand, the pins, rings, and lockets sixteen thousand, an ornament of emeralds and sapphires fourteen thousand; a diamond solitaire on a gold chain forty thousand; the whole reached a total of a hundred and ninety-six thousand francs.

The merchant said with bantering good humor: "All this comes from a person whose savings were placed entirely in jewels."

Lantin said gravely: "It is a way, like any other, to invest one's money." And he went out, after having arranged with the purchaser that a confirming appraisal would take place the next day.

When he found himself in the street he looked at the Vendome column with the longing to climb it as though it were a greased pole. He felt so buoyant he thought he could play leap frog over the statue of the emperor perched on the top away up in the sky.

He went for lunch to Voisin's and drank wine at twenty francs a bottle.

Then he took a taxicab and rode in the Bois de Boulogne. He looked at the other vehicles with a certain scorn, filled with an urge to cry out to those passing by: "I am rich, too! I have two hundred thousand francs!"

Memory of his office returned. He had himself taken there, entered his boss's office boldly, and declared:

"I come, sir, to give you my resignation. I have just inherited three hundred thousand francs." He went around shaking hands with his old colleagues, and telling them of his plans for his new life; then he dined at the Café Anglais.

Finding himself near a distinguished-looking gentleman, he could not resist the itch to confide in him, with a certain coyness, that he had just inherited four hundred thousand francs.

For the first time in his life he was not bored at the theater and he spent the night with women.

Six months later, he married again. His second wife was completely respectable, but she had a difficult temperament. She made him suffer a good deal.

GOOSEBERRIES

Anton Chekhov

Anton Chekhov (1860–1904) was born in Taganrog, Russia. He studied medicine at the University of Moscow, supporting himself by hack-work journalism. Later, although he practiced medicine briefly, the drive to write took over his life. Today he is considered to be the father of modern literary impressionism. After Chekhov, truth in narrative becomes more intimate and more refined. Subtle exploration of character, mood, and situation with a vast and penetrating sympathy, together with a minimum attention to formal plot, are the distinguishing features of his work—all qualities that eventually come to dominate the modern short story.

The sky had been overcast since early morning; it was a still day, not hot, but tedious, as it usually is when the weather is gray and dull, when clouds have been hanging over the fields for a long time, and you wait for the rain that does not come. Ivan Ivanych, a veterinary, and Burkin, a high school teacher, were already tired with walking, and the plain seemed endless to them. Far ahead were the scarcely visible windmills of the village of Mironositzkoe; to the right lay a range of hills that disappeared in the distance beyond the village, and both of them knew that over there were the river, and fields, green willows, homesteads, and if you stood on one of the hills, you could see from there another vast plain, telegraph poles, and a train that from afar looked like a caterpillar crawling, and in clear weather you could even see the town. Now, when it was still and when nature seemed mild and pensive, Ivan Ivanych and Burkin were filled with love for this plain, and both of them thought what a beautiful land it was.

"Last time when we were in Elder Prokofy's barn," said Burkin, "you were going to tell me a story."

"Yes; I wanted to tell you about my brother."

Ivan Ivanych heaved a slow sigh and lit his pipe before beginning his story, but just then it began to rain. And five minutes later there was a downpour, and it was hard to tell when it would be over. The two men halted, at a loss; the dogs, already wet, stood with their tails between their legs and looked at them feelingly.

"We must find shelter somewhere," said Burkin. "Let's go to Alyohin's; it's quite near."

"Let's."

They turned aside and walked across a mown meadow, now going straight ahead, now bearing to the right, until they reached the road. Soon poplars came into view, a garden, then the red roofs of barns; the river gleamed, and the view opened on a broad expanse of water with a mill and a white bathing-cabin. That was Sofyino, Alyohin's place.

The mill was going, drowning out the sound of the rain; the dam was shaking. Wet horses stood near the carts, their heads drooping, and men were walking about, their heads covered with sacks. It was damp, muddy, dreary; and the water looked cold and unkind. Ivan Ivanych and Burkin felt cold and messy and uncomfortable through and through; their feet were heavy with mud and when, having crossed the dam, they climbed up to the barns, they were silent as though they were cross with each other.

The noise of a winnowing-machine came from one of the barns, the door was open, and clouds of dust were pouring from within. On the threshold stood Alyohin himself, a man of forty, tall and rotund, with long hair, looking more like a professor or an artist than a gentleman farmer. He was wearing a white blouse, badly in need of washing, that was belted with a rope, and drawers, and his high boots were plastered with mud and straw. His eyes and nose were black with dust. He recognized Ivan Ivanych and Burkin and was apparently very glad to see them.

"Please go up to the house, gentlemen," he said, smiling; "I'll be there directly, in a moment."

It was a large structure of two stories. Alyohin lived downstairs in what was formerly the stewards' quarters: two rooms that had arched ceilings and small windows; the furniture was plain, and the place smelled of rye bread, cheap vodka, and harness. He went into the showy rooms upstairs only rarely, when he had guests. Once in the house, the two visitors were met by a chambermaid, a young woman so beautiful that both of them stood still at the same moment and glanced at each other.

"You can't imagine how glad I am to see you, gentlemen," said Alyohin, joining them in the hall. "What a surprise! Pelageya," he said, turning to the chambermaid, "give the guests a change of clothes. And, come to think of it, I will change, too. But I must go and bathe first, I don't think I've had a wash since spring. Don't you want to go into the bathing-cabin? In the meanwhile things will be got ready here."

The beautiful Pelageya, with her soft, delicate air, brought them bath towels and soap, and Alyohin went to the bathing-cabin with his guests.

"Yes, it's a long time since I've bathed," he said, as he undressed. "I've an excellent bathing-cabin, as you see—it was put up by my father—but somehow I never find time to use it." He sat down on the steps and lathered his long hair and neck, and the water around him turned brown.

"I say—" observed Ivan Ivanych significantly, looking at his head.

"I haven't had a good wash for a long time," repeated Alyohin, embarrassed, and soaped himself once more; the water about him turned dark-blue, the color of ink.

Ivan Ivanych came out of the cabin, plunged into the water with a splash and swam in the rain, thrusting his arms out wide; he raised waves on which white lilies swayed. He swam out to the middle of the river and dived and a minute later came up in another spot and swam on and kept diving, trying to touch bottom. "By God!" he kept repeating delightedly, "by God!" He swam to the mill, spoke to the peasants there, and turned back and in the middle of the river lay floating, exposing his face to the rain. Burkin and Alyohin were already dressed and ready to leave, but he kept on swimming and diving. "By God!" he kept exclaiming. "Lord, have mercy on me."

"You've had enough!" Burkin shouted to him.

They returned to the house. And only when the lamp was lit in the big drawing room upstairs, and the two guests, in silk dressing-gowns and warm slippers, were lounging in armchairs, and Alyohin himself, washed and combed, wearing a new jacket, was walking about the room, evidently savoring the warmth, the cleanliness, the dry clothes and light footwear, and when pretty Pelageya, stepping noiselessly across the carpet and smiling softly, brought in a tray with tea and jam, only then did Ivan Ivanych begin his story, and it was as though not only Burkin and Alyohin were listening, but also the ladies, old and young, and the military men who looked down upon them, calmly and severely, from their gold frames.

"We are two brothers," he began, "I, Ivan Ivanych, and my brother, Nikolay Ivanych, who is two years my junior. I went in for a learned profession and became a veterinary; Nikolay at nineteen began to clerk in a provincial branch of the Treasury. Our father was a *kantonist,** but he rose to be an officer and so a nobleman, a rank that he bequeathed to us together with a small estate. After his death there was a lawsuit and we lost the estate to creditors, but be that as it may, we spent our childhood in the country. Just like peasant children we passed days and nights in the fields and the woods, herded horses, stripped bast from the trees, fished, and so on. And, you know, whoever even once in his life has caught a perch or seen thrushes migrate in the autumn, when on clear, cool days they sweep in flocks over the village, will never really be a townsman and to the day of his death will have a longing for the open. My brother was unhappy in the government office. Years passed, but he went on warming the same seat, scratching away at the same papers, and thinking of one and the same thing: how to get away to the country. And little by little this vague longing turned into a definite desire, into a dream of buying a little property somewhere on the banks of a river or a lake.

"He was a kind and gentle soul and I loved him, but I never sympathized with his desire to shut himself up for the rest of his life on a little property of his own. It is a common saying that a man needs only six feet of earth. But six

* The son of a private, registered at birth in the army and trained in a military school.

feet is what a corpse needs, not a man. It is also asserted that if our educated class is drawn to the land and seeks to settle on farms, that's a good thing. But these farms amount to the same six feet of earth. To retire from the city, from the struggle, from the hubbub, to go off and hide on one's own farm—that's not life, it is selfishness, sloth, it is a kind of monasticism, but monasticism without works. Man needs not six feeth of earth, not a farm, but the whole globe, all of Nature, where unhindered he can display all the capacities and peculiarities of his free spirit.

"My brother Nikolay, sitting in his office, dreamed of eating his own *shchi,* which would fill the whole farmyard with a delicious aroma, of picnicking on the green grass, of sleeping in the sun, of sitting for hours on the seat by the gate gazing at field and forest. Books on agriculture and the farming items in almanacs were his joy, the delight of his soul. He liked newspapers too, but the only things he read in them were advertisements of land for sale, so many acres of tillable land and pasture, with house, garden, river, mill, and millpond. And he pictured to himself garden paths, flowers, fruit, bird-houses with starlings in them, crucians in the pond, and all that sort of thing, you know. These imaginary pictures varied with the advertisements he came upon, but somehow gooseberry bushes figured in every one of them. He could not picture to himself a single country-house, a single rustic nook, without gooseberries.

" 'Country life has its advantages,' he used to say. 'You sit on the veranda having tea, and your ducks swim in the pond, and everything smells delicious and—the gooseberries are ripening.'

"He would draw a plan of his estate and invariably it would contain the following features: a) the master's house; b) servants' quarters; c) kitchen-garden; d) a gooseberry patch. He lived meagerly: he deprived himself of food and drink; he dressed God knows how, like a beggar, but he kept on saving and salting money away in the bank. He was terribly stingy. It was painful for me to see it, and I used to give him small sums and send him something on holidays, but he would put that away too. Once a man is possessed by an idea, there is no doing anything with him.

"Years passed. He was transferred to another province, he was already past forty, yet he was still reading newspaper advertisements and saving up money. Then I heard that he was married. Still for the sake of buying a property with a gooseberry patch he married an elderly, homely widow, without a trace of affection for her, but simply because she had money. After marrying her, he went on living parsimoniously, keeping her half-starved, and he put her money in the bank in his own name. She had previously been the wife of a postmaster, who had got her used to pies and cordials. This second husband did not even give her enough black bread. She began to sicken, and some three years later gave up the ghost. And, of course, it never for a moment occurred to my brother that he was to blame for her death. Money, like vodka, can do queer things to a man. Once in our town a merchant lay on his deathbed; before he died, he ordered a plateful of honey and he ate up all his money and lottery tickets with the honey, so that no one should get it. One day when I was inspecting a drove of cattle at a railway station, a cattle dealer fell under a locomotive and it sliced off his leg. We carried him to the infirmary, the blood was gushing from the wound—a terrible business, but he kept begging us to find his leg and was very anxious about it: he had twenty rubles in the boot that was on that leg, and he was afraid they would be lost."

"That's a tune from another opera," said Burkin.

Ivan Ivanych paused a moment and then continued:

"After his wife's death, my brother began to look around for a property. Of course, you may scout about for five years and in the end make a mistake, and buy something quite different from what you have been dreaming of. Through an agent my brother bought a mortgaged estate of three hundred acres with a house, servants' quarters, a park, but with no orchard, no gooseberry patch, no duck-pond. There was a stream, but the water in it was the color of coffee, for on one of its banks there was a brickyard and on the other a glue factory. But my brother was not at all disconcerted: he ordered a score of gooseberry bushes, planted them, and settled down to the life of a country gentleman.

"Last year I paid him a visit. I thought I would go and see how things were with him. In his letter to me my brother called his estate 'Chumbaroklov Waste, or Himalaiskoe' (our surname was Chimsha-Himalaisky). I reached the place in the afternoon. It was hot. Everywhere there were ditches, fences, hedges, rows of fir trees, and I was at a loss as to how to get to the yard and where to leave my horse. I made my way to the house and was met by a fat dog with reddish hair that looked like a pig. It wanted to bark, but was too lazy. The cook, a fat, barelegged woman, who also looked like a pig, came out of the kitchen and said that the master was resting after dinner. I went in to see my brother, and found him sitting up in bed, with a quilt over his knees. He had grown older, stouter, flabby; his cheeks, his nose, his lips jutted out: it looked as though he might grunt into the quilt at any moment.

"We embraced and dropped tears of joy and also of sadness at the thought that the two of us had once been young, but were now gray and nearing death. He got dressed and took me out to show me his estate.

" 'Well, how are you getting on here?' I asked.

" 'Oh, all right, thank God. I am doing very well.'

"He was no longer the poor, timid clerk he used to be but a real landowner, a gentleman. He had already grown used to his new manner of living and developed a taste for it. He ate a great deal, steamed himself in the bathhouse, was growing stout, was already having a lawsuit with the village commune and the two factories and was very much offended when the peasants failed to address him as 'Your Honor.' And he concerned himself with his soul's welfare too in a substantial, upper-class manner, and performed good deeds not simply, but pompously. And what good works! He dosed the peasants with bicarbonate and castor oil for all their ailments and on his name day he had a thanksgiving service celebrated in the center of the village, and then treated the villagers to a gallon of vodka, which he thought was the thing to do. Oh, those horrible gallons of vodka! One day a fat landowner hauls the peasants up before the rural police officer for trespassing, and the next, to mark a feast day, treats them to a gallon of vodka, and they drink and shout 'Hurrah' and when they are drunk bow down at his feet. A higher standard of living, overeating and idleness develop the most insolent self-conceit in a Russian. Nikolay Ivanych, who when he was a petty official was afraid to have opinions of his own even if he kept them to himself, now uttered nothing but incontrovertible truths and did so in the tone of a minister of state: 'Education is necessary, but the masses are not ready for it; corporal punishment is generally harmful, but in some cases it is useful and nothing else will serve.'

" 'I know the common people, and I know how to deal

with them,' he would say. 'They love me. I only have to raise my little finger, and they will do anything I want.'

"And all this, mark you, would be said with a smile that bespoke kindness and intelligence. Twenty times over he repeated: 'We, of the gentry,' 'I, as a member of the gentry.' Apparently he no longer remembered that our grandfather had been a peasant and our father just a private. Even our surname, 'Chimsha-Himalaisky,' which in reality is grotesque, seemed to him sonorous, distinguished, and delightful.

"But I am concerned now not with him, but with me. I want to tell you about the change that took place in me during the few hours that I spent on his estate. In the evening when we were having tea, the cook served a plateful of gooseberries. They were not bought, they were his own gooseberries, the first ones picked since the bushes were planted. My brother gave a laugh and for a minute looked at the gooseberries in silence, with tears in his eyes—he could not speak for excitement. Then he put one berry in his mouth, glanced at me with the triumph of a child who has at last been given a toy he was longing for and said: 'How tasty!' And he ate the gooseberries greedily, and kept repeating: 'Ah, how delicious! Do taste them!'

"They were hard and sour, but as Pushkin has it,

> The falsehood that exalts we cherish more
> Than meaner truths that are a thousand strong.

I saw a happy man, one whose cherished dream had so obviously come true, who had attained his goal in life, who had got what he wanted, who was satisfied with his lot and with himself. For some reason an element of sadness had always mingled with my thoughts of human happiness, and now at the sight of a happy man I was assailed by an oppressive feeling bordering on despair. It weighed on me particularly at night. A bed was made up for me in a room next to my brother's bedroom, and I could hear that he was wakeful, and that he would get up again and again, go to the plate of gooseberries and eat one after another. I said to myself: how many contented, happy people there really are! What an overwhelming force they are! Look at life: the insolence and idleness of the strong, the ignorance and brutishness of the weak, horrible poverty everywhere, overcrowding, degeneration, drunkenness, hypocrisy, lying— Yet in all the houses and on all the streets there is peace and quiet; of the fifty thousand people who live in our town there is not one who would cry out, who would vent his indignation aloud. We see the people who go to market, eat by day, sleep by night, who babble nonsense, marry, grow old, good-naturedly drag their dead to the cemetery, but we do not see or hear those who suffer, and what is terrible in life goes on somewhere behind the scenes. Everything is peaceful and quiet and only mute statistics protest: so many people gone out of their minds, so many gallons of vodka drunk, so many children dead from malnutrition— And such a state of things is evidently necessary; obviously the happy man is at ease only because the unhappy ones bear their burdens in silence, and if there were not this silence, happiness would be impossible. It is a general hypnosis. Behind the door of every contented, happy man there ought to be someone standing with a little hammer and continually reminding him with a knock that there are unhappy people, that however happy he may be, life will sooner or later show him its claws, and trouble will come to him—illness, poverty, losses, and then no one will see or hear him, just as now he neither sees nor hears others. But there is no man with a hammer. The happy man lives at his ease, faintly fluttered by small daily cares, like an aspen in the wind—and all is well.

"That night I came to understand that I too had been contented and happy," Ivan Ivanych continued, getting up. "I too over the dinner table or out hunting would hold forth on how to live, what to believe, the right way to govern the people. I too would say that learning was the enemy of darkness, that education was necessary but that for the common people the three R's were sufficient for the time being. Freedom is a boon, I used to say, it is as essential as air, but we must wait awhile. Yes, that's what I used to say, and now I ask: Why must we wait?" said Ivan Ivanych, looking wrathfully at Burkin. "Why must we wait, I ask you? For what reason? I am told that nothing can be done all at once, that every idea is realized gradually, in its own time. But who is it that says so? Where is the proof that it is just? You cite the natural order of things, the law governing all phenomena, but is there law, is there order in the fact that I, a living, thinking man, stand beside a ditch and wait for it to close up of itself or fill up with silt, when I could jump over it or throw a bridge across it? And again, why must we wait?

Wait, until we have no strength to live, and yet we have to live and are eager to live!

"I left my brother's place early in the morning, and ever since then it has become intolerable for me to stay in town. I am oppressed by the peace and the quiet, I am afraid to look at the windows, for there is nothing that pains me more than the spectacle of a happy family sitting at table having tea. I am an old man now and unfit for combat, I am not even capable of hating. I can only grieve inwardly, get irritated, worked up, and at night my head is ablaze with the rush of ideas and I cannot sleep. Oh, if I were young!"

Ivan Ivanych paced up and down the room excitedly and repeated, "If I were young!"

He suddenly walked up to Alyohin and began to press now one of his hands, now the other.

"Pavel Konstantinych," he said imploringly, "don't quiet down, don't let yourself be lulled to sleep! As long as you are young, strong, alert, do not cease to do good! There is no happiness and there should be none, and if life has a meaning and a purpose, that meaning and purpose is not our happiness but something greater and more rational. Do good!"

All this Ivan Ivanych said with a pitiful, imploring smile, as though he were asking a personal favor.

Afterwards all three of them sat in armchairs in different corners of the drawing room and were silent. Ivan Ivanych's story satisfied neither Burkin nor Alyohin. With the ladies and generals looking down from the golden frames, seeming alive in the dim light, it was tedious to listen to the story of the poor devil of a clerk who ate gooseberries. One felt like talking about elegant people, about women. And the fact that they were sitting in a drawing room where everything—the chandelier under its cover, the armchairs, the carpets underfoot—testified that the very people who were now looking down from the frames had once moved about here, sat and had tea, and the fact that lovely Pelageya was noiselessly moving about—that was better than any story.

Alyohin was very sleepy; he had gotten up early, before three o'clock in the morning, to get some work done, and now he could hardly keep his eyes open, but he was afraid his visitors might tell an interesting story in his absence, and he would not leave. He did not trouble to ask himself if what Ivan Ivanych had just said was intelligent or right. The guests were not talking about groats, or hay, or tar, but about something that had no direct bearing on his life, and he was glad of it and wanted them to go on.

"However, it's bedtime," said Burkin, rising. "Allow me to wish you good night."

Alyohin took leave of his guests and went downstairs to his own quarters, while they remained upstairs. They were installed for the night in a big room in which stood two old wooden beds decorated with carvings and in the corner was an ivory crucifix. The wide cool beds which had been made by the lovely Pelageya gave off a pleasant smell of clean linen.

Ivan Ivanych undressed silently and got into bed.

"Lord forgive us sinners!" he murmured, and drew the bedclothes over his head.

His pipe, which lay on the table, smelled strongly of burnt tobacco, and Burkin, who could not sleep for a long time, kept wondering where the unpleasant odor came from.

The rain beat against the window panes all night.

THE TREE OF KNOWLEDGE

Henry James

Henry James (1843–1916) is, with Hemingway, one of the two most influential and original stylists among American short-story writers. His popularity today is, if anything, on the increase. A master of artful irony and an unsurpassed analyst of the delicate social interplay of highly sensitive and highly civilized human beings, James weaves a spell of deeply personal magic. Within its range, "The Tree of Knowledge" comes about as close to perfection as a short story can.

It was one of the secret opinions, such as we all have, of Peter Brench that his main success in life would have consisted in his never having committed himself about the work, as it was called, of his friend Morgan Mallow. This was a subject on which it was, to the best of his belief, impossible with veracity to quote him, and it was nowhere on record that he had, in the connexion, on any occasion and in any embarrassment, either lied or spoken the truth. Such a triumph had its honour even for a man of other triumphs—a man who had reached fifty, who had escaped marriage, who had lived within his means, who had been in love with Mrs. Mallow for years without breathing it, and who, last not least, had judged himself once for all. He had so judged himself in fact that he felt an extreme and general humility to be his proper portion; yet there was nothing that made him think so well of his parts as the course he had steered so often through the shallows just mentioned. It became thus a real wonder that the friends in whom he had most confidence were just those with whom he had most reserves. He couldn't tell Mrs. Mallow—or at least he supposed, excellent man, he couldn't—that she was the one beautiful reason he had never married; any more than he could tell her husband that the sight of the multiplied marbles in that gentleman's studio was an affliction of which even time had never blunted the edge. His victory, however, as I have intimated, in regard to these productions, was not simply in his not having let it out that he deplored them; it was, remarkably, in his not having kept it in by anything else.

The whole situation, among these good people, was verily a marvel, and there was probably not such another for a long way from the spot that engages us—the point at which the soft declivity of Hampstead began at that time to confess in broken accents to Saint John's Wood. He despised Mallow's statues and adored Mallow's wife, and yet was distinctly fond of Mallow, to whom, in turn, he was equally dear. Mrs. Mallow rejoiced in the statues—though she preferred, when pressed, the busts; and if she was visibly attached to Peter Brench it was because of his affection for Morgan. Each loved the other moreover for the love borne in each case to Lancelot, whom the Mallows respectively cherished as their only child and whom the friend of their fireside identified as the third—but decidedly the handsomest—of his godsons. Already in the old years it had come to that—that no one, for such a relation, could possibly have occurred to any of them, even to the baby itself, but Peter. There was luckily a certain independence, of the pecuniary sort, all round: the Master could never otherwise have spent his solemn *Wanderjahre* in Florence and Rome, and continued by the Thames as well as by the Arno and the Tiber to add unpurchased group to group and model, for what was too apt to prove in the event mere love, fancy-heads of celebrities either too busy or too buried—too much of the age or too little of it—to sit. Neither could Peter, lounging in almost daily, have found time to keep the whole complicated tradition so alive by his presence. He was massive but mild, the depositary of these mysteries—large and loose and ruddy and curly, with deep tones, deep eyes, deep pockets, to say nothing of the habit of long pipes, soft hats and brownish greyish weather-faded clothes, apparently always the same.

He had "written," it was known, but had never spoken, never spoken in particular of that; and he had the air (since, as was believed, he continued to write) of keeping it up in order to have something more—as if he hadn't at the worst enough—to be silent about. Whatever his air, at any rate, Peter's occasional unmentioned prose and verse were quite truly the result of an impulse to maintain the purity of his taste by establishing still more firmly the right relation of fame to feebleness. The little green door of his domain was in a garden-wall on which the discoloured stucco made patches, and in the small detached villa behind it everything was old, the furniture, the servants, the books, the prints, the immemorial habits and the new improvements. The Mallows, at Carrara Lodge, were within ten minutes, and the studio there was on their little land, to which they had added, in their happy faith, for building it. This was the good fortune, if it was not the ill, of her having brought him in marriage a portion that put them in a manner at their ease and enabled them thus, on their side, to keep it up. And they did keep it up—they always had—the infatuated sculptor and his wife, for whom nature had refined on the impossible by relieving them of the sense of the difficult. Morgan had at all events everything of the sculptor but the spirit of Phidias—the brown velvet, the becoming *beretto*, the "plastic" presence, the fine fingers, the beautiful accent in Italian and the old Italian factotum. He seemed to make up for everything when he addressed Egidio with the "tu" and waved him to turn one of the rotary pedestals of which the place was full. They were tremendous Italians at Carrara Lodge, and the secret of the part played by this fact in Peter's life was in a large degree that it gave him, sturdy Briton as he was, just the amount of "going abroad" he could bear. The Mallows were all his Italy, but it was in a measure for Italy he liked them. His one worry was that Lance—to which they had shortened his godson—was, in spite of a public school, perhaps a shade too Italian. Morgan meanwhile looked like somebody's flattering idea of somebody's own person as expressed in the great room provided at the Uffizzi Museum for the general illustration of that idea by eminent hands. The Master's sole regret that he hadn't been born rather to the brush than to the chisel sprang from his wish that he might have contributed to that collection.

It appeared with time at any rate to be to the brush that Lance had been born; for Mrs. Mallow, one day when the boy was turning twenty, broke it to their friend, who shared, to the last delicate morsel, their problems and pains, that it seemed as if nothing would really do but that he should embrace the career. It had been impossible longer to remain blind to the fact that he was gaining no glory at Cambridge, where Brench's own college had for a year tempered its tone to him as for Brench's own sake. Therefore why renew the vain form of preparing him for the impossible? The impossible—it had become clear—was that he should be anything but an artist.

"Oh dear, dear!" said poor Peter.

"Don't you believe in it?" asked Mrs. Mallow, who still, at more than forty, had her violet velvet eyes, her creamy satin skin and her silken chestnut hair.

"Believe in what?"

"Why in Lance's passion."

"I don't know what you mean by 'believing in it.' I've never been unaware, certainly, of his disposition, from his earliest time, to daub and draw; but I confess I've hoped it would burn out."

"But why should it," she sweetly smiled, "with his wonderful heredity? Passion is passion—though of course indeed *you*, dear Peter, know nothing of that. Has the Master's ever burned out?"

Peter looked off a little and, in his familiar formless way, kept up for a moment, a sound between a smothered whistle and a subdued hum. "Do you think he's going to be another Master?"

She seemed scarce prepared to go that length, yet she had on the whole a marvellous trust. "I know what you mean by that. Will it be a career to incur the jealousies and provoke the machinations that have been at times almost too much for his father? Well—say it may be, since nothing but claptrap, in these dreadful days, *can*, it would seem, make its way, and since, with the curse of refinement and distinction, one may easily find one's self begging one's bread. Put it at the worst—say he *has* the misfortune to wing his flight further than the vulgar taste of his stupid countrymen can follow. Think, all the same, of the happiness—the same the Master has had. He'll *know*."

Peter looked rueful. "Ah but *what* will he know?"

"Quiet joy!" cried Mrs. Mallow, quite impatient and turning away.

II

He had of course before long to meet the boy himself on it and to hear that practically everything was settled. Lance was not to go up again, but to go instead to Paris where, since the die was cast, he would find the best advantages. Peter had always felt he must be taken as he was, but had never perhaps found him so much of that pattern as on this occasion. "You chuck Cambridge then altogether? Doesn't that seem rather a pity?"

Lance would have been like his father, to his friend's sense, had he had less humour, and like his mother had he had more beauty. Yet it was a good middle way for Peter that, in the modern manner, he was, to the eye, rather the young stockbroker than the young artist. The youth reasoned that it was a question of time—there was such a mill to go through, such an awful lot to learn. He had talked with fellows and had judged. "One has got, today," he said, "don't you see? to know."

His interlocutor, at this, gave a groan. "Oh hang it, *don't* know!"

Lance wondered. " 'Don't'? Then what's the use—?"

"The use of what?"

"Why of anything. Don't you think I've talent?"

Peter smoked away for a little in silence; then went on: "It isn't knowledge, it's ignorance that—as we've been beautifully told—is bliss."

"Don't you think I've talent?" Lance repeated.

Peter, with his trick of queer kind demonstrations, passed his arm round his godson and held him a moment. "How do I know?"

"Oh," said the boy, "if it's your own ignorance you're defending—!"

Again, for a pause, on the sofa, his godfather smoked. "It isn't. I've the misfortune to be omniscient."

"Oh, well," Lance laughed again, "if you know *too* much—!"

"That's what I do, and it's why I'm so wretched."

Lance's gaiety grew. "Wretched? Come, I say!"

"But I forgot," his companion went on—"you're not to know about that. It would indeed for you too make the too much. Only I'll tell you what I'll do." And Peter got up from the sofa. "If you'll go up again I'll pay your way at Cambridge."

Lance stared, a little rueful in spite of being still more amused. "Oh Peter! You disapprove so of Paris?"

"Well, I'm afraid of it."

"Ah I see!"

"No, you don't see—yet. But you will—that is you would. And you mustn't."

The young man thought more gravely. "But one's innocence, already—!"

"Is considerably damaged? Ah that won't matter," Peter persisted—"we'll patch it up here."

"Here? Then you want me to stay at home?"

Peter almost confessed to it. "Well, we're so right—we four together—just as we are. We're so safe. Come, don't spoil it."

The boy, who had turned to gravity, turned from this, on the real pressure in his friend's tone, to consternation. "Then what's a fellow to be?"

"My particular care. Come, old man"—and Peter now fairly pleaded—"*I'll* look out for you."

Lance, who had remained on the sofa with his legs out and his hands in his pockets, watched him with eyes that showed suspicion. Then he got up. "You think there's something the matter with me—that I can't make a success."

"Well, what do you call a success?"

Lance thought again. "Why the best sort, I suppose, is to please one's self. Isn't that the sort that, in spite of cabals and things, is—in his own peculair line—the Master's?"

There were so much too many things in this question to be answered at once that they practically checked the discussion, which became particularly difficult in the light of such renewed proof that, though the young man's innocence might, in the course of his studies, as he contended, somewhat have shrunken, the finer essence of it still remained. That was indeed exactly what Peter had assumed and what above all he desired; yet perversely enough it gave him a chill. The boy believed in the cabals and things, believed in the peculiar line, believed, to be brief, in the Master. What happened a month or two later wasn't that he went up again at the expense of his godfather, but that a fortnight after he had got settled in Paris this personage sent him fifty pounds.

He had meanwhile at home, this personage, made up his

mind to the worst; and what that might be had never yet grown quite so vivid to him as when, on his presenting himself one Sunday might, as he never failed to do, for supper, the mistress of Carrara Lodge met him with an appeal as to —of all things in the world—the wealth of the Canadians. She was earnest, she was even excited. "Are many of them *really* rich?"

He had to confess he knew nothing about them, but he often thought afterwards of that evening. The room in which they sat was adorned with sundry specimens of the Master's genius, which had the merit of being, as Mrs. Mallow herself frequently suggested, of an unusually convenient size. They were indeed of dimensions not customary in the products of the chisel, and they had the singularity that, if the objects and features intended to be small looked too large, the objects and features intended to be large looked too small. The Master's idea, either in respect to this matter or to any other, had in almost any case, even after years, remained undiscoverable to Peter Brench. The creations that so failed to reveal it stood about on pedestals and brackets, on tables and shelves, a little staring white population, heroic, idyllic, allegoric, mythic, symbolic, in which "scale" had so strayed and lost itself that the public square and the chimney-piece seemed to have changed places, the monumental being all diminutive and the diminutive all monumental; branches at any rate, markedly, of a family in which stature was rather oddly irrespective of function, age and sex. They formed, like the Mallows themselves, poor Brench's own family—having at least to such a degree the note of familiarity. The occasion was one of those he had long ago learnt to know and to name—short flickers of the faint flame, soft gusts of a kinder air. Twice a year regularly the Master believed in his fortune, in addition to believing all the year round in his genius. This time it was to be made by a bereaved couple from Toronto, who had given him the handsomest order for a tomb to three lost children, each of whom they desired to see, in the composition, emblematically and characteristically represented.

Such was naturally the moral of Mrs. Mallow's question: if their wealth was to be assumed, it was clear, from the nature of their admiration, as well as from mysterious hints thrown out (they were a little odd!) as to other possibilities of the same mortuary sort, that their further patronage might be; and not less evident that should the Master become at all known in those climes nothing would be more inevitable than a run of Canadian custom. Peter had been present before at runs of custom, colonial and domestic—present at each of those of which the aggregation had left so few gaps in the marble company round him; but it was his habit never at these junctures to prick the bubble in advance. The fond illusion, while it lasted, eased the wound of elections never won, the long ache of medals and diplomas carried off, on every chance, by every one but the Master; it moreover lighted the lamp that would glimmer through the next eclipse. They lived, however, after all—as it was always beautiful to see—at a height scarce susceptible of ups and downs. They strained a point at times charmingly, strained it to admit that the public was here and there not too bad to buy; but they would have been nowhere without their attitude that the Master was always too good to sell. They were at all events deliciously formed, Peter often said to himself, for their fate; the Master had a vanity, his wife had a loyalty, of which success, depriving these things of innocence, would have diminished the merit and the grace. Any one could be charming under a charm, and as he looked about him at a world of prosperity more void of proportion even than the Master's museum he wondered if he knew another pair that so completely escaped vulgarity.

"What a pity Lance isn't with us to rejoice!" Mrs. Mallow on this occasion sighed at supper.

"We'll drink to the health of the absent," her husband replied, filling his friend's glass and his own and giving a drop to their companion; "but we must hope he's preparing himself for a happiness much less like this of ours this evening—excusable as I grant it to be!—than like the comfort we have always (whatever has happened or has not happened) been able to trust ourselves to enjoy. The comfort," the Master explained, leaning back in the pleasant lamplight and firelight, holding up his glass and looking round at his marble family, quartered more or less, a monstrous brood, in every room—"the comfort of art in itself!"

Peter looked a little shyly at his wine. "Well—I don't care what you may call it when a fellow doesn't—but Lance must learn to *sell*, you know. I drink to his acquisition of the secret of a base popularity!"

"Oh yes, *he* must sell," the boy's mother, who was still

more, however, this seemed to give out, the Master's wife, rather artlessly allowed.

"Ah," the sculptor after a moment confidently pronounced, "Lance *will*. Don't be afraid. He'll have learnt."

"Which is exactly what Peter," Mrs. Mallow gaily returned—"why in the world were you so perverse, Peter?—wouldn't when he told him hear of."

Peter, when this lady looked at him with accusatory affection—a grace on her part not infrequent—could never find a word; but the Master, who was always all amenity and tact, helped him out now as he had often helped him before. "That's his old idea, you know—on which we've so often differed: his theory that the artist should be all impulse and instinct. *I* go in of course for a certain amount of school. Not too much—but a due proportion. There's where his protest came in," he continued to explain to his wife, "as against what *might*, don't you see? be in question for Lance."

"Ah well"—and Mrs. Mallow turned the violet eyes across the table at the subject of this discourse—"he's sure to have meant of course nothing but good. Only that wouldn't have prevented him, if Lance *had* taken his advice, from being in effect horribly cruel."

They had a sociable way of talking of him to his face as if he had been in the clay or—at most—in the plaster, and the Master was unfailingly generous. He might have been waving Egidio to make him revolve. "Ah but poor Peter wasn't so wrong as to what it may after all come to that he *will* learn."

"Oh but nothing artistically bad," she urged—still, for poor Peter, arch and dewy.

"Why just the little French tricks," said the Master: on which their friend had to pretend to admit, when pressed by Mrs. Mallow, that these aesthetic vices had been the objects of his dread.

III

"I know now," Lance said to him the next year, "why you were so much against it." He had come back supposedly for a mere interval and was looking about him at Carrara Lodge, where indeed he had already on two or three occasions since his expatriation briefly reappeared. This had the air of a longer holiday. "Something rather awful has happened to me. It *isn't* so very good to know."

"I'm bound to say high spirits don't show in your face," Peter was rather ruefully forced to confess. "Still, are you very sure you do know?"

"Well, I at least know about as much as I can bear." These remarks were exchanged in Peter's den, and the young man, smoking cigarettes, stood before the fire with his back against the mantel. Something of his bloom seemed really to have left him.

Poor Peter wondered. "You're clear then as to what in particular I wanted you not to go for?"

"In particular?" Lance thought. "It seems to me that in particular there can have been only one thing."

They stood for a little sounding each other. "Are you quite sure?"

"Quite sure I'm a beastly duffer? Quite—by this time."

"Oh!"—and Peter turned away as if almost with relief.

"It's *that* that isn't pleasant to find out."

"Oh I don't care for 'that,' " said Peter, presently coming round again. "I mean I personally don't."

"Yet I hope you can understand a little that I myself should!"

"Well, what do you mean by it?" Peter sceptically asked.

And on this Lance had to explain—how the upshot of his studies in Paris had inexorably proved a mere deep doubt of his means. These studies had so waked him up that a new light was in his eyes; but what the new light did was really to show him too much. "Do you know what's the matter with me? I'm too horribly intelligent. Paris was really the last place for me. I've learnt what I can't do."

Poor Peter stared—it was a staggerer; but even after they had had, on the subject, a longish talk in which the boy brought out to the full the hard truth of his lesson, his friend betrayed less pleasure than usually breaks into a face to the happy tune of "I told you so!" Poor Peter himself made now indeed so little a point of having told him so that Lance broke ground in a different place a day or two after. "What was it then that—before I went—you were afraid I should find out?" This, however, Peter refused to tell him—on the ground that if he hadn't yet guessed perhaps he never would, and that in any case nothing at all for either of them was to be gained by giving the thing a name. Lance eyed him on this an instant with the bold curiosity of youth—with the air indeed of having in his mind two or three names, of which one or other would be right. Peter nevertheless, turning his back again, offered no encouragement, and when they parted afresh it was with some show of impatience on the side of the boy. Accordingly on their next encounter Peter saw at a glance that he had now, in the interval, divined and that, to sound his note, he was only waiting till they should find themselves alone. This he had soon arranged and he then broke straight out. "Do you know your conundrum has been keeping me awake? But in the watches of the night the answer came over me—so that, upon my honour, I quite laughed out. Had you been supposing I had to go to Paris to learn *that?*" Even now, to see him still so sublimely on his guard, Peter's young friend had to laugh afresh. "You won't give a sign till you're sure? Beautiful old Peter!" But Lance at last produced it. "Why, hang it, the truth about the Master."

It made between them for some minutes a lively passage, full of wonder for each at the wonder of the other. "Then how long have you understood—"

"The true value of his work? I understood it," Lance recalled, "as soon as I began to understand anything. But I didn't begin fully to do that, I admit, till I got *là-bas*."

"Dear, dear!"—Peter gasped with retrospective dread.

"But for what have you taken me? I'm a hopeless muff—that I *had* to have rubbed in. But I'm not such a muff as the Master!" Lance declared.

"Then why did you never tell me—?"

"That I hadn't, after all"—the boy took him up—"remained such an idiot? Just because I never dreamed *you* knew. But I beg your pardon. I only wanted to spare you. And what I don't now understand is how the deuce then for so long you've managed to keep bottled."

Peter produced his explanation, but only after some delay, and with a gravity not void of embarrassment. "It was for your mother."

"Oh!" said Lance.

"And that's the great thing now—since the murder *is* out. I want a promise from you. I mean"—and Peter almost feverishly followed it up—"a vow from you, solemn and such as you owe me here on the spot, that you'll sacrifice anything rather than let her ever guess—"

"That *I've* guessed?"—Lance took it in. "I see." He evidently after a moment had taken in much. "But what is it you've in mind that I may have a chance to sacrifice?"

"Oh one has always something."

Lance looked at him hard. "Do you mean that *you've* had—?" The look he received back, however, so put the question by that he found soon enough another. "Are you really sure my mother doesn't know?"

Peter, after renewed reflexion, was really sure. "If she does she's too wonderful."

"But aren't we all too wonderful?"

"Yes," Peter granted—"but in different ways. The thing's so desperately important because your father's little public consists only, as you know then," Peter developed—"well, of how many?"

"First of all," the Master's son risked, "of himself. And last of all too. I don't quite see of whom else."

Peter had an approach to impatience. "Of your mother, I say—*always*."

Lance cast it all up. "You absolutely feel that?"

"Absolutely."

"Well then with yourself that makes three."

"Oh *me!*"—and Peter, with a wag of his kind old head, modestly excused himself. "The number's at any rate small enough for any individual dropping out to be too dreadfully missed. Therefore, to put it in a nutshell, take care, my boy—that's all—that *you're* not!"

"I've got to keep on humbugging?" Lance wailed.

"It's just to warn you of the danger of your failing of that that I've seized this opportunity."

"And what do you regard in particular," the young man asked, "as the danger?"

"Why this certainly: that the moment your mother, who feels so strongly, should suspect your secret—well," said Peter desperately, "the fat would be on the fire."

Lance for a moment seemed to stare at the blaze. "She'd throw me over?"

"She'd throw *him* over."

"And come round to us?"

Peter, before he answered, turned away. "Come round to *you*." But he had said enough to indicate—and, as he evidently trusted, to avert—the horrid contingency.

IV

Within six months again, none the less, his fear was on more occasions than one all before him. Lance had returned to Paris for another trial; then had reappeared at home and had had, with his father, for the first time in his life, one of the scenes that strike sparks. He described it with much expression to Peter, touching whom (since they had never done so before) it was the sign of a new reserve on the part of the pair at Carrara Lodge that they at present failed, on a matter of intimate interest, to open themselves—if not in joy then in sorrow—to their good friend. This produced perhaps practically between the parties a shade of alienation and a slight intermission of commerce—marked mainly indeed by the fact that to talk at his ease with his old playmate Lance had in general to come to see him. The closest if not quite the gayest relation they had yet known together was thus ushered in. The difficulty for poor Lance was a tension at home—begotten by the fact that his father wished him to be at least the sort of success he himself had been. He hadn't "chucked" Paris—though nothing appeared more vivid to him than that Paris had chucked him: he would go back again because of the fascination in trying, in seeing, in sounding the depths—in learning one's lesson, briefly, even if the lesson were simply that of one's impotence in the presence of one's larger vision. But what did the Master, all aloft in his senseless fluency, know of impotence, and what vision—to be called such—had he in all his blind life ever had? Lance, heated and indignant, frankly appealed to his godparent on this score.

His father, it appeared, had come down on him for having, after so long, nothing to show, and hoped that on his next return this deficiency would be repaired. *The* thing, the Master complacently set forth was—for any artist, however inferior to himself—at least to "do" something. "What can you do? That's all I ask!" *He* had certainly done enough, and there was no mistake about what he had to show. Lance had tears in his eyes when it came thus to letting his old friend know how great the strain might be on the "sacrifice" asked of him. It wasn't so easy to continue humbugging—as from son to parent—after feeling one's self despised for not grovelling in mediocrity. Yet a noble duplicity was what, as they intimately faced the situation, Peter went on requiring; and it was still for a time what his young friend, bitter and sore, managed loyally to comfort him with. Fifty pounds more than once again, it was true, rewarded both in London and in Paris the young friend's loyalty; none the less sensibly, doubtless, at the moment, that the money was a direct advance on a decent sum for which Peter had long since privately prearranged an ultimate function. Whether by these arts or others, at all events, Lance's just resentment was kept for a season—but only for a season—at bay. The day arrived when he warned his companion that he could hold out —or hold in—no longer. Carrara Lodge had had to listen to another lecture delivered from a great height—an infliction really heavier at last than, without striking back or in some way letting the Master have the truth, flesh and blood could bear.

"And what I don't see is," Lance observed with a certain irritated eye for what was after all, if it came to that, owing to himself too; "what I don't see is, upon my honour, how *you*, as things are going, can keep the game up."

"Oh the game for me is only to hold my tongue," said placid Peter. "And I have my reason."

"Still my mother?"

Peter showed a queer face as he had often shown it before—that is by turning it straight away. "What will you have? I haven't ceased to like her."

"She's beautiful—she's a dear of course," Lance allowed; "but what is she to you, after all, and what is it to you that, as to anything whatever, she should or she shouldn't?"

Peter, who had turned red, hung fire a little. "Well—it's all simply what I make of it."

There was now, however, in his young friend a strange, an adopted insistence. "What are you after all to *her?*"

"Oh nothing. But that's another matter."

"She cares only for my father," said Lance the Parisian.

"Naturally—and that's just why."

"Why you've wished to spare her?"

"Because she cares so tremendously much."

Lance took a turn about the room, but with his eyes still on his host. "How awfully—always—you must have liked her!"

"Awfully. Always," said Peter Brench.

The young man continued for a moment to muse—then

stopped again in front of him. "Do you know how much she cares?" Their eyes met on it, but Peter, as if his own found something new in Lance's, appeared to hesitate, for the first time in an age, to say he did know. *"I've* only just found out," said Lance. "She came to my room last night, after being present, in silence and only with her eyes on me, at what I had had to take from him: she came—and she was with me an extraordinary hour."

He had paused again and they had again for a while sounded each other. Then something—and it made him suddenly turn pale—came to Peter. "She *does* know?"

"She does know. She let it all out to me—so as to demand of me no more than 'that,' as she said, of which she herself had been capable. She has always, always known," said Lance without pity.

Peter was silent a long time; during which his companion might have heard him gently breathe, and on touching him might have felt within him the vibration of a long low sound suppressed. By the time he spoke at last he had taken everything in. "Then I do see how tremendously much."

"Isn't it wonderful?" Lance asked.

"Wonderful," Peter mused.

"So that if your original effort to keep me from Paris was to keep me from knowledge—!" Lance exclaimed as if with a sufficient indication of this futility.

It might have been at the futility Peter appeared for a little to gaze. "I think it must have been—without my quite at the time knowing it—to keep *me!*" he replied at last as he turned away.

THE CAT, A GOLDFINCH, AND THE STARS

Luigi Pirandello

Luigi Pirandello was born in Girgenti, Sicily, in 1867, the son of a mine owner. He was educated at Rome and at the University of Bonn, Germany. He is most famous as a dramatist, having written approximately fifty plays; the best known of these in America is Six Characters in Search of an Author *(1921). In 1934 he received the Nobel Prize for his drama. He died in 1936. Pirandello writes in a bare but intensely poetic style and possesses a deeper metaphysical awareness than is characteristic of most American short-story writers.*

A stone. Another stone. Man passes and sees the two lying side by side. But what does this stone know of the one beside it? Or what does the water know of the drain in which it flows? Man sees the water and the drain; he sees the water running in the drain, and he comes to fancy that the water, as it goes, may be confiding to the drain—who knows what secrets?

Ah, what a starry night over the roofs of this little mountain hamlet! Looking up at the sky from these roofs, one would swear that those brightly shining orbs beheld nothing else.

Yet the stars do not even know there is an earth.

Those mountains? Is it possible that they are not aware of this little hamlet which has nestled between them since time immemorial? Their names are known: Monte Corno; Monte Moro; and yet, can it be, they do not even know they are mountains? And it is possible that that house over there, the oldest in the village, does not know that it came to be there on account of the road that runs by it, which is the oldest of all roads? Can it, really, be?

And supposing that it *is* so?

Go ahead and believe, then, if you like, that the stars see nothing but the roofs of your little mountain hamlet.

I once knew an old couple who had a goldfinch. And the question, certainly, never occurred to them as to how their faces, its cage, the house with its old-fashioned furnishings might look to the goldfinch, or what the latter might think of all the care and caresses lavished upon it; for they were sure that, when the goldfinch came to alight upon one of their shoulders and began pecking at their wrinkled necks or the lobes of their ears—they were sure that it knew very well that this was a shoulder upon which it had alighted, and that the shoulder or the ear belonged to one of them and not to the other. Was it possible that it did not know them both very well, that it did not know that this was Grandpa and this Grandma? Or that it was not very well-aware that the reason they both loved it so was because it had been their little dead granddaughter's goldfinch, and it was she who had trained it so nicely to come perch upon her shoulder and peck at her ear, and to leave its cage and fly about the house?

For the goldfinch's cage, between the curtains, upon the window shelf, was its home only at night; by day, it spent but a few moments there, pecking at its millet seed or cunningly throwing back its head to swallow a tiny drop of water. The cage, in short, was its palace, while the house was its boundless realm. And oftentimes, it would alight upon the shade of the hanging lamp in the dining-room or upon the back of Grandfather's chair, and there it would sit and trill, or—well, you know what goldfinches are!

"Nasty thing!" the old lady would scold, when she caught sight of it doing this. And she would come running with the dustcloth, always ready to clean up after it, just as if there were a baby in the house that simply could not learn to do certain things in a certain time and place. And as she did so, the old lady would think of her granddaughter, little angel, and of how, for more than a year, she had given her this task to do, until—

"You remember, eh?"

And the old man—did he remember? He could still see her running through the house, such a tiny little mite! And he would shake his head, long and sadly.

The old couple had been left with this orphan on their hands, and she had grown up in the house with them. They had hoped that she might be the joy of their old age; but instead, when she was fifteen— But her memory had remained alive, in the trilling and the fluttering of that goldfinch. It was strange they had not thought of it sooner! But in the depths of despair into which they had fallen after their great grief, how were they ever to have thought of a goldfinch? Upon their bent shoulders, shaking with sobs, it, the goldfinch—yes, the goldfinch—had come to alight, moving its little head from side to side; and then it had stretched out its neck and, with its little beak, had pecked at their ears, as if to say—yes, it was something of hers, something alive—something that was alive still, and which still had need of their care, need of the same love that they had shown her.

Ah, how the old lady had trembled as she took it in her hand and showed it to her aged husband, sobbing all the while! What kisses they had showered upon its little head, upon its beak! It did not like to be held a prisoner in the hand, but had struggled with its tiny feet and head, and had returned the old couple's kisses with sharp little pecks.

The old lady was as sure as could be that, when the goldfinch trilled, it was calling for its lost mistress, and that, when it flew here and there through the rooms of the house, it was searching for her, searching for her ceaselessly, and that it was inconsolable at not finding her; it was certain, too, that all those prolonged trills were for her,—questions that spoke plainer than words, questions repeated three and four times in succession, the bird waiting for an answer and displaying its anger at not receiving one.

What did this mean, she would like to know, if not that the goldfinch knew all about death? But did the goldfinch really know whom it was calling, who it was from whom it awaited a response to those questions that spoke louder than words?

Ah, good heavens, it was a goldfinch after all! Now it called for her, now it wept for her. How, after all, could anyone doubt that, at this moment, for example, sitting there all huddled up on the perch of its cage, with its little head tucked in and its beak sticking up and its eyes half-closed—how could anyone doubt that it was thinking of her, the dead? At such times, it would let out a few submissive cheeps, which were obvious proof that it was thinking of her, weeping for her, lamenting her absence. They were a torture, those cheeps.

The old man did not contradict his wife. For he was as certain of it as she! He would get up on a chair as if to whisper a few words of comfort to this poor little distressed soul; and scarcely letting himself see what he did, he would open once more the door of the cage.

"There he goes! There he goes! the little rascal!" he would exclaim, turning upon the chair to watch it with a smile in his eyes, his two hands up in front of his face as if to ward it off. And then, Grandpa and Grandma would have a quarrel; for the reason that she, time and time again, had told him that he should leave it alone when it was like that, and not disturb it in its sorrow.

"It's singing," the old man would say.

"What do you mean, it's singing!" the old lady would snap back at him, with a shrug of her shoulders. "You are talking nonsense! It's fairly frantic!"

And she would come running up to soothe it. But how was she to soothe it? It would flutter away disdainfully, first in one direction and then in the other; and quite right it was in so doing, for it must have thought that they had no consideration for it whatsoever at such a time as that.

And lo, the old man not only took all these scoldings from his wife, without telling her that the cage door had been shut, and that it was, possibly, on account of this that the goldfinch had been cheeping so pitifully; but he even wept at her words—wept and shook his head.

"That's right, poor little thing! That's right, poor little thing! He feels that we aren't considerate!"

He knew what it meant, the old man did, not to have consideration shown one. For the old couple were the talk of their neighbors, who severely criticized them for living the way they did, all wrapped up in that goldfinch, and with their windows all the time closed. The old man no longer so much as stuck his nose out of the door; for after all, he was an old man; and so, he stayed at home crying like a baby. But all the same, there were no flies on him; and if anyone in the street should have had the bad taste to crack a joke about him, his life (but what did his life mean to him now?)—his life would not have meant anything to him—it would have meant nothing at all, had he felt that he was an object of ridicule. Yes, sir, on account of that goldfinch there, if anyone had had the bad taste to say anything— Three times, when he was a young fellow, he had been within a hair's breadth—give him liberty or give him death! Ah, it no longer meant much to him, if his blind old eyes went out!

Every once in a while, these violent impulses would boil up in the old man, and he would rise and go, often with the goldfinch on his shoulder, to gaze with truculent eyes through the windowpane at the windows of the house across the way.

Of the reality of those houses across the way, those windows with the fancy panes, those balustrades, those vases of flowers and everything, or of the reality of those roofs, tiles and chimneys up above, the old man could not doubt, since he knew well enough to whom they belonged, who lived there, and how they lived. But the sad part is, he never once put to himself the question what either his own house or those others opposite could mean to the goldfinch upon his shoulder; and then, there was that big white tabby-cat, crouching and sunning itself on the window-sill directly facing him. Windows? panes? roofs? tiles? my house? your house? What was my house, your house for that big white cat, sleeping there in the sun? All houses were its houses, all that it could enter. What houses? Wherever it could find something to filch, wherever it could doze comfortably, or pretend to doze.

Did the old couple believe that, by thus keeping their doors and windows always shut, a cat, if it wanted to, could not find some other means of getting in to eat their goldfinch?

Was it too much to assume that the cat knew all about that goldfinch, knew that it was the very breath of life to that old couple, for the reason that it had belonged to their little granddaughter who was dead, and who had trained it so nicely to come out of its cage and fly around the house? And who could have foretold that the old man, once having caught the cat peering intently through the closed panes at the goldfinch in its heedless flight about the room, would go to warn the cat's mistress that—woe, woe, if he caught that cat there another time? There? Where? How was that? The cat's mistress—the old couple—the window—? the goldfinch?

And so, one day, it did eat it—yes, ate that goldfinch which, for it, might very well have been another. Entering the old couple's house, no one could say from where or how, the cat proceeded to eat the goldfinch up. It was near evening, and all the old lady heard was a little anguished peep and a moan. The old man came running in and caught a glimpse of a white object scampering away through the kitchen and, on the floor, a few delicate little white feathers which, as he opened the door, fluttered over the carpet. What a scream he let out! Despite the old lady's attempts to restrain him, he seized a weapon and ran like a madman to the house across the way. No, it was not the neighbor woman, but the cat—it was the cat that the old man wanted to kill, there, under her very eyes; and so, he fired into the dining-room, for he had caught sight of the cat there, quietly perched on the cupboard; he fired one, two, three times, and there was a great crashing of pottery. Then the neighbors' son came running out; he was armed, too, and he fired on the old man.

A tragedy. Weeping and screaming, the old man was taken back to his own house, in a dying condition; he had been shot through the lungs, and they carried him home to his aged wife.

The neighbors' son fled the country. A catastrophe in two homes; the whole countryside in an uproar for a night.

As for the cat, it scarcely remembered, a moment later, having eaten the goldfinch, any goldfinch; and it is doubtful if it understood that the old man was firing at it. It had taken a quick and nimble leap and had escaped; and now—there it was, all white against the black roof, gazing up at the stars which, from the darkening depths of interplanetary space, saw—and of this we may be quite certain—nothing whatsoever of the humble roofs of this mountain hamlet; and yet, so brilliantly did they shine up there, one would have sworn that they beheld nothing else that night.

YOUTH

Joseph Conrad

Born in Poland in 1857, Joseph Conrad is that rare figure, the writer who becomes a master in a foreign tongue. An orphan at the age of twelve, he acquired an early passion for the sea, finally setting sail from Marseilles as an apprentice in 1875. There followed a long and adventurous career as seaman, officer, and eventually captain. His writing career began relatively late in life, his first novel, Almayer's Folly, *being published in England in 1895. It was followed by a long and distinguished list of novels and short stories, many of them major works of our century. He died in England in 1924.*

In a period inclined to pessimism and emotional sterility, Conrad maintains a genuinely tragic view of existence. The central theme of his works is the moral victory achieved through heroic struggle against overwhelming calamity. Among his short stories, "Youth" (1902) is felt by most critics to be the best, and many believe it is the greatest of all modern short stories of the sea.

This could have occurred nowhere but in England, where men and sea interpenetrate, so to speak—the sea entering into the life of most men, and the men knowing something or everything about the sea, in the way of amusement, of travel, or of bread-winning.

We were sitting round a mahogany table that reflected the

bottle, the claret glasses, and our faces as we leaned on our elbows. There was a director of companies, an accountant, a lawyer, Marlow, and myself. The director had been a *Conway* boy, the accountant had served four years at sea, the lawyer —a fine crusted Tory, High Churchman, the best of old fellows, the soul of honor—had been chief officer in the P. & O. service in the good old days when mail-boats were square-rigged at least on two masts, and used to come down the China Sea before a fair monsoon with stun'-sails set alow and aloft. We all began life in the merchant service. Between the five of us there was the strong bond of the sea, and also the fellowship of the craft, which no amount of enthusiasm for yachting, cruising, and so on can give, since one is only the amusement of life and the other is life itself.

Marlow (at least I think that is how he spelt his name) told the story, or rather the chronicle, of a voyage:

"Yes, I have seen a little of the Eastern seas; but what I remember best is my first voyage there. You fellows know there are those voyages that seem ordered for the illustration of life, that might stand for a symbol of existence. You fight, work, sweat, nearly kill yourself, sometimes do kill yourself, trying to accomplish something—and you can't. Not from any fault of yours. You simply can do nothing, neither great nor little—not a thing in the world—not even marry an old maid, or get a wretched 600-ton cargo of coal to its port of destination.

"It was altogether a memorable affair. It was my first voyage to the East, and my first voyage as second mate; it was also my skipper's first command. You'll admit it was time. He was sixty if a day; a little man, with a broad, not very straight back, with bowed shoulders and one leg more bandy than the other, he had that queer twisted-about appearance you see so often in men who work in the fields. He had a nut-cracker face—chin and nose trying to come together over a sunken mouth—and it was framed in iron-gray fluffy hair, that looked like a chin strap of cotton-wool sprinkled with coal dust. And he had blue eyes in that old face of his, which were amazingly like a boy's, with that candid expression some quite common men preserve to the end of their days by a rare internal gift of simplicity of heart and rectitude of soul. What induced him to accept me was a wonder. I had come out of a crack Australian clipper, where I had been third officer, and he seemed to have a prejudice against crack clippers as aristocratic and high-toned. He said to me, 'You know, in this ship you will have to work.' I said I had to work in every ship I had ever been in. 'Ah, but this is different, and you gentlemen out of them big ships; . . . but there! I dare say you will do. Join tomorrow.'

"I joined tomorrow. It was twenty-two years ago; and I was just twenty. How time passes! It was one of the happiest days of my life. Fancy! Second mate for the first time—a really responsible officer! I wouldn't have thrown up my new billet for a fortune. The mate looked me over carefully. He was also an old chap, but of another stamp. He had a Roman nose, a snow-white, long beard, and his name was Mahon, but he insisted that it should be pronounced Mann. He was well connected; yet there was something wrong with his luck, and he had never got on.

"As to the captain, he had been for years in coasters, then in the Mediterranean, and last in the West Indian trade. He had never been round the Capes. He could just write a kind of sketchy hand, and didn't care for writing at all. Both were thorough good seamen of course, and between those two old chaps I felt like a small boy between two grandfathers.

"The ship also was old. Her name was the *Judea*. Queer name, isn't it? She belonged to a man Wilmer, Wilcox—some name like that; but he has been bankrupt and dead these twenty years or more, and his name don't matter. She had been laid up in Shadwell basin for ever so long. You can imagine her state. She was all rust, dust, grime—soot aloft, dirt on deck. To me it was like coming out of a palace into a ruined cottage. She was about 400 tons, had a primitive windlass, wooden latches on the doors, not a bit of brass about her, and a big square stern. There was on it, below her name in big letters, a lot of scroll work, with the gilt off, and some sort of a coat of arms, with the motto 'Do or Die' underneath. I remember it took my fancy immensely. There was a touch of romance in it, something that made me love the old thing—something that appealed to my youth!

"We left London in ballast—sand ballast—to load a cargo of coal in a northern port for Bankok. Bankok! I thrilled. I had been six years at sea, but had only seen Melbourne and Sydney, very good places, charming places in their way—but Bankok!

"We worked out of the Thames under canvas, with a North Sea pilot on board. His name was Jermyn, and he dodged all day long about the galley drying his handkerchief before the stove. Apparently he never slept. He was a dismal man, with a perpetual tear sparkling at the end of his nose, who either had been in trouble, or was in trouble, or expected to be in trouble—couldn't be happy unless something went wrong. He mistrusted my youth, my common sense, and my seamanship, and made a point of showing it in a hundred little ways. I dare say he was right. It seems to me I knew very little then, and I know not much more now; but I cherish a hate for that Jermyn to this day.

"We were a week working up as far as Yarmouth Roads, and then we got into a gale—the famous October gale of twenty-two years ago. It was wind, lightning, sleet, snow, and a terrific sea. We were flying light, and you may imagine how bad it was when I tell you we had smashed bulwarks and a flooded deck. On the second night she shifted her ballast into the lee bow, and by that time we had been blown off somewhere on the Dogger Bank. There was nothing for it but go below with shovels and try to right her, and there we were in that vast hold, gloomy like a cavern, the tallow dips stuck and flickering on the beams, the gale howling above, the ship tossing about like mad on her side; there we all were, Jermyn, the captain, everyone, hardly able to keep our feet, engaged on that gravedigger's work, and trying to toss shovelfuls of wet sand up to windward. At every tumble of the ship you could see vaguely in the dim light men falling down with a great flourish of shovels. One of the ship's boys (we had two), impressed by the weirdness of the scene, wept as if his heart would break. We could hear him blubbering somewhere in the shadows.

"On the third day the gale died out, and by-and-by a north-country tug picked us up. We took sixteen days in all to get from London to the Tyne! When we got into dock we had lost our turn for loading, and they hauled us off to a tier where we remained for a month. Mrs. Beard (the captain's name was Beard) came from Colchester to see the old man. She lived on board. The crew of runners had left, and there remained only the officers, one boy, and the steward, a mulatto who answered to the name of Abraham. Mrs. Beard was an old woman, with a face all wrinkled and ruddy like a winter apple, and the figure of a young girl. She caught sight of me once, sewing on a button, and insisted on having my shirts to repair. This was something different from the captains' wives I had known on board crack clippers. When I brought her the shirts, she said: 'And the socks? They want mending, I am sure, and John's—Captain Beard's—things are all in order now. I would be glad of something to do.' Bless the old woman. She overhauled my outfit for me, and meantime I read for the first time 'Sartor Resartus' and Burnaby's 'Ride to Khiva.' I didn't understand much of the first then; but I remember I preferred the soldier to the philosopher at the time; a preference which life has only confirmed. One was a man, and the other was either more—or less. However, they are both dead, and Mrs. Beard is dead, and youth, strength, genius, thoughts, achievements, simple hearts—all die. . . . No matter.

"They loaded us at last. We shipped a crew. Eight able seamen and two boys. We hauled off one evening to the buoys at the dock-gates, ready to go out, and with a fair prospect of beginning the voyage next day. Mrs. Beard was to start for home by a late train. When the ship was fast we went to tea. We sat rather silent through the meal—Mahon, the old couple, and I. I finished first, and slipped away for a smoke, my cabin being in a deckhouse just against the poop. It was high water, blowing fresh with a drizzle; the double dock-gates were opened, and the steam colliers were going in and out in the darkness with their lights burning bright, a great plashing of propellers, rattling of winches, and a lot of hailing on the pier-heads. I watched the procession of headlights gliding high and of green lights gliding low in the night, when suddenly a red gleam flashed at me, vanished, came into view again, and remained. The fore-end of a steamer loomed up close. I shouted down the cabin, 'Come up, quick!' and then heard a startled voice saying afar in the dark, 'Stop her, sir.' A bell jingled. Another voice cried warningly, 'We are going right into that bark, sir.' The answer to this was a gruff 'All right,' and the next thing was a heavy crash as the steamer struck a glancing blow with the bluff of her bow about our fore-rigging. There was a moment of confusion, yelling, and running about. Steam roared. Then somebody was heard saying, 'All clear, sir.' . . . 'Are you all right?' asked the gruff voice. I had jumped forward to see the damage, and hailed back, 'I think so.' 'Easy astern,' said the gruff voice. A bell jingled. 'What steamer is that?' screamed Mahon. By that time she was no more to us than a bulky shadow maneuvering a little way off. They shouted at us some name—a woman's name, Miranda or Melissa—or some such thing. 'This means another month in this beastly hole,' said Mahon to me, as we peered with lamps about the splintered bulwarks and broken braces. 'But where's the captain?'

"We had not heard or seen anything of him all that time. We went aft to look. A doleful voice arose hailing somewhere in the middle of the dock, '*Judea* ahoy!' . . . How the devil did he get there? . . . 'Hallo!' we shouted. 'I am adrift in our boat without oars,' he cried. A belated waterman offered his services, and Mahon struck a bargain with him for half-a-crown to tow our skipper alongside; but it was Mrs. Beard that came up the ladder first. They had been floating about the dock in that mizzly cold rain for nearly an hour. I was never so surprised in my life.

"It appears that when he heard my shout 'Come up,' he understood at once what was the matter, caught up his wife, ran on deck, and across, and down into our boat, which was fast to the ladder. Not bad for a sixty-year-old. Just imagine that old fellow saving heroically in his arms that old woman—the woman of his life. He set her down on a thwart, and was ready to climb back on board when the painter came adrift somehow, and away they went together. Of course in the confusion we did not hear him shouting. He looked abashed. She said cheerfully, 'I suppose it does not matter my losing the train now?' 'No, Jenny—you go below and get warm,' he growled. Then to us: 'A sailor has no business with a wife—I say. There I was, out of the ship. Well, no harm done this time. Let's go and look at what that fool of a steamer smashed.'

"It wasn't much, but it delayed us three weeks. At the end of that time, the captain being engaged with his agents, I carried Mrs. Beard's bag to the railway station and put her all comfy into a third-class carriage. She lowered the window to say, 'You are a good young man. If you see John—Captain Beard—without his muffler at night, just remind him from me to keep his throat well wrapped up.' 'Certainly, Mrs. Beard,' I said. 'You are a good young man; I noticed how attentive you are to John—to Captain—' The train pulled out suddenly; I took my cap off to the old woman: I never saw her again. . . . Pass the bottle.

"We went to sea next day. When we made that start for Bankok we had been already three months out of London. We had expected to be a fortnight or so—at the outside.

"It was January, and the weather was beautiful—the beautiful sunny winter weather that has more charm than in the summertime, because it is unexpected, and crisp, and you know it won't, it can't, last long. It's like a windfall, like a godsend, like an unexpected piece of luck.

"It lasted all down the North Sea, all down Channel; and it lasted till we were three hundred miles or so to the westward of the Lizards: then the wind went round to the sou'west and began to pipe up. In two days it blew a gale. The *Judea,* hove to, wallowed on the Atlantic like an old candlebox. It blew day after day: it blew with spite, without interval, without mercy, without rest. The world was nothing but an immensity of great foaming waves rushing at us, under a sky low enough to touch with the hand and dirty like a smoked ceiling. In the stormy space surrounding us there was as much flying spray as air. Day after day and night after night there was nothing round the ship but the howl of the wind, the tumult of the sea, the noise of water pouring over her deck. There was no rest for her and no rest for us. She tossed, she pitched, she stood on her head, she sat on her tail, she rolled, she groaned, and we had to hold on while on deck and cling to our bunks when below, in a constant effort of body and worry of mind.

"One night Mahon spoke through the small window of my berth. It opened right into my very bed, and I was lying there sleepless, in my boots, feeling as though I had not slept for years, and could not if I tried. He said excitedly—

" 'You got the sounding-rod in here, Marlow? I can't get the pumps to suck. By God! it's no child's play.'

"I gave him the sounding-rod and lay down again, trying to think of various things—but I thought only of the pumps. When I came on deck they were still at it, and my watch relieved at the pumps. By the light of the lantern brought on deck to examine the sounding-rod I caught a glimpse of their weary, serious faces. We pumped all the four hours. We pumped all night, all day, all the week,—watch and watch. She was working herself loose, and leaked badly—not enough to drown us at once, but enough to kill us with the work at the pumps. And while we pumped the ship was going from us piecemeal: the bulwarks went, the stanchions were torn out, the ventilators smashed, the cabin door burst in. There was not a dry spot in the ship. She was being gutted bit by bit. The longboat changed, as if by magic, into matchwood where she stood in her gripes. I had lashed her myself, and was rather proud of my handiwork, which had withstood so long the malice of the sea. And we pumped. And there was no break in the weather. The sea was white like a sheet of foam, like a caldron of boiling milk; there was not a break in the clouds, no—not the size of a man's hand—no, not for so much as ten seconds. There was for us no sky, there were for us no stars, no sun, no universe—nothing but angry clouds and an infuriated sea. We pumped watch and watch, for dear life; and it seemed to last for months, for years, for all eternity, as though we had been dead and gone to a hell for sailors. We forgot the day of the week, the name of the month, what year it was, and whether we had ever been ashore. The sails blew away, she lay broadside on under a weather-cloth, the ocean poured over her, and we did not care. We turned those handles, and had the eyes of idiots. As soon as we had crawled on deck I used to take a round turn with a rope about the men, the pumps, and the mainmast, and we turned, we turned incessantly, with the water to our waists, to our necks, over our heads. It was all one. We had forgotten how it felt to be dry.

"And there was somewhere in me the thought: By Jove! this is the deuce of an adventure—something you read about; and it is my first voyage as second mate—and I am only twenty—and here I am lasting it out as well as any of these men, and keeping my chaps up to the mark. I was pleased. I would not have given up the experience for worlds. I had moments of exultation. Whenever the old dismantled craft pitched heavily with her counter high in the air, she seemed to me to throw up, like an appeal, like a defiance, like a cry to the clouds without mercy, the words written on her stern: '*Judea*, London, Do or Die.'

"O youth! The strength of it, the faith of it, the imagination of it! To me she was not an old rattletrap carting about the world a lot of coal for a freight—to me she was the endeavor, the test, the trial of life. I think of her with pleasure, with affection, with regret—as you would think of someone dead you have loved. I shall never forget her. . . . Pass the bottle.

"One night when, tied to the mast, as I explained, we were pumping on, deafened with the wind, and without spirit enough in us to wish ourselves dead, a heavy sea crashed aboard and swept clean over us. As soon as I got my breath

I shouted, as in duty bound, 'Keep on, boys!' when suddenly I felt something hard floating on deck strike the calf of my leg. I made a grab at it and missed. It was so dark we could not see each other's faces within a foot—you understand.

"After that thump the ship kept quiet for a while, and the thing, whatever it was, struck my leg again. This time I caught it—and it was a saucepan. At first, being stupid with fatigue and thinking of nothing but the pumps, I did not understand what I had in my hand. Suddenly it dawned upon me, and I shouted, 'Boys, the house on deck is gone. Leave this, and let's look for the cook.'

"There was a deckhouse forward, which contained the galley, the cook's berth, and the quarters of the crew. As we had expected for days to see it swept away, the hands had been ordered to sleep in the cabin—the only safe place in the ship. The steward, Abraham, however, persisted in clinging to his berth, stupidly, like a mule—from sheer fright I believe, like an animal that won't leave a stable falling in an earthquake. So we went to look for him. It was chancing death, since once out of our lashings we were as exposed as if on a raft. But we went. The house was shattered as if a shell had exploded inside. Most of it had gone overboard—stove, men's quarters, and their property, all was gone; but two posts, holding a portion of the bulkhead to which Abraham's bunk was attached, remained as if by a miracle. We groped in the ruins and came upon this, and there he was, sitting in his bunk, surrounded by foam and wreckage, jabbering cheerfully to himself. He was out of his mind; completely and for ever mad, with this sudden shock coming upon the fag-end of his endurance. We snatched him up, lugged him aft, and pitched him head-first down the cabin companion. You understand there was no time to carry him down with infinite precautions and wait to see how he got on. Those below would pick him up at the bottom of the stairs all right. We were in a hurry to go back to the pumps. That business could not wait. A bad leak is an inhuman thing.

"One would think that the sole purpose of that fiendish gale had been to make a lunatic of that poor devil of a mulatto. It eased before morning, and next day the sky cleared, and as the sea went down the leak took up. When it came to bending a fresh set of sails the crew demanded to put back—and really there was nothing else to do. Boats gone, decks swept clean, cabin gutted, men without a stitch but what they stood in, stores spoiled, ship strained. We put her head for home, and—would you believe it? The wind came east right in our teeth. It blew fresh, it blew continuously. We had to beat up every inch of the way, but she did not leak so badly, the water keeping comparatively smooth. Two hours' pumping in every four is no joke—but it kept her afloat as far as Falmouth.

"The good people there live on casualties of the sea, and no doubt were glad to see us. A hungry crowd of shipwrights sharpened their chisels at the sight of that carcass of a ship. And, by Jove! they had pretty pickings off us before they were done. I fancy the owner was already in a tight place. There were delays. Then it was decided to take part of the cargo out and calk her topsides. This was done, the repairs finished, cargo reshipped; a new crew came on board, and we went out—for Bankok. At the end of a week we were back again. The crew said they weren't going to Bankok—a hundred and fifty days' passage—in a something hooker that wanted pumping eight hours out of the twenty-four; and the nautical papers inserted again the little paragraph: '*Judea.* Bark. Tyne to Bankok; coals; put back to Falmouth leaky and with crew refusing duty.'

"There were more delays—more tinkering. The owner came down for a day, and said she was as right as a little fiddle. Poor old Captain Beard looked like the ghost of a Geordie skipper—through the worry and humiliation of it. Remember he was sixty, and it was his first command. Mahon said it was a foolish business, and would end badly. I loved the ship more than ever, and wanted awfully to get to Bankok. To Bankok! Magic name, blessed name. Mesopotamia wasn't a patch on it. Remember I was twenty, and it was my first second mate's billet, and the East was waiting for me.

"We went out and anchored in the outer roads with a fresh crew—the third. She leaked worse than ever. It was as if those confounded shipwrights had actually made a hole in her. This time we did not even go outside. The crew simply refused to man the windlass.

"They towed us back to the inner harbor, and we became a fixture, a feature, an institution of the place. People pointed us out to visitors as 'That 'ere bark that's going to Bankok—has been here six months—put back three times.' On holidays the small boys pulling about in boats would hail, '*Judea*, ahoy!' and if a head showed above the rail shouted, 'Where you bound to?—Bankok?' and jeered. We were only three on board. The poor old skipper mooned in the cabin. Mahon undertook the cooking, and unexpectedly developed all a Frenchman's genius for preparing nice little messes. I looked languidly after the rigging. We became citizens of Falmouth. Every shopkeeper knew us. At the barber's or tobacconist's they asked familiarly, 'Do you think you will ever get to Bankok?' Meantime the owner, the underwriters, and the charterers squabbled amongst themselves in London, and our pay went on. . . . Pass the bottle.

"It was horrid. Morally it was worse than pumping for life. It seemed as though we had been forgotten by the world, belonged to nobody, would get nowhere; it seemed that, as if bewitched, we would have to live for ever and ever in that inner harbor, a derision and a byword to generations of longshore loafers and dishonest boatmen. I obtained three months' pay and a five days' leave, and made a rush for London. It took me a day to get there and pretty well another to come back—but three months' pay went all the same. I don't know what I did with it. I went to a music hall, I believe, lunched, dined, and supped in a swell place in Regent Street, and was back to time, with nothing but a complete set of Byron's works and a new railway rug to show for three months' work. The boatman who pulled me off to the ship said: 'Hallo! I thought you had left the old thing. *She* will never get to Bankok.' 'That's all *you* know about it,' I said scornfully—but I didn't like that prophecy at all.

"Suddenly a man, some kind of agent to somebody, appeared with full powers. He had grog blossoms all over his face, an indomitable energy, and was a jolly soul. We leaped into life again. A hulk came alongside, took our cargo, and then we went into dry dock to get our copper stripped. No wonder she leaked. The poor thing, strained beyond endurance by the gale, had, as if in disgust, spat out all the oakum of her lower seams. She was recalked, new coppered, and made as tight as a bottle. We went back to the hulk and reshipped our cargo.

"Then on a fine moonlight night, all the rats left the ship.

"We had been infested with them. They had destroyed our sails, consumed more stores than the crew, affably shared our beds and our dangers, and now, when the ship was made seaworthy, concluded to clear out. I called Mahon to enjoy the spectacle. Rat after rat appeared on our rail, took a last look over his shoulder, and leaped with a hollow thud into the empty hulk. We tried to count them, but soon lost the tale. Mahon said: 'Well, well! don't talk to me about the intelligence of rats. They ought to have left before, when we had that narrow squeak from foundering. There you have the proof how silly is the superstition about them. They leave a good ship for an old rotten hulk, where there is nothing to eat, too, the fools! . . . I don't believe they know what is safe or what is good for them, any more than you or I.'

"And after some more talk we agreed that the wisdom of rats had been grossly overrated, being in fact no greater than that of men.

"The story of the ship was known, by this, all up the Channel from Land's End to the Forelands, and we could get no crew on the south coast. They sent us one all complete from Liverpool, and we left once more—for Bankok.

"We had fair breezes, smooth water right into the tropics, and the old *Judea* lumbered along in the sunshine. When she went eight knots everything cracked aloft, and we tied our caps to our heads; but mostly she strolled on at the rate of three miles an hour. What could you expect? She was tired—that old ship. Her youth was where mine is—where yours is—you fellows who listen to this yarn; and what friend would throw your years and your weariness in your face? We didn't grumble at her. To us aft, at least, it seemed as though we had been born in her, reared in her, had lived in her for ages, had never known any other ship. I would just as soon have abused the old village church at home for not being a cathedral.

"And for me there was also my youth to make me patient. There was all the East before me, and all life, and the thought that I had been tried in that ship and had come out pretty well. And I thought of men of old who, centuries ago, went that road in ships that sailed no better, to the land of palms, and spices, and yellow sands, and of brown nations ruled by kings more cruel than Nero the Roman and more splendid than Solomon the Jew. The old bark lumbered on, heavy with her age and the burden of her cargo, while I lived the life of youth in ignorance and hope. She lumbered on through an interminable procession of days; and the fresh gilding flashed back at the setting sun, seemed to cry out over the darkening sea the words painted on her stern, '*Judea*, London. Do or Die.'

"Then we entered the Indian Ocean and steered northerly for Java Head. The winds were light. Weeks slipped by. She crawled on, do or die, and people at home began to think of posting us as overdue.

"One Saturday evening, I being off duty, the men asked me to give them an extra bucket of water or so—for washing clothes. As I did not wish to screw on the fresh-water pump so late, I went forward whistling, and with a key in my hand to unlock the forepeak scuttle, intending to serve the water out of a spare tank we kept there.

"The smell down below was as unexpected as it was frightful. One would have thought hundreds of paraffin lamps had been flaring and smoking in that hole for days. I was glad to get out. The man with me coughed and said, 'Funny smell, sir.' I answered negligently, 'It's good for the health, they say,' and walked aft.

"The first thing I did was to put my head down the square of the midship ventilator. As I lifted the lid a visible breath, something like a thin fog, a puff of faint haze, rose from the opening. The ascending air was hot, and had a heavy, sooty, paraffiny smell. I gave one sniff, and put down the lid gently. It was no use choking myself. The cargo was on fire.

"Next day she began to smoke in earnest. You see it was to be expected, for though the coal was of a safe kind, that cargo had been so handled, so broken up with handling, that it looked more like smithy coal than anything else. Then it had been wetted—more than once. It rained all the time we were taking it back from the hulk, and now with this long passage it got heated, and there was another case of spontaneous combustion.

"The captain called us into the cabin. He had a chart spread on the table, and looked unhappy. He said, 'The coast of West Australia is near, but I mean to proceed to our destination. It is the hurricane month too; but we will just keep her head for Bankok, and fight the fire. No more putting back anywhere, if we all get roasted. We will try first to stifle this 'ere damned combustion by want of air.'

"We tried. We battened down everything, and still she smoked. The smoke kept coming out through imperceptible crevices; it forced itself through bulkheads and covers; it oozed here and there and everywhere in slender threads, in an invisible film, in an incomprehensible manner. It made its way into the cabin, into the forecastle; it poisoned the sheltered places on the deck; it could be sniffed as high as the mainyard. It was clear that if the smoke came out the air came in. This was disheartening. This combustion refused to be stifled.

"We resolved to try water, and took the hatches off. Enormous volumes of smoke, whitish, yellowish, thick, greasy, misty, choking, ascended as high as the trucks. All hands cleared out aft. Then the poisonous cloud blew away, and we went back to work in a smoke that was no thicker now than that of an ordinary factory chimney.

"We rigged the force pump, got the hose along, and by-and-by it burst. Well, it was as old as the ship—a prehistoric hose, and past repair. Then we pumped with the feeble head-pump, drew water with buckets, and in this way managed in time to pour lots of Indian Ocean into the main hatch. The bright stream flashed in sunshine, fell into a layer of white crawling smoke, and vanished on the black surface of coal. Steam ascended mingling with the smoke. We poured salt water as into a barrel without a bottom. It was our fate to pump in that ship, to pump out of her, to pump into her; and after keeping water out of her to save ourselves from being drowned, we frantically poured water into her to save ourselves from being burnt.

"And she crawled on, do or die, in the serene weather. The sky was a miracle of purity, a miracle of azure. The sea was polished, was blue, was pellucid, was sparkling like a precious stone, extending on all sides, all round to the horizon—as if the whole terrestrial globe had been one jewel, one colossal sapphire, a single gem fashioned into a planet. And on the luster of the great calm waters the *Judea* glided imperceptibly, enveloped in languid and unclean vapors, in a lazy cloud that drifted to leeward, light and slow: a pestiferous cloud defiling the splendor of sea and sky.

"All this time of course we saw no fire. The cargo smoldered at the bottom somewhere. Once Mahon, as we were working side by side, said to me with a queer smile: 'Now, if she only would spring a tidy leak—like that time when we first left the Channel—it would put a stopper on this fire. Wouldn't it?' I remarked irrelevantly, 'Do you remember the rats?'

"We fought the fire and sailed the ship too as carefully as though nothing had been the matter. The steward cooked and attended on us. Of the other twelve men, eight worked while four rested. Everyone took his turn, captain included. There was equality, and if not exactly fraternity, then a deal of good feeling. Sometimes a man, as he dashed a bucketful of water down the hatchway, would yell out, 'Hurrah for Bankok!' and the rest laughed. But generally we were taciturn and serious—and thirsty. Oh! how thirsty! And we had to be careful with the water. Strict allowance. The ship smoked, the sun blazed. . . . Pass the bottle.

"We tried everything. We even made an attempt to dig down to the fire. No good, of course. No man could remain more than a minute below. Mahon, who went first, fainted there, and the man who went to fetch him out did likewise. We lugged them out on deck. Then I leaped down to show how easily it could be done. They had learned wisdom by that time, and contented themselves by fishing for me with a chain-hook tied to a broom handle, I believe. I did not offer to go and fetch up my shovel, which was left down below.

"Things began to look bad. We put the longboat into the water. The second boat was ready to swing out. We had also another, a fourteen-foot thing, on davits aft, where it was quite safe.

"Then behold, the smoke suddenly decreased. We redoubled our efforts to flood the bottom of the ship. In two days there was no smoke at all. Everybody was on the broad grin. This was on a Friday. On Saturday no work, but sailing the ship of course was done. The men washed their clothes and their faces for the first time in a fortnight, and had a special dinner given them. They spoke of spontaneous combustion with contempt, and implied *they* were the boys to put out combustions. Somehow we all felt as though we each had inherited a large fortune. But a beastly smell of burning hung about the ship. Captain Beard had hollow eyes and sunken cheeks. I had never noticed so much before how twisted and bowed he was. He and Mahon prowled soberly about hatches and ventilators, sniffing. It struck me suddenly poor Mahon was a very, very old chap. As to me, I was as pleased and proud as though I had helped to win a great naval battle. O! Youth!

"The night was fine. In the morning a homeward-bound ship passed us hull down—the first we had seen for months; but we were nearing the land at last, Java Head being about 190 miles off, and nearly due north.

"Next day it was my watch on deck from eight to twelve. At breakfast the captain observed, 'It's wonderful how that smell hangs about the cabin.' About ten, the mate being on the poop, I stepped down on the main deck for a moment. The carpenter's bench stood abaft the mainmast: I leaned against it sucking at my pipe, and the carpenter, a young chap, came to talk to me. He remarked, 'I think we have done very well, haven't we?' and then I perceived with annoyance the fool was trying to tilt the bench. I said curtly, 'Don't, Chips,' and immediately became aware of a queer sensation, of an absurd delusion—I seemed somehow to be in the air. I heard all round me like a pent-up breath released—as if a thousand giants simultaneously had said Phoo!—and felt a dull concussion which made my ribs ache suddenly. No doubt about it—I was in the air, and my body was describing a short parabola. But short as it was, I had the time to think several thoughts in, as far as I can remember, the following order: 'This can't be the carpenter—What is it?—Some accident—Submarine volcano?—Coals, gas!—By Jove! we are being blown up—Everybody's dead—I am falling into the afterhatch—I see fire in it.'

"The coal dust suspended in the air of the hold had glowed dull red at the moment of the explosion. In the twinkling of an eye, in an infinitesimal fraction of a second since the first tilt of the bench, I was sprawling full length on the cargo. I picked myself up and scrambled out. It was quick like a rebound. The deck was a wilderness of smashed timber, lying crosswise like trees in a wood after a hurricane; an immense curtain of soiled rags waved gently before me—it was the mainsail blown to strips. I thought, The masts will be toppling over directly; and to get out of the way bolted on all fours towards the poop-ladder. The first person I saw was Mahon, with eyes like saucers, his mouth open, and the long white hair standing straight on end round his head like a silver halo. He was just about to go down when the sight of the main deck stirring, heaving up, and changing into splinters before his eyes, petrified him on the top step. I stared at him in unbelief, and he stared at me with a queer kind of shocked curiosity. I did not know that I had no hair, no eyebrows, no eyelashes, that my young mustache was burnt off, that my face was black, one cheek laid open, my nose cut, and my chin bleeding. I had lost my cap, one of my slippers, and my shirt was torn to rags. Of all this I was not aware. I was amazed to see the ship still afloat, the poop-deck whole—and, most of all, to see anybody alive. Also the peace of the sky and the serenity of the sea were distinctly surprising. I suppose I expected to see them convulsed with horror. . . . Pass the bottle.

"There was a voice hailing the ship from somewhere—in the air, in the sky—I couldn't tell. Presently I saw the captain—and he was mad. He asked me eagerly, 'Where's the cabin-table?' and to hear such a question was a frightful shock. I had just been blown up, you understand, and vibrated with that experience—I wasn't quite sure whether I was alive. Mahon began to stamp with both feet and yelled at him, 'Good God! don't you see the deck's blown out of her?' I found my voice, and stammered out as if conscious of some gross neglect of duty, 'I don't know where the cabin-table is.' It was like an absurd dream.

"Do you know what he wanted next? Well, he wanted to trim the yards. Very placidly, and as if lost in thought, he insisted on having the foreyard squared. 'I don't know if there's anybody alive,' said Mahon, almost tearfully. 'Surely,' he said, gently, 'there will be enough left to square the foreyard.'

"The old chap, it seems, was in his own berth, winding up the chronometers, when the shock sent him spinning. Immediately it occurred to him—as he said afterwards—that the ship had struck something, and he ran out into the cabin. There, he saw, the cabin-table had vanished somewhere. The deck being blown up, it had fallen down into the lazarette of course. Where we had our breakfast that morning he saw only a great hole in the floor. This appeared to him so awfully mysterious, and impressed him so immensely, that what he saw and heard after he got on deck were mere trifles in comparison. And, mark, he noticed directly the wheel deserted and his bark off her course—and his only thought was to get that miserable, stripped, undecked, smoldering shell of a ship back again with her head pointing at her port of destination. Bankok! That's what he was after. I tell you this quiet, bowed, bandy-legged, almost deformed little man was immense in the singleness of his idea and in his placid ignorance of our agitation. He motioned us forward with a commanding gesture, and went to take the wheel himself.

"Yes; that was the first thing we did—trim the yards of that wreck! No one was killed, or even disabled, but everyone was more or less hurt. You should have seen them! Some were in rags, with black faces, like coal-heavers, like sweeps, and had bullet heads that seemed closely cropped, but were in fact singed to the skin. Others, of the watch below, awakened by being shot out from their collapsing bunks, shivered incessantly, and kept on groaning even as we went about our work. But they all worked. That crew of Liverpool hard cases had in them the right stuff. It's my experience they always have. It is the sea that gives it—the vastness, the loneliness surrounding their dark stolid souls. Ah! Well! we stumbled, we crept, we fell, we barked our shins on the wreckage, we hauled. The masts stood, but we did not know how much they might be charred down below. It was nearly calm, but a long swell ran from the west and made her roll. They might go at any moment. We looked at them with apprehension. One could not foresee which way they would fall.

"Then we retreated aft and looked about us. The deck was a tangle of planks on edge, of planks on end, of splinters, of ruined woodwork. The masts rose from that chaos like big trees above a matted undergrowth. The interstices of that mass of wreckage were full of something whitish, sluggish, stirring—of something that was like a greasy fog. The smoke of the invisible fire was coming up again, was trailing, like a poisonous thick mist in some valley choked with dead wood. Already lazy wisps were beginning to curl upwards amongst the mass of splinters. Here and there a piece of timber, stuck upright, resembled a post. Half of a fife-rail had been shot through the foresail, and the sky made a patch of glorious blue in the ignobly soiled canvas. A portion of several boards holding together had fallen across the rail, and one end protruded overboard, like a gangway leading upon nothing, like a gangway leading over the deep sea, leading to death—as if inviting us to walk the plank at once and be done with our ridiculous troubles. And still the air, the sky—a ghost, something invisible was hailing the ship.

"Someone had the sense to look over, and there was the

helmsman, who had impulsively jumped overboard, anxious to come back. He yelled and swam lustily like a merman, keeping up with the ship. We threw him a rope, and presently he stood amongst us streaming with water and very crestfallen. The captain had surrendered the wheel, and apart, elbow on rail and chin in hand, gazed at the sea wistfully. We asked ourselves, What next? I thought, Now, that is something like. This is great. I wonder what will happen. O youth!

"Suddenly Mahon sighted a steamer far astern. Captain Beard said, 'We may do something with her yet.' We hoisted two flags, which said in the international language of the sea, 'On fire. Want immediate assistance.' The steamer grew bigger rapidly, and by-and-by spoke with two flags on her foremast, 'I am coming to your assistance.'

"In half an hour she was abreast, to windward, within hail, and rolling slightly, with her engines stopped. We lost our composure, and yelled all together with excitement, 'We've been blown up.' A man in a white helmet, on the bridge, cried, 'Yes! All right! all right!' and he nodded his head, and smiled, and made soothing motions with his hand as though at a lot of frightened children. One of the boats dropped in the water, and walked towards us upon the sea with her long oars. Four Calashes pulled a swinging stroke. This was my first sight of Malay seamen. I've known them since, but what struck me then was their unconcern: they came alongside, and even the bowman standing up and holding to our main-chains with the boat-hook did not deign to lift his head for a glance. I thought people who had been blown up deserved more attention.

"A little man, dry like a chip and agile like a monkey, clambered up. It was the mate of the steamer. He gave one look, and cried, 'O boys—you had better quit.'

"We were silent. He talked apart with the captain for a time—seemed to argue with him. Then they went away together to the steamer.

"When our skipper came back we learned that the steamer was the *Sommerville*, Captain Nash, from West Australia to Singapore via Batavia with mails, and that the agreement was she should tow us to Anjer or Batavia, if possible, where we could extinguish the fire by scuttling, and then proceed on our voyage—to Bankok! The old man seemed excited.

'We will do it yet,' he said to Mahon, fiercely. He shook his fist at the sky. Nobody else said a word.

"At noon the steamer began to tow. She went ahead slim and high, and what was left of the *Judea* followed at the end of seventy fathom of tow-rope—followed her swiftly like a cloud of smoke with mastheads protruding above. We went aloft to furl the sails. We coughed on the yards, and were careful about the bunts. Do you see the lot of us there, putting a neat furl on the sails of that ship doomed to arrive nowhere? There was not a man who didn't think that at any moment the masts would topple over. From aloft we could not see the ship for smoke, and they worked carefully, passing the gaskets with even turns. 'Harbor furl—aloft there!' cried Mahon from below.

"You understand this? I don't think one of those chaps expected to get down in the usual way. When we did I heard them saying to each other, 'Well, I thought we would come down overboard, in a lump—sticks and all—blame me if I didn't.' 'That's what I was thinking to myself,' would answer wearily another battered and bandaged scarecrow. And, mind, these were men without the drilled-in habit of obedience. To an onlooker they would be a lot of profane scallywags without a redeeming point. What made them do it—what made them obey me when I, thinking consciously how fine it was, made them drop the bunt of the foresail twice to try and do it better? What? They had no professional reputation—no examples, no praise. It wasn't a sense of duty; they all knew well enough how to shirk, and laze, and dodge—when they had a mind to it—and mostly they had. Was it the two pounds ten a month that sent them there? They didn't think their pay half good enough. No; it was something in them, something inborn and subtle and everlasting. I don't say positively that the crew of a French or German merchantman wouldn't have done it, but I doubt whether it would have been done in the same way. There was a completeness in it, something solid like a principle, and masterful like an instinct—a disclosure of something secret—of that hidden something, that gift, of good or evil that makes racial difference, that shapes the fate of nations.

"It was that night at ten that, for the first time since we had been fighting it, we saw the fire. The speed of the towing had fanned the smoldering destruction. A blue gleam appeared forward, shining below the wreck of the deck. It wavered in patches, it seemed to stir and creep like the light of a glowworm. I saw it first, and told Mahon. 'Then the game's up,' he said. 'We had better stop this towing, or she will burst out suddenly fore and aft before we can clear out.' We set up a yell; rang bells to attract their attention; they towed on. At last Mahon and I had to crawl forward and cut the rope with an ax. There was no time to cast off the lashings. Red tongues could be seen licking the wilderness of splinters under our feet as we made our way back to the poop.

"Of course they very soon found out in the steamer that the rope was gone. She gave a loud blast of her whistle, her lights were seen sweeping in a wide circle, she came up ranging close alongside, and stopped. We were all in a tight group on the poop looking at her. Every man had saved a little bundle or a bag. Suddenly a conical flame with a twisted top shot up forward and threw upon the black sea a circle of light, with the two vessels side by side and heaving gently in its center. Captain Beard had been sitting on the gratings still and mute for hours, but now he rose slowly and advanced in front of us, to the mizzen-shrouds. Captain Nash hailed: 'Come along! Look sharp. I have mail bags on board. I will take you and your boats to Singapore.'

" 'Thank you! No!' said our skipper. 'We must see the last of the ship.'

" 'I can't stand by any longer,' shouted the other. 'Mails —you know.'

" 'Ay! ay! We are all right.'

" 'Very well! I'll report you in Singapore. . . . Good-by!'

"He waved his hand. Our men dropped their bundles quietly. The steamer moved ahead, and passing out of the circle of light, vanished at once from our sight, dazzled by the fire which burned fiercely. And then I knew that I would see the East first as commander of a small boat. I thought it fine; and the fidelity to the old ship was fine. We should see the last of her. Oh the glamour of youth! Oh the fire of it, more dazzling than the flames of the burning ship, throwing a magic light on the wide earth, leaping audaciously to the sky, presently to be quenched by time, more cruel, more pitiless, more bitter than the sea—and like the flames of the burning ship surrounded by an impenetrable night.

"The old man warned us in his gentle and inflexible way

that it was part of our duty to save for the underwriters as much as we could of the ship's gear. Accordingly we went to work aft, while she blazed forward to give us plenty of light. We lugged out a lot of rubbish. What didn't we save? An old barometer fixed with an absurd quantity of screws nearly cost me my life: a sudden rush of smoke came upon me, and I just got away in time. There were various stores, bolts of canvas, coils of rope; the poop looked like a marine bazaar, and the boats were lumbered to the gunwales. One would have thought the old man wanted to take as much as he could of his first command with him. He was very, very quiet, but off his balance evidently. Would you believe it? He wanted to take a length of old stream-cable and a kedge-anchor with him in the longboat. We said, 'Ay, ay, sir,' deferentially, and on the quiet let the thing slip overboard. The heavy medicine chest went that way, two bags of green coffee, tins of paint—fancy, paint!—a whole lot of things. Then I was ordered with two hands into the boats to make a stowage and get them ready against the time it would be proper for us to leave the ship.

"We put everything straight, stepped the longboat's mast for our skipper, who was to take charge of her, and I was not sorry to sit down for a moment. My face felt raw, every limb ached as if broken, I was aware of all my ribs, and would have sworn to a twist in the backbone. The boats, fast astern, lay in a deep shadow, and all around I could see the circle of the sea lighted by the fire. A gigantic flame arose forward straight and clear. It flared fierce, with noises like the whir of wings, with rumbles as of thunder. There were cracks, detonations, and from the cone of flame the sparks flew upwards, as man is born to trouble, to leaky ships, and to ships that burn.

"What bothered me was that the ship, lying broadside to the swell and to such wind as there was—a mere breath—the boats would not keep astern where they were safe, but persisted, in a pig-headed way boats have, in getting under the counter and then swinging alongside. They were knocking about dangerously and coming near the flame, while the ship rolled on them, and, of course, there was always the danger of the masts going over the side at any moment. I and my two boat-keepers kept them off as best we could with oars and boat-hooks; but to be constantly at it became exasperating, since there was no reason why we should not leave at once. We could not see those on board, nor could we imagine what caused the delay. The boat-keepers were swearing feebly, and I had not only my share of the work, but also had to keep at it two men who showed a constant inclination to lay themselves down and let things slide.

"At last I hailed 'On deck there,' and someone looked over. 'We're ready here,' I said. The head disappeared, and very soon popped up again. 'The captain says, All right, sir, and to keep the boats well clear of the ship.'

"Half an hour passed. Suddenly there was a frightful racket, rattle, clanking of chain, hiss of water, and millions of sparks flew up into the shivering column of smoke that stood leaning slightly above the ship. The catheads had burned away, and the two red-hot anchors had gone to the bottom, tearing out after them two hundred fathom of red-hot chain. The ship trembled, the mass of flame swayed as if ready to collapse, and the fore top-gallant-mast fell. It darted down like an arrow of fire, shot under, and instantly leaping up within an oar's-length of the boats, floated quietly, very black on the luminous sea. I hailed the deck again. After some time a man in an unexpectedly cheerful but also muffled tone, as though he had been trying to speak with his mouth shut, informed me, 'Coming directly, sir,' and vanished. For a long time I heard nothing but the whir and roar of the fire. There were also whistling sounds. The boats jumped, tugged at the painters, ran at each other playfully, knocked their sides together, or, do what we would, swung in a bunch against the ship's side. I couldn't stand it any longer, and swarming up a rope, clambered aboard over the stern.

"It was as bright as day. Coming up like this, the sheet of fire facing me was a terrifying sight, and the heat seemed hardly bearable at first. On a settee cushion dragged out of the cabin, Captain Beard, with his legs drawn up and one arm under his head, slept with the light playing on him. Do you know what the rest were busy about? They were sitting on deck right aft, round an open case, eating bread and cheese and drinking bottled stout.

"On the background of flames twisting in fierce tongues above their heads they seemed at home like salamanders, and looked like a band of desperate pirates. The fire sparkled in the whites of their eyes, gleamed on patches of white skin seen through the torn shirts. Each had the marks as of a battle about him—bandaged heads, tied-up arms, a strip of dirty rag round a knee—and each man had a bottle between his legs and a chunk of cheese in his hand. Mahon got up. With his handsome and disreputable head, his hooked profile, his long white beard, and with an uncorked bottle in his hand, he resembled one of those reckless sea-robbers of old making merry amidst violence and disaster. 'The last meal on board,' he explained solemnly. 'We had nothing to eat all day, and it was no use leaving all this.' He flourished the bottle and indicated the sleeping skipper. 'He said he couldn't swallow anything, so I got him to lie down,' he went on; and as I stared, 'I don't know whether you are aware, young fellow, the man had no sleep to speak of for days—and there will be dam' little sleep in the boats.' 'There will be no boats by-and-by if you fool about much longer,' I said, indignantly. I walked up to the skipper and shook him by the shoulder. At last he opened his eyes, but did not move. 'Time to leave her, sir,' I said quietly.

"He got up painfully, looked at the flames, at the sea sparkling round the ship, and black, black as ink farther away; he looked at the stars shining dim through a thin veil of smoke in a sky black, black as Erebus.

" 'Youngest first,' he said.

"And the ordinary seaman, wiping his mouth with the back of his hand, got up, clambered over the taffrail, and vanished. Others followed. One, on the point of going over, stopped short to drain his bottle, and with a great swing of his arm flung it at the fire. 'Take this!' he cried.

"The skipper lingered disconsolately, and we left him to commune alone for a while with his first command. Then I went up again and brought him away at last. It was time. The ironwork on the poop was hot to the touch.

"Then the painter of the long-boat was cut, and the three boats, tied together, drifted clear of the ship. It was just sixteen hours after the explosion when we abandoned her. Mahon had charge of the second boat, and I had the smallest—the 14-foot thing. The long-boat would have taken the lot of us; but the skipper said we must save as much property as we could—for the underwriters—and so I got my first command. I had two men with me, a bag of biscuits, a few tins of meat, and a breaker of water. I was ordered to keep close to the long-boat, that in case of bad weather we might be taken into her.

"And do you know what I thought? I thought I would

part company as soon as I could. I wanted to have my first command all to myself. I wasn't going to sail in a squadron if there were a chance for independent cruising. I would make land by myself. I would beat the other boats. Youth! All youth! The silly, charming, beautiful youth.

"But we did not make a start at once. We must see the last of the ship. And so the boats drifted about that night, heaving and setting on the swell. The men dozed, waked, sighed, groaned. I looked at the burning ship.

"Between the darkness of earth and heaven she was burning fiercely upon a disc of purple sea shot by the blood-red play of gleams; upon a disc of water glittering and sinister. A high, clear flame, an immense and lonely flame, ascended from the ocean, and from its summit the black smoke poured continuously at the sky. She burned furiously; mournful and imposing like a funeral pile kindled in the night, surrounded by the sea, watched over by the stars. A magnificent death had come like a grace, like a gift, like a reward to that old ship at the end of her laborious days. The surrender of her weary ghost to the keeping of stars and sea was stirring like the sight of a glorious triumph. The masts fell just before daybreak, and for a moment there was a burst and turmoil of sparks that seemed to fill with flying fire the night patient and watchful, the vast night lying silent upon the sea. At daylight she was only a charred shell, floating still under a cloud of smoke and bearing a glowing mass of coal within.

"Then the oars were got out, and the boats forming in a line moved round her remains as if in procession—the long-boat leading. As we pulled across her stern a slim dart of fire shot out viciously at us, and suddenly she went down, head first, in a great hiss of steam. The unconsumed stern was the last to sink; but the paint had gone, had cracked, had peeled off, and there were no letters, there was no word, no stubborn device that was like her soul, to flash at the rising sun her creed and her name.

"We made our way north. A breeze sprang up, and about noon all the boats came together for the last time. I had no mast or sail in mine, but I made a mast out of a spare oar and hoisted a boat-awning for a sail, with a boat-hook for a yard. She was certainly over-masted, but I had the satisfaction of knowing that with the wind aft I could beat the other two. I had to wait for them. Then we all had a look at the captain's chart, and, after a sociable meal of hard bread and water, got our last instructions. These were simple: steer north, and keep together as much as possible. 'Be careful with that jury-rig, Marlow,' said the captain; and Mahon, as I sailed proudly past his boat, wrinkled his curved nose and hailed, 'You will sail that ship of yours under water, if you don't look out, young fellow.' He was a malicious old man—and may the deep sea where he sleeps now rock him gently, rock him tenderly to the end of time!

"Before sunset a thick rain-squall passed over the two boats, which were far astern, and that was the last I saw of them for a time. Next day I sat steering my cockle-shell—my first command—with nothing but water and sky around me. I did sight in the afternoon the upper sails of a ship far away, but said nothing, and my men did not notice her. You see I was afraid she might be homeward bound, and I had no mind to turn back from the portals of the East. I was steering for Java—another blessed name—like Bankok, you know. I steered many days.

"I need not tell you what it is to be knocking about in an open boat. I remember nights and days of calm, and we pulled, we pulled, and the boat seemed to stand still, as if bewitched within the circle of the sea horizon. I remember the heat, the deluge of rain-squalls that kept us baling for dear life (but filled our water-cask), and I remember sixteen hours on end with a mouth dry as a cinder and a steering-oar over the stern to keep my first command head on to a breaking sea. I did not know how good a man I was till then. I remember the drawn faces, the dejected figures of my two men, and I remember my youth and the feeling that will never come back any more—the feeling that I could last for ever, outlast the sea, the earth, and all men; the deceitful feeling that lures us on to joys, to perils, to love, to vain effort—to death; the triumphant conviction of strength, the heat of life in the handful of dust, the glow in the heart that with every year grows dim, grows cold, grows small, and expires—and expires, too soon, too soon—before life itself.

"And this is how I see the East. I have seen its secret places and have looked into its very soul; but now I see it always from a small boat, a high outline of mountains, blue and afar in the morning; like faint mist at noon; a jagged wall of purple at sunset. I have the feel of the oar in my hand, the vision of a scorching blue sea in my eyes. And I see a bay, a wide bay, smooth as glass and polished like ice, shimmering in the dark. A red light burns far off upon the gloom of the land, and the night is soft and warm. We drag at the oars with aching arms, and suddenly a puff of wind, a puff faint and tepid and laden with strange odours of blossoms, of aromatic wood, comes out of the still night—the first sigh of the East on my face. That I can never forget. It was impalpable and enslaving, like a charm, like a whispered promise of mysterious delight.

"We had been pulling this finishing spell for eleven hours. Two pulled, and he whose turn it was to rest sat at the tiller. We had made out the red light in that bay and steered for it, guessing it must mark some small coasting port. We passed two vessels, outlandish and high-sterned, sleeping at anchor, and, approaching the light, now very dim, ran the boat's nose against the end of a jutting wharf. We were blind with fatigue. My men dropped the oars and fell off the thwarts as if dead. I made fast to a pile. A current rippled softly. The scented obscurity of the shore was grouped into vast masses, a density of colossal clumps of vegetation, probably—mute and fantastic shapes. And at their foot the semicircle of a beach gleamed faintly, like an illusion. There was not a light, not a stir, not a sound. The mysterious East faced me, perfumed like a flower, silent like death, dark like a grave.

"And I sat weary beyond expression, exulting like a conqueror, sleepless and entranced as if before a profound, a fateful enigma.

"A splashing of oars, a measured dip reverberating on the level of water, intensified by the silence of the shore into loud claps, made me jump up. A boat, a European boat, was coming in. I invoked the name of the dead; I hailed: *Judea* ahoy! A thin shout answered.

"It was the captain. I had beaten the flagship by three hours, and I was glad to hear the old man's voice again, tremulous and tired. 'Is it you, Marlow?' 'Mind the end of that jetty, sir,' I cried.

"He approached cautiously, and brought up with the deep-sea lead-line which we had saved—for the underwriters. I eased my painter and fell alongside. He sat, a broken figure at the stern, wet with dew, his hands clasped in his lap. His men were asleep already. 'I had a terrible time of it,' he murmured. 'Mahon is behind—not very far.' We conversed whispers, in low whispers, as if afraid to wake up th

Guns, thunder, earthquakes would not have awakened the men just then.

"Looking round as we talked, I saw away at sea a bright light travelling in the night. 'There's a steamer passing the bay,' I said. She was not passing, she was entering, and she even came close and anchored. 'I wish,' said the old man, 'you would find out whether she is English. Perhaps they could give us a passage somewhere.' He seemed nervously anxious. So by dint of punching and kicking I started one of my men into a state of somnambulism, and giving him an oar, took another and pulled towards the lights of the steamer.

"There was a murmur of voices in her, metallic hollow clangs of the engine-room, footsteps on the deck. Her ports shone, round like dilated eyes. Shapes moved about, and there was a shadowy man high up on the bridge. He heard my oars.

"And then, before I could open my lips, the East spoke to me, but it was in a Western voice. A torrent of words was poured into the enigmatical, the fateful silence: outlandish, angry words, mixed with words and even whole sentences of good English, less strange but even more surprising. The voice swore and cursed violently; it riddled the solemn peace of the bay by a volley of abuse. It began by calling me Pig, and from that went crescendo into unmentionable adjectives —in English. The man up there raged aloud in two languages, and with a sincerity in his fury that almost convinced me I had, in some way, sinned against the harmony of the universe. I could hardly see him, but began to think he would work himself into a fit.

"Suddenly he ceased, and I could hear him snorting and blowing like a porpoise. I said—

" 'What steamer is this, pray?'

" 'Eh? What's this? And who are you?'

" 'Castaway crew of an English barque burnt at sea. We came here tonight. I am the second mate. The captain is in the long-boat, and wishes to know if you would give us a passage somewhere.'

" 'Oh, my goodness! I say. . . . This is the *Celestial* from Singapore on her return trip. I'll arrange with your captian [illegible]e morning, . . . and, . . . I say, . . . did you hear me [illegible]y?'"

[illegible]uld think the whole bay heard you.'

[illegible]ht you were a shore-boat. Now, look here—this [illegible]oundrel of a caretaker has gone to sleep again

—curse him. The light is out, and I nearly ran foul of the end of this damned jetty. This is the third time he plays me this trick. Now, I ask you, can anybody stand this kind of thing? It's enough to drive a man out of his mind. I'll report him. . . . I'll get the Assistant Resident to give him the sack, by . . . ! See—there's no light. It's out, isn't it! I take you to witness the light's out. There should be a light, you know. A red light on the——'

" 'There was a light,' I said, mildly.

" 'But it's out, man! What's the use of talking like this? You can see for yourself it's out—don't you? If you had to take a valuable steamer along this God-forsaken coast you would want a light, too. I'll kick him from end to end of his miserable wharf. You'll see if I don't. I will——'

" 'So I may tell my captain you'll take us?' I broke in.

" 'Yes, I'll take you. Good-night,' he said, brusquely.

"I pulled back, made fast again to the jetty, and then went to sleep at last. I had faced the silence of the East. I had heard some of its language. But when I opened my eyes again the silence was as complete as though it had never been broken. I was lying in a flood of light, and the sky had never looked so far, so high, before. I opened my eyes and lay without moving.

"And then I saw the men of the East—they were looking at me. The whole length of the jetty was full of people. I saw brown, bronze, yellow faces, the black eyes, the glitter, the colour of an Eastern crowd. And all these beings stared without a murmur, without a sigh, without a movement. They stared down at the boats, at the sleeping men who at night had come to them from the sea. Nothing moved. The fronds of palms stood still against the sky. Not a branch stirred along the shore, and the brown roofs of hidden houses peeped through the green foliage, through the big leaves that hung shining and still like leaves forged of heavy metal. This was the East of the ancient navigators, so old, so mysterious, resplendent and sombre, living and unchanged, full of danger and promise. And these were the men. I sat up suddenly. A wave of movement passed through the crowd from end to end, passed along the heads, swayed the bodies, ran along the jetty like a ripple on the water, like a breath of wind on a field—and all was still again. I see it now—the wide sweep of the bay, the glittering sands, the wealth of green infinite and varied, the sea blue like the sea of a dream, the crowd of attentive faces, the blaze of vivid colour—the water reflecting it all, the curve of the shore, the jetty, the high-sterned outlandish craft floating still, and the three boats with the tired men from the West sleeping, unconscious of the land and the people and of the violence of sunshine. They slept thrown across the thwarts, curled on bottom-boards, in the careless attitudes of death. The head of the old skipper, leaning back in the stern of the long-boat, had fallen on his breast, and he looked as though he would never wake. Farther out old Mahon's face was upturned to the sky, with the long white beard spread out on his breast, as though he had been shot where he sat at the tiller; and a man, all in a heap in the bows of the boat, slept with both arms embracing the stem-head and with his cheek laid on the gunwale. The East looked at them without a sound.

"I have known its fascination since; I have seen the mysterious shores, the still water, the lands of brown nations, where a stealthy Nemesis lies in wait, pursues, overtakes so many of the conquering race, who are proud of their wisdom, of their knowledge, of their strength. But for me all the East is contained in that vision of my youth. It is all in that moment when I opened my young eyes on it. I came upon it from a tussle with the sea—and I was young—and I saw it looking at me. And this is all that is left of it! Only a moment; a moment of strength, of romance, of glamour—of youth! . . . A flick of sunshine upon a strange shore, the time to remember, the time for a sigh, and—good-bye!—Night—Goodbye . . . !"

He drank.

"Ah! The good old time—the good old time. Youth and the sea. Glamour and the sea! The good, strong sea, the salt, bitter sea, that could whisper to you and roar at you and knock your breath out of you."

He drank again.

"By all that's wonderful it is the sea, I believe, the sea itself—or is it youth alone? Who can tell? But you here—you all had something out of life: money, love—whatever one gets on shore—and, tell me, wasn't that the best time, that time when we were young at sea; young and had nothing, on the sea that gives nothing, except hard knocks—and sometimes a chance to feel your strength—that only—what you all regret?"

And we all nodded at him: the man of finance, the man

of accounts, the man of law, we all nodded at him over the polished table that like a still sheet of brown water reflected our faces, lined, wrinkled; our faces marked by toil, by deceptions, by success, by love; our weary eyes looking still, looking always, looking anxiously for something out of life, that while it is expected is already gone—has passed unseen, in a sigh, in a flash—together with the youth, with the strength, with the romance of illusions.

THE ROCKING-HORSE WINNER

D. H. Lawrence

D. H. Lawrence (1885-1930) was born in Nottinghamshire, England, but after the publication of his first novel, The White Peacock *(1911), he lived mainly on the continent and, for a brief period, in America. His best-known novels are* Sons and Lovers *(1913),* The Rainbow *(1915),* Women in Love *(1920), and* Lady Chatterley's Lover *(1928). He also wrote several collections of short stories, and is one of the major poets of the twentieth century as well as a brilliant letter writer. Restless, unconventional, possessed himself with neurotic tendencies at least partially due to family discord during his childhood, he is one of the most original and powerful writers of the twentieth century. His daringly frank analysis of the inner sexual conflicts of modern civilized man made him a highly controversial figure. "The Rocking-Horse Winner"* (1932), *his most famous story, reveals his amazing insight into family tension, registered through the sensitive mind of a child.*

There was a woman who was beautiful, who started with all the advantages, yet she had no luck. She married for love, and the love turned to dust. She had bonny children, yet she felt they had been thrust upon her, and she could not love them. They looked at her coldly, as if they were finding fault with her. And hurriedly she felt she must cover up some fault in herself. Yet what it was that she must cover up she never knew. Nevertheless, when her children were present, she always felt the centre of her heart go hard. This troubled her, and in her manner she was all the more gentle and anxious for her children, as if she loved them very much. Only she herself knew that at the centre of her heart was a hard little place that could not feel love, no, not for anybody. Everybody else said of her: "She is such a good mother. She adores her children." Only she herself, and her children themselves, knew it was not so. They read it in each other's eyes.

There were a boy and two little girls. They lived in a pleasant house, with a garden, and they had discreet servants, and felt themselves superior to anyone in the neighbourhood.

Although they lived in style, they felt always an anxiety in the house. There was never enough money. The mother had a small income, and the father had a small income, but not nearly enough for the social position which they had to keep up. The father went into town to some office. But though he had good prospects, these prospects never materialized. There was always the grinding sense of the shortage of money, though the style was always kept up.

At last the mother said: "I will see if I can't make something." But she did not know where to begin. She racked her brains, and tried this thing and the other, but could not find anything successful. The failure made deep lines come into her face. Her children were growing up, they would have to go to school. There must be more money, there must be more money. The father, who was always very handsome and expensive in his tastes, seemed as if he never would be able to do anything worth doing. And the mother, who had a great belief in herself, did not succeed any better, and her tastes were just as expensive.

And so the house came to be haunted by the unspoken phrase: There must be more money! There must be more money! The children could hear it all the time, though nobody said it aloud. They heard it at Christmas, when the expensive and splendid toys filled the nursery. Behind the shining modern rocking-horse, behind the smart doll's house, a voice would start whispering: "There must be more money! There must be more money!" And the children would stop playing, to listen for a moment. They would look into each other's eyes, to see if they had all heard. And each one saw in the eyes of the other two that they too had heard. "There must be more money! There must be more money!"

It came whispering from the springs of the still-swaying rocking-horse, and even the horse, bending his wooden, champing head, heard it. The big doll, sitting so pink and smirking in her new pram, could hear it quite plainly, and seemed to be smirking all the more self-consciously because of it. The foolish puppy, too, that took the place of the teddy-bear, he was looking so extraordinarily foolish for no other reason but that he heard the secret whisper all over the house: "There must be more money!"

Yet nobody ever said it aloud. The whisper was everywhere, and therefore no one spoke it. Just as no one ever says: "We are breathing!" in spite of the fact that breath is coming and going all the time.

"Mother," said the boy Paul one day, "why don't we keep a car of our own? Why do we always use uncle's, or else a taxi?"

"Because we're the poor members of the family," said the mother.

"But why are we, mother?"

"Well—I suppose," she said slowly and bitterly, "it's because your father has no luck."

The boy was silent for some time.

"Is luck money, mother?" he asked, rather timidly.

"No, Paul. Not quite. It's what causes you to have money."

"Oh!" said Paul vaguely. "I thought when Uncle Oscar said filthy lucker, it meant money."

"Filthy lucre does mean money," said the mother. "But it's lucre, not luck."

"Oh!" said the boy. "Then what is luck, mother?"

"It's what causes you to have money. If you're lucky you have money. That's why it's better to be born lucky than rich. If you're rich, you may lose your money. But if you're lucky, you will always get more money."

"Oh! Will you? And is father not lucky?"

"Very unlucky, I should say," she said bitterly.

The boy watched her with unsure eyes.

"Why?" he asked.

"I don't know. Nobody ever knows why one person is lucky and another unlucky."

"Don't they? Nobody at all? Does nobody know?"

"Perhaps God. But He never tells."

"He ought to, then. And aren't you lucky either, mother?"

"I can't be, if I married an unlucky husband."

"But by yourself, aren't you?"

"I used to think I was, before I married. Now I think I am very unlucky indeed."

"Why?"

"Well—never mind! Perhaps I'm not really," she said.

The child looked at her, to see if she meant it. But he saw, by the lines of her mouth, that she was only trying to hide something from him.

"Well, anyhow," he said stoutly, "I'm a lucky person."

"Why?" said his mother, with a sudden laugh.

He stared at her. He didn't even know why he had said it.

"God told me," he asserted, brazening it out.

"I hope He did, dear!" she said, again with a laugh, but rather bitter.

"He did, mother!"

"Excellent!" said the mother, using one of her husband's exclamations.

The boy saw she did not believe him; or, rather, that she paid no attention to his assertion. This angered him somewhat, and made him want to compel her attention.

He went off by himself, vaguely, in a childish way, seeking for the clue to "luck." Absorbed, taking no heed of other people, he went about with a sort of stealth, seeking inwardly for luck. He wanted luck, he wanted it, he wanted it. When the two girls were playing dolls in the nursery, he would sit on his big rocking-horse, charging madly into space, with a frenzy that made the little girls peer at him uneasily. Wildly the horse careered, the waving dark hair of the boy tossed, his eyes had a strange glare in them. The little girls dared not speak to him.

When he had ridden to the end of his mad little journey, he climbed down and stood in front of his rocking-horse, staring fixedly into its lowered face. Its red mouth was slightly open, its big eye was wide and glassy-bright.

"Now!" he would silently command the snorting steed. "Now, take me to where there is luck! Now take me!"

And he would slash the horse on the neck with the little whip he had asked Uncle Oscar for. He knew the horse could take him to where there was luck, if only he forced it. So he would mount again, and start on his furious ride, hoping at last to get there. He knew he could get there.

"You'll break your horse, Paul!" said the nurse.

"He's always riding like that! I wish he'd leave off!" said his elder sister Joan.

But he only glared down on them in silence. Nurse gave him up. She could make nothing of him. Anyhow he was growing beyond her.

One day his mother and his Uncle Oscar came in when he was on one of his furious rides. He did not speak to them.

"Hallo, you young jockey! Riding a winner?" said his uncle.

"Aren't you growing too big for a rocking-horse? You're not a very little boy any longer, you know," said his mother.

But Paul only gave a blue glare from his big, rather close-set eyes. He would speak to nobody when he was in full tilt. His mother watched him with an anxious expression on her face.

At last he suddenly stopped forcing his horse into the mechanical gallop, and slid down.

"Well, I got there!" he announced fiercely, his blue eyes still flaring, and his sturdy long legs straddling apart.

"Where did you get to?" asked his mother.

"Where I wanted to go," he flared back at her.

"That's right, son!" said Uncle Oscar. "Don't you stop till you get there. What's the horse's name?"

"He doesn't have a name," said the boy.

"Gets on without all right?" asked the uncle.

"Well, he has different names. He was called Sansovino last week."

"Sansovino, eh? Won the Ascot. How did you know his name?"

"He always talks about horse-races with Bassett," said Joan.

The uncle was delighted to find that his small nephew was posted with all the racing news. Bassett, the young gardener, who had been wounded in the left foot in the war and had got his present job through Oscar Cresswell, whose batman he had been, was a perfect blade of the "turf." He lived in the racing events, and the small boy lived with him.

Oscar Cresswell got it all from Bassett.

"Master Paul comes and asks me, so I can't do more than tell him, sir," said Bassett, his face terribly serious, as if he were speaking of religious matters.

"And does he ever put anything on a horse he fancies?"

"Well—I don't want to give him away—he's a young sport, a fine sport, sir. Would you mind asking him yourself? He sort of takes a pleasure in it, and perhaps he'd feel I was giving him away, sir, if you don't mind."

Bassett was serious as a church.

The uncle went back to his nephew, and took him off for a ride in the car.

"Say, Paul, old man, do you ever put anything on a horse?" the uncle asked.

The boy watched the handsome man closely.

"Why, do you think I oughtn't to?" he parried.

"Not a bit of it! I thought perhaps you might give me a tip for the Lincoln."

The car sped on into the country, going down to Uncle Oscar's place in Hampshire.

"Honour bright?" said the nephew.

"Honour bright, son!" said the uncle.

"Well, then, Daffodil."

"Daffodil! I doubt it, sonny. What about Mirza?"

"I only know the winner," said the boy. "That's Daffodil."

"Daffodil, eh?"

There was a pause. Daffodil was an obscure horse comparatively.

"Uncle!"

"Yes, son?"

"You won't let it go any further, will you? I promised Bassett."

"Bassett be damned, old man! What's he got to do with it?"

"We're partners. We've been partners from the first. Uncle, he lent me my first five shillings, which I lost. I promised him, honour bright, it was only between me and him; only you gave me that ten-shilling note I started winning with, so I thought you were lucky. You won't let it go any further, will you?"

The boy gazed at his uncle from those big, hot, blue eyes, set rather close together. The uncle stirred and laughed uneasily.

"Right you are, son! I'll keep your tip private. Daffodil, eh? How much are you putting on him?"

"All except twenty pounds," said the boy. "I keep that in reserve."

The uncle thought it a good joke.

"You keep twenty pounds in reserve, do you, you young romancer? What are you betting, then?"

"I'm betting three hundred," said the boy gravely. "But it's between you and me, Uncle Oscar! Honour bright?"

The uncle burst into a roar of laughter.

"It's between you and me all right, you young Nat Gould," he said, laughing. "But where's your three hundred?"

"Bassett keeps it for me. We're partners."

"You are, are you? And what is Bassett putting on Daffodil?"

"He won't go quite as high as I do, I expect. Perhaps he'll go a hundred and fifty."

"What, pennies?" laughed the uncle.

"Pounds," said the child, with a surprised look at his uncle. "Bassett keeps a bigger reserve than I do."

Between wonder and amusement Uncle Oscar was silent. He pursued the matter no further, but he determined to take his nephew with him to the Lincoln races.

"Now, son," he said, "I'm putting twenty on Mirza, and I'll put five for you on any horse you fancy. What's your pick?"

"Daffodil, uncle."

"No, not the fiver on Daffodil!"

"I should if it was my own fiver," said the child.

"Good! Good! Right you are! A fiver for me and a fiver for you on Daffodil."

The child had never been to a race-meeting before, and his eyes were blue fire. He pursed his mouth tight, and watched. A Frenchman just in front had put his money on Lancelot. Wild with excitement, he flayed his arms up and down, yelling "Lancelot! Lancelot!" in his French accent.

Daffodil came in first, Lancelot second, Mirza third. The child, flushed and with eyes blazing, was curiously serene. His uncle brought him four five-pound notes, four to one.

"What am I to do with these?" he cried, waving them before the boy's eyes.

"I suppose we'll talk to Bassett," said the boy. "I expect I have fifteen hundred now; and twenty in reserve; and this twenty."

His uncle studied him for some moments.

"Look here, son!" he said. "You're not serious about Bassett and that fifteen hundred, are you?"

"Yes, I am. But it's between you and me, uncle. Honour bright!"

"Honour bright all right, son! But I must talk to Bassett."

"If you'd like to be a partner, uncle, with Bassett and me, we could all be partners. Only, you'd have to promise, honour bright, uncle, not to let it go beyond us three. Bassett and I are lucky, and you must be lucky, because it was your ten shillings I started winning with. . . ."

Uncle Oscar took both Bassett and Paul into Richmond Park for an afternoon, and there they talked.

"It's like this, you see, sir," Bassett said. "Master Paul would get me talking about racing events, spinning yarns, you know, sir. And he was always keen on knowing if I'd made or if I'd lost. It's about a year since, now, that I put five shillings on Blush of Dawn for him—and we lost. Then the luck turned, with that ten shillings he had from you, that we put on Singhalese. And since that time, it's been pretty steady, all things considering. What do you say, Master Paul?"

"We're all right when we're sure," said Paul. "It's when we're not quite sure that we go down."

"Oh, but we're careful then," said Bassett.

"But when are you sure?" smiled Uncle Oscar.

"It's Master Paul, sir," said Bassett, in a secret, religious voice. "It's as if he had it from heaven. Like Daffodil, now, for the Lincoln. That was as sure as eggs."

"Did you put anything on Daffodil?" asked Oscar Cresswell.

"Yes, sir. I made my bit."

"And my nephew?"

Bassett was obstinately silent, looking at Paul.

"I made twelve hundred, didn't I, Bassett? I told uncle I was putting three hundred on Daffodil."

"That's right," said Bassett, nodding.

"But where's the money?" asked the uncle.

"I keep it safe locked up, sir. Master Paul he can have it any minute he likes to ask for it."

"What, fifteen hundred pounds?"

"And twenty! And forty, that is, with the twenty he made on the course."

"It's amazing!" said the uncle.

"If Master Paul offers you to be partners, sir, I would, if I were you; if you'll excuse me," said Bassett.

Oscar Cresswell thought about it.

"I'll see the money," he said.

They drove home again, and sure enough, Bassett came round to the garden-house with fifteen hundred pounds in notes. The twenty pounds reserve was left with Joe Glee, in the Turf Commission deposit.

"You see, it's all right, uncle, when I'm sure! Then we go strong, for all we're worth. Don't we, Bassett?"

"We do that, Master Paul."

"And when are you sure?" said the uncle, laughing.

"Oh, well, sometimes I'm absolutely sure, like about Daffodil," said the boy; "and sometimes I have an idea; and sometimes I haven't even an idea, have I, Bassett? Then we're careful, because we mostly go down."

"You do, do you! And when you're sure, like about Daffodil, what makes you sure, sonny?"

"Oh, well, I don't know," said the boy uneasily. "I'm sure, you know, uncle; that's all."

"It's as if he had it from heaven, sir," Bassett reiterated.

"I should say so!" said the uncle.

But he became a partner. And when the Leger was coming on, Paul was "sure" about Lively Spark, which was a quite inconsiderable horse. The boy insisted on putting a thousand on the horse, Bassett went for five hundred, and Oscar Cresswell two hundred. Lively Spark came in first, and the betting had been ten to one against him. Paul had made ten thousand.

"You see," he said. "I was absolutely sure of him."

Even Oscar Cresswell had cleared two thousand.

"Look here, son," he said, "this sort of thing makes me nervous."

"It needn't, uncle! Perhaps I shan't be sure again for a long time."

"But what are you going to do with your money?" asked the uncle.

"Of course," said the boy, "I started it for mother. She said she had no luck, because father is unlucky, so I thought if I was lucky, it might stop whispering."

"What might stop whispering?"

"Our house. I hate our house for whispering."

"What does it whisper?"

"Why—why"—the boy fidgeted—"why, I don't know. But it's always short of money, you know, uncle."

"I know it, son, I know it."

"You know people send mother writs, don't you, uncle?"

"I'm afraid I do," said the uncle.

"And then the house whispers, like people laughing at

you behind your back. It's awful, that is! I thought if I was lucky . . ."

"You might stop it," added the uncle.

The boy watched him with big blue eyes that had an uncanny cold fire in them, and he said never a word.

"Well, then!" said the uncle. "What are we doing?"

"I shouldn't like mother to know I was lucky," said the boy.

"Why not, son?"

"She'd stop me."

"I don't think she would."

"Oh!"—and the boy writhed in an odd way—"I don't want her to know, uncle."

"All right, son! We'll manage it without her knowing."

They managed it very easily. Paul, at the other's suggestion, handed over five thousand pounds to his uncle, who deposited it with the family lawyer, who was then to inform Paul's mother that a relative had put five thousand pounds into his hands, which sum was to be paid out a thousand pounds at a time, on the mother's birthday, for the next five years.

"So she'll have a birthday present of a thousand pounds for five successive years," said Uncle Oscar. "I hope it won't make it all the harder for her later."

Paul's mother had her birthday in November. The house had been "whispering" worse than ever lately, and, even in spite of his luck, Paul could not bear up against it. He was very anxious to see the effect of the birthday letter, telling his mother about the thousand pounds.

When there were no visitors, Paul now took his meals with his parents, as he was beyond the nursery control. His mother went into town nearly every day. She had discovered that she had an odd knack of sketching furs and dress materials, so she worked secretly in the studio of a friend who was the chief "artist" for the leading drapers. She drew the figures of ladies in furs and ladies in silk and sequins for the newspaper advertisements. This young woman artist earned several thousand pounds a year, but Paul's mother only made several hundreds, and she was again dissatisfied. She so wanted to be first in something, and she did not succeed, even in making sketches for drapery advertisements.

She was down to breakfast on the morning of her birthday. Paul watched her face as she read her letters. He knew the lawyer's letter. As his mother read it, her face hardened and became more expressionless. Then a cold, determined look came on her mouth. She hid the letter under the pile of others, and said not a word about it.

"Didn't you have anything nice in the post for your birthday, mother?" said Paul.

"Quite moderately nice," she said, her voice cold and absent.

She went away to town without saying more.

But in the afternoon Uncle Oscar appeared. He said Paul's mother had had a long interview with the lawyer, asking if the whole five thousand could be advanced at once, as she was in debt.

"What do you think, uncle?" said the boy.

"I leave it to you, son."

"Oh, let her have it, then! We can get some more with the other," said the boy.

"A bird in the hand is worth two in the bush, laddie!"

"But I'm sure to know for the Grand National; or the Lincolnshire; or else the Derby. I'm sure to know for one of them," said Paul.

So Uncle Oscar signed the agreement, and Paul's mother touched the whole five thousand. Then something very curious happened. The voices in the house suddenly went mad, like a chorus of frogs on a spring evening. There were certain new furnishings, and Paul had a tutor. He was really going to Eton, his father's school, in the following autumn. There were flowers in the winter, and a blossoming of the luxury Paul's mother had been used to. And yet the voices in the house, behind the sprays of mimosa and almond blossom, and from under the piles of iridescent cushions, simply trilled and screamed in a sort of ecstasy: "There must be more money! Oh-h-h, there must be more money. Oh, now, now-w! Now-w-w—there must be more money!—more than ever! More than ever!"

It frightened Paul terribly. He studied away at his Latin and Greek with his tutors. But his intense hours were spent with Bassett. The Grand National had gone by: he had not "known," and had lost a hundred pounds. Summer was at hand. He was in agony for the Lincoln. But even for the Lincoln he didn't "know" and he lost fifty pounds. He became wild-eyed and strange, as if something were going to explode in him.

"Let it alone, son! Don't you bother about it!" urged Uncle Oscar. But it was as if the boy couldn't really hear what his uncle was saying.

"I've got to know for the Derby! I've got to know for the Derby!" the child reiterated, his big blue eyes blazing with a sort of madness.

His mother noticed how overwrought he was.

"You'd better go to the seaside. Wouldn't you like to go now to the seaside, instead of waiting? I think you'd better," she said, looking down at him anxiously, her heart curiously heavy because of him.

But the child lifted his uncanny blue eyes.

"I couldn't possibly go before the Derby, mother!" he said. "I couldn't possibly!"

"Why not?" she said, her voice becoming heavy when she was opposed. "Why not? You can still go from the seaside to see the Derby with your Uncle Oscar, if that's what you wish. No need for you to wait here. Besides, I think you care too much about these races. It's a bad sign. My family has been a gambling family, and you won't know till you grow up how much damage it has done. But it has done damage. I shall have to send Bassett away, and ask Uncle Oscar not to talk racing to you, unless you promise to be reasonable about it; go away to the seaside and forget it. You're all nerves!"

"I'll do what you like, mother, so long as you don't send me away till after the Derby," the boy said.

"Send you away from where? Just from this house?"

"Yes," he said, gazing at her.

"Why, you curious child, what makes you care about this house so much, suddenly? I never knew you loved it."

He gazed at her without speaking. He had a secret within a secret, something he had not divulged, even to Bassett or to his Uncle Oscar.

But his mother, after standing undecided and a little bit sullen for some moments, said:

"Very well, then! Don't go to the seaside till after the Derby, if you don't wish it. But promise me you won't let your nerves go to pieces. Promise you won't think so much about horse-racing and events, as you call them!"

"Oh, no," said the boy casually. "I won't think much about them, mother. You needn't worry. I wouldn't worry, mother, if I were you."

"If you were me and I were you," said his mother, "I wonder what we should do!"

"But you know you needn't worry, mother, don't you?" the boy repeated.

"I should be awfully glad to know it," she said wearily.

"Oh, well, you can, you know. I mean, you ought to know you needn't worry," he insisted.

"Ought I? Then I'll see about it," she said.

Paul's secret of secrets was his wooden horse, that which had no name. Since he was emancipated from a nurse and a nursery-governess, he had had his rocking-horse removed to his own bedroom at the top of the house.

"Surely, you're too big for a rocking-horse!" his mother had remonstrated.

"Well, you see, mother, till I can have a real horse, I like to have some sort of animal about," had been his quaint answer.

"Do you feel he keeps you company?" she laughed.

"Oh, yes! He's very good, he always keeps me company, when I'm there," said Paul.

So the horse, rather shabby, stood in an arrested prance in the boy's bedroom.

The Derby was drawing near, and the boy grew more and more tense. He hardly heard what was spoken to him, he was very frail, and his eyes were really uncanny. His mother had sudden seizures of uneasiness about him. Sometimes, for half-an-hour, she would feel a sudden anxiety about him that was almost anguish. She wanted to rush to him at once, and know he was safe.

Two nights before the Derby, she was at a big party in town, when one of her rushes of anxiety about her boy, her first-born, gripped her heart till she could hardly speak. She fought with the feeling, might and main, for she believed in common sense. But it was too strong. She had to leave the dance and go downstairs to telephone to the country. The children's nursery-governess was terribly surprised and startled at being rung up in the night.

"Are the children all right, Miss Wilmot?"

"Oh, yes, they are quite all right."

"Master Paul? Is he all right?"

"He went to bed as right as a trivet. Shall I run up and look at him?"

"No," said Paul's mother reluctantly. "No! Don't trouble.

It's all right. Don't sit up. We shall be home fairly soon." She did not want her son's privacy intruded upon.

"Very good," said the governess.

It was about one o'clock when Paul's mother and father drove up to their house. All was still. Paul's mother went to her room and slipped off her white fur cloak. She had told her maid not to wait up for her. She heard her husband downstairs, mixing a whisky-and-soda.

And then, because of the strange anxiety at her heart, she stole upstairs to her son's room. Noiselessly she went along the upper corridor. Was there a faint noise. What was it?

She stood, with arrested muscles, outside his door, listening. There was a strange, heavy, and yet not loud noise. Her heart stood still. It was a soundless noise, yet rushing and powerful. Something huge, in violent, hushed motion. What was it? What in God's name was it? She ought to know. She felt that she knew the noise. She knew what it was.

Yet she could not place it. She couldn't say what it was. And on and on it went, like a madness.

Softly, frozen with anxiety and fear, she turned the door-handle.

The room was dark. Yet in the space near the window, she heard and saw something plunging to and fro. She gazed in fear and amazement.

Then suddenly she switched on the light, and saw her son, in his green pyjamas, madly surging on the rocking-horse. The blaze of light suddenly lit him up, as he urged the wooden horse, and lit her up, as she stood, blonde, in her dress of pale green and crystal, in the doorway.

"Paul!" she cried. "Whatever are you doing?"

"It's Malabar!" he screamed, in a powerful, strange voice. "It's Malabar."

His eyes blazed at her for one strange and senseless second, as he ceased urging his wooden horse. Then he fell with a crash to the ground, and she, all her tormented motherhood flooding upon her, rushed to gather him up.

But he was unconscious, and unconscious he remained, with some brain-fever. He talked and tossed, and his mother sat stonily by his side.

"Malabar! It's Malabar! Bassett, Bassett, I know! It's Malabar!"

So the child tried, trying to get up and urge the rocking-horse that gave him his inspiration.

"What does he mean by Malabar?" asked the heart-frozen mother.

"I don't know," said the father stonily.

"What does he mean by Malabar?" she asked her brother Oscar.

"It's one of the horses running for the Derby," was the answer.

And, in spite of himself, Oscar Creswell spoke to Bassett, and himself put a thousand on Malabar: at fourteen to one.

The third day of the illness was critical: they were waiting for a change. The boy, with his rather long, curly hair, was tossing ceaselessly on the pillow. He neither slept nor regained consciousness, and his eyes were like blue stones. His mother sat, feeling her heart had gone, turned actually into a stone.

In the evening, Oscar Cresswell did not come, but Bassett sent a message, saying could he come up for one moment, just one moment? Paul's mother was very angry at the intrusion, but on second thought she agreed. The boy was the same. Perhaps Bassett might bring him to consciousness.

The gardener, a shortish fellow with a little brown moustache, and sharp little brown eyes, tiptoed into the room, touched his imaginary cap to Paul's mother, and stole to the bedside, staring with glittering, smallish eyes, at the tossing, dying child.

"Master Paul!" he whispered. "Master Paul! Malabar come in first all right, a clean win. I did as you told me. You've made over seventy thousand pounds, you have; you've got over eighty thousand. Malabar came in all right, Master Paul!"

"Malabar! Malabar! Did I say Malabar, mother? Did I say Malabar? Do you think I'm lucky, mother? I knew Malabar, didn't I? Overy eighty thousand pounds! I call that lucky, don't you, mother? Over eighty thousand pounds! I knew, didn't I know I knew? Malabar came in all right. If I ride my horse till I'm sure, then I tell you, Bassett, you can go as high as you like. Did you go for all you were worth, Bassett?"

"I went a thousand on it, Master Paul."

"I never told you, mother, that if I can ride my horse, and get there, then I'm absolutely sure—oh, absolutely! Mother, did I ever tell you? I am lucky."

"No, you never did," said the mother.

But the boy died in the night.

And even as he lay dead, his mother heard her brother's voice saying to her: "My God, Hester, you're eighty-odd thousand to the good and a poor devil of a son to the bad. But, poor devil, poor devil, he's best gone out of a life where he rides his rocking-horse to find a winner."

BLISS

Katherine Mansfield

Katherine Mansfield was born in Wellington, New Zealand, in 1888, but settled in London in 1909. In 1919 she married the English critic John Middleton Murry, an intimate friend of D. H. Lawrence. Before her death in 1923 she published over seventy short stories. Her work reflects the impressionistic techniques of Chekhov. She is especially gifted in recording elusive emotional states with both delicacy and power.

Although Bertha Young was thirty she still had moments like this when she wanted to run instead of walk, to take dancing steps on and off the pavement, to bowl a hoop, to throw something up in the air and catch it again, or to stand still and laugh at—nothing—at nothing, simply.

What can you do if you are thirty and, turning the corner of your own street, you are overcome, suddenly, by a feeling of bliss—absolute bliss!—as though you'd suddenly swallowed a bright piece of that late afternoon sun and it burned in your bosom, sending out a little shower of sparks into every particle, into every finger and toe? . . .

Oh, is there no way you can express it without being "drunk and disorderly"? How idiotic civilization is! Why be given a body if you have to keep it shut up in a case like a rare, rare fiddle?

"No, that about the fiddle is not quite what I mean," she thought, running up the steps and feeling in her bag for the key—she'd forgotten it, as usual—and rattling the letterbox.

"It's not what I mean, because—Thank you, Mary"—she went into the hall. "Is Nurse back?"

"Yes, M'm."

"And has the fruit come?"

"Yes, M'm. Everything's come."

"Bring the fruit up to the dining-room, will you? I'll arrange it before I go upstairs."

It was dusky in the dining-room and quite chilly. But all the same Bertha threw off her coat; she could not bear the tight clasp of it another moment, and the cold air fell on her arms.

But in her bosom there was still that bright glowing place—that shower of little sparks coming from it. It was almost unbearable. She hardly dared to breathe for fear of fanning it higher, and yet she breathed deeply, deeply. She hardly dared to look into the cold mirror—but she did look, and it gave her back a woman, radiant, with smiling, trembling lips, with big, dark eyes and an air of listening, waiting for something . . . divine to happen . . . that she knew must happen . . . infallibly.

Mary brought in the fruit on a tray and with it a glass bowl, and a blue dish, very lovely, with a strange sheen on it as though it had been dipped in milk.

"Shall I turn on the light, M'm?"

"No, thank you. I can see quite well."

There were tangerines and apples stained with strawberry pink. Some yellow pears, smooth as silk, some white grapes covered with a silver bloom and a big cluster of purple ones. These last she had bought to tone in with the new dining-room carpet. Yes, that did sound rather far-fetched and absurd, but it was really why she had bought them. She had thought in the shop: "I must have some purple ones to bring the carpet up to the table." And it had seemed quite sensible at the time.

When she had finished with them and had made two pyramids of these bright round shapes, she stood away from the table to get the effect—and it really was most curious. For the dark table seemed to melt into the dusky light and the glass dish and the blue bowl to float in the air. This, of course in her present mood, was so incredibly beautiful. . . . She began to laugh.

"No, no. I'm getting hysterical." And she seized her bag and coat and ran upstairs to the nursery.

Nurse sat at a low table giving Little B her supper after her bath. The baby had on a white flannel gown and a blue woollen jacket, and her dark, fine hair was brushed up into a funny little peak. She looked up when she saw her mother and began to jump.

"Now, my lovey, eat it up like a good girl," said Nurse, setting her lips in a way that Bertha knew, and that meant she had come into the nursery at another wrong moment.

"Has she been good, Nanny?"

"She's been a little sweet all the afternoon," whispered Nanny. "We went to the park and I sat down on a chair and took her out of the pram and a big dog came along and put its head on my knee and she clutched its ear, tugged it. Oh, you should have seen her."

Bertha wanted to ask if it wasn't rather dangerous to let her clutch at a strange dog's ear. But she did not dare to. She stood watching them, her hands by her sides, like the poor little girl in front of the rich little girl with the doll.

The baby looked up at her again, stared, and then smiled so charmingly that Bertha couldn't help crying:

"Oh, Nanny, do let me finish giving her her supper while you put the bath things away."

"Well, M'm, she oughtn't to be changed hands while she's eating," said Nanny, still whispering. "It unsettles her; it's very likely to upset her."

How absurd it was. Why have a baby if it has to be kept —not in a case like a rare, rare fiddle—but in another woman's arms? "Oh, I must!" she said.

Very offended, Nanny handed her over.

"Now, don't excite her after her supper. You know you do, M'm. And I have such a time with her after!"

Thank heaven! Nanny went out of the room with the bath towels.

"Now I've got you to myself, my little precious," said Bertha, as the baby leaned against her.

She ate delightfully, holding up her lips for the spoon and then waving her hands. Sometimes she wouldn't let the spoon go; and sometimes, just as Bertha had filled it, she waved it away to the four winds.

When the soup was finished Bertha turned round to the fire.

"You're nice—you're very nice!" said she, kissing her warm baby. "I'm fond of you. I like you."

And, indeed, she loved Little B so much—her neck as she bent forward, her exquisite toes as they shone transparent in the firelight—that all her feeling of bliss came back again, and again she didn't know how to express it—what to do with it.

"You're wanted on the telephone," said Nanny, coming back in triumph and seizing *her* Little B.

Down she flew. It was Harry.

"Oh, is that you, Ber? Look here. I'll be late. I'll take a taxi and come along as quickly as I can, but get dinner put back ten minutes—will you? All right?"

"Yes, perfectly. Oh, Harry!"

"Yes?"

What had she to say? She'd nothing to say. She only wanted to get in touch with him for a moment. She couldn't absurdly cry: "Hasn't it been a divine day!"

"What is it?" rapped out the little voice.

"Nothing. *Entendu*," said Bertha, and hung up the receiver, thinking how more than idiotic civilization was.

They had people coming to dinner. The Norman Knights—a very sound couple—he was about to start a theatre, and she was awfully keen on interior decoration, a young man, Eddie Warren, who had just published a little book of poems and whom everybody was asking to dine, and a "find" of Bertha's called Pearl Fulton. What Miss Fulton did, Bertha didn't know. They had met at the club and Bertha had fallen in love with her, as she always did fall in love with beautiful women who had something strange about them.

The provoking thing was that, though they had been about together and met a number of times and really talked, Bertha couldn't yet make her out. Up to a certain point Miss Fulton was rarely, wonderfully frank, but the certain point was there, and beyond that she would not go.

Was there anything beyond it? Harry said, "No." Voted her dullish, and "cold like all blond women, with a touch, perhaps, of anæmia of the brain." But Bertha wouldn't agree with him; not yet, at any rate.

"No, the way she has of sitting with her head a little on one side, and smiling, has something behind it, Harry, and I must find out what that something is."

"Most likely it's a good stomach," answered Harry.

He made a point of catching Bertha's heels with replies of that kind . . . "liver frozen, my dear girl," or "pure flatulence," or "kidney disease," . . . and so on. For some strange reason Bertha liked this, and almost admired it in him very much.

She went into the drawing-room and lighted the fire; then, picking up the cushions, one by one, that Mary had disposed so carefully, she threw them back on to the chairs and the couches. That made all the difference; the room came alive at once. As she was about to throw the last one she surprised herself by suddenly hugging it to her, passionately, passionately. But it did not put out the fire in her bosom. Oh, on the contrary!

The windows of the drawing-room opened on to a balcony overlooking the garden. At the far end, against the wall, there was a tall, slender pear tree in fullest, richest bloom; it stood perfect, as though becalmed against the jade-green sky. Bertha couldn't help feeling, even from this distance, that it had not a single bud or a faded petal. Down below, in the garden beds, the red and yellow tulips, heavy with flowers, seemed to lean upon the dusk. A grey cat, dragging its belly, crept across the lawn, and a black one, its shadow, trailed after. The sight of them, so intent and so quick, gave Bertha a curious shiver.

"What creepy things cats are!" she stammered, and she turned away from the window and began walking up and down. . . .

How strong the jonquils smelled in the warm room. Too strong? Oh, no. And yet, as though overcome, she flung down on a couch and pressed her hands to her eyes.

"I'm too happy—too happy!" she murmured.

And she seemed to see on her eyelids the lovely pear tree with its wide open blossoms as a symbol of her own life.

Really—really—she had everything. She was young. Harry and she were as much in love as ever, and they got on together splendidly and were really good pals. She had an adorable baby. They didn't have to worry about money. They had this absolutely satisfactory house and garden. And friends—modern, thrilling friends, writers and painters and poets or people keen on social questions—just the kind of friends they wanted. And then there were books, and there was music, and she had found a wonderful little dressmaker, and they were going abroad in the summer, and their new cook made the most superb omelettes. . . .

"I'm absurd. Absurd!" She sat up; but she felt quite dizzy, quite drunk. It must have been the spring.

Yes, it was the spring. Now she was so tired she could not drag herself upstairs to dress.

A white dress, a string of jade beads, green shoes and stockings. It wasn't intentional. She had thought of this scheme hours before she stood at the drawing-room window.

Her petals rustled softly into the hall, and she kissed Mrs. Norman Knight, who was taking off the most amusing orange coat with a procession of black monkeys round the hem and up the fronts.

". . . Why! Why! Why is the middle-class so stodgy—so utterly without a sense of humour! My dear, it's only by a fluke that I am here at all—Norman being the protective fluke. For my darling monkeys so upset the train that it rose to a man and simply ate me with its eyes. Didn't laugh—wasn't amused—that I should have loved. No, just stared—and bored me through and through."

"But the cream of it was," said Norman, pressing a large tortoise-shell-rimmed monocle into his eye, "you don't mind me telling this, Face, do you?" (In their home and among their friends they called each other Face and Mug.) "The cream of it was when she, being full red, turned to the woman beside her and said: 'Haven't you ever seen a monkey before?' "

"Oh, yes!" Mrs. Norman Knight joined in the laughter. "Wasn't that too absolutely creamy?"

And a funnier thing still was that now her coat was off she did look like a very intelligent monkey—who had even made that yellow silk dress out of scraped banana skins. And her amber ear-rings; they were like little dangling nuts.

"This is a sad, sad fall!" said Mug, pausing in front of Little B's perambulator. "When the perambulator comes into the hall—" and he waved the rest of the quotation away.

The bell rang. It was lean, pale Eddie Warren (as usual) in a state of acute distress.

"It *is* the right house, *isn't* it?" he pleaded.

"Oh, I think so—I hope so," said Bertha brightly.

"I have had such a *dreadful* experience with a taxi-man; he was *most* sinister. I couldn't get him to stop. The *more* I knocked and called the *faster* he went. And *in* the moonlight this *bizarre* figure with the *flattened* head *crouching* over the *lit-tle* wheel . . ."

He shuddered, taking off an immense white silk scarf. Bertha noticed that his socks were white, too—most charming.

"But how dreadful!" she cried.

"Yes, it really was," said Eddie, following her into the drawing-room. "I saw myself *driving* through Eternity in a *timeless* taxi."

He knew the Norman Knights. In fact, he was going to write a play for N.K. when the theatre scheme came off.

"Well, Warren, how's the play?" said Norman Knight, dropping his monocle and giving his eye a moment in which to rise to the surface before it was screwed down again.

And Mrs. Norman Knight: "Oh, Mr. Warren, what happy socks!"

"I *am* so glad you like them," said he, staring at his feet. "They seem to have got so *much* whiter since the moon rose." And he turned his lean sorrowful young face to Bertha. "There *is* a moon, you know."

She wanted to cry: "I am sure there is—often—often!"

He really was a most attractive person. But so was Face, crouched before the fire in her banana skins, and so was Mug, smoking a cigarette and saying as he flicked the ash: "Why doth the bridegroom tarry?"

"There he is, now."

Bang went the front door open and shut. Harry shouted: "Hullo, you people. Down in five minutes." And they heard him swarm up the stairs. Bertha couldn't help smiling; she knew how he loved doing things at high pressure. What, after all, did an extra five minutes matter? But he would pretend to himself that they mattered beyond measure. And then he would make a great point of coming into the drawing-room, extravagantly cool and collected.

Harry had such a zest for life. Oh, how she appreciated it in him. And his passion for fighting—for seeking in everything that came up against him another test of his power and of his courage—that, too, she understood. Even when it made him just occasionally to other people, who didn't know him well, a little ridiculous perhaps. . . . For there were moments when he rushed into battle where no battle was. . . . She talked and laughed and postively forgot until he had come in (just as she had imagined) that Pearl Fulton had not turned up.

"I wonder if Miss Fulton has forgotten?"

"I expect so," said Harry. "Is she on the 'phone?"

"Ah! There's a taxi, now." And Bertha smiled with that little air of proprietorship that she always assumed while her women finds were new and mysterious. "She lives in taxis."

"She'll run to fat if she does," said Harry coolly, ringing the bell for dinner. "Frightful danger for blond women."

"Harry—don't," warned Bertha, laughing up at him.

Came another tiny moment, while they waited, laughing and talking, just a trifle too much at their ease, a trifle too unaware. And then Miss Fulton, all in silver, with a silver fillet binding her pale blond hair, came in smiling, her head a little on one side. "Am I late?"

"No, not at all," said Bertha. "Come along." And she took her arm and they moved into the dining-room.

What was there in the touch of that cool arm that could fan—fan—start blazing—blazing—the fire of bliss that Bertha did not know what to do with?

Miss Fulton did not look at her; but then she seldom did look at people directly. Her heavy eyelids lay upon her eyes and the strange half smile came and went upon her lips as though she lived by listening rather than seeing. But Bertha knew, suddenly, as if the longest, most intimate look had passed between them—as if they had said to each other: "You, too?"—that Pearl Fulton, stirring the beautiful red soup in the grey plate, was feeling just what she was feeling.

And the others? Face and Mug, Eddie and Harry, their spoons rising and falling—dabbing their lips with their napkins, crumbling bread, fiddling with the forks and glasses and talking.

"I met her at the Alpha show—the weirdest little person. She'd not only cut off her hair, but she seemed to have taken a dreadfully good snip off her legs and arms and her neck and her poor little nose as well."

"Isn't she very *liée* with Michael Oat?"

"The man who wrote *Love in False Teeth?*"

"He wants to write a play for me. One act. One man. Decides to commit suicide. Gives all the reasons why he should and why he shouldn't. And just as he has made up his mind either to do it or not to do it—curtain. Not half a bad idea."

"What's he going to call it—'Stomach Trouble'?"

"I *think* I've come across the *same* idea in a lit-tle French review, *quite* unknown in England."

No, they didn't share it. They were dears—dears—and she loved having them there, at her table, and giving them delicious food and wine. In fact, she longed to tell them how delightful they were, and what a decorative group they made, how they seemed to set one another off and how they reminded her of a play by Chekhov!

Harry was enjoying his dinner. It was part of his—well, not his nature, exactly, and certainly not his pose—his—something or other—to talk about food and to glory in his "shameless passion for the white flesh of the lobster" and "the green of pistachio ices—green and cold like the eyelids of Egyptian dancers."

When he looked up at her and said: "Bertha, this is a very admirable *soufflée!*" she almost could have wept with childlike pleasure.

Oh, why did she feel so tender towards the whole world tonight? Everything was good—was right. All that happened seemed to fill again her brimming cup of bliss.

And still, in the back of her mind, there was the pear tree. It would be silver now, in the light of poor dear Eddie's moon, silver as Miss Fulton, who sat there turning a tangerine in her slender fingers that were so pale a light seemed to come from them.

What she simply couldn't make out—what was miraculous—was how she should have guessed Miss Fulton's mood so exactly and so instantly. For she never doubted for a moment that she was right, and yet what had she to go on? Less than nothing. "I believe this does happen very, very rarely between women. Never between men," thought Bertha. "But while I am making the coffee in the drawing-room perhaps she will 'give a sign.' "

What she meant by that she did not know, and what would happen after that she could not imagine.

While she thought like this she saw herself talking and laughing. She had to talk because of her desire to laugh.

"I must laugh or die."

But when she noticed Face's funny little habit of tucking something down the front of her bodice—as if she kept a tiny, secret hoard of nuts there, too—Bertha had to dig her nails into her hands—so as not to laugh too much.

It was over at last. And: "Come and see my new coffee machine," said Bertha.

"We only have a new coffee machine once a fortnight,"

said Harry. Face took her arm this time; Miss Fulton bent her head and followed after.

The fire had died down in the drawing-room to a red, flickering "nest of baby phœnixes," said Face.

"Don't turn up the light for a moment. It is so lovely." And down she crouched by the fire again. She was always cold . . . "without her little red flannel jacket, of course," thought Bertha.

At that moment Miss Fulton "gave the sign."

"Have you a garden?" said the cool, sleepy voice.

This was so exquisite on her part that all Bertha could do was to obey. She crossed the room, pulled the curtains apart, and opened those long windows. "There!" she breathed.

And the two women stood side by side looking at the slender, flowering tree. Although it was so still it seemed, like the flame of a candle, to stretch up, to point, to quiver in the bright air, to grow taller and taller as they gazed—almost to touch the rim of the round, silver moon.

How long did they stand there? Both, as it were, caught in that circle of unearthly light, understanding each other perfectly, creatures of another world, and wondering what they were to do in this one with all this blissful treasure that burned in their bosoms and dropped, in silver flowers, from their hair and hands?

For ever—for a moment? And did Miss Fulton murmur: "Yes, just *that*." Or did Bertha dream it?

Then the light was snapped on and Face made the coffee and Harry said: "My dear Mrs. Knight, don't ask me about my baby. I never see her. I shan't feel the slightest interest in her until she has a lover," and Mug took his eye out of the conservatory for a moment and then put it under glass again and Eddie Warren drank his coffee and set down the cup with a face of anguish as though he had drunk and seen the spider.

"What I want to do is to give the young men a show. I believe London is simply teeming with first-chop, unwritten plays. What I want to say to 'em is: 'Here's the theatre. Fire ahead.' "

"You know, my dear, I am going to decorate a room for the Jacob Nathans. Oh, I am so tempted to do a fried-fish scheme, with the backs of the chairs shaped like frying pans and lovely chip potatoes embroidered all over the curtains."

"The trouble with our young writing men is that they are

still too romantic. You can't put out to sea without being seasick and wanting a basin. Well, why won't they have the courage of those basins?"

"A *dreadful* poem about a *girl* who was *violated* by a beggar *without* a nose in a lit-tle wood. . . ."

Miss Fulton sank into the lowest, deepest chair and Harry handed round the cigarettes.

From the way he stood in front of her shaking the silver box and saying abruptly: "Egyptian? Turkish? Virginian? They're all mixed up," Bertha realized that she not only bored him; he really disliked her. And she decided from the way Miss Fulton said "No, thank you, I won't smoke," that she felt it, too, and was hurt.

"Oh, Harry, don't dislike her. You are quite wrong about her. She's wonderful, wonderful. And, besides, how can you feel so differently about someone who means so much to me. I shall try to tell you when we are in bed to-night what has been happening. What she and I have shared."

At those last words something strange and almost terrifying darted into Bertha's mind. And this something blind and smiling whispered to her: "Soon these people will go. The house will be quiet—quiet. The lights will be out. And you and he will be alone together in the dark room—the warm bed. . . ."

She jumped up from her chair and ran over to the piano.

"What a pity someone does not play!" she cried. "What a pity somebody does not play."

For the first time in her life Bertha Young desired her husband.

Oh, she loved him—she'd been in love with him, of course, in every other way, but just not in that way. And, equally, of course, she'd understood that he was different. They'd discussed it so often. It had worried her dreadfully at first to find that she was so cold, but after a time it had not seemed to matter. They were so frank with each other—such good pals. That was the best of being modern.

But now—ardently! ardently! The word ached in her ardent body! Was this what that feeling of bliss had been leading up to? But then—

"My dear," said Mrs. Norman Knight, "you know our shame. We are the victims of time and train. We live in Hampstead. It's been so nice."

"I'll come with you into the hall," said Bertha. "I loved having you. But you must not miss the last train. That's so awful, isn't it?"

"Have a whisky, Knight, before you go?" called Harry.

"No, thanks, old chap."

Bertha squeezed his hand for that as she shook it.

"Good night, good-bye," she cried from the top step, feeling that this self of hers was taking leave of them for ever.

When she got back into the drawing-room the others were on the move.

". . . Then you can come part of the way in my taxi."

"I shall be *so* thankful *not* to have to face *another* drive *alone* after my *dreadful* experience."

"You can get a taxi at the rank just at the end of the street. You won't have to walk more than a few yards."

"That's a comfort. I'll go and put on my coat."

Miss Fulton moved towards the hall and Bertha was following when Harry almost pushed past.

"Let me help you."

Bertha knew that he was repenting his rudeness—she let him go. What a boy he was in some ways—so impulsive—so —simple. And Eddie and she were left by the fire.

"I *wonder* if you have seen Bilks' *new* poem called *Table d'Hôte*," said Eddie softly. "It's *so* wonderful. In the last Anthology. Have you got a copy? I'd *so* like to *show* it to you. It begins with an *incredibly* beautiful line: 'Why Must it Always be Tomato Soup?' "

"Yes," said Bertha. And she moved noiselessly to a table opposite the drawing-room door and Eddie glided noiselessly after her. She picked up the little book and gave it to him; they had not made a sound.

While he looked it up she turned her head towards the hall. And she saw . . . Harry with Miss Fulton's coat in his arms and Miss Fulton with her back turned to him and her head bent. He tossed the coat away, put his hands on her shoulders and turned her violently to him. His lips said: "I adore you," and Miss Fulton laid her moonbeam fingers on his cheeks and smiled her sleepy smile. Harry's nostrils quivered; his lips curled back in a hideous grin while he whispered: "To-morrow," and with her eyelids Miss Fulton said: "Yes."

"Here it is," said Eddie. " 'Why Must it Always be Tomato

Soup?' It's so *deeply* true, don't you feel? Tomato soup is so *dreadfully* eternal."

"If you prefer," said Harry's voice, very loud, from the hall, "I can phone you a cab to come to the door."

"Oh, no. It's not necessary," said Miss Fulton, and she came up to Bertha and gave her the slender fingers to hold.

"Good-bye. Thank you so much."

"Good-bye," said Bertha.

Miss Fulton held her hand a moment longer.

"Your lovely pear tree!" she murmured.

And then she was gone, with Eddie following, like the black cat following the grey cat.

"I'll shut up shop," said Harry, extravagantly cool and collected.

"Your lovely pear tree—pear tree—pear tree!"

Bertha simply ran over to the long windows.

"Oh, what is going to happen now?" she cried.

But the pear tree was as lovely as ever and as full of flower and as still.

THE DEAD

James Joyce

James Joyce is probably the most significant writer of fiction in the twentieth century. Born in Dublin in 1882, he left Ireland for good in 1904, and spent most of his adult life on the continent. He died in 1941. His three famous novels are A Portrait of the Artist as a Young Man *(1916),* Ulysses *(1920), and* Finnegan's Wake *(1939). Moving through impressionism to expressionism and surrealism, Joyce's lively mind succeeds beyond the efforts of any other novelist in encompassing the complexity of modern civilization. Of all his short stories "The Dead" (1914) is the most richly illustrative of the unique powers of this great modern writer.*

Lily, the caretaker's daughter, was literally run off her feet. Hardly had she brought one gentleman into the little pantry behind the office on the ground floor and helped him off with his overcoat, than the wheezy hall-door bell clanged again and she had to scamper along the bare hallway to let in another guest. It was well for her she had not to attend to the ladies also. But Miss Kate and Miss Julia had thought of that and had converted the bathroom upstairs into a ladies' dressing-room. Miss Kate and Miss Julia were there, gossiping and laughing and fussing, walking after each other to the head of the stairs, peering down over the banisters and calling down to Lily to ask her who had come.

It was always a great affair, the Misses Morkan's annual

dance. Everybody who knew them came to it, members of the family, old friends of the family, the members of Julia's choir, any of Kate's pupils that were grown up enough, and even some of Mary Jane's pupils too. Never once had it fallen flat. For years and years it had gone off in splendid style, as long as anyone could remember: ever since Kate and Julia, after the death of their brother Pat, had left the house in Stoney Batter and taken Mary Jane, their only niece, to live with them in the dark, gaunt house on Usher's Island, the upper part of which they had rented from Mr. Fulham, the corn-factor on the ground floor. That was a good thirty years ago if it was a day. Mary Jane, who was then a little girl in short clothes, was now the main prop of the household, for she had the organ in Haddington Road. She had been through the Academy and gave a pupils' concert every year in the upper room of the Antient Concert Rooms. Many of her pupils belonged to the better-class families on the Kingstown and Dalkey line. Old as they were, her aunts also did their share. Julia, though she was quite grey, was still the leading soprano in Adam and Eve's, and Kate, being too feeble to go about much, gave music lessons to beginners on the old square piano in the back room. Lily, the caretaker's daughter, did housemaid's work for them. Though their life was modest, they believed in eating well; the best of everything: diamond-bone sirloins, three-shilling tea and the best bottled stout. But Lily seldom made a mistake in the orders, so that she got on well with her three mistresses. They were fussy, that was all. But the only thing they would not stand was back answers.

Of course, they had good reason to be fussy on such a night. And then it was long after ten o'clock and yet there was no sign of Gabriel and his wife. Besides they were dreadfully afraid that Freddy Malins might turn up screwed. They would not wish for worlds that any of Mary Jane's pupils should see him under the influence; and when he was like that it was sometimes very hard to manage him. Freddy Malins always came late, but they wondered what could be keeping Gabriel: and that was what brought them every two minutes to the banisters to ask Lily had Gabriel or Freddy come.

"Oh, Mr. Conroy," said Lily to Gabriel when she opened the door for him, "Miss Kate and Miss Julia thought you were never coming. Good night, Mrs. Conroy."

"I'll engage they did," said Gabriel, "but they forget that my wife here takes three mortal hours to dress herself."

He stood on the mat, scraping the snow from his goloshes, while Lily led his wife to the foot of the stairs and called out:

"Miss Kate, here's Mrs. Conroy."

Kate and Julia came toddling down the dark stairs at once. Both of them kissed Gabriel's wife, said she must be perished alive, and asked was Gabriel with her.

"Here I am as right as the mail, Aunt Kate! Go on up. I'll follow," called out Gabriel from the dark.

He continued scraping his feet vigorously while the three women went upstairs, laughing, to the ladies' dressing-room. A light fringe of snow lay like a cape on the shoulders of his overcoat and like toecaps on the toes of his goloshes; and, as the buttons of his overcoat slipped with a squeaking noise through the snow-stiffened frieze, a cold, fragrant air from out-of-doors escaped from crevices and folds.

"Is it snowing again, Mr. Conroy?" asked Lily.

She had preceded him into the pantry to help him off with his overcoat. Gabriel smiled at the three syllables she had given his surname and glanced at her. She was a slim, growing girl, pale in complexion and with hay-coloured hair. The gas in the pantry made her look still paler. Gabriel had known her when she was a child and used to sit on the lowest step nursing a rag doll.

"Yes, Lily," he answered, "and I think we're in for a night of it."

He looked up at the pantry ceiling, which was shaking with the stamping and shuffling of feet on the floor above, listened for a moment to the piano and then glanced at the girl, who was folding his overcoat carefully at the end of a shelf.

"Tell me, Lily," he said in a friendly tone, "do you still go to school?"

"Oh no, sir," she answered. "I'm done schooling this year and more."

"Oh, then," said Gabriel gaily, "I suppose we'll be going to your wedding one of these fine days with your young man, eh?"

The girl glanced back at him over her shoulder and said with great bitterness:

"The men that is now is only all palaver and what they can get out of you."

Gabriel coloured, as if he felt he had made a mistake and, without looking at her, kicked off his goloshes and flicked actively with his muffler at his patent-leather shoes.

He was a stout, tallish young man. The high colour of his cheeks pushed upwards even to his forehead, where it scattered itself in a few formless patches of pale red; and on his hairless face there scintillated restlessly the polished lenses and the bright gilt rims of the glasses which screened his delicate and restless eyes. His glossy black hair was parted in the middle and brushed in a long curve behind his ears where it curled slightly beneath the groove left by his hat.

When he had flicked lustre into his shoes he stood up and pulled his waistcoat down more tightly on his plump body. Then he took a coin rapidly from his pocket.

"O Lily," he said, thrusting it into her hands, "it's Christmas-time, isn't it? Just . . . here's a little. . . ."

He walked rapidly towards the door.

"O no, sir!" cried the girl, following him. "Really, sir, I wouldn't take it."

"Christmas-time! Christmas-time!" said Gabriel, almost trotting to the stairs and waving his hand to her in deprecation.

The girl, seeing that he had gained the stairs, called out after him:

"Well, thank you, sir."

He waited outside the drawing-room door until the waltz should finish, listening to the skirts that swept against it and to the shuffling of feet. He was still discomposed by the girl's bitter and sudden retort. It had cast a gloom over him which he tried to dispel by arranging his cuffs and the bows of his tie. He then took from his waistcoat pocket a little paper and glanced at the headings he had made for his speech. He was undecided about the lines from Robert Browning, for he feared they would be above the heads of his hearers. Some quotation that they would recognize from Shakespeare or from the Melodies would be better. The indelicate clacking of the men's heels and the shuffling of their soles reminded him that their grade of culture differed from his. He would only make himself ridiculous by quoting poetry to them which they could not understand. They would think that he was airing his superior education. He would fail with them just as he had failed with the girl in the pantry. He had taken up a wrong tone. His whole speech was a mistake from first to last, an utter failure.

Just then his aunts and his wife came out of the ladies' dressing-room. His aunts were two small, plainly dressed old women. Aunt Julia was an inch or so the taller. Her hair, drawn low over the tops of her ears, was grey; and grey also, with darker shadows, was her large flaccid face. Though she was stout in build and stood erect, her slow eyes and parted lips gave her the appearance of a woman who did not know where she was or where she was going. Aunt Kate was more vivacious. Her face, healthier than her sister's, was all puckers and creases, like a shrivelled red apple, and her hair, braided in the same old-fashioned way, had not lost its ripe nut colour.

They both kissed Gabriel frankly. He was their favourite nephew, the son of their dead elder sister, Ellen, who had married T. J. Conroy of the Port and Docks.

"Gretta tells me you're not going to take a cab back to Monkstown to-night, Gabriel," said Aunt Kate.

"No," said Gabriel, turning to his wife, "we had quite enough of that last year, hadn't we? Don't you remember, Aunt Kate, what a cold Gretta got out of it? Cab windows rattling all the way, and the east wind blowing in after we passed Merrion. Very jolly it was. Gretta caught a dreadful cold."

Aunt Kate frowned severely and nodded her head at every word.

"Quite right, Gabriel, quite right," she said. "You can't be too careful."

"But as for Gretta there," said Gabriel, "she'd walk home in the snow if she were let."

Mrs. Conroy laughed.

"Don't mind him, Aunt Kate," she said. "He's really an awful bother, what with green shades for Tom's eyes at night and making him do the dumb-bells, and forcing Eva to eat the stirabout. The poor child! And she simply hates the sight of it! . . . Oh, but you'll never guess what he makes me wear now!"

She broke out into a peal of laughter and glanced at her husband, whose admiring and happy eyes had been wandering from her dress to her face and hair. The two aunts laughed heartily, too, for Gabriel's solicitude was a standing joke with them.

"Goloshes!" said Mrs. Conroy. "That's the latest. Whenever it's wet underfoot I must put on my goloshes. To-night even, he wanted me to put them on, but I wouldn't. The next thing he'll buy me will be a diving suit."

Gabriel laughed nervously and patted his tie reassuringly, while Aunt Kate nearly doubled herself, so heartily did she enjoy the joke. The smile soon faded from Aunt Julia's face and her mirthless eyes were directed towards her nephew's face. After a pause she asked:

"And what are goloshes, Gabriel?"

"Goloshes, Julia!" exclaimed her sister. "Goodness me, don't you know what goloshes are? You wear them over your . . . over your boots, Gretta, isn't it?"

"Yes," said Mrs. Conroy. "Gutta-percha things. We both have a pair now. Gabriel says everyone wears them on the Continent."

"Oh, on the Continent," murmured Aunt Julia, nodding her head slowly.

Gabriel knitted his brows and said, as if he were slightly angered:

"It's nothing very wonderful, but Gretta thinks it very funny, because she says the word reminds her of Christy Minstrels."

"But tell me, Gabriel," said Aunt Kate, with brisk tact. "Of course, you've seen about the room. Gretta was saying . . ."

"Oh, the room is all right," replied Gabriel. "I've taken one in the Gresham."

"To be sure," said Aunt Kate, "by far the best thing to do. And the children, Gretta, you're not anxious about them?"

"Oh, for one night," said Mrs. Conroy. "Besides, Bessie will look after them."

"To be sure," said Aunt Kate again. "What a comfort it is to have a girl like that, one you can depend on! There's that Lily, I'm sure I don't know what has come over her lately. She's not the girl she was at all."

Gabriel was about to ask his aunt some questions on this point, but she broke off suddenly to gaze after her sister, who had wandered down the stairs and was craning her neck over the banisters.

"Now, I ask you," she said almost testily, "where is Julia going? Julia! Julia! Where are you going?"

Julia, who had gone half-way down one flight, came back and announced blandly:

"Here's Freddy."

At the same moment a clapping of hands and a final flourish of the pianist told that the waltz had ended. The drawing-room door was opened from within and some couples came out. Aunt Kate drew Gabriel aside hurriedly and whispered into his ear:

"Slip down, Gabriel, like a good fellow and see if he's all right, and don't let him up if he's screwed. I'm sure he's screwed. I'm sure he is."

Gabriel went to the stairs and listened over the banisters. He could hear two persons talking in the pantry. Then he recognized Freddy Malin's laugh. He went down the stairs noisily.

"It's such a relief," said Aunt Kate to Mrs. Conroy, "that Gabriel is here. I always feel easier in my mind when he's here . . . Julia, there's Miss Daly and Miss Power will take some refreshment. Thanks for your beautiful waltz, Miss Daly. It made lovely time."

A tall wizen-faced man, with a stiff grizzled moustache and swarthy skin, who was passing out with his partner, said:

"And may we have some refreshment, too, Miss Morkan?"

"Julia," said Aunt Kate summarily, "and here's Mr. Browne and Miss Furlong. Take them in, Julia, with Miss Daly and Miss Power."

"I'm the man for the ladies," said Mr. Browne, pursing his lips until his moustache bristled and smiling in all his wrinkles. "You know, Miss Morkan, the reason they are so fond of me is . . ."

He did not finish his sentence, but, seeing that Aunt Kate was out of earshot, at once lead the three young ladies into the back room. The middle of the room was occupied by two square tables placed end to end, and on these Aunt Julia and the caretaker were straightening and smoothing a large cloth. On the sideboard were arrayed dishes and plates, and glasses and bundles of knives and forks and spoons. The top of the closed square piano served also as a sideboard for viands and sweets. At a smaller sideboard in one corner two young men were standing, drinking hop-bitters.

Mr. Browne led his charges thither and invited them all, in jest, to some ladies' punch, hot, strong and sweet. As they said they never took anything strong, he opened three bottles of lemonade for them. Then he asked one of the young men to move aside, and, taking hold of the decanter, filled out for himself a goodly measure of whisky. The young men eyed him respectfully while he took a trial sip.

"God help me," he said, smiling, "it's the doctor's orders."

His wizened face broke into a broader smile, and the three young ladies laughed in musical echo to his pleasantry, swaying their bodies to and fro, with nervous jerks of their shoulders. The boldest said:

"Oh, now, Mr. Browne, I'm sure the doctor never ordered anything of the kind."

Mr. Browne took another sip of his whisky and said, with sidling mimicry:

"Well, you see, I'm like the famous Mrs. Cassidy, who is reported to have said: 'Now, Mary Grimes, if I don't take it, make me take it, for I feel I want it.' "

His hot face had leaned forward a little too confidentially and he had assumed a very low Dublin accent, so that the young ladies, with one instinct, received his speech in silence. Miss Furlong, who was one of Mary Jane's pupils, asked Miss Daly what was the name of the pretty waltz she had played; and Mr. Browne, seeing that he was ignored, turned promptly to the two young men, who were more appreciative.

A red-faced young woman, dressed in pansy, came into the room, excitedly clapping her hands and crying:

"Quadrilles! Quadrilles!"

Close on her heels came Aunt Kate, crying:

"Two gentlemen and three ladies, Mary Jane!"

"Oh, here's Mr. Bergin and Mr. Kerrigan,' said Mary Jane. "Mr. Kerrigan, will you take Miss Power? Miss Furlong, may I get you a partner, Mr. Bergin. Oh, that'll just do now."

"Three ladies, Mary Jane," said Aunt Kate.

The two young gentlemen asked the ladies if they might have the pleasure, and Mary Jane turned to Miss Daly.

"Oh, Miss Daly, you're really awful good, after playing for the last two dances, but really we're so short of ladies tonight."

"I don't mind in the least, Miss Morkan."

"But I've a nice partner for you, Mr. Bartell D'Arcy, the tenor. I'll get him to sing later on. All Dublin is raving about him."

"Lovely voice, lovely voice!" said Aunt Kate.

As the piano had twice begun the prelude to the first figure Mary Jane led her recruits quickly from the room. They had hardly gone when Aunt Julia wandered slowly into the room, looking behind her at something.

"What is the matter, Julia?" asked Aunt Kate anxiously. "Who is it!"

Julia, who was carrying in a column of table-napkins, turned to her sister and said, simply, as if the question had surprised her:

"It's only Freddy, Kate, and Gabriel with him."

In fact, right behind her Gabriel could be seen piloting Freddy Malins across the landing. The latter, a young man of about forty, was of Gabriel's size and build, with very round shoulders. His face was fleshy and pallid, touched with colour only at the thick hanging lobes of his ears and at the wide wings of his nose. He had coarse features, a blunt nose, a convex and receding brow, tumid and protruded lips. His heavy-lidded eyes and the disorder of his scanty hair made him look sleepy. He was laughing heartily in a high key at a story which he had been telling Gabriel on the stairs and at the same time rubbing the knuckles of his left fist backwards and forwards into his left eye.

"Good evening, Freddy," said Aunt Julia.

Freddy Malins bade the Misses Morkan good evening in what seemed an offhand fashion by reason of the habitual catch in his voice and then, seeing that Mr. Browne was grinning at him from the sideboard, crossed the room on rather shaky legs and began to repeat in an undertone the story he had just told to Gabriel.

"He's not so bad, is he?" said Aunt Kate to Gabriel.

Gabriel's brows were dark, but he raised them quickly and answered:

"Oh, no, hardly noticeable."

"Now, isn't he a terrible fellow!" she said. "And his poor mother made him take the pledge on New Year's Eve. But come on, Gabriel, into the drawing-room."

Before leaving the room with Gabriel she signalled to Mr. Browne by frowning and shaking her forefinger in warning to and fro. Mr. Browne nodded in answer and, when she had gone, said to Freddy Malins:

"Now, then, Teddy, I'm going to fill you out a good glass of lemonade just to buck you up."

Freddy Malins, who was nearing the climax of his story, waved the offer aside impatiently, but Mr. Browne, having first called Freddy Malin's attention to a disarray in his dress, filled out and handed him a full glass of lemonade. Freddy Malins' left hand accepted the glass mechanically, his right hand being engaged in the mechanical readjustment of his dress. Mr. Browne, whose face was once more wrinkling with mirth, poured out for himself a glass of whisky while Freddy Malins exploded, before he had well reached the climax of his story, in a kind of high-pitched bronchitic laughter and, setting down his untasted and overflowing glass, began to rub the knuckles of his left fist backwards and forwards into his left eye, repeating words of his last phrase as well as his fit of laughter would allow him.

Gabriel could not listen while Mary Jane was playing her Academy piece, full of runs and difficult passages, to the hushed drawing-room. He liked music, but the piece she was playing had no melody for him and he doubted whether it had any melody for the other listeners, though they had begged Mary Jane to play something. Four young men, who had come from the refreshment-room to stand in the doorway at the sound of the piano, had gone away quietly in couples after a few minutes. The only persons who seemed to follow the music were Mary Jane herself, her hands racing along the keyboard or lifted from it at the pauses like those of a priestess in momentary imprecation, and Aunt Kate standing at her elbow to turn the page.

Gabriel's eyes, irritated by the floor, which glittered with beeswax under the heavy chandelier, wandered to the wall above the piano. A picture of the balcony scene in *Romeo and Juliet* hung there and beside it was a picture of the two murdered princes in the Tower which Aunt Julia had worked in red, blue and brown wools when she was a girl. Probably in the school they had gone to as girls that kind of work had been taught for one year. His mother had worked for him as a birthday present a waistcoat of purple tabinet, with little foxes' heads upon it, lined with brown satin and having round mulberry buttons. It was strange that his mother had had no musical talent, though Aunt Kate used to call her the brains carrier of the Morkan family. Both she and Julia had always seemed a little proud of their serious and matronly sister. Her photograph stood before the pierglass. She held an open book on her knees and was pointing out something in it to Constantine who, dressed in a man-o'-war suit, lay at her feet. It was she who had chosen the names of her sons for she was very sensible of the dignity of family life. Thanks to her, Constantine was now senior curate in Balbriggan and, thanks to her, Gabriel himself had taken his degree in the Royal University. A shadow passed over his face as he remembered her sullen opposition to his marriage. Some slighting phrases she had used still rankled in his memory; she had once spoke of Gretta as being country cute and that was not true of Gretta at all. It was Gretta who had nursed her during all her last long illness in their house at Monkstown.

He knew that Mary Jane must be near the end of her piece, for she was playing again the opening melody with runs of scales after every bar, and while he waited for the end the resentment died down in his heart. The piece ended with a trill of octaves in the treble and a final deep octave in the bass. Great applause greeted Mary Jane as, blushing and rolling up her music nervously, she escaped from the room. The most vigorous clapping came from the four young men in the doorway who had gone away to the refreshment-room at the beginning of the piece but had come back when the piano had stopped.

Lancers were arranged. Gabriel found himself partnered with Miss Ivors. She was a frank-mannered, talkative young lady, with a freckled face and prominent brown eyes. She did not wear a low-cut bodice, and the large brooch which was fixed in the front of her collar bore on it an Irish device and motto.

When they had taken their places she said abruptly:

"I have a crow to pluck with you."

"With me?" said Gabriel.

She nodded her head gravely.

"What is it?" asked Gabriel, smiling at her solemn manner.

"Who is G. C.?" answered Miss Ivors, turning her eyes upon him.

Gabriel coloured and was about to knit his brows, as if he did not understand, when she said bluntly:

"Oh, innocent Amy! I have found out that you write for the *Daily Express*. Now, aren't you ashamed of yourself?"

"Why should I be ashamed of myself?" asked Gabriel, blinking his eyes and trying to smile.

"Well, I'm ashamed of you," said Miss Ivors frankly. "To say you'd write for a paper like that. I didn't think you were a West Briton."

A look of perplexity appeared on Gabriel's face. It was true that he wrote a literary column every Wednesday in the *Daily Express*, for which he was paid fifteen shillings. But that did not make him a West Briton surely. The books he received for review were almost more welcome than the paltry cheque. He loved to feel the covers and turn over the pages of newly printed books. Nearly every day when his teaching in the college was ended he used to wander down the quays to the second-hand booksellers, to Hickey's on Bachelor's Walk, to Webb's or Massey's on Aston's Quay, or to O'Clohissey's in the by-street. He did not know how to meet her charge. He wanted to say that literature was above politics. But they were friends of many years' standing and their careers had been parallel, first at the University and then as teachers: he could not risk a grandiose phrase with her. He continued blinking his eyes and trying to smile and murmured lamely that he saw nothing political in writing reviews of books.

When their turn to cross had come he was still perplexed and inattentive. Miss Ivors promptly took his hand in a warm grasp and said in a soft friendly tone:

"Of course, I was only joking. Come, we cross now."

When they were together again she spoke of the University question and Gabriel felt more at ease. A friend of hers had shown her his review of Browning's poems. That was how she had found out the secret: but she liked the review immensely. Then she said suddenly:

"Oh, Mr. Conroy, will you come for an excursion to the Aran Isles this summer? We're going to stay there a whole month. It will be splendid out in the Atlantic. You ought to come. Mr. Clancy is coming, and Mr. Kilkelly and Kathleen Kearney. It would be splendid for Gretta too is she'd come. She's from Connacht, isn't she?"

"Her people are," said Gabriel shortly.

"But you will come, won't you?" said Miss Ivors, laying her warm hand eagerly on his arm.

"The fact is," said Gabriel, "I have just arranged to go . . ."

"Go where?" asked Miss Ivors.

"Well, you know, every year I go for a cycling tour with some fellows and so . . ."

"But where?" asked Miss Ivors.

"Well, we usually go to France or Belgium or perhaps Germany," said Gabriel awkwardly.

"And why do you go to France and Belgium," said Miss Ivors, "instead of visting your own land?"

"Well," said Gabriel, "it's partly to keep in touch with the languages and partly for a change."

"And haven't you your own language to keep in touch with —Irish?" asked Miss Ivors.

"Well," said Gabriel, "if it comes to that, you know, Irish is not my language."

Their neighbours had turned to listen to the cross-examination. Gabriel glanced right and left nervously and tried to keep his good humour under the ordeal, which was making a blush invade his forehead.

"And haven't you your own land to visit," continued Miss Ivors, "that you know nothing of, your own people, and your own country?"

"Oh, to tell you the truth," retorted Gabriel suddenly, "I'm sick of my own country, sick of it!"

"Why?" asked Miss Ivors.

Gabriel did not answer, for his retort had heated him.

"Why?" repeated Miss Ivors.

They had to go visiting together and, as he had not answered her, Miss Ivors said warmly:

"Of course, you've no answer."

Gabriel tried to cover his agitation by taking part in the dance with great energy. He avoided her eyes, for he had seen a sour expression on her face. But when they met in the long chain he was surprised to feel his hand firmly pressed. She looked at him from under her brows for a moment quizzically until he smiled. Then, just as the chain was about to start again, she stood on tiptoe and whispered into his ear:

"West Briton!"

When the lancers were over Gabriel went away to a remote corner of the room where Freddy Malins' mother was sitting. She was a stout, feeble old woman with white hair. Her voice had a catch in it like her son's and she stuttered slightly. She had been told that Freddy had come and that he was nearly all right. Gabriel asked her whether she had had a good crossing. She lived with her married daughter in Glasgow and came to Dublin on a visit once a year. She answered placidly that she had had a beautiful crossing and that the captain had been most attentive to her. She spoke also of the beautiful house her daughter kept in Glasgow, and of all the friends they had there. While her tongue rambled on Gabriel tried to banish from his mind all memory of the unpleasant incident with Miss Ivors. Of course the girl, or woman, or whatever she was, was an enthusiast, but there was a time for all things. Perhaps he ought not to have answered her like that. But she had no right to call him a West Briton before people, even in joke. She had tried to make him ridiculous before people, heckling him and staring at him with her rabbit's eyes.

He saw his wife making her way towards him through the waltzing couples. When she reached him she said into his ear:

"Gabriel, Aunt Kate wants to know won't you carve the goose as usual. Miss Daly will carve the ham and I'll do the pudding."

"All right," said Gabriel.

"She's sending in the younger ones first as soon as this waltz is over so that we'll have the table to ourselves."

"Were you dancing?" asked Gabriel.

"Of course I was. Didn't you see me? What row had you with Molly Ivors?"

"No row. Why? Did she say so?"

"Something like that. I'm trying to get that Mr. D'Arcy to sing. He's full of conceit, I think."

"There was no row," said Gabriel moodily, "only she wanted me to go for a trip to the west of Ireland and I said I wouldn't."

His wife clasped her hands excitedly and gave a little jump.

"Oh, do go, Gabriel," she cried. "I'd love to see Galway again."

"You can go if you like," said Gabriel coldly.

She looked at him for a moment, then turned to Mrs. Malins and said:

"There's a nice husband for you, Mrs. Malins."

While she was threading her way back across the room Mrs. Malins, without adverting to the interruption, went on to tell Gabriel what beautiful places there were in Scotland and beautiful scenery. Her son-in-law brought them every year to the lakes and they used to go fishing. Her son-in-law was a splendid fisher. One day he caught a beautiful big fish and the man in the hotel cooked it for their dinner.

Gabriel hardly heard what she said. Now that supper was

coming near he began to think again about his speech and about the quotation. When he saw Freddy Malins coming across the room to visit his mother Gabriel left the chair free for him and retired into the embrasure of the window. The room had already cleared and from the back room came the clatter of plates and knives. Those who still remained in the drawing-room seemed tired of dancing and were conversing quietly in little groups. Gabriel's warm, trembling fingers tapped the cold pane of the window. How cool it must be outside! How pleasant it would be to walk out alone, first along by the river and then through the park! The snow would be lying on the branches of the trees and forming a bright cap on the top of the Wellington Monument. How much more pleasant it would be there than at the supper-table!

He ran over the headings of his speech: Irish hospitality, sad memories, the Three Graces, Paris, the quotation from Browning. He repeated to himself a phrase he had written in his review: "One feels that one is listening to a thought-tormented music." Miss Ivors had praised the review. Was she sincere? Had she really any life of her own behind all her propagandism? There had never been any ill-feeling between them until that night. It unnerved him to think that she would be at the supper-table, looking up at him while he spoke with her critical quizzing eyes. Perhaps she would not be sorry to see him fail in his speech. An idea came into his mind and gave him courage. He would say, alluding to Aunt Kate and Aunt Julia: "Ladies and Gentlemen, the generation which is now on the wane among us may have had its faults, but for my part I think it had certain qualities of hospitality, of humour, of humanity, which the new and very serious and hypereducated generation that is growing up around us seems to me to lack." Very good: that was one for Miss Ivors. What did he care that his aunts were only two ignorant old women?

A murmur in the room attracted his attention. Mr. Browne was advancing from the door, gallantly escorting Aunt Julia, who leaned upon his arm, smiling and hanging her head. An irregular musketry of applause escorted her also as far as the piano and then, as Mary Jane seated herself on the stool, and Aunt Julia, no longer smiling, half turned so as to pitch her voice fairly into the room, gradually ceased. Gabriel recognized the prelude. It was that of an old song of Aunt

Julia's—"Arrayed for the Bridal." Her voice, strong and clear in tone, attacked with great spirit the runs which embellish the air, and though she sang very rapidly she did not miss even the smallest of the grace notes. To follow the voice, without looking at the singer's face, was to feel and share the excitement of swift and secure flight. Gabriel applauded loudly with all the others at the close of the song, and loud applause was borne in from the invisible supper-table. It sounded so genuine that a little colour struggled into Aunt Julia's face as she bent to replace in the music-stand the old leather-bound song-book that had her initials on the cover. Freddy Malins, who had listened with his head perched sideways to hear her better, was still applauding when everyone else had ceased and talking animatedly to his mother, who nodded her head gravely and slowly in acquiescence. At last, when he could clap no more, he stood up suddenly and hurried across the room to Aunt Julia whose hand he seized and held in both his hands, shaking it when words failed him or the catch in his voice proved too much for him.

"I was just telling my mother," he said, "I never heard you sing so well, never. No, I never heard your voice so good as it is to-night. Now! Would you believe that now? That's the truth. Upon my word and honour that's the truth. I never heard your voice sound so fresh and so . . . so clear and fresh, never."

Aunt Julia smiled broadly and murmured something about compliments as she released her hand from his grasp. Mr. Browne extended his open hand towards her and said to those who were near him in the manner of a showman introducing a prodigy to an audience:

"Miss Julia Morkan, my latest discovery!"

He was laughing very heartily at this himself when Freddy Malins turned to him and said:

"Well, Browne, if you're serious you might make a worse discovery. All I can say is I never heard her sing half so well as long as I am coming here. And that's the honest truth."

"Neither did I," said Mr. Browne. "I think her voice has greatly improved."

Aunt Julia shrugged her shoulders and said with meek pride:

"Thirty years ago I hadn't a bad voice as voices go."

"I often told Julia," said Aunt Kate emphatically, "that

she was simply thrown away in that choir. But she never would be said by me."

She turned as if to appeal to the good sense of the others against a refractory child, while Aunt Julia gazed in front of her, a vague smile of reminiscence playing on her face.

"No," continued Aunt Kate, "she wouldn't be said or led by anyone, slaving there in that choir night and day, night and day. Six o'clock on Christmas morning! And all for what?"

"Well, isn't it for the honour of God, Aunt Kate?" asked Mary Jane, twisting round on the piano-stool and smiling.

Aunt Kate turned fiercely on her niece and said:

"I know all about the honour of God, Mary Jane, but I think it's not at all honourable for the pope to turn out the women out of the choirs that have slaved there all their lives and put little whipper-snappers of boys over their heads. I suppose it is for the good of the Church, if the pope does it. But it's not just, Mary Jane, and it's not right."

She had worked herself into a passion and would have continued in defence of her sister, for it was a sore subject with her, but Mary Jane, seeing that all the dancers had come back, intervened pacifically.

"Now, Aunt Kate, you're giving scandal to Mr. Browne, who is of the other persuasion."

Aunt Kate turned to Mr. Browne, who was grinning at this allusion to his religion, and said hastily:

"Oh, I don't question the pope's being right. I'm only a stupid old woman and I wouldn't presume to do such a thing. But there's such a thing as common everyday politeness and gratitude. And if I were in Julia's place I'd tell that Father Healey straight up to his face . . ."

"And besides, Aunt Kate," said Mary Jane, "we really are all hungry and when we are hungry we are all very quarrelsome."

"And when we are thirsty we are also quarrelsome," added Mr. Browne.

"So that we had better go to supper," said Mary Jane, "and finish the discussion afterwards."

On the landing outside the drawing-room Gabriel found his wife and Mary Jane trying to persuade Miss Ivors to stay for supper. But Miss Ivors, who had put on her hat and was buttoning her cloak, would not stay. She did not feel in the least hungry and she had already overstayed her time.

"But only for ten minutes, Molly," said Mrs. Conroy. "That won't delay you."

"To take a pick itself," said Mary Jane, "after all your dancing."

"I really couldn't," said Miss Ivors.

"I am afraid you didn't enjoy yourself at all," said Mary Jane hopelessly.

"Ever so much I assure you," said Miss Ivors, "but you really must let me run off now."

"But how can you get home?" asked Mrs. Conroy.

"Oh, it's only two steps up the quay."

Gabriel hesitated a moment and said:

"If you will allow me, Miss Ivors, I'll see you home if you are really obliged to go."

But Miss Ivors broke away from them.

"I won't hear of it," she cried. "For goodness' sake go in to your suppers and don't mind me. I'm quite well able to take care of myself."

"Well, you're the comical girl, Molly," said Mrs. Conroy frankly.

"Beannacht libh," cried Miss Ivors, with a laugh, as she ran down the staircase.

Mary Jane gazed after her, a moody puzzled expression on her face, while Mrs. Conroy leaned over the banisters to listen for the hall-door. Gabriel asked himself was he the cause of her abrupt departure. But she did not seem to be in ill humour—she had gone away laughing. He stared blankly down the staircase.

At the moment Aunt Kate came toddling out of the supper-room, almost wringing her hands in despair.

"Where is Gabriel!" she cried. "Where on earth is Gabriel? There's every one waiting in there, stage to let, and nobody to carve the goose!"

"Here I am, Aunt Kate!" cried Gabriel, with sudden animation, "ready to carve a flock of geese, if necessary."

A fat brown goose lay at one end of the table, and at the other end, on a bed of creased paper strewn with sprigs of parsley, lay a great ham, stripped of its outer skin and peppered over with crust crumbs, a neat paper frill round its shin, and beside this was a round of spiced beef. Between these rival ends ran parallel lines of side-dishes: two little minsters of jelly, red and yellow; a shallow dish full of blocks of blancmange and red jam, a large green leaf-shaped dish with a stalk-shaped handle, on which lay bunches of purple raisins and peeled almonds, a companion dish on which lay a solid rectangle of Smyrna figs, a dish of custard topped with grated nutmeg, a small bowl full of chocolates and sweets wrapped in gold and silver papers and a glass vase in which stood some tall celery stalks. In the centre of the table there stood, as sentries to a fruit-stand which upheld a pyramid of oranges and American apples, two squat old-fashioned decanters of cut glass, one containing port and the other dark sherry. On the closed square piano a pudding in a huge yellow dish lay in waiting, and behind it were three squads of bottles of stout and ale and minerals, drawn up according to the colours of their uniforms, the first two black, with brown and red labels, the third and smallest squad white, with transverse green sashes.

Gabriel took his seat boldly at the head of the table and, having looked to the edge of the carver, plunged his fork firmly into the goose. He felt quite at ease now, for he was an expert carver and liked nothing better than to find himself at the head of a well-laden table.

"Miss Furlong, what shall I send you?" he asked. "A wing or a slice of the breast?"

"Just a small slice of the breast."

"Miss Higgins, what for you?"

"Oh, anything at all, Mr. Conroy."

While Gabriel and Miss Daly exchanged plates of goose and plates of ham and spiced beef, Lily went from guest to guest with a dish of hot floury potatoes wrapped in a white napkin. This was Mary Jane's idea and she had also suggested apple sauce for the goose, but Aunt Kate had said that plain roast goose without any apple sauce had always been good enough for her and she hoped she might never eat worse. Mary Jane waited on her pupils and saw that they got the best slices, and Aunt Kate and Aunt Julia opened and carried across from the piano bottles of stout and ale for the gentlemen and bottles of minerals for the ladies. There was a great deal of confusion and laughter and noise, the noise of orders and counter-orders, of knives and forks, of corks and glass-stoppers. Gabriel began to carve second helpings as soon as he had finished the first round without serving himself. Everyone protested loudly, so that he compromised by taking a long draught of stout, for he had found the carving hot work. Mary Jane settled down quietly to her supper, but Aunt Kate and Aunt Julia were still toddling round the table, walking on each other's heels, getting in each other's way and giving each other unheeded orders. Mr. Browne begged of them to sit down and eat their suppers and so did Gabriel, but they said there was time enough, so that at last Freddy Malins stood up and, capturing Aunt Kate, plumped her down on her chair amid general laughter.

When everyone had been well served Gabriel said, smiling:

"Now, if anyone wants a little more of what vulgar people call stuffing let him or her speak."

A chorus of voices invited him to begin his own supper, and Lily came forward with three potatoes which she had reserved for him.

"Very well," said Gabriel amiably, as he took another preparatory draught, "kindly forget my existence, ladies and gentlemen, for a few minutes."

He set to his supper and took no part in the conversation with which the table covered Lily's removal of the plates. The subject of talk was the opera company which was then at the Theatre Royal. Mr. Bartell D'Arcy, the tenor, a dark-complexioned young man with a smart moustache, praised very highly the leading contralto of the company, but Miss Furlong thought she had a rather vulgar style of production. Freddy Malins said there was a negro chieftain singing in the second part of the Gaiety pantomime who had one of the finest tenor voices he had ever heard.

"Have you heard him?" he asked Mr. Bartell D'Arcy across the table.

"No," answered Mr. Bartell D'Arcy carelessly.

"Because," Freddy Malins explained, "now I'd be curious to hear your opinion of him. I think he has a grand voice."

"It takes Teddy to find out the really good things," said Mr. Browne familiarly to the table.

"And why couldn't he have a voice too?" asked Freddy Malins sharply. "Is it because he's only a black?"

Nobody answered this question and Mary Jane led the table back to the legitimate opera. One of her pupils had given her a pass for *Mignon*. Of course it was very fine, she said, but it made her think of poor Georgina Burns. Mr. Browne could go back farther still, to the old Italian companies that used to come to Dublin—Tietjens, Ilma de Murzka, Campanini, the great Trebelli, Giuglini, Ravelli, Aramburo. Those were the days, he said, when there was something like singing to be heard in Dublin. He told too of how the top gallery of the old Royal used to be packed night after night, of how one night an Italian tenor had sung five encores to "Let me like a Soldier fall," introducing a high C every time, and of how the gallery boys would sometimes in their enthusiasm unyoke the horses from the carriage of some great *prima donna* and pull her themselves through the streets to her hotel. "Why did they never play the grand old operas now," he asked, *"Dinorah, Lucrezia Borgia?* Because they could not get the voices to sing them: that was why."

"Oh, well," said Mr. Bartell D'Arcy, "I presume there are as good singers to-day as there were then."

"Where are they?" asked Mr. Browne defiantly.

"In London, Paris, Milan," said Mr. Bartell D'Arcy warmly. "I suppose Caruso, for example, is quite as good, if not better than any of the men you have mentioned."

"Maybe so," said Mr. Browne. "But I may tell you I doubt it strongly."

"Oh, I'd give anything to hear Caruso sing," said Mary Jane.

"For me," said Aunt Kate, who had been picking a bone, "there was only one tenor. To please me, I mean. But I suppose none of you ever heard of him."

"Who was he, Miss Morkan?" asked Mr. Bartell D'Arcy politely.

"His name," said Aunt Kate, "was Parkinson. I heard him when he was in his prime and I think he had then the purest tenor voice that was ever put into a man's throat."

"Strange," said Mr. Bartell D'Arcy. "I never even heard of him."

"Yes, yes, Miss Morkan is right," said Mr. Browne. "I remember hearing of old Parkinson, but he's too far back for me."

"A beautiful, pure, sweet, mellow English tenor," said Aunt Kate with enthusiasm.

Gabriel having finished, the huge pudding was transferred to the table. The clatter of forks and spoons began again. Gabriel's wife served out spoonfuls of the pudding and passed the plates down the table. Midway down they were held up by Mary Jane, who replenished them with raspberry of orange jelly or with blancmange and jam. The pudding was of Aunt Julia's making, and she received praises for it from all quarters. She herself said that it was not quite brown enough.

"Well, I hope, Miss Morkan," said Mr. Browne, "that I'm brown enough for you because, you know, I'm all brown."

All the gentlemen, except Gabriel, ate some of the pudding out of compliment to Aunt Julia. As Gabriel never ate sweets the celery had been left for him. Freddy Malins also took a stalk of celery and ate it with his pudding. He had been told that celery was a capital thing for the blood and he was just then under the doctor's care. Mrs. Malins who had been silent all through the supper, said that her son was going down to Mount Melleray in a week or so. The table then spoke of Mount Melleray, how bracing the air was down there, how hospitable the monks were and how they never asked for a penny-piece from their guests.

"And do you mean to say," asked Mr. Browne incredulously, "that a chap can go down there and put up there as if it were an hotel and live on the fat of the land and then come away without paying anything?"

"Oh, most people give some donation to the monastery when they leave," said Mary Jane.

"I wish we had an institution like that in our Church," said Mr. Browne candidly.

He was astonished to hear that the monks never spoke, got up at two in the morning and slept in their coffins. He asked what they did it for.

"That's the rule of the order," said Aunt Kate firmly.

"Yes, but why?" asked Mr. Browne.

Aunt Kate repeated that it was the rule, that was all. Mr. Browne still seemed not to understand. Freddy Malins explained to him, as best he could, that the monks were trying to make up for the sins committed by all the sinners in the outside world. The explanation was not very clear, for Mr. Browne grinned and said:

"I like that idea very much, but wouldn't a comfortable spring bed do them as well as a coffin?"

"The coffin," said Mary Jane, "is to remind them of their last end."

As the subject had grown lugubrious it was buried in a silence of the table, during which Mrs. Malins could be heard saying to her neighbour in an indistinct undertone:

"They are very good men, the monks, very pious men."

The raisins and almonds and figs and apples and oranges and chocolates and sweets were now passed about the table, and Aunt Julia invited all the guests to have either port or sherry. At first Mr. Bartell D'Arcy refused to take either, but one of his neighbours nudged him and whispered something to him, upon which he allowed his glass to be filled. Gradually as the last glasses were being filled the conversation ceased. A pause followed, broken only by the noise of the wine and by unsettlings of chairs. The Misses Morkan, all three, looked down at the table-cloth. Someone coughed once or twice, and then a few gentlemen patted the table gently as a signal for silence. The silence came and Gabriel pushed back his chair and stood up.

The patting at once grew louder in encouragement and then ceased altogether. Gabriel leaned his ten trembling fingers on the table-cloth and smiled nervously at the company. Meeting a row of upturned faces he raised his eyes to the chandelier. The piano was playing a waltz tune and he could hear the skirts sweeping against the drawing-room door. People, perhaps, were standing in the snow on the quay outside, gazing up at the lighted windows and listening to the waltz music. The air was pure there. In the distance lay the park, where the trees were weighted with snow. The Wellington Monument wore a gleaming cap of snow that flashed westward over the white field of Fifteen Acres.

He began:

"Ladies and Gentlemen,

"It has fallen to my lot this evening, as in years past, to perform a very pleasing task, but a task for which I am afraid my poor powers as a speaker are all too inadequate."

"No, no!" said Mr. Browne.

"But, however that may be, I can only ask you to-night to take the will for the deed, and to lend me your attention for a few moments while I endeavour to express to you in words what my feelings are on this occasion.

"Ladies and Gentlemen, it is not the first time that we have gathered together under this hospitable roof, around this hospitable board. It is not the first time that we have been the recipients—or perhaps, I had better say, the victims—of the hospitality of certain good ladies."

He made a circle in the air with his arm and paused. Every one laughed or smiled at Aunt Kate and Aunt Julia and Mary Jane, who all turned crimson with pleasure. Gabriel went on more boldly:

"I feel more strongly with every recurring year that our

country has no tradition which does it so much honour and which it should guard so jealously as that of its hospitality. It is a tradition that is unique as far as my experience goes (and I have visited not a few places abroad) among the modern nations. Some would say, perhaps, that with us it is rather a failing than anything to be boasted of. But granted even that, it is, to my mind, a princely failing, and one that I trust will long be cultivated among us. Of one thing, at least, I am sure. As long as this one roof shelters the good ladies aforesaid—and I wish from my heart it may do so for many and many a long year to come—the tradition of genuine warm-hearted courteous Irish hospitality, which our forefathers have handed down to us and which we in turn must hand down to our descendants, is still alive among us."

A hearty murmur of assent ran round the table. It shot through Gabriel's mind that Miss Ivors was not there and that she had gone away discourteously: and he said with confidence in himself:

"Ladies and Gentlemen,

"A new generation is growing up in our midst, a generation actuated by new ideas and new principles. It is serious and enthusiastic, for these new ideas and its enthusiasm, even when it is misdirected, is, I believe, in the main sincere. But we are living in a sceptical and, if I may use the phrase, a thought-tormented age: and sometimes I fear that this new generation, educated or hyper-educated as it is, will lack those qualities of humanity, of hospitality, of kindly humour which belonged to an older day. Listening to-night to the names of all those great singers of the past it seemed to me, I must confess, that we were living in a less spacious age. Those days might, without exaggeration, be called spacious days: and if they are gone beyond recall, let us hope, at least, that in gatherings such as this we shall still speak of them with pride and affection, still cherish in our hearts the memory of those dead and gone great ones whose fame the world will not willingly let die."

"Hear, hear!" said Mr. Browne loudly.

"But yet," continued Gabriel, his voice falling into a softer inflection, "there are always in gatherings such as this sadder thoughts that will recur to our minds: thoughts of the past, of youth, of changes, of absent faces that we miss here to-night. Our path through life is strewn with many such sad memories: and were we to brood upon them always we could not find the heart to go on bravely with our work among the living. We have all of us living duties and living affections which claim, and rightly claim, our strenuous endeavours.

"Therefore, I will not linger on the past, I will not let any gloomy moralizing intrude upon us here to-night. Here we are gathered together for a brief moment from the bustle and rush of our everyday routine. We are met here as friends, in the spirt of good-fellowship, as colleagues, also, to a certain extent, in the true spirit of *camaraderie,* and as the guests of—what shall I call them?—the Three Graces of the Dublin musical world."

The table burst into applause and laughter at this allusion. Aunt Julia vainly asked each of her neighbours in turn to tell her what Gabriel had said.

"He says we are the Three Graces, Aunt Julia," said Mary Jane.

Aunt Julia did not understand, but she looked up, smiling, at Gabriel, who continued in the same vein:

"Ladies and Gentlemen,

"I will not attempt to play to-night the part that Paris played on another occasion. I will not attempt to choose between them. The task would be an invidious one and one beyond my poor powers. For when I view them in turn, whether it be our chief hostess herself, whose good heart, whose too good heart, has become a byword with all who know her; or her sister, who seems to be gifted with perennial youth and whose singing must have been a surprise and a revelation to us all to-night; or, last but not least, when I consider our youngest hostess, talented, cheerful, hard-working and the best of nieces, I confess, Ladies and Gentlemen, that I do not know to which of them I should award the prize."

Gabriel glanced down at his aunts and, seeing the large smile on Aunt Julia's face and the tears which had risen to Aunt Kate's eyes, hastened to his close. He raised his glass of port gallantly, while every member of the company fingered a glass expectantly, and said loudly:

"Let us toast them all three together. Let us drink to their health, wealth, long life, happiness and prosperity, and may they long continue to hold the proud and self-won position which they hold in their profession and the position of honour and affection which they hold in our hearts."

All the guests stood up, glass in hand, and turning towards

the three seated ladies, sang in unison, with Mr. Browne as leader:

For they are jolly gay fellows,
For they are jolly gay fellows,
For they are jolly gay fellows,
Which nobody can deny.

Aunt Kate was making frank use of her handkerchief and even Aunt Julia seemed moved. Freddy Malins beat time with his pudding-fork and the singers turned towards one another, as if in melodious conference, while they sang with emphasis:

Unless he tells a lie,
Unless he tells a lie,

Then, turning once more towards their hostesses, they sang:

For they are jolly gay fellows,
For they are jolly gay fellows,
For they are jolly gay fellows,
Which nobody can deny.

The acclamation which followed was taken up beyond the door of the supper-room by many of the other guests and renewed time after time, Freddy Malins acting as officer with his fork on high.

The piercing morning air came into the hall where they were standing so that Aunt Kate said:

"Close the door, somebody. Mrs. Malins will get her death of cold."

"Browne is out there, Aunt Kate," said Mary Jane.

"Browne is everywhere," said Aunt Kate, lowering her voice.

Mary Jane laughed at her tone.

"Really," she said archly, "he is very attentive."

"He has been laid on here like the gas," said Aunt Kate in the same tone, "all during the Christmas."

She laughed herself this time good-humouredly and then added quickly:

"But tell him to come in, Mary Jane, and close the door. I hope to goodness he didn't hear me."

At that moment the hall-door was opened and Mr. Browne came in from the doorstep, laughing as if his heart would break. He was dressed in a long green overcoat with mock Astrakhan cuffs and collar and wore on his head an oval fur cap. He pointed down the snow-covered quay from where the sound of shrill prolonged whistling was borne in.

"Teddy will have all the cabs in Dublin out," he said.

Gabriel advanced from the little pantry behind the office, struggling into his overcoat and, looking round the hall, said:

"Gretta not down yet?"

"She's getting on her things, Gabriel," said Aunt Kate.

"Who's playing up there?" asked Gabriel.

"Nobody. They're all gone."

"Oh, no, Aunt Kate," said Mary Jane. "Bartell D'Arcy and Miss O'Callaghan aren't gone yet."

"Someone is fooling at the piano anyhow," said Gabriel.

Mary Jane glanced at Gabriel and Mr. Browne and said with a shiver:

"It makes me feel cold to look at you two gentlemen muffled up like that. I wouldn't like to face your journey home at this hour."

"I'd like nothing better this minute," said Mr. Browne stoutly, "than a rattling fine walk in the country or a fast drive with a good spanking goer between the shafts."

"We used to have a very good horse and trap at home," said Aunt Julia, sadly.

"The never-to-be-forgotten Johnny," said Mary Jane, laughing.

Aunt Kate and Gabriel laughed too.

"Why, what was wonderful about Johnny?" asked Mr. Browne.

"The late lamented Patrick Morkan, our grandfather, that is," explained Gabriel, "commonly known in his later years as the old gentleman, was a glue-boiler."

"Oh, now, Gabriel," said Aunt Kate, laughing, "he had a starch mill."

"Well, glue or starch," said Gabriel, "the old gentleman had a horse by the name of Johnny. And Johnny used to work in the old gentleman's mill, walking round and round in order to drive the mill. That was all very well; but now comes the tragic part about Johnny. One fine day the old gentleman thought he'd like to drive out with the quality to a military review in the park."

"The Lord have mercy on his soul," said Aunt Kate compassionately.

"Amen," said Gabriel. "So the old gentleman, as I said, harnessed Johnny and put on his very best tall hat and his very best stock collar and drove out in grand style from his ancestral mansion somewhere near Back Lane, I think."

Every one laughed, even Mrs. Malins, at Gabriel's manner, and Aunt Kate said:

"Oh, now, Gabriel, he didn't live in Back Lane, really. Only the mill was there."

"Out from the mansion of his forefathers," continued Gabriel, "he drove with Johnny. And everything went on beautifully until Johnny came in sight of King Billy's statue: and whether he fell in love with the horse King Billy sits on or whether he thought he was back again in the mill, anyhow he began to walk round the statue."

Gabriel paced in a circle round the hall in his goloshes amid the laughter of the others.

"Round and round he went," said Gabriel, "and the old gentleman, who was a very pompous old gentleman, was highly indignant. 'Go on, sir! What do you mean, sir? Johnny! Johnny! Most extraordinary conduct! Can't understand the horse!' "

The peals of laughter which followed Gabriel's imitation of the incident was interrupted by a resounding knock at the hall door. Mary Jane ran to open it and let in Freddy Malins. Freddy Malins, with his hat well back on his head and his shoulders humped with cold, was puffing and steaming after his exertions.

"I could only get one cab," he said.

"Oh, we'll find another along the quay," said Gabriel.

"Yes," said Aunt Kate. "Better not keep Mrs. Malins standing in the draught."

Mrs. Malins was helped down the front steps by her son and Mr. Browne and, after many manœuvres, hoisted into the cab. Freddy Malins clambered in after her and spent a long time settling her on the seat, Mr. Browne helping him with advice. At last she was settled comfortably and Freddy Malins invited Mr. Browne into the cab. There was a good deal of confused talk, and then Mr. Browne got into the cab. The cabman settled his rug over his knees, and bent down for the address. The confusion grew greater and the cabman was directed differently by Freddy Malins and Mr. Browne, each of whom had his head out through a window of the cab. The difficulty was to know where to drop Mr. Browne along the route, and Aunt Kate, Aunt Julia and Mary Jane helped the discussion from the doorstep with cross-directions and contradictions and abundance of laughter. As for Freddy Malins he was speechless with laughter. He popped his head in and out of the window every moment to the great danger of his hat, and told his mother how the discussion was progressing, till at last Mr. Browne shouted to the bewildered cabman above the din of everybody's laughter:

"Do you know Trinity College?"

"Yes, sir," said the cabman.

"Well, drive bang up against Trinity College gates," said Mr. Browne, "and then we'll tell you where to go. You understand now?"

"Yes, sir," said the cabman.

"Make like a bird for Trinity College."

"Right, sir," said the cabman.

The horse was whipped up and the cab rattled off along the quay amid a chorus of laughter and adieux.

Gabriel had not gone to the door with the others. He was in a dark part of the hall gazing up the staircase. A woman was standing near the top of the first flight, in the shadow also. He could not see her face but he could see the terracotta and salmon-pink panels of her skirt which the shadow made appear black and white. It was his wife. She was leaning on the banisters, listening to something. Gabriel was surprised at her stillness and strained his ear to listen also. But he could hear little save the noise of laugher and dispute on the front steps, a few chords struck on the piano and a few notes of a man's voice singing.

He stood still in the gloom of the hall, trying to catch the air that the voice was singing and gazing up at his wife. There was grace and mystery in her attitude as if she were a symbol of something. He asked himself what is a woman standing on the stairs in the shadow, listening to distant music, a symbol of. If he were a painter he would paint her in that attitude. Her blue felt hat would show off the bronze of her hair against the darkness and the dark panels of her skirt would show off the light ones. "Distant Music" he would call the picture if he were a painter.

The hall-door was closed, and Aunt Kate, Aunt Julia and Mary Jane came down the hall, still laughing.

"Well, isn't Freddy terrible?" said Mary Jane. "He's really terrible."

Gabriel said nothing, but pointed up the stairs towards where his wife was standing. Now that the hall-door was closed the voice and the piano could be heard more clearly. Gabriel held up his hand for them to be silent. The song seemed to be in the old Irish tonality and the singer seemed uncertain both of his words and of his voice. The voice, made plaintive by distance and by the singer's hoarseness, faintly illuminated the cadence of the air with words expressing grief:

O, the rain falls on my heavy locks
And the dew wets my skin,
My babe lies cold . . .

"Oh," exclaimed Mary Jane. "It's Bartell D'Arcy singing, and he wouldn't sing all the night. Oh, I'll get him to sing a song before he goes."

"Oh, do, Mary Jane," said Aunt Kate.

Mary Jane brushed past the others and ran to the staircase, but before she reached it the singing stopped and the piano was closed abruptly.

"Oh, what a pity!" she cried. "Is he coming down, Gretta?"

Gabriel heard his wife answer yes and saw her come down towards them. A few steps behind her were Mr. Bartell D'Arcy and Miss O'Callaghan.

"Oh, Mr. D'Arcy," cried Mary Jane, "it's downright mean of you to break off like that when we were all in raptures listening to you."

"I have been at him all the evening," said Miss O'Callaghan, "and Mrs. Conroy, too, and he told us he had a dreadful cold and couldn't sing."

"Oh, Mr. D'Arcy," said Aunt Kate, "now that was a great fib to tell."

"Can't you see that I'm as hoarse as a crow?" said Mr. D'Arcy roughly.

He went into the pantry hastily and put on his overcoat. The others, taken back by his rude speech, could find nothing to say. Aunt Kate wrinkled her brows and made signs to the others to drop the subject. Mr. D'Arcy stood swathing his neck carefully and frowning.

"It's the weather," said Aunt Julia, after a pause.

"Yes, everybody has colds," said Aunt Kate readily, "everybody."

"They say," said Mary Jane, "we haven't had snow like it for thirty years, and I read this morning in the newspapers that the snow is general all over Ireland."

"I love the look of snow," said Aunt Julia sadly.

"So do I," said Miss O'Callaghan. "I think Christmas is never really Christmas unless we have the snow on the ground."

"But poor Mr. D'Arcy doesn't like the snow," said Aunt Kate, smiling.

Mr. D'Arcy came from the pantry, fully swathed and buttoned, and in a repentant tone told them the history of his cold. Everyone gave him advice and said it was a great pity and urged him to be very careful of his throat in the night air. Gabriel watched his wife, who did not join in the conversation. She was standing right under the dusty fanlight and the flame of the gas lit up the rich bronze of her hair, which he had seen her drying at the fire a few days before. She was in the same attitude and seemed unaware of the talk about her. At last she turned towards them and Gabriel saw that there was colour on her cheeks and that her eyes were shining. A sudden tide of joy went leaping out of his heart.

"Mr. D'Arcy," she said, "what is the name of that song you were singing?"

"It's called 'The Lass of Aughrim'," said Mr. D'Arcy, "but I couldn't remember it properly. Why? Do you know it?"

" 'The Lass of Aughrim,' " she repeated. "I couldn't think of the name."

"It's a very nice air," said Mary Jane. "I'm sorry you were not in voice to-night."

"Now, Mary Jane," said Aunt Kate, "don't annoy Mr. D'Arcy. I won't have him annoyed."

Seeing that all were ready to start she shepherded them to the door, where good night was said:

"Well, good night, Aunt Kate, and thanks for the pleasant evening."

"Good night, Gabriel. Good night, Gretta!"

"Good night, Aunt Kate, and thanks ever so much. Good night, Aunt Julia."

"Oh, good night, Gretta, I didn't see you."

"Good night, Mr. D'Arcy. Good night, Miss O'Callaghan."

"Good night, Miss Morkan."

"Good night, again."

"Good night, all. Safe home."

"Good night. Good night."

The morning was still dark. A dull, yellow light brooded over the houses and the river; and the sky seemed to be descending. It was slushy underfoot, and only streaks and patches of snow lay on the roofs, on the parapets of the quay and on the area railings. The lamps were still burning redly in the murky air, and, across the river, the palace of the Four Courts stood out menacingly against the heavy sky.

She was walking on before him with Mr. Bartell D'Arcy, her shoes in a brown parcel tucked under one arm and her hands holding her skirt up from the slush. She had no longer any grace of attitude, but Gabriel's eyes were still bright with happiness. The blood went bounding along his veins and the thoughts went rioting through his brain, proud, joyful, tender, valorous.

She was walking on before him so lightly and so erect that he longed to run after her noiselessly, catch her by the shoulders and say something foolish and affectionate into her ear. She seemed to him so frail that he longed to defend her against something and then to be alone with her. Moments of their secret life together burst like stars upon his memory. A heliotrope envelope was lying beside his breakfast cup and he was caressing it with his hand. Birds were twittering in the ivy and the sunny web of the curtain was shimmering along the floor: he could not eat for happiness. They were standing on the crowded platform and he was placing a ticket inside the warm palm of her glove. He was standing with her in the cold, looking in through a grated window at a man making bottles in a roaring furnace. It was very cold. Her face, fragrant in the cold air, was quite close to his, and suddenly he called out to the man at the furnace:

"Is the fire hot, sir?"

But the man could not hear with the noise of the furnace. It was just as well. He might have answered rudely.

A wave of yet more tender joy escaped from his heart and

went coursing in warm flood along his arteries. Like the tender fire of stars moments of their life together, that no one knew of or would ever know of, broke upon and illumined his memory. He longed to recall to her those moments, to make her forget the years of their dull existence together and remember only their moments of ecstasy. For the years, he felt, had not quenched his soul or hers. Their children, his writing, her household cares had not quenched all their souls' tender fire. In one letter that he had written to her then he had said: "Why is it that words like these seem to me so dull and cold? Is it because there is no word tender enough to be your name?"

Like distant music these words that he had written years before were borne towards him from the past. He longed to be alone with her. When the others had gone away, when he and she were in the room in the hotel, then they would be alone together. He would call her softly:

"Gretta!"

Perhaps she would not hear at once: she would be undressing. Then something in his voice would strike her. She would turn and look at him. . . .

At the corner of Winetavern Street they met a cab. He was glad of its rattling noise as it saved him from conversation. She was looking out of the window and seemed tired. The others spoke only a few words, pointing out some building or street. The horse galloped along wearily under the murky morning sky, dragging his old rattling box after his heels, and Gabriel was again in a cab with her, galloping to catch the boat, galloping to their honeymoon.

As the cab drove across O'Connell Bridge Miss O'Callaghan said:

"They say you never cross O'Connell Bridge without seeing a white horse."

"I see a white man this time," said Gabriel.

"Where?" asked Mr. Bartell D'Arcy.

Gabriel pointed to the statue, on which lay patches of snow. Then he nodded familiarly to it and waved his hand.

"Good night, Dan," he said gaily.

When the cab drew up before the hotel, Gabriel jumped out and, in spite of Mr. Bartell D'Arcy's protest, paid the driver. He gave the man a shilling over his fare. The man saluted and said:

"A prosperous New Year to you, sir."

"The same to you," said Gabriel cordially.

She leaned for a moment on his arm in getting out of the cab and while standing at the kerbstone, bidding the others good night. She leaned lightly on his arm, as lightly as when she had danced with him a few hours before. He had felt proud and happy then, happy that she was his, proud of her grace and wifely carriage. But now, after the kindling again of so many memories, the first touch of her body, musical and strange and perfumed, sent through him a keen pang of lust. Under cover of her silence he pressed her arm closely to his side, and, as they stood at the hotel door, he felt that they had escaped from their lives and duties, escaped from home and friends and run away together with wild and radiant hearts to a new adventure.

An old man was dozing in a great hooded chair in the hall. He lit a candle in the office and went before them to the stairs. They followed him in silence, their feet falling in soft thuds on the thickly carpeted stairs. She mounted the stairs behind the porter, her head bowed in the ascent, her frail shoulders curved as with a burden, her skirt girt tightly about her. He could have flung his arms about her hips and held her still, for his arms were trembling with desire to seize her and only the stress of his nails against the palms of his hands held the wild impulse of his body in check. The porter halted on the stairs to settle his guttering candle. They halted, too, on the steps below him. In the silence Gabriel could hear the falling of the molten wax into the tray and the thumping of his own heart against his ribs.

The porter led them along a corridor and opened a door. Then he set his unstable candle down on a toilet-table and asked at what hour they were to be called in the morning.

"Eight," said Gabriel.

The porter pointed to the switch of the electric-light and began a muttered apology, but Gabriel cut him short.

"We don't want any light. We have light enough from the street. And I say," he added, pointing to the candle, "you might remove that handsome article, like a good man."

The porter took up his candle again, but slowly, for he was surprised by such a novel idea. Then he mumbled good night and went out. Gabriel shot the lock to.

A ghastly light from the street lamp lay in a long shaft from one window to the door. Gabriel threw his overcoat and hat on a couch and crossed the room towards the window.

He looked down into the street in order that his emotion might calm a little. Then he turned and leaned against a chest of drawers with his back to the light. She had taken off her hat and cloak and was standing before a large swinging mirror, unhooking her waist. Gabriel paused for a few moments, watching her, and then said:

"Gretta!"

She turned away from the mirror slowly and walked along the shaft of light towards him. Her face looked so serious and weary that the words would not pass Gabriel's lips. No, it was not the moment yet.

"You looked tired." he said.

"I am a little," she answered.

"You don't feel ill or weak?"

"No, tired: that's all."

She went on to the window and stood there, looking out. Gabriel waited again and then, fearing that diffidence was about to conquer him, he said abruptly:

"By the way, Gretta!"

"What is it?"

"You know that poor fellow Malins?" he said quickly.

"Yes. What about him?"

"Well, poor fellow, he's a decent sort of chap, after all," continued Gabriel in a false voice. "He gave me back that sovereign I lent him, and I didn't expect it, really. It's a pity he wouldn't keep away from that Browne, because he's not a bad fellow, really."

He was trembling now with annoyance. Why did she seem so abstracted? He did not know how he could begin. Was she annoyed, too, about something? If she would only turn to him or come to him of her own accord! To take her as she was would be brutal. No, he must see some ardour in her eyes first. He longed to be master of her strange mood.

"When did you lend him the pound?" she asked, after a pause.

Gabriel strove to restrain himself from breaking out into brutal language about the sottish Malins and his pound. He longed to cry to her from his soul, to crush her body against his, to overmaster her. But he said:

"Oh, at Christmas, when he opened that little Christmas-card shop, in Henry Street."

He was in such a fever of rage and desire that he did not hear her come from the window. She stood before him for an instant, looking at him strangely. Then, suddenly raising herself on tiptoe and resting her hands lightly on his shoulders, she kissed him.

"You are a very generous person, Gabriel," she said.

Gabriel, trembling with delight at her sudden kiss and at the quaintness of her phrase, put his hands on her hair and began smoothing it back, scarcely touching it with his fingers. The washing had made it fine and brilliant. His heart was brimming over with happiness. Just when he was wishing for it she had come to him of her own accord. Perhaps her thoughts had been running with his. Perhaps she had felt the impetuous desire that was in him, and then, the yielding mood had come upon her. Now that she had fallen to him so easily, he wondered why he had been so diffident.

He stood, holding her head between his hands. Then, slipping one arm swiftly about her body and drawing her towards him, he said softly: "Gretta, dear, what are you thinking about?"

She did not answer nor yield wholly to his arm. He said again, softly:

"Tell me what it is, Gretta. I think I know what is the matter. Do I know?"

She did not answer at once. Then she said in an outburst of tears:

"Oh, I am thinking about that song, 'The Lass of Aughrim'."

She broke loose from him and ran to the bed and, throwing her arms across the bed-rail, hid her face. Gabriel stood stock-still for a moment in astonishment and then followed her. As he passed in the way of the cheval-glass he caught sight of himself in full length, his broad, well-filled shirt-front, the face whose expression always puzzled him when he saw it in a mirror, and his glimmering gilt-rimmed eyeglasses. He halted a few paces from her and said:

"What about the song? Why does that make you cry?"

She raised her head from her arms and dried her eyes with the back of her hand like a child. A kinder note than he had intended went into his voice.

"Why, Gretta?" he asked.

"I am thinking about a person long ago who used to sing that song."

"And who was that person long ago?" asked Gabriel, smiling.

"It was a person I used to know in Galway when I was living with my grandmother," she said.

The smile passed away from Gabriel's face. A dull anger began to gather again at the back of his mind and the dull fires of his lust began to glow angrily in his veins.

"Someone you were in love with?" he asked ironically.

"It was a young boy I used to know," she answered, "named Michael Furey. He used to sing that song, 'The Lass of Aughrim.' He was very delicate."

Gabriel was silent. He did not wish her to think that he was interested in this delicate boy.

"I can see him so plainly," she said, after a moment. "Such eyes as he had: big, dark eyes! And such an expression in them—an expression!"

"Oh, then, you are in love with him?" said Gabriel.

"I used to go out walking with him," she said, "when I was in Galway."

A thought flew across Gabriel's mind.

"Perhaps that was why you wanted to go to Galway with that Ivory girl?" he said coldly.

She looked at him and asked in surprise:

"What for?"

Her eyes made Gabriel feel awkward. He shrugged his shoulders and said:

"How do I know? To see him, perhaps."

She looked away from him along the shaft of light towards the window in silence.

"He is dead," she said at length. "He died when he was only seventeen. Isn't it a terrible thing to die so young as that?"

"What was he?" asked Gabriel, still ironically.

"He was in the gasworks," she said.

Gabriel felt humiliated by the failure of his irony and by the evocation of this figure from the dead, a boy in the gasworks. While he had been full of memories of their secret life together, full of tenderness and joy and desire, she had been comparing him in her mind with another. A shameful consciousness of his own person assailed him. He saw himself as a ludicrous figure, acting as a pennyboy for his aunts, a nervous, well-meaning sentimentalist, orating to vulgarians and idealizing his own clownish lusts, the pitiable fatuous fellow he had caught a glimpse of in the mirror. Instinctively he turned his back more to the light lest she might see the shame that burned upon his forehead.

He tried to keep up his tone of cold interrogation, but his voice when he spoke was humble and indifferent.

"I suppose you were in love with this Michael Furey, Gretta," he said.

"I was great with him at that time," she said.

Her voice was veiled and sad. Gabriel, feeling now how vain it would be to try to lead her whither he had purposed, caressed one of her hands and said, also sadly:

"And what did he die of so young, Gretta? Consumption, was it?"

"I think he died for me," she answered.

A vague terror seized Gabriel at this answer, as if, at that hour when he had hoped to triumph, some impalpable and vindictive being was coming against him, gathering forces against him in its vague world. But he shook himself free of it with an effort of reason and continued to caress her hand. He did not question her again, for he felt that she would tell him of herself. Her hand was warm and moist; it did not respond to his touch, but he continued to caress it just as he had caressed her first letter to him that spring morning.

"It was in the winter," she said, "about the beginning of the winter when I was going to leave my grandmother's and come up here to the convent. And he was ill at the time in his lodgings in Galway and wouldn't be let out, and his people in Oughterard were written to. He was in decline, they said, or something like that. I never knew rightly."

She paused for a moment and sighed.

"Poor fellow," she said. "He was very fond of me and he was such a gentle boy. We used to go out together, walking, you know, Gabriel, like the way they do in the country. He was going to study singing only for his health. He had a very good voice, poor Michael Furey."

"Well; and then?" asked Gabriel.

"And then when it came time for me to leave Galway and come up to the convent he was much worse and I wouldn't be let see him, so I wrote him a letter saying I was going up to Dublin and would be back in the summer, and hoping he would be better then."

She paused for a moment to get her voice under control, and then went on:

"Then the night before I left, I was in my grandmother's

house in Nun's Island, packing up, and I heard gravel thrown up against the window. The window was so wet I couldn't see, so I ran downstairs as I was and slipped out the back into the garden and there was the poor fellow at the end of the garden, shivering."

"And did you not tell him to go back?" asked Gabriel.

"I implored of him to go home at once and told him he would get his death in the rain. But he said he did not want to live. I can see his eyes as well as well! He was standing at the end of the wall where there was a tree."

"And did he go home?" asked Gabriel.

"Yes, he went home. And when I was only a week in the convent he died and he was buried in Oughterard, where his people came from. Oh, the day I heard that, that he was dead!"

She stopped, choking with sobs, and, overcome by emotion, flung herself face downward on the bed, sobbing in the quilt. Gabriel held her hand for a moment longer, irresolutely, and then, shy of intruding on her grief, let it fall gently and walked quietly to the window.

She was fast asleep.

Gabriel, leaning on his elbow, looked for a few moments unresentfully on her tangled hair and half-open mouth, listening to her deep-drawn breath. So she had had that romance in her life: a man had died for her sake. It hardly pained him now to think how poor a part he, her husband, had played in her life. He watched her while she slept, as though he and she had never lived together as man and wife. His curious eyes rested long upon her face and on her hair: and, as he thought of what she must have been then, in that time of her first girlish beauty, a strange, friendly pity for her entered his soul. He did not like to say even to himself that her face was no longer beautiful, but he knew that it was no longer the face for which Michael Furey had braved death.

Perhaps she had not told him all the story. His eyes moved to the chair over which she had thrown some of her clothes. A petticoat string dangled to the floor. One boot stood upright, its limp upper fallen down: the fellow of it lay upon its side. He wondered at his riot of emotions of an hour before. From what had it proceeded? From his aunt's supper, from his own foolish speech, from the wine and dancing, the merry-making when saying good night in the hall, the pleasure of the walk along the river in the snow. Poor Aunt Julia! She, too, would soon be a shade with the shade of Patrick Morkan and his horse. He had caught that haggard look upon her face for a moment when she was singing "Arrayed for the Bride." Soon, perhaps, he would be sitting in that same drawing-room, dressed in black, his silk hat on his knees. The blinds would be drawn down and Aunt Kate would be sitting beside him, crying and blowing her nose and telling him how Julia had died. He would cast about his mind for some words that might console her, and would find only lame and useless ones. Yes, yes: that would happen very soon.

The air of the room chilled his shoulders. He stretched himself cautiously along under the sheets and lay down beside his wife. One by one, they were all becoming shades. Better pass boldly into that other world, in the full glory of some passion, than fade and wither dismally with age. He thought of how she who lay beside him had locked in her heart for so many years that image of her lover's eyes when he had told her that he did not wish to live.

Generous tears filled Gabriel's eyes. He had never felt like that himself towards any woman, but he knew that such a feeling must be love. The tears gathered more thickly in his eyes and in the partial darkness he imagined he saw the form of a young man standing under a dripping tree. Other forms were near. His soul had approached that region where dwell the vast hosts of the dead. He was conscious of, but could not apprehend, their wayward and flickering existence. His own identity was fading out into a grey impalpable world: the solid world itself, which these dead had one time reared and lived in, was dissolving and dwindling.

A few light taps upon the pane made him turn to the window. It had begun to snow again. He watched sleepily the flakes, silver and dark, falling obliquely against the lamp-light. The time had come for him to set out his journey westward. Yes, the newspapers were right: snow was general all over Ireland. It was falling on every part of the dark central plain, on the treeless hills, falling softly upon the Bog of Allen, and farther westward, softly falling into the dark mutinous Shannon waves. It was falling, too, upon every part of the lonely churchyard on the hill where Michael Furey lay buried. It lay thickly drifted on the crooked crosses and headstones, on the spears of the little gate, on the barren thorns. His soul swooned slowly as he heard the snow falling faintly through the universe and faintly falling, like the descent of their last end, upon all the living and the dead.

LITTLE HERR FRIEDEMANN

Thomas Mann

Thomas Mann (1875–1955) grew up in the ancient German city of Lübeck, conscious of the conflict in his nature between the contrasting backgrounds of his father—a former mayor, of solid burgher stock—and his mother—musical and temperamental, the daughter of a German planter and his Portuguese-Creole wife.

Mann's magazine stories appeared in book form in 1899, under the title, Little Herr Friedemann. *Two years later came his first novel,* Buddenbrooks; *in 1924, his acknowledged masterpiece,* The Magic Mountain. *Depth psychology, anthropology, and Jung's theories of racial memory influenced the writing of* Joseph and His Brothers *(1943). These interests, plus his deep human sympathy and his use of the leitmotif—the repetition of certain themes, words and images in a manner reminiscent of Wagnerian music—are the distinctive characteristics of Mann's work. They are revealed clearly in this intensely moving story.*

It was the nurse's fault. When they first suspected, Frau Consul Friedemann had spoken to her very gravely about the need of controlling her weakness. But what good did that do? Or the glass of red wine which she got daily besides the beer which was needed for the milk? For they suddenly discovered that she even sank so low as to drink the methylated spirit which was kept for the spirit lamp. Before they could send her away and get someone to take her place, the mischief was done. One day the mother and sisters came home to find that little Johannes, then about a month old, had fallen from the couch and lay on the floor, uttering an appallingly faint little cry, while the nurse stood beside him quite stupefied.

The doctor came and with firm, gentle hands tested the little creature's contracted and twitching limbs. He made a very serious face. The three girls stood sobbing in a corner and the Frau Consul in the anguish of her heart prayed aloud.

The poor mother, just before the child's birth, had already suffered a crushing blow: her husband, the Dutch Consul, had been snatched away from her by sudden and violent illness, and now she was too broken to cherish any hope that little Johannes would be spared to her. But by the second day the doctor had given her hand an encouraging squeeze and told her that all immediate danger was over. There was no longer any sign that the brain was affected. The facial expression was altered, it had lost the fixed and staring look. . . . Of course, they must see how things went on—and hope for the best, hope for the best.

The grey gabled house in which Johannes Friedemann grew up stood by the north gate of the little old commercial city. The front door led into a large flag-paved entry, out of which a stair with a white wooden balustrade led up into the second storey. The faded wall-paper in the living-room had a landscape pattern, and straight-backed chairs and sofas in dark-red plush stood round the heavy mahogany table.

Often in his childhood Johannes sat here at the window, which always had a fine showing of flowers, on a small footstool at his mother's feet, listening to some fairy-tale she told him, gazing at her smooth grey head, her mild and gentle face, and breathing in the faint scent she exhaled. She showed him the picture of his father, a kindly man with grey side-whiskers—he was now in heaven, she said, and awaiting them there.

Behind the house was a small garden where in summer they spent much of their time, despite the smell of burnt sugar which came over from the refinery close by. There was a gnarled old walnut tree in whose shade little Johannes would sit, on a low wooden stool, cracking walnuts, while Frau Friedemann and her three daughters, now grown women, took refuge from the sun under a grey canvas tent. The mother's gaze often strayed from her embroidery to look with sad and loving eyes at her child.

He was not beautiful, little Johannes, as he crouched on his stool industriously cracking his nuts. In fact, he was a strange sight, with his pigeon breast, humped back, and disproportionately long arms. But his hands and feet were delicately formed, he had soft red-brown eyes like a doe's, a sensitive mouth, and fine, light-brown hair. His head, had it not sat so deep between his shoulders, might almost have been called pretty.

When he was seven he went to school, where time passed swiftly and uniformly. He walked every day, with the strut deformed people often have, past the quaint gabled houses and shops to the old schoolhouse with the vaulted arcades. When he had done his preparation he would read in his books with the lovely title-page illustrations in colour, or else work in the garden, while his sisters kept house for their invalid mother. They went out too, for they belonged to the best society of the town; but unfortunately they had not married, for they had not much money nor any looks to recommend them.

Johannes too was now and then invited out by his schoolmates, but it is not likely that he enjoyed it. He could not take part in their games, and they were always embarrassed in his company, so there was no feeling of good fellowship.

There came a time when he began to hear certain matters talked about, in the courtyard at school. He listened wide-eyed and large-eared, quite silent, to his companions' raving over this or that little girl. Such things, though they entirely engrossed the attention of these others, were not, he felt, for him; they belonged in the same category as the ball games and gymnastics. At times he felt a little sad. But at length he had become quite used to standing on one side and not taking part.

But after all it came about—when he was sixteen—that he felt suddenly drawn to a girl of his own age. She was the sister of a classmate of his, a blonde, hilarious hoyden, and he met her when calling at her brother's house. He felt strangely embarrassed in her neighbourhood; she too was embarrassed and treated him with such artificial cordiality that it made him sad.

One summer afternoon as he was walking by himself on

the wall outside the town, he heard a whispering behind a jasmine bush and peeped cautiously through the branches. There she sat on a bench beside a long-legged, red-haired youth of his acquaintance. They had their arms about each other and he was imprinting on her lips a kiss, which she returned amid giggles. Johannes looked, turned round, and went softly away.

His head was sunk deeper than ever between his shoulders, his hands trembled, and a sharp pain shot upwards from his chest to his throat. But he choked it down, straightening himself as well as he could. "Good," said he to himself. "That is over. Never again will I let myself in for any of it. To the others it brings joy and happiness, for me it can only mean sadness and pain. I am done with it. For me that is all over. Never again."

The resolution did him good. He had renounced, renounced forever. He went home, took up a book, or else played on his violin, which despite his deformed chest he had learned to do.

At seventeen Johannes left school to go into business, like everybody else he knew. He was apprenticed to the big lumber firm of Herr Schlievogt down on the river-bank. They were kind and considerate, he on his side was responsive and friendly, time passed with peaceful regularity. But in his twenty-first year his mother died, after a lingering illness.

This was a sore blow for Johannes Friedemann, and the pain of it endured. He cherished this grief, he gave himself up to it as one gives oneself to a great joy, he fed it with a thousand childhood memories; it was the first important event in his life and he made the most of it.

Is not life in and for itself a good, regardless of whether we may call its content "happiness"? Johannes Friedemann felt that it was so, and he loved life. He, who had renounced the greatest joy it can bring us, taught himself with infinite, incredible care to take pleasure in what it had still to offer. A walk in the spring time in the parks surrounding the town; the fragrance of a flower; the song of a bird—might not one feel grateful for such things as these?

And that we need to be taught how to enjoy, yes, that our education is always and only equal to our capacity for enjoyment—he knew that too, and he trained himself. Music he loved, and attended all the concerts that were given in the town. He came to play the violin not so badly himself, no matter what a figure of fun he made when he did it; and took delight in every beautiful soft tone he succeeded in producing. Also, by much reading he came in time to possess a literary taste the like of which did not exist in the place. He kept up with the new books, even the foreign ones; he knew how to savour the seductive rhythm of a lyric or the ultimate flavour of a subtly told tale—yes, one might almost call him a connoisseur.

He learned to understand that to everything belongs its own enjoyment and that it is absurd to distinguish between an experience which is "happy" and one which is not. With a right good will he accepted each emotion as it came, each mood, whether sad or gay. Even he cherished the unfulfilled desires, the longings. He loved them for their own sakes and told himself that with fulfilment the best of them would be past. The vague, sweet, painful yearning and hope of quiet spring evenings—are they not richer in joy than all the fruition the summer can bring? Yes, he was a connoisseur, our little Herr Friedemann.

But of course they did not know that, the people whom he met on the street, who bowed to him with the kindly, compassionate air he knew so well. They could not know that this unhappy cripple, strutting comically along in his light overcoat and shiny top hat—strange to say, he was a little vain—they could not know how tenderly he loved the mild flow of his life, charged with no great emotions, it is true, but full of a quiet and tranquil happiness which was his own creation.

But Herr Friedemann's great preference, his real passion, was for the theatre. He possessed a dramatic sense which was unusually strong; at a telling theatrical effect or the catastrophe of a tragedy his whole small frame would shake with emotion. He had his regular seat in the first row of boxes at the opera-house; was an assiduous frequenter and often took his sisters with him. Since their mother's death they kept house for their brother in the old home which they all owned together.

It was a pity they were unmarried still; but with the decline of hope had come resignation—Friederike, the eldest, was seventeen years further on than Herr Friedemann. She and her sister Henriette were over-tall and thin, whereas Pfiffi, the youngest, was too short and stout. She had a funny way, too, of shaking herself as she talked, and water came in the corners of her mouth.

Little Herr Friedemann did not trouble himself overmuch about his three sisters. But they stuck together loyally and were always of one mind. Whenever an engagement was announced in their circle they with one voice said how very gratifying that was.

Their brother continued to live with them even after he became independent, as he did by leaving Herr Schlievogt's firm and going into business for himself, in an agency of sorts, which was no great tax on his time. His offices were in a couple of rooms on the ground floor of the house so that at mealtimes he had but the pair of stairs to mount—for he suffered now and then from asthma.

His thirtieth birthday fell on a fine warm June day, and after dinner he sat out in the grey canvas tent, with a new head-rest embroidered by Henriette. He had a good cigar in his mouth and a good book in his hand. But sometimes he would put the latter down to listen to the sparrows chirping blithely in the old nut tree and look at the clean gravel path leading up to the house between lawns bright with summer flowers.

Little Herr Friedemann wore no beard, and his face had scarcely changed at all, save that the features were slightly sharper. He wore his fine light-brown hair parted on one side.

Once, as he let the book fall on his knee and looked up into the sunny blue sky, he said to himself: "Well, so that is thirty years. Perhaps there may be ten or even twenty more. God knows. They will mount up without a sound or a stir and pass by like those that are gone; and I look forward to them with peace in my heart."

Now, it happened in July of the same year that a new appointment to the office of District Commandant had set the whole town talking. The stout and jolly gentleman who had for many years occupied the post had been very popular in social circles and they saw him go with great regret. It was in compliance with goodness knows what regulations that Herr von Rinnlingen and no other was sent hither from the capital.

In any case the exchange was not such a bad one. The new Commandant was married but childless. He rented a spacious villa in the southern suburbs of the city and seemed to intend to set up an establishment. There was a report that he was very rich—which received confirmation in the fact that he brought with him four servants, five riding and carriage horses, a landau and a light hunting-cart.

Soon after their arrival the husband and wife left cards on all the best society, and their names were on every tongue. But it was not Herr von Rinnlingen, it was his wife who was the centre of interest. All the men were dazed, for the moment too dazed to pass judgment; but their wives were quite prompt and definite in the view that Gerda von Rinnlingen was not their sort.

"Of course, she comes from the metropolis, her ways would naturally be different," Frau Hagenström, the lawyer's wife, said, in conversation with Henriette Friedemann. "She smokes, and she rides. That is of course. But it is her manners—they are not only free, they are positively brusque, or even worse. You see, no one could call her ugly, one might even say she is pretty; but she has not a trace of feminine charm in her looks or gestures or her laugh—they completely lack everything that makes a man fall in love with a woman. She is not a flirt—and goodness knows I would be the last to disparage her for that. But it is strange to see so young a woman—she is only twenty-four—so entirely wanting in natural charm. I am not expressing myself very well, my dear, but I know what I mean. All the men are simply bewildered. In a few weeks, you will see, they will be disgusted."

"Well," Fräulein Friedemann said, "she certainly has everything she wants."

"Yes," cried Frau Hagenström, "look at her husband! And how does she treat him? You ought to see it—you will see it! I would be the first to approve of a married woman behaving with a certain reserve towards the other sex. But how does she behave to her own husband? She has a way of fixing him with an ice-cold stare and saying 'My dear friend!' with a pitying expression that drives me mad. For when you look at him—upright, correct, gallant, a brilliant officer and a splendidly preserved man of forty! They have been married four years, my dear."

Herr Friedemann was first vouchsafed a glimpse of Frau von Rinnlingen in the main street of the town, among all the rows of shops, at midday, when he was coming from the Bourse, where he had done a little bidding.

He was strolling along beside Herr Stephens, looking tiny and important, as usual. Herr Stephens was in the wholesale trade, a huge stocky man with round side-whiskers and bushy eyebrows. Both of them wore top hats; their overcoats were unbuttoned on account of the heat. They tapped their canes along the pavement and talked of the political situation; but half-way down the street Stephens suddenly said:

"Deuce take it if there isn't the Rinnlingen driving along."

"Good," answered Herr Friedemann in his high, rather sharp voice, looking expectantly ahead. "Because I have never set eyes on her. And here we have the yellow cart we hear so much about."

It was in fact that hunting-cart which Frau von Rinnlingen was herself driving today with a pair of thoroughbreds; a groom sat behind her, with folded arms. She wore a loose beige coat and skirt and a small round straw hat with a brown leather band, beneath which her well-waved red-blond hair, a good, thick crop, was drawn into a knot at the nape of her neck. Her face was oval, with a dead-white skin and faint bluish shadows lurking under the close-set eyes. Her nose was short but well-shaped, with a becoming little saddle of freckles; whether her mouth was as good or no could not be told, for she kept it in continual motion, sucking the lower and biting the upper lip.

Herr Stephens, as the cart came abreast of them, greeted her with a great show of deference; little Herr Friedemann lifted his hat too and looked at her with wide-eyed attention. She lowered her whip, nodded slightly, and drove slowly past, looking at the houses and shop-windows.

After a few paces Herr Stephens said:

"She has been taking a drive and was on her way home."

Little Herr Friedemann made no answer, but stared before him at the pavement. Presently he started, looked at his companion, and asked: "What did you say?"

And Herr Stephens repeated his acute remark.

Three days after that Johannes Friedemann came home at midday from his usual walk. Dinner was at half past twelve, and he would spend the interval in his office at the right of the entrance door. But the maid came across the entry and told him that there were visitors.

"In my office?" he asked.

"No, upstairs with the mistress."

"Who are they?"

"Herr and Frau Colonel von Rinnlingen."

"Ah," said Johannes Friedemann. "Then I will—"

And he mounted the stairs. He crossed the lobby and laid his hand on the knob of the high white door leading into the "landscape room." And then he drew back, turned round, and slowly returned as he had come. And spoke to himself, for there was no one else there, and said: "No, better not."

He went into his office, sat down at his desk, and took up the paper. But after a little he dropped it again and sat looking to one side out of the window. Thus he sat until the maid came to say that luncheon was ready; then he went up into the dining-room where his sisters were already waiting, and sat down in his chair, in which there were three music-books.

As she ladled the soup Henriette said:

"Johannes, do you know who were here?"

"Well?" he asked.

"The new Commandant and his wife."

"Indeed? That was friendly of them."

"Yes," said Pfiffi, a little water coming in the corners of her mouth. "I found them both very agreeable."

"And we must lose no time in returning the call," said Friederike. "I suggest that we go next Sunday, the day after tomorrow."

"Sunday," Henriette and Pfiffi said.

"You will go with us, Johannes?" asked Friederike.

"Of course he will," said Pfiffi, and gave herself a little shake. Herr Friedemann had not heard her at all; he was eating his soup, with a hushed and troubled air. It was as though he were listening to some strange noise he heard.

Next evening *Lohengrin* was being given at the opera, and everybody in society was present. The small auditorium was crowded, humming with voices and smelling of gas and perfumery. And every eyeglass in the stalls was directed towards box thirteen, next to the stage; for this was the first appearance of Herr and Frau von Rinnlingen and one could give them a good looking-over.

When little Herr Friedemann, in flawless dress clothes and glistening white pigeon-breasted shirt-front, entered his box, which was number thirteen, he started back at the door, making a gesture with his hand towards his brow. His nostrils dilated feverishly. Then he took his seat, which was next to Frau von Rinnlingen's.

She contemplated him for a little while, with her under lip stuck out; then she turned to exchange a few words with her husband, a tall, broad-shouldered gentleman with a brown, good-natured face and turned-up moustaches.

When the overture began and Frau von Rinnlingen leaned over the balustrade Herr Friedemann gave her a quick, searching side glance. She wore a light-coloured evening frock, the only one in the theatre which was slightly low in the neck. Her sleeves were full and her white gloves came up to her elbows. Her figure was statelier than it had looked under the loose coat; her full bosom slowly rose and fell and the knot of red-blond hair hung low and heavy at the nape of her neck.

Herr Friedemann was pale, much paler than usual, and little beads of perspiration stood on his brow beneath the smoothly parted brown hair. He could see Frau von Rinnlingen's left arm, which lay upon the balustrade. She had taken off her glove and the rounded, dead-white arm and ringless hand, both of them shot with pale blue veins, were directly under his eye—he could not help seeing them.

The fiddles sang, the trombones crashed, Telramund was slain, general jubilation reigned in the orchestra, and little Herr Friedemann sat there motionless and pallid, his head drawn in between his shoulders, his forefinger to his lips and one hand thrust into the opening of his waistcoat.

As the curtain fell, Frau von Rinnlingen got up to leave the box with her husband. Johannes Friedemann saw her without looking, wiped his handkerchief across his brow, then rose suddenly and went as far as the door into the foyer, where he turned, came back to his chair, and sat down in the same posture as before.

When the bell rang and his neighbours re-entered the box he felt Frau von Rinnlingen's eyes upon him, so that finally against his will he raised his head. As their eyes met, hers did not swerve aside; she continued to gaze without embarrassment until he himself, deeply humiliated, was forced to look away. He turned a shade paler and felt a strange, sweet pang of anger and scorn. The music began again.

Towards the end of the act Frau von Rinnlingen chanced

to drop her fan; it fell at Herr Friedemann's feet. They both stooped at the same time, but she reached it first and gave a little mocking smile as she said: "Thank you."

Their heads were quite close together and just for a second he got the warm scent of her breast. His face was drawn, his whole body twitched, and his heart thumped so horribly that he lost his breath. He sat without moving for half a minute, then he pushed back his chair, got up quietly, and went out.

He crossed the lobby, pursued by the music; got his top hat from the cloak-room, his light overcoat and his stick, went down the stairs and out of doors.

It was a warm, still evening. In the gas-lit street the gabled houses towered towards a sky where stars were softly beaming. The pavement echoed the steps of a few passers-by. Someone spoke to him, but he heard and saw nothing; his head was bowed and his deformed chest shook with the violence of his breathing. Now and then he murmured to himself:

"My God, my God!"

He was gazing horror-struck within himself, beholding the havoc which had been wrought with his tenderly cherished, scrupulously managed feelings. Suddenly he was quite overpowered by the strength of his tortured longing. Giddy and drunken he learned against a lamppost and his quivering lips uttered the one word: "Gerda!"

The stillness was complete. Far and wide not a soul was to be seen. Little Herr Friedemann pulled himself together and went on, up the street in which the opera-house stood and which ran steeply down to the river, then along the main street northwards to his home.

How she had looked at him! She had forced him, actually, to cast down his eyes! She had humiliated him with her glance. But was she not a woman and he a man? And those strange brown eyes of hers—had they not positively glittered with unholy joy?

Again he felt the same surge of sensual, impotent hatred mount up in him; then he relived the moment when her head had touched his, when he had breathed in the fragrance of her body—and for the second time he halted, bent his deformed torso backwards, drew in the air through clenched teeth, and murmured helplessly, desperately, uncontrollably:

"My God, my God!"

Then went on again, slowly, mechanically, through the heavy evening air, through the empty echoing streets until he stood before his own house. He paused a minute in the entry, breathing the cool, dank inside air; then he went into his office.

He sat down at his desk by the open window and stared straight ahead of him at a large yellow rose which somebody had set there in a glass of water. He took it up and smelt it with his eyes closed, then put it down with a gesture of weary sadness. No, no. That was all over. What was even that fragrance to him now? What any of all those things that up to now had been the well-springs of his joy?

He turned away and gazed into the quiet street. At intervals steps passed and the sound died away. The stars stood still and glittered. He felt so weak, so utterly tired to death. His head was quite vacant, and suddenly his despair began to melt into a gentle, pervading melancholy. A few lines of a poem flickered through his head, he heard the *Lohengrin* music in his ears, he saw Frau von Rinnlingen's face and her round white arm on the red velvet—then he fell into a heavy fever-burdened sleep.

Often he was near waking, but feared to do so and managed to sink back into forgetfulness again. But when it had grown quite light, he opened his eyes and looked round him with a wide and painful gaze. He remembered everything, it was as though the anguish had never been intermitted by sleep.

His head was heavy and his eyes burned. But when he had washed up and bathed his head with cologne he felt better and sat down in his place by the still open window. It was early, perhaps only five o'clock. Now and then a baker's boy passed; otherwise there was no one to be seen. In the opposite house the blinds were down. But birds were twittering and the sky was luminously blue. A wonderfully beautiful Sunday morning.

A feeling of comfort and confidence came over little Herr Friedemann. Why had he been distressing himself? Was not everything just as it had been? The attack of yesterday had been a bad one. Granted. But it should be the last. It was not too late, he could still escape destruction. He must avoid every occasion of a fresh seizure; he felt sure he could do this. He felt the strength to conquer and suppress his weakness.

It struck half past seven and Friederike came in with the coffee, setting it on the round table in front of the leather sofa against the rear wall.

"Good morning, Johannes," said she; "here is your breakfast."

"Thanks," said little Herr Friedemann. And then: "Dear Friederike, I am sorry, but you will have to pay your call without me, I do not feel well enough to go. I have slept badly and have a headache—in short, I must ask you—"

"What a pity!" answered Friederike. "You must go another time. But you do look ill. Shall I lend you my menthol pencil?"

"Thanks," said Herr Friedemann. "It will pass." And Friederike went out.

Standing at the table he slowly drank his coffee and ate a croissant. He felt satisfied with himself and proud of his firmness. When he had finished he sat down again by the open window, with a cigar. The food had done him good and he felt happy and hopeful. He took a book and sat reading and smoking and blinking into the sunlight.

Morning had fully come, wagons rattled past, there were many voices and the sound of the bells on passing trams. With and among it all was woven the twittering and chirping; there was a radiant blue sky, a soft mild air.

At ten o'clock he heard his sisters cross the entry; the front door creaked, and he idly noticed that they passed his window. An hour went by. He felt more and more happy.

A sort of hubris mounted in him. What a heavenly air—and how the birds were singing! He felt like taking a little walk. Then suddenly, without any transition, yet accompanied by a terror namelessly sweet, came the thought: "Suppose I were to go to her!" And suppressing, as though by acutal muscular effort, every warning voice within him, he added with blissful resolution: "I will go to her!"

He changed into his Sunday clothes, took his top hat and his stick, and hurried with quickened breath through the town and into the southern suburbs. Without looking at a soul he kept raising and dropping his head with each eager step, completely rapt in his exalted state until he arrived at the avenue of chestnut trees and the red brick villa with the name of Commandant von Rinnlingen on the gatepost.

But here he was seized by a tremor, his heart throbbed and pounded in his breast. He went across the vestibule and rang at the inside door. The die was cast, there was no retreating now. "Come what come may," thought he, and felt the stillness of death within him.

The door suddenly opened and the maid came towards him across the vestibule; she took his card and hurried away up the red-carpeted stair. Herr Friedemann gazed fixedly at the bright colour until she came back and said that her mistress would like him to come up.

He put down his stick beside the door leading into the salon and stole a look at himself in the glass. His face was pale, the eyes red, his hair was sticking to his brow, the hand that held his top hat kept on shaking.

The maid opened the door and he went in. He found himself in a rather large, half-darkened room, with drawn curtains. At his right was a piano, and about the round table in the centre stood several arm-chairs covered in brown silk. The sofa stood along the left-hand wall, with a landscape painting in a heavy gilt frame hanging above it. The wall-paper too was dark in tone. There was an alcove filled with potted palms.

A minute passed, then Frau von Rinnlingen opened the portières on the right and approached him noiselessly over the thick brown carpet. She wore a simply cut frock of red and black plaid. A ray of light, with motes dancing in it, streamed from the alcove and fell upon her heavy red hair so that it shone like gold. She kept her strange eyes fixed upon him with a searching gaze and as usual stuck out her under lip.

"Good morning, Frau Commandant," began little Herr Friedemann, and looked up at her, for he came only as high as her chest. "I wished to pay you my respects too. When my sisters did so I was unfortunately out . . . I regretted sincerely . . ."

He had no idea at all what else he should say; and there she stood and gazed ruthlessly at him as though she would force him to go on. The blood rushed to his head. "She sees through me," he thought, "she will torture and despise me. Her eyes keep flickering. . . ."

But at last she said, in a very high, clear voice:

"It is kind of you to have come. I have also been sorry not to see you before. Will you please sit down?"

She took her seat close beside him, leaned back, and put

her arm along the arm of the chair. He sat bent over, holding his hat between his knees. She went on:

"Did you know that your sisters were here a quarter of an hour ago? They told me you were ill."

"Yes," he answered, "I did not feel well enough to go out, I thought I should not be able to. That is why I am late."

"You do not look very well even now," said she tranquilly, not shifting her gaze. "You are pale and your eyes are inflamed. You are not very strong, perhaps?"

"Oh," said Herr Friedemann, stammering, "I've not much to complain of, as a rule."

"I am ailing a good deal too," she went on, still not turning her eyes from him, "but nobody notices it. I am nervous, and sometimes I have the strangest feelings."

She paused, lowered her chin to her breast, and looked up expectantly at him. He made no reply, simply sat with his dreamy gaze directed upon her. How strangely she spoke, and how her clear and thrilling voice affected him! His heart beat more quietly and he felt as though he were in a dream. She began again:

"I am not wrong in thinking that you left the opera last night before it was over?"

"Yes, madam."

"I was sorry to see that. You listened like a music-lover—though the performance was only tolerable. You are fond of music, I am sure. Do you play the piano?"

"I play the violin, a little," said Herr Friedemann. "That is, really not very much—"

"You play the violin?" she asked, and looked past him consideringly. "But we might play together," she suddenly said. "I can accompany a little. It would be a pleasure to find somebody here—would you come?"

"I am quite at your service—with pleasure," said he, stiffly. He was still as though in a dream. A pause ensued. Then suddenly her expression changed. He saw it alter for one of cruel, though hardly perceptible mockery, and again she fixed him with that same searching, uncannily flickering gaze. His face burned, he knew not where to turn; drawing his head down between his shoulders he stared confusedly at the carpet, while there shot through him once more that strangely sweet and torturing sense of impotent rage.

He made a desperate effort and raised his eyes. She was

looking over his head at the door. With the utmost difficulty he fetched out a few words:

"And you are so far not too dissatisfied with your stay in our city?"

"Oh, no," said Frau Rinnlingen indifferently. "No, certainly not; why should I not be satisfied? To be sure, I feel a little hampered, as though everybody's eyes were upon me, but—oh before I forget it," she went on quickly, "we are entertaining a few people next week, a small, informal company. A little music perhaps, and conversation. . . . There is a charming garden at the back, it runs down to the river. You and your sisters will be receiving an invitation in due course, but perhaps I may ask you now to give us the pleasure of your company?"

Herr Friedemann was just expressing his gratitude for the invitation when the door-knob was seized energetically from without and the Commandant entered. They both rose and Frau von Rinnlingen introduced the two men to each other. Her husband bowed to them both with equal courtesy. His bronze face glistened with the heat.

He drew off his gloves, addressing Herr Friedemann in a powerful, rather sharp-edged voice. The latter looked up at him with large vacant eyes and had the feeling that he would presently be clapped benevolently on the shoulder. Heels together, inclining from the waist, the Commandant turned to his wife and asked, in a much gentler tone:

"Have you asked Herr Friedemann if he will give us the pleasure of his company at our little party, my love? If you are willing I should like to fix the date for next week and I hope that the weather will remain fine so that we can enjoy ourselves in the garden."

"Just as you say," answered Frau von Rinnlingen, and gazed past him.

Two minutes later Herr Friedemann got up to go. At the door he turned and bowed to her once more, meeting her expressionless gaze still fixed upon him.

He went away, but he did not go back to the town; unconsciously he struck into a path that led away from the avenue towards the old ruined fort by the river, among well-kept lawns and shady avenues with benches.

He walked quickly and absently, with bent head. He felt

intolerably hot, as though aware of flames leaping and sinking within him and his head throbbed with fatigue.

It was as though her gaze still rested on him—not vacantly as it had at the end, but with that flickering cruelty which went with the strange still way she spoke. Did it give her pleasure to put him beside himself, to see him helpless? Looking through and through him like that, could she not feel a little pity?

He had gone along the river-bank under the moss-grown wall; he sat down on a bench within a half-circle of blossoming jasmine. The sweet, heavy scent was all about him, the sun brooded upon the dimpling water.

He was weary, he was worn out; and yet within him all was tumult and anguish. Were it not better to take one last look and then to go down into that quiet water; after a brief struggle to be free and safe and at peace? Ah, peace, peace—that was what he wanted! Not peace in an empty and soundless void, but a gentle, sunlit peace, full of good, of tranquil thoughts.

All his tender love of live thrilled through him in that moment, all his profound yearning for his vanished "happiness." But then he looked about him into the silent, endlessly indifferent peace of nature, saw how the river went its own way in the sun, how the grasses quivered and the flowers stood up where they blossomed, only to fade and be blown away; saw how all that was bent submissively to the will of life; and there came over him all at once that sense of acquaintance and understanding with the inevitable which can make those who know it superior to the blows of fate.

He remembered the afternoon of his thirtieth birthday and the peaceful happiness with which he, untroubled by fears or hopes, had looked forward to what was left of his life. He had seen no light and no shadow there, only a mild twilight radiance gently declining into the dark. With what a calm and superior smile had he contemplated the years still to come—how long ago was that?

Then this woman had come, she had to come, it was his fate that she should, for she herself was his fate and she alone. He had known it from the first moment. She had come—and though he had tried his best to defend his peace, her coming had roused in him all those forces which from his youth up he had sought to suppress, feeling, as he did, that they spelled torture and destruction. They had seized upon him with frightful, irresistible power and flung him to the earth.

They were his destruction, well he knew it. But why struggle, then, and why torture himself? Let everything take its course. He would go his appointed way, closing his eyes before the yawning void, bowing to his fate, bowing to the overwhelming, anguishingly sweet, irresistible power.

The water glittered, the jasmine gave out its strong, pungent scent, the birds chattered in the tree-tops that gave glimpses among them of a heavy, velvety-blue sky. Little hump-backed Herr Friedemann sat long upon his bench; he sat bent over, holding his head in his hands.

Everybody agreed that the Rinnlingens entertained very well. Some thirty guests sat in the spacious dining-room, at the long, prettily decorated table, and the butler and two hired waiters were already handing round the ices. Dishes clattered, glasses rang, there was a warm aroma of food and perfumes. Here were comfortable merchants with their wives and daughters; most of the officers of the garrison; a few professional men, lawyers and the popular old family doctor—in short, all the best society.

A nephew of the Commandant, on a visit, a student of mathematics, sat deep in conversation with Fräulein Hagenström, whose place was directly opposite Herr Friedemann's, at the lower end of the table. Johannes Friedemann sat there on a rich velvet cushion, beside the unbeautiful wife of the Colonial Director and not far off Frau von Rinnlingen, who had been escorted to table by Consul Stephens. It was astonishing, the change which had taken place in little Herr Friedemann in these few days. Perhaps the incandescent lighting in the room was partly to blame; but his cheeks looked sunken, he made a more crippled impression even than usual, and his inflamed eyes, with their dark rings, glowed with an inexpressibly tragic light. He drank a great deal of wine and now and then addressed a remark to his neighbour.

Frau von Rinnlingen had not so far spoken to him at all; but now she leaned over and called out:

"I have been expecting you in vain these days, you and your fiddle."

He looked vacantly at her for a while before he replied. She wore a light-coloured frock with a low neck that left the white throat bare; a Maréchal Niel rose in full bloom was fastened in her shining hair. Her cheeks were a little flushed, but the same bluish shadows lurked in the corners of her eyes.

Herr Friedemann looked at his plate and forced himself to make some sort of reply; after which the school superintendent's wife asked him if he did not love Beethoven and he had to answer that too. But at this point the Commandant, sitting at the head of the table, caught his wife's eyes, tapped on his glass and said:

"Ladies and gentlemen, I suggest that we drink our coffee in the next room. It must be fairly decent out in the garden too, and whoever wants a little fresh air, I am for him."

Lieutenant von Deidesheim made a tactful little joke to cover the ensuing pause, and the table rose in the midst of laughter. Herr Friedemann and his partner were among the last to quit the room; he escorted her through the "old German" smoking-room to the dim and pleasant living-room, where he took his leave.

He was dressed with great care: his evening clothes were irreproachable, his shirt was dazzlingly white, his slender, well-shaped feet were encased in patent-leather pumps, which now and then betrayed the fact that he wore red silk stockings.

He looked out into the corridor and saw a good many people descending the steps into the garden. But he took up a position at the door of the smoking-room, with his cigar and coffee, where he could see into the living-room.

Some of the men stood talking in this room, and at the right of the door a little knot had formed round a small table, the centre of which was the mathematics student, who was eagerly talking. He had made the assertion that one could draw through a given point more than one parallel to a straight line; Frau Hagenström had cried that this was impossible, and he had gone on to prove it so conclusively that his hearers were constrained to behave as though they understood.

At the rear of the room, on the sofa beside the red-shaded lamp, Gerda von Rinnlingen sat in conversation with young Fräulein Stephens. She leaned back among the yellow silk cushions with one knee slung over the other, slowly smoking a cigarette, breathing out the smoke through her nose and sticking out her lower lip. Fräulein Stephens sat stiff as a graven image beside her, answering her questions with an assiduous smile.

Nobody was looking at little Herr Friedemann, so nobody saw that his large eyes were constantly directed upon Frau von Rinnlingen. He sat rather droopingly and looked at her. There was no passion in his gaze nor scarcely any pain. But there was something dull and heavy there, a dead weight of impotent, involuntary adoration.

Some ten minutes went by. Then as though she had been secretly watching him the whole time, Frau von Rinnlingen approached and paused in front of him. He got up as he heard her say:

"Would you care to go into the garden with me, Herr Friedemann?"

He answered:

"With pleasure, madam."

"You have never seen our garden?" she asked him as they went down the steps. "It is fairly large. I hope that there are not too many people in it; I should like to get a breath of fresh air. I got a headache during supper; perhaps the red wine was too strong for me. Let us go this way." They passed through a glass door, the vestibule, and a cool little courtyard, whence they gained the open air by descending a couple more steps.

The scent of all the flower-beds rose into the wonderful, warm, starry night. The garden lay in full moonlight and the guests were strolling up and down the white gravel paths, smoking and talking as they went. A group had gathered round the old fountain, where the much-loved old doctor was making them laugh by sailing paper boats.

With a little nod Frau von Rinnlingen passed them by, and pointed ahead of her, where the fragrant and well-cared-for garden blended into the darker park.

"Shall we go down this middle path?" asked she. At the beginning of it stood two low, squat obelisks.

In the vista at the end of the chestnut alley they could see the river shining green and bright in the moonlight. All about them was darkness and coolness. Here and there side paths branched off, all of them probably curving down to the river. For a long time there was not a sound.

"Down by the water," she said, "there is a pretty spot where I often sit. We could stop and talk a little. See the stars glittering here and there through the trees."

He did not answer, gazing, as they approached it, at the

river's shimmering green surface. You could see the other bank and the park along the city wall. They left the alley and came out on the grassy slope down to the river, and she said:

"Here is our place, a little to the right, and there is no one there."

The bench stood facing the water, some six paces away, with its back to the trees. It was warmer here in the open. Crickets chirped among the grass, which at the river's edge gave way to sparse reeds. The moonlit water gave off a soft light.

For a while they both looked in silence. Then he heard her voice; it thrilled him to recognize the same low, gentle, pensive tone of a week ago, which now as then moved him strongly:

"How long have you had your infirmity, Herr Friedemann? Were you born so?"

He swallowed before he replied, for his throat felt as though he were choking. Then he said, politely and gently:

"No, *gnädige Frau*. It comes from their having let me fall, when I was an infant."

"And how old are you now?" she asked again.

"Thirty years old."

"Thirty years old," she repeated. "And these thirty years were not happy ones?"

Little Herr Friedemann shook his head, his lips quivered.

"No," he said, "that was all lies and my imagination."

"Then you have thought that you were happy?" she asked.

"I have tried to be," he replied, and she responded:

"That was brave of you."

A minute passed. The crickets chirped and behind them the boughs rustled lightly.

"I understand a good deal about unhappiness," she told him. "These summer nights by the water are the best thing for it."

He made no direct answer, but gestured feebly across the water, at the opposite bank, lying peaceful in the darkness.

"I was sitting over there not long ago," he said.

"When you came from me?" she asked. He only nodded.

Then suddenly he started up from his seat, trembling all over; he sobbed and gave vent to a sound, a wail which yet seemed like a release from strain, and sank slowly to the ground before her. He had touched her hand with his as it lay beside him on the bench, and clung to it now, seizing the other as he knelt before her, this little cripple, trembling and shuddering; he buried his face in her lap and stammered between his gasps in a voice which was scarcely human:

"You know, you understand . . . let me . . . I can no longer . . . my God, oh, my God!"

She did not repulse him, neither did she bend her face towards him. She sat erect, leaning a little away, and her close-set eyes, wherein the liquid shimmer of the water seemed to be mirrored, stared beyond him into space.

Then she gave him an abrupt push and uttered a short, scornful laugh. She tore her hands from his burning fingers, clutched his arm, and flung him sidewise upon the ground. Then she sprang up and vanished down the wooded avenue.

He lay there with his face in the grass, stunned, unmanned, shudders coursing swiftly through his frame. He pulled himself together, got up somehow, took two steps, and fell again, close to the water. What were his sensations at this moment? Perhaps he was feeling that same luxury of hate which he had felt before when she had humiliated him with her glance, degenerated now, when he lay before her on the ground and she had treated him like a dog, into an insane rage which must at all costs find expression even against himself—a disgust, perhaps of himself, which filled him with a thirst to destroy himself, to tear himself to pieces, to blot himself utterly out.

On his belly he dragged his body a little further, lifted its upper part, and let it fall into the water. He did not raise his head nor move his legs, which still lay on the bank.

The crickets stopped chirping a moment at the noise of the little splash. Then they went on as before, the boughs lightly rustled, and down the long alley came the faint sound of laughter.

SOPHISTICATION

Sherwood Anderson

Sherwood Anderson (1876–1941) was born in Camden, Ohio. His novels include Windy McPherson's Son *(1916),* Marching Men *(1917),* Poor White *(1920), and* Dark Laughter *(1925). But his fame rests almost entirely upon his short stories, of which the three best-known collections are* Winesburg, Ohio *(1919),* The Triumph of the Egg *(1921) and* Death in the Woods and Other Stories *(1933). Of all American writers Anderson is most like Chekhov. Extremely sensitive characterization colored by unusual sympathy, a highly poetic style, and an easy naturalness and frequent looseness of form are the most striking qualities of his writing.*

It was early evening of a day in the late fall and the Winesburg County Fair had brought crowds of country people into town. The day had been clear and the night came on warm and pleasant. On the Trunion Pike, where the road after it left town stretched away between berry fields now covered with dry brown leaves, the dust from passing wagons arose in clouds. Children, curled into little balls, slept on the straw scattered on wagon beds. Their hair was full of dust and their fingers black and sticky. The dust rolled away over the fields and the departing sun set it ablaze with colors.

In the main street of Winesburg crowds filled the stores and the sidewalks. Night came on, horses whinnied, the clerks in the stores ran madly about, children became lost and cried lustily, an American town worked terribly at the task of amusing itself.

Pushing his way through the crowds in Main Street, young George Willard concealed himself in the stairway leading to Doctor Reefy's office and looked at the people. With feverish eyes he watched the faces drifting past under the store lights. Thoughts kept coming into his head and he did not want to think. He stamped impatiently on the wooden steps and looked sharply about. "Well, is she going to stay with him all day? Have I done all this waiting for nothing?" he muttered.

George Willard, the Ohio village boy, was fast growing into manhood and new thoughts had been coming into his mind. All that day, amid the jam of people at the Fair, he had gone about feeling lonely. He was about to leave Winesburg to go away to some city where he hoped to get work on a city newspaper and he felt grown up. The mood that had taken possession of him was a thing known to men and unknown to boys. He felt old and a little tired. Memories awoke in him. To his mind his new sense of maturity set him apart, made of him a half-tragic figure. He wanted someone to understand the feeling that had taken possession of him after his mother's death.

There is a time in the life of every boy when he for the first time takes the backward view of life. Perhaps that is the moment when he crosses the line into manhood. The boy is walking through the street of his town. He is thinking of the future and of the figure he will cut in the world. Ambitions and regrets awake within him. Suddenly something happens; he stops under a tree and waits as for a voice calling his name. Ghosts of old things creep into his consciousness; the voices outside of himself whisper a message concerning the limitations of life. From being quite sure of himself and his future he becomes not at all sure. If he be an imaginative boy a door is torn open and for the first time he looks out upon the world, seeing, as though they marched in procession before him, the countless figures of men who before his time have come out of nothingness into the world, lived their lives and again disappeared into nothingness. The sadness of sophistication has come to the boy. With a little gasp he sees himself as merely a leaf blown by the wind through the streets of his village. He knows that in spite of all the stout talk of his fellows he must live and die in uncertainty, a thing blown by the winds, a thing destined like corn to wilt in the sun. He shivers and looks eagerly about. The eighteen years he has lived seem but a moment, a breathing space in the long march of humanity. Already he hears death calling. With all his heart he wants to come close to some other human, touch someone with his hands, be touched by the hand of another. If he prefers that the other be a woman, that is because he believes that a woman will be gentle, that she will understand. He wants, most of all, understanding.

When the moment of sophistication came to George Willard his mind turned to Helen White, the Winesburg banker's daughter. Always he had been conscious of the girl growing into womanhood as he grew into manhood. Once on a summer night when he was eighteen, he had walked with her on a country road and in her presence had given way to an impulse to boast, to make himself appear big and significant in her eyes. Now he wanted to see her for another purpose. He wanted to tell her of the new impulses that had come to him. He had tried to make her think of him as a man when he knew nothing of manhood and now he wanted to be with her and to try to make her feel the change he believed had taken place in his nature.

As for Helen White, she also had come to a period of change. What George felt, she in her young woman's way felt also. She was no longer a girl and hungered to reach into the grace and beauty of womanhood. She had come home from Cleveland, where she was attending college, to spend a day at the Fair. She also had begun to have memories. During the day she sat in the grand-stand with a young man, one of the instructors from the college, who was a guest of her mother's. The young man was of a pedantic turn of mind and she felt at once he would not do for her purpose. At the Fair she was glad to be seen in his company as he was well dressed and a stranger. She knew that the fact of his presence would create an impression. During the day she was happy, but when night came on she began to grow restless. She wanted to drive the instructor away, to get out of his presence. While they sat together in the grand-stand and while the eyes of former schoolmates were upon them, she paid so much attention to her escort that he grew interested. "A scholar needs money. I should marry a woman with money," he mused.

Helen White was thinking of George Willard even as he wandered gloomily through the crowds thinking of her. She remembered the summer evening when they had walked together and wanted to walk with him again. She thought that the months she had spent in the city, the going to theatres and the seeing of great crowds wandering in lighted thoroughfares, had changed her profoundly. She wanted him to feel and be conscious of the change in her nature.

The summer evening together that had left its mark on the memory of both the young man and woman had, when looked at quite sensibly, been rather stupidly spent. They had walked out of town along a country road. Then they had stopped by a fence near a field of young corn and George had taken off his coat and let it hang on his arm. "Well, I've stayed here in Winesburg—yes—I've not yet gone away but I'm growing up," he had said. "I've been reading books and I've been thinking. I'm going to try to amount to something in life."

"Well," he explained, "that isn't the point. Perhaps I'd better quit talking."

The confused boy put his hand on the girl's arm. His voice trembled. The two started to walk back along the road toward town. In his desperation George boasted, "I'm going to be a big man, the biggest that ever lived here in Winesburg," he declared. "I want you to do something, I don't know what. Perhaps it is none of my business. I want you to try to be different from other women. You see the point. It's none of my business I tell you. I want you to be a beautiful woman. You see what I want."

The boy's voice failed and in silence the two came back into town and went along the street to Helen White's house. At the gate he tried to say something impressive. Speeches he had thought out came into his head, but they seemed utterly pointless. "I thought—I used to think—I had it in my mind you would marry Seth Richmond. Now I know you won't," was all he could find to say as she went through the gate and toward the door of her house.

On the warm fall evening as he stood in the stairway and looked at the crowd drifting through Main Street, George thought of the talk beside the field of young corn and was ashamed of the figure he had made of himself. In the street the people surged up and down like cattle confined in a pen. Buggies and wagons almost filled the narrow thoroughfare. A band played and small boys raced along the sidewalk, diving between the legs of men. Young men with shining red faces walked awkwardly about with girls on their arms. In a room above one of the stores, where a dance was to be held, the fiddlers tuned their instruments. The broken sounds floated down through an open window and out across the murmur of voices and the loud blare of the horns of the band. The medley of sounds got on young Willard's nerves. Everywhere, on all sides, the sense of crowding, moving life closed in about him. He wanted to run away by himself and think. "If she wants to stay with that fellow she may. Why should I care? What difference does it make to me?" he growled and went along Main Street and through Hern's grocery into a side street.

George felt so utterly lonely and dejected that he wanted to weep but pride made him walk rapidly along, swinging his arms. He came to Westley Moyer's livery barn and stopped in the shadows to listen to a group of men who talked of a race Westley's stallion, Tony Tip, had won at the Fair during the afternoon. A crowd had gathered in front of the barn and before the crowd walked Westley, prancing up and down and boasting. He held a whip in his hand and kept tapping the ground. Little puffs of dust arose in the lamplight. "Hell, quit your talking," Westley exclaimed. "I wasn't afraid, I knew I had 'em beat all the time. I wasn't afraid."

Ordinarily George Willard would have been intensely interested in the boasting of Moyer, the horseman. Now it made him angry. He turned and hurried away along the street. "Old windbag," he sputtered. "Why does he want to be bragging? Why don't he shut up?"

George went into a vacant lot and as he hurried along, fell over a pile of rubbish. A nail protruding from an empty barrel tore his trousers. He sat down on the ground and swore. With a pin he mended the torn place and then arose and went on. "I'll go to Helen White's house, that's what I'll do. I'll walk right in. I'll say that I want to see her. I'll walk right in and sit down, that's what I'll do," he declared, climbing over a fence and beginning to run.

On the veranda of Banker White's house Helen was restless and distraught. The instructor sat between the mother and daughter. His talk wearied the girl. Although he had also been raised in an Ohio town, the instructor began to put on the airs of the city. He wanted to appear cosmopolitan. "I like the chance you have given me to study the background out of which most of our girls come," he declared. "It was good of you, Mrs. White, to have me down for the day." He turned to Helen and laughed. "Your life is still bound up with the life of this town?" he asked. "There are people here in whom you are interested?" To the girl his voice sounded pompous and heavy.

Helen arose and went into the house. At the door leading to a garden at the back she stopped and stood listening. Her mother began to talk. "There is no one here fit to associate with a girl of Helen's breeding," she said.

Helen ran down a flight of stairs at the back of the house and into the garden. In the darkness she stopped and stood trembling. It seemed to her that the world was full of meaningless people saying words. Afire with eagerness she ran through a garden gate and turning a corner by the banker's barn, went into a little side street. "George! Where are you, George?" she cried, filled with nervous excitement. She stopped running, and leaned against a tree to laugh hysterically. Along the dark little street came George Willard, still saying words. "I'm going to walk right into her house. I'll go right in and sit down," he declared as he came up to her. He stopped and stared stupidly. "Come on," he said and took hold of her hand. With hanging heads they walked away along the street under the trees. Dry leaves rustled under foot. Now that he had found her George wondered what he had better do and say.

At the upper end of the fair ground, in Winesburg, there is a half decayed old grand-stand. It has never been painted and the boards are all warped out of shape. The fair ground stands on top of a low hill rising out of the valley of Wine Creek and from the grand-stand one can see at night, over a cornfield, the lights of the town reflected against the sky.

George and Helen climbed the hill to the fair ground, coming by the path past Waterworks Pond. The feeling of loneliness and isolation that had come to the young man in the crowded streets of his town was both broken and intensified by the presence of Helen. What he felt was reflected in her.

In youth there are always two forces fighting in people. The warm unthinking little animal struggles against the thing that reflects and remembers, and the older, the more sophisticated thing had possession of George Willard. Sensing his mood, Helen walked beside him filled with respect. When they got to the grand-stand they climbed up under the roof and sat down on one of the long bench-like seats.

There is something memorable in the experience to be had by going into a fair ground that stands at the edge of a Middle Western town on a night after the annual fair has been held. The sensation is one never to be forgotten. On all sides are ghosts, not of the dead, but of living people. Here, during the day just passed, have come the people pouring in from the town and the country around. Farmers with their wives and children and all the people from the hundreds of little frame houses have gathered within these board walls. Young girls have laughed and men with beards have talked of the affairs of their lives. The place has been filled to overflowing with life. It has itched and squirmed with life and now it is night and the life has all gone away. The silence is almost terrifying. One conceals oneself standing silently beside the trunk of a tree and what there is of a reflective tendency in his nature is intensified. One shudders at the thought of the meaninglessness of life while at the same instant, and if the people of the town are his people, one loves life so intensely that tears come into the eyes.

In the darkness under the roof of the grand-stand, George Willard sat beside Helen White and felt very keenly his own insignificance in the scheme of existence. Now that he had come out of town where the presence of the people stirring about, busy with a multitude of affairs, had been so irritating the irritation was all gone. The presence of Helen renewed and refreshed him. It was as though her woman's hand was assisting him to make some minute readjustment of the machinery of his life. He began to think of the people in the town where he had always lived with something like reverence. He had reverence for Helen. He wanted to love and to be loved by her, but he did not at the moment want to be confused by her womanhood. In the darkness he took hold of her hand and when she crept close put a hand on her shoulder. A wind began to blow and he shivered. With all his strength he tried to hold and to understand the mood that had come upon him. In that high place in the darkness the two oddly sensitive human atoms held each other tightly and waited. In the mind of each was the same thought. "I have come to this lonely place and here is this other," was the substance of the thing felt.

In Winesburg the crowded day had run itself out into the long night of the late fall. Farm horses jogged away along lonely country roads pulling their portion of weary people. Clerks began to bring samples of goods in off the sidewalks and lock the doors of stores. In the Opera House a crowd had gathered to see a show and further down Main Street the fiddlers, their instruments tuned, sweated and worked to keep the feet of youth flying over a dance floor.

In the darkness in the grand-stand Helen White and George Willard remained silent. Now and then the spell that held them was broken and they turned and tried in the dim light to see into each other's eyes. They kissed but that impulse did not last. At the upper end of the fair ground a half dozen men worked over horses that had raced during the afternoon. The men had built a fire and were heating kettles of water. Only their legs could be seen as they passed back and forth in the light. When the wind blew the little flames of the fire danced crazily about.

George and Helen arose and walked away into the darkness. They went along a path past a field of corn that had not yet been cut. The wind whispered among the dry corn blades. For a moment during the walk back into town the spell that held them was broken. When they had come to the crest of Waterworks Hill they stopped by a tree and George again put his hands on the girl's shoulders. She embraced him eagerly and then again they drew quickly back from that impulse. They stopped kissing and stood a little apart. Mutual respect grew big in them. They were both embarrassed and to relieve their embarrassment dropped into the animalism of youth. They laughed and began to pull and haul at each other. In some way chastened and purified by the mood they had been in they became, not man and woman, not boy and girl, but excited little animals.

It was so they went down the hill. In the darkness they played like two splendid young things in a young world. Once, running swiftly forward, Helen tripped George and he fell. He squirmed and shouted. Shaking with laughter, he rolled down the hill. Helen ran after him. For just a moment she stopped in the darkness. There is no way of knowing what woman's thoughts went through her mind but, when the bottom of the hill was reached and she came up to the boy, she took his arm and walked beside him in dignified silence. For some reason they could not have explained they had both got from their silent evening together the thing needed. Man or boy, woman or girl, they had for a moment taken hold of the thing that makes the mature life of men and women in the modern world possible.

THE STORY OF MY DOVECOT

Isaac Babel

Isaac Babel was a Jew, born in Odessa in 1894, writing under the Soviet régime during the late twenties and early thirties. "The Story of My Dovecot" (1925), and Red Cavalry *(1926), a book of sketches about the Soviet-Polish War of 1920, won him considerable popularity, but his position in Russian letters was not secure enough to save him from a Russian concentration camp, where he died, in 1939 or 1940. In 1955, his collected stories were published in this country. Writing under stresses unknown to Western authors, Babel has a unique and most important view of life to bring us.*

When I was a kid I longed for a dovecot. Never in all my life have I wanted a thing more. But not till I was nine did father promise the wherewithal to buy the wood to make one, and three pairs of pigeons to stock it with. It was then 1904, and I was studying for the entrance exam to the preparatory class of the secondary school at Nikolayev in the Province of Kherson, where my people were at that time living. This province of course no longer exists, and our town has been incorporated in the Odessa Region.

I was only nine, and I was scared stiff of the exams. In both subjects, Russian Language and arithmetic, I couldn't afford to get less than top marks. At our secondary school the *numerus clausus* was stiff: a mere five percent. So that out of forty boys only two that were Jews could get into the preparatory class. The teachers used to put cunning questions to Jewish boys; no one else was asked such devilish questions. So when Father promised to buy the pigeons he demanded top marks with distinction in both subjects. He absolutely tortured me to death. I fell into a state of permanent daydream, into an endless, despairing, childish reverie. I went to the exam deep in this dream, and nevertheless did better than everybody else.

I had a knack for book-learning. Even though they asked cunning questions, the teachers could not rob me of my intelligence and my avid memory. I was good at learning, and got top marks in both subjects. But then everything went wrong. Khariton Efrussi, the corn-dealer who exported wheat to Marseille, slipped someone a 500-rouble bribe. My mark was changed from A to A-, and Efrussi Junior went to the secondary school instead of me. Father took it very badly. From the time I was six he had been cramming me with every scrap of learning he could, and that A- drove him to despair. He wanted to beat Efrussi up, or at least bribe two longshoremen to beat Efrussi up, but mother talked him out of the idea, and I started studying for the second exam the following year, the one for the lowest class. Behind my back, my people got the teacher to take me, in one year, through the preparatory and first-year courses simultaneously, and conscious of the family's despair, I got three whole books by heart. These were Smirnovsky's *Russian Grammar,* Yevtushevsky's *Problems,* and Putsykovich's *Manual of Early Russian History*. Children no longer cram from these books, but I learned them by heart, line for line, and the following year in the Russian exam Karavayev gave me an unrivaled A+.

This Karavayev was a red-faced, irritable fellow, a graduate of Moscow University. He was hardly more than thirty. Crimson glowed in his manly cheeks as it does in the cheeks of peasant children. A wart sat perched on one cheek, and from it there sprouted a tuft of ash-colored cat's whiskers. At the exam, besides Karavayev, there was the Assistant Curator Pyatnitsky, who was reckoned a big noise in the school and throughout the province. When the Assistant Curator asked me about Peter the Great, a feeling of complete oblivion came over me, and awareness that the end was near: an abyss seemed to yawn before me, an arid abyss lined with exultation and despair.

About Peter the Great, I knew things by heart from Putsykovich's book and Pushkin's verses. Sobbing, I recited these verses, while the faces before me suddenly turned upside down, were shuffled as a pack of cards is shuffled. This card-shuffling went on, and meanwhile, shivering, jerking my back straight, galloping headlong, I was shouting Pushkin's stanzas at the top of my voice. On and on I yelled them, and no one broke into my crazy mouthings. Through a crimson blindness, through the sense of absolute freedom that had filled me, I was aware of nothing but Pyatnitsky's old face with its silver-touched beard bent toward me. He didn't interrupt me, and merely said to Karavayev, who was rejoicing for my sake and Pushkin's:

"What a people," the old man whispered, "those little Jews of yours! There's a devil in them!"

And when at last I could shout no more, he said:

"Very well, run along, my little friend."

I went out of the classroom into the corridor, and there, leaning against a wall that needed a coat of whitewash, I began to awake from my trance. About me Russian boys were playing, the school bell hung not far away above the stairs, the caretaker was snoozing on a chair with a broken seat. I looked at the caretaker, and gradually woke up. Boys were creeping toward me from all sides. They wanted to give me a jab, or perhaps just have a game, but Pyatnitsky suddenly loomed up in the corridor. As he passed me, he halted for a moment, the frock coat flowing down his back in a slow heavy wave. I discerned embarrassment in that large, fleshy, upper-class back, and got closer to the old man.

"Children," he said to the boys, "don't touch this lad." And he laid a fat hand tenderly on my shoulder.

"My little friend," he went on, turning me towards him, "tell your father that you are admitted to the first class."

On his chest a great star flashed, and decorations jingled in his lapel. His great black uniformed body started to move away on its stiff legs. Hemmed in by the shadowy walls, moving between them as a barge moves through a deep canal, it disappeared in the doorway of the headmaster's study. The little servingman took in a tray of tea, clinking solemnly, and I ran home to the shop.

In the shop, a peasant customer, tortured by doubt, sat

scratching himself. When he saw me, my father stopped trying to help the peasant to make up his mind, and without a moment's hesitation believed everything I had to say. Calling to the assistant to start shutting up shop, he dashed out into Cathedral Street to buy me a school cap with a badge on it. My poor mother had her work cut out getting me away from the crazy fellow. She was pale at that moment, she was experiencing destiny. She kept smoothing me, and pushing me away as though she hated me. She said there was always a notice in the paper about those who had been admitted to the school, and that God would punish us, and that folk would laugh at us if we bought a school cap too soon. My mother was pale; she was experiencing destiny through my eyes. She looked at me with bitter compassion as one might look at a little cripple boy, because she alone knew what a family ours was for misfortunes.

All the men in our family were trusting by nature, and quick to ill-considered actions. We were unlucky in everything we undertook. My grandfather had been a rabbi somewhere in the Belaya Tserkov region. He had been thrown out for blasphemy, and for another forty years he lived noisily and sparsely, teaching foreign languages. In his eightieth year he started going off his head. My Uncle Leo, my father's brother, had studied at the Talmudic Academy in Volozhin. In 1892 he ran away to avoid doing military service, eloping with the daughter of someone serving in the commissariat in the Kiev military district. Uncle Leo took this woman to California, to Los Angeles, and there he abandoned her, and died in a house of ill fame among Negroes and Malays. After his death the American police sent us a heritage from Los Angeles, a large trunk bound with brown iron hoops. In this trunk there were dumbbells, locks of women's hair, uncle's talith, horsewhips with gilt handles, scented tea in boxes trimmed with imitation pearls. Of all the family there remained only crazy Uncle Simon-Wolf who lived in Odessa, my father, and I. But my father had faith in people, and he used to put them off with the transports of first love. People could not forgive him for this, and used to play him false. So my father believed that his life was guided by an evil fate, an inexplicable being that pursued him, a being in every respect unlike him. And so I alone of all our family was left to my mother. Like all Jews I was short, weakly, and had headaches from studying. My mother saw all this. She had never been dazzled by her husband's pauper pride, by his incomprehensible belief that our family would one day be richer and more powerful than all others on earth. She desired no success for us, was scared of buying a school jacket too soon, and all she would consent to was that I should have my photo taken.

On September 20, 1905, a list of those admitted to the first class was hung up at the school. In the list my name figured too. All our kith and kin kept going to look at this paper, and even Shoyl, my granduncle, went along. I loved that boastful old man, for he sold fish at the market. His fat hands were moist, covered with fish-scales, and smelt of worlds chill and beautiful. Shoyl also differed from ordinary folk in the lying stories he used to tell about the Polish Rising of 1861. Years ago, Shoyl had been a tavernkeeper at Skvira. He had seen Nicholas I's soldiers shooting Count Godlevski and other Polish insurgents. But perhaps he hadn't. *Now* I know that Shoyl was just an old ignoramus and a simple-minded liar, but his cock-and-bull stories I have never forgotten: they were good stories. Well now, even silly old Shoyl went along to the school to read the list with my name on it, and that evening he danced and pranced at our pauper ball.

My father got up the ball to celebrate my success, and asked all his pals—grain-dealers, real-estate brokers, and the traveling salesmen who sold agricultural machinery in our parts. These salesmen would sell a machine to anyone. Peasants and landowners went in fear of them: you couldn't break loose without buying something or other. Of all Jews, salesmen are the widest-awake and the jolliest. At our party they sang Hasidic songs consisting of three words only but which took an awful long time to sing, songs performed with endless comical intonations. The beauty of these intonations may only be recognized by those who have had the good fortune to spend Passover with the Hasidim or who have visited their noisy Volhynian synagogues. Besides the salesmen, old Lieberman who had taught me the Torah and ancient Hebrew honored us with his presence. In our circle he was known as Monsieur Lieberman. He drank more Bessarabian wine than he should have. The ends of the traditional silk tassels poked out from beneath his waistcoat, and in ancient Hebrew he proposed my health. In this toast the old man congratulated my parents and said that I had vanquished all my foes in single combat: I had vanquished the Russian boys with their fat cheeks, and I had vanquished the sons of our own vulgar parvenus. So, too, in ancient times David King of Judah had overcome Goliath, and just as I had triumphed over Goliath, so, too, would our people by the strength of their intellect conquer the foes who had encircled us and were thirsting for our blood. Monsieur Lieberman wept and shouted *"Vivat!"* The guests formed a circle and danced an old-fashioned quadrille with him in the middle, just as at a wedding in a little Jewish town. Everyone was happy at our ball. Even mother took a sip of vodka, though she neither liked the stuff nor understood how anyone else could—because of this she considered all Russians cracked, and just couldn't imagine how women managed with Russian husbands.

But our happy days came later. For mother they came when of a morning, before I set off for school, she would start making me sandwiches; when we went shopping to buy my school things—pencil box, money box, satchel, new books in cardboard bindings, and exercise books in shiny covers. No one in the world has a keener feeling for new things than children have. Children shudder at the smell of newness as a dog does when it scents a hare, experiencing the madness which later, when we grow up, is called inspiration. And mother acquired this pure and childish sense of the ownership of new things. It took us a whole month to get used to the pencil box, to the morning twilight as I drank my tea on the corner of the large, brightly-lit table and packed my books in my satchel. It took us a month to grow accustomed to our happiness, and it was only after the first half-term that I remembered about the pigeons.

I had everything ready for them: one rouble fifty and a dovecot made from a box by Grandfather Shoyl, as we called him. The dovecot was painted brown. It had nests for twelve pairs of pigeons, carved strips on the roof, and a special grating that I had devised to facilitate the capture of strange birds. All was in readiness. On Sunday, October 20, I set out for the bird market, but unexpected obstacles arose in my path.

The events I am relating, that is to say my admission to the first class at the secondary school, occurred in the autumn of 1905. The Emperor Nicholas was then bestowing a constitution on the Russian people. Orators in shabby overcoats were clambering onto tall curbstones and haranguing the people. At night shots had been heard in the streets, and so mother didn't want me to go to the bird market. From early morning on October 20 the boys next door were flying a kite right by the police station, and our water carrier, abandoning all his buckets, was walking about the streets with a red face and brilliantined hair. Then we saw baker Kalistov's sons drag a leather vaulting-horse out into the street and start doing gym in the middle of the roadway. No one tried to stop them: Semernikov the policeman even kept inciting them to jump higher. Semernikov was girt with a silk belt his wife had made him, and his boots had been polished that day as they had never been polished before. Out of his customary uniform, the policeman frightened my mother more than anything else. Because of him she didn't want me to go out, but I sneaked out by the back way and ran to the bird market, which in our town was behind the station.

At the bird market Ivan Nikodimych, the pigeon-fancier, sat in his customary place. Apart from pigeons, he had rabbits for sale, too, and a peacock. The peacock, spreading its tail, sat on a perch moving a passionless head from side to side. To its paw was tied a twisted cord, and the other end of the cord was caught beneath one leg of Ivan Nikodimych's wicker chair. The moment I got there I bought from the old man a pair of cherry-colored pigeons with luscious tousled tails, and a pair of crowned pigeons, and put them away in a bag on my chest under my shirt. After these purchases I had only forty copecks left, and for this price the old man was not prepared to let me have a male and female pigeon of the Kryukov breed. What I liked about Kryukov pigeons was their short, knobbly, good natured beaks. Forty copecks was the proper price, but the fancier insisted on haggling, averting from me a yellow face scorched by the unsociable passions of bird-snarers. At the end of our bargaining, seeing that there were no other customers, Ivan Nikodimych beckoned me closer. All went as I wished, and all went badly.

Toward twelve o'clock, or perhaps a bit later, a man in felt boots passed across the square. He was stepping lightly on swollen feet, and in his worn-out face lively eyes glittered.

"Ivan Nikodimych," he said as he walked past the bird-fancier, "pack up your gear. In town the Jerusalem aristocrats are being granted a constitution. On Fish Street Grandfather Babel has been constitutioned to death."

He said this and walked lightly on between the cages like a barefoot ploughman walking along the edge of a field.

"They shouldn't," murmured Ivan Nikodimych in his wake. "They shouldn't!" he cried more sternly. He started collecting his rabbits and his peacock, and shoved the Kryukov pigeons at me for forty copecks. I hid them in my bosom and watched the people running away from the bird market. The peacock on Ivan Nikodimych's shoulder was last of all to depart. It sat there like the sun in a raw autumnal sky; it sat as July sits on a pink riverbank, a white-hot July in the long cool grass. No one was left in the market, and not far off shots were rattling. Then I ran to the station, cut across a square that had gone topsy-turvy, and flew down an empty lane of trampled yellow earth. At the end of the lane, in a little wheeled armchair, sat the legless Makarenko, who rode about town in his wheel-chair selling cigarettes from a tray. The boys in our street used to buy smokes from him; children loved him; I dashed toward him down the lane.

"Makarenko," I gasped, panting from my run, and I stroked the legless one's shoulder, "have you seen Shoyl?"

The cripple did not reply. A light seemed to be shining through his coarse face built up of red fat, clenched fists, chunks of iron. He was fidgeting on his chair in his excitement, while his wife Kate, presenting a wadded behind, was sorting out some things scattered on the ground.

"How far have you counted?" asked the legless man, and moved his whole bulk away from the woman, as though aware in advance that her answer would be unbearable.

"Fourteen pair of leggings," said Kate, still bending over, "six undersheets. Now I'm a-counting the bonnets."

"Bonnets!" cried Makarenko, with a choking sound like a sob, "it's clear, Catherine, that God has picked on me, that I must answer for all. People are carting off whole rolls of cloth, people have everything they should, and we're stuck with bonnets."

And, indeed, a woman with a beautiful burning face ran past us down the lane. She was clutching an armful of fezzes in one arm and a piece of cloth in the other, and in a voice of joyful despair she was yelling for her children, who had strayed. A silk dress and a blue blouse fluttered after her as she flew, and she paid no attention to Makarenko who was rolling his chair in pursuit of her. The legless man couldn't catch up. His wheels clattered as he turned the handles for all he was worth.

"Little lady," he cried in a deafening voice, "where did you get that striped stuff?"

But the woman with the fluttering dress was gone. Round the corner to meet her leaped a rickety cart in which a peasant lad stood upright.

"Where've they all run to?" asked the lad, raising a red rein above the nags, jerking in their collars.

"Everybody's on Cathedral Street," said Makarenko pleadingly. "Everybody's there, sonny. Anything you happen to pick up, bring it along to me. I'll give you a good price."

The lad bent down over the front of the cart and whipped up his piebald nags. Tossing their filthy croups like calves, the horses shot off at a gallop. The yellow lane was once more yellow and empty. Then the legless man turned his quenched eyes upon me.

"God's picked on me, I reckon," he said lifelessly. "I'm a son of man, I reckon."

And he stretched a hand spotted with leprosy toward me.

"What's that you've got in your sack?" he demanded, and took the bag that had been warming my heart.

With his fat hand the cripple fumbled among the tumbler pigeons and dragged to light a cherry-colored she-bird. Jerking back its feet, the bird lay still on his palm.

"Pigeons," said Makarenko, and squeaking his wheels he rode right up to me. "Damned pigeons," he repeated, and struck me on the cheek.

He dealt me a flying blow with the hand that was clutching the bird. Kate's wadded back seemed to turn upside down, and I fell to the ground in my new overcoat.

"Their spawn must be wiped out," said Kate, straightening up over the bonnets. "I can't a-bear their spawn, nor their stinking menfolk."

She said more things about our spawn, but I heard nothing of it. I lay on the ground, and the guts of the crushed bird trickled down from my temple. They flowed down my cheek, winding this way and that, splashing, blinding me. The tender pigeon-guts slid down over my forehead, and I closed my solitary unstopped-up eye so as not to see the world that spread out before me. This world was tiny, and it was awful. A stone lay just before my eyes, a little stone so chipped as to resemble the face of an old woman with a large jaw. A piece of string lay not far away, and a bunch of feathers that still breathed. My world was tiny, and it was awful. I closed my eyes so as not to see it, and pressed myself tight into the ground that lay beneath me in soothing dumbness. This trampled earth in no way resembled real life, waiting for exams in real life. Somewhere far away Woe rode across it on a great steed, but the noise of the hoofbeats grew weaker and died away, and silence, the bitter silence that sometimes overwhelms children in their sorrow, suddenly deleted the boundary between my body and the earth that was moving nowhither. The earth smelled of raw depths, of the tomb, of flowers. I smelled its smell and started crying, unafraid. I was walking along an unknown street set on either side with white boxes, walking in a getup of bloodstained feathers, alone between the pavements swept clean as on Sunday, weeping bitterly, fully and happily as I never wept again in all my life. Wires that had grown white hummed above my head, a watchdog trotted on in front, in the lane on one side a young peasant in a waistcoat was smashing a window frame in the house of Khariton Efrussi. He was smashing it with a wooden mallet, striking out with his whole body. Sighing, he smiled all around with the amiable grin of drunkenness, sweat, and spiritual power. The whole street was filled with a splitting, a snapping, the song of flying wood. The peasant's whole existence consisted in bending over, sweating, shouting queer words in some unknown, non-Russian language. He shouted the words and sang, shot out his blue eyes; till in the street there appeared a procession bearing the Cross and moving from the Municipal Building. Old men bore aloft the portrait of the neatly-combed Tsar, banners with graveyard saints swayed above their heads, inflamed old women flew on in front. Seeing the procession, the peasant pressed his mallet to his chest and dashed off in pursuit of the banners, while I, waiting till the tail-end of the procession had passed, made my furtive way home. The house was empty. Its white doors were open, the grass by the dovecot had been trampled down. Only Kuzma was still in the yard. Kuzma the yardman was sitting in the shed laying out the dead Shoyl.

"The wind bears you about like an evil wood-chip," said the old man when he saw me. "You've been away ages. And now look what they've done to granddad."

Kuzma wheezed, turned away from me, and started pulling a fish out of a rent in grandfather's trousers. Two pike perch had been stuck into grandfather: one into the rent in his trousers, the other into his mouth. And while grandfather was dead, one of the fish was still alive, and struggling.

"They've done grandfather in, but nobody else," said Kuzma, tossing the fish to the cat. "He cursed them all good and proper, a wonderful damning and blasting it was. You might fetch a couple of pennies to put on his eyes."

But then, at ten years of age, I didn't know what need the dead had of pennies.

"Kuzma," I whispered, "save us."

And I went over to yardman, hugged his crooked old back with its one shoulder higher than the other, and over this back I saw grandfather. Shoyl lay in the sawdust, his chest squashed in, his beard twisted upwards, battered shoes on his bare feet. His feet, thrown wide apart, were dirty, lilac-colored, dead. Kuzma was fussing over him. He tied the dead man's jaws and kept glancing over the body to see what else he could do. He fussed as though over a newly-purchased garment, and only cooled down when he had given the dead man's beard a good combing.

"He cursed the lot of 'em right and left," he said, smiling, and cast a loving look over the corpse. "If Tartars had crossed his path he'd have sent them packing, but Russians came, and their women with them, Rooski women. Russians just can't bring themselves to forgive, I know what Rooskis are."

The yardman spread some more sawdust beneath the body, threw off his carpenter's apron, and took me by the hand.

"Let's go to father," he mumbled, squeezing my hand tighter and tighter. "Your father has been searching for you since morning, sure as fate you was dead."

And so with Kuzma I went to the house of the tax-inspector, where my parents, escaping the pogrom, had sought refuge.

THE DEVIL AND DANIEL WEBSTER

Stephen Vincent Benét

Stephen Vincent Benét (1898-1943) was born in Pennsylvania and graduated from Yale in 1919. Novelist, poet, and short-story writer, Benét won the Pulitzer Prize in 1929 for his long narrative poem, John Brown's Body. *His brilliant fantasy "The Devil and Daniel Webster" (1939) is a recognized classic of American short fiction, and is a* tour de force *of plot interweaving, containing at least half a dozen distinct themes borrowed from sources as far apart as the American tall tale, the Book of Job, and the Faust story.*

It's a story they tell in the border country, where Massachusetts joins Vermont and New Hampshire.

Yes, Dan'l Webster's dead—or, at least, they buried him. But every time there's a thunderstorm around Marshfield, they say you can hear his rolling voice in the hollows of the sky. And they say that if you go to his grave and speak loud and clear, "Dan'l Webster—Dan'l Webster!" the ground'll begin to shiver and the trees begin to shake. And after a while you'll hear a deep voice saying, "Neighbor, how stands the Union?" Then you better answer the Union stands as she stood, rock bottomed and copper sheathed, one and indivisible, or he's liable to rear right out of the ground. At least, that's what I was told when I was a youngster.

You see, for a while, he was the biggest man in the country. He never got to be President, but he was the biggest man. There were thousands that trusted in him right next to God Almighty, and they told stories about him and all the things that belonged to him that were like the stories of patriarchs and such. They said, when he stood up to speak, stars and stripes came right out in the sky, and once he spoke against a river and made it sink into the ground. They said, when he walked the woods with his fishing rod, Killall, the trout would jump out of the streams right into his pockets, for they knew it was no use putting up a fight against him; and, when he argued a case, he could turn on the harps of the blessed and the shaking of the earth underground. That was the kind of man he was, and his big farm up at Marshfield was suitable to him. The chickens he raised were all white meat down through the drumsticks, the cows were tended like children, and the big ram he called Goliath had horns with a curl like a morning-glory vine and could butt through an iron door. But Dan'l wasn't one of your gentleman farmers; he knew all the ways of the land, and he'd be up by candlelight to see that the chores got done. A man with a mouth like a mastiff, a brow like a mountain and eyes like burning anthracite—that was Dan'l Webster in his prime. And the biggest case he argued never got written down in the books, for he argued it against the devil, nip and tuck and no holds barred. And this is the way I used to hear it told.

There was a man named Jabez Stone, lived at Cross Corners, New Hampshire. He wasn't a bad man to start with, but he was an unlucky man. If he planted corn, he got borers; if he planted potatoes, he got blight. He had good-enough land, but it didn't prosper him; he had a decent wife and children, but the more children he had, the less there was to feed them. If stones cropped up in his neighbor's field, boulders boiled up in his; if he had a horse with the spavins, he'd trade it for one with the staggers and give something extra. There's some folks bound to be like that, apparently. But one day Jabez Stone got sick of the whole business.

He'd been plowing that morning and he'd just broke the plowshare on a rock that he could have sworn hadn't been there yesterday. And, as he stood looking at the plowshare, the off horse began to cough—that ropy kind of cough that means sickness and horse doctors. There were two children down with the measles, his wife was ailing, and he had a whitlow on his thumb. It was about the last straw for Jabez Stone. "I vow," he said, and he looked around him kind of desperate, "I vow it's enough to make a man want to sell his soul to the devil! And I would, too, for two cents!"

Then he felt a kind of queerness come over him at having said what he'd said; though, naturally, being a New Hampshireman, he wouldn't take it back. But, all the same, when it got to be evening and, as far as he could see, no notice had been taken, he felt relieved in his mind, for he was a religious man. But notice is always taken, sooner or later, just like the Good Book says. And, sure enough, next day, about suppertime, a soft-spoken, dark-dressed stranger drove up in a handsome buggy and asked for Jabez Stone.

Well, Jabez told his family it was a lawyer, come to see him about a legacy. But he knew who it was. He didn't like the looks of the stranger, nor the way he smiled with his teeth. They were white teeth, and plentiful—some say they were filed to a point, but I wouldn't vouch for that. And he didn't like it when the dog took one look at the stranger and ran away howling, with his tail between his legs. But having passed the word, more or less, he stuck to it, and they went out behind the barn and made their bargain. Jabez Stone had to prick his finger to sign, and the stranger lent him a silver pin. The wound healed clean, but it left a little white scar.

After that, all of a sudden, things began to pick up and prosper for Jabez Stone. His cows got fat and his horses sleek, his crops were the envy of the neighborhood, and lightning might strike all over the valley, but it wouldn't strike his barn. Pretty soon he was one of the prosperous people of the county; they asked him to stand for selectman, and he stood for it; there began to be talk of running him for state senate. All in all, you might say the Stone family was as happy and contented as cats in a dairy. And so they were, except for Jabez Stone.

He'd been contented enough for the first few years. It's a great thing when bad luck turns; it drives most other things out of your head. True, every now and then, especially in rainy weather, the little white scar on his finger would give him a twinge. And once a year, punctual as clockwork, the stranger with the handsome buggy would come driving by. But the sixth year the stranger lighted, and, after that, his peace was over for Jabez Stone.

The stranger came up through the lower field, switching his boots with a cane—they were handsome black boots, but

Jabez Stone never liked the look of them, particularly the toes. And, after he'd passed the time of day, he said, "Well, Mr. Stone, you're a hummer! It's a very pretty property you've got here, Mr. Stone."

"Well, some might favor it and others might not," said Jabez Stone, for he was a New Hampshireman.

"Oh, no need to decry your industry!" said the stranger, very easy, showing his teeth in a smile. "After all, we know what's been done, and it's been according to contract and specifications. So when—ahem—the mortgage falls due next year, you shouldn't have any regrets."

"Speaking of that mortgage, mister," said Jabez Stone, and he looked around for help to the earth and the sky, "I'm beginning to have one or two doubts about it."

"Doubts?" said the stranger not quite so pleasantly.

"Why, yes," said Jabez Stone. "This being the U.S.A. and me always having been a religious man." He cleared his throat and got bolder. "Yes, sir," he said, "I'm beginning to have considerable doubts as to that mortgage holding in court."

"There's courts and courts," said the stranger, clicking his teeth. "Still, we might as well have a look at the original document." And he hauled out a big black pocketbook, full of papers. "Sherwin, Slater, Stevens, Stone," he muttered. " 'I, Jabez Stone, for a term of seven years——' Oh, it's quite in order, I think."

But Jabez Stone wasn't listening, for he saw something else flutter out of the black pocketbook. It was something that looked like a moth, but it wasn't a moth. And as Jabez Stone stared at it, it seemed to speak to him in a small sort of piping voice, terrible small and thin, but terrible human. "Neighbor Stone!" it squeaked. "Neighbor Stone! Help me! For God's sake, help me!"

But before Jabez Stone could stir hand or foot, the stranger whipped out a big bandanna handkerchief, caught the creature in it, just like a butterfly, and started tying up the ends of the bandanna.

"Sorry for the interruption," he said. "As I was saying——"

But Jabez Stone was shaking all over like a scared horse.

"That's Miser Stevens' voice!" he said in a croak. "And you've got him in your handkerchief!"

The stranger looked a little embarrassed.

"Yes, I really should have transferred him to the collecting box," he said with a simper, "but there were some rather unusual specimens there and I don't want them crowded. Well, well, these little contretemps will occur."

"I don't know what you mean by contertan," said Jabez Stone, "but that was Miser Stevens' voice! And he ain't dead! You can't tell me he is! He was just as spry and mean as a woodchuck Tuesday!"

"In the midst of life . . ." said the stranger, kind of pious. "Listen!" Then a bell began to toll in the valley and Jabez Stone listened, with the sweat running down his face. For he knew it was tolled for Miser Stevens and that he was dead.

"These long-standing accounts," said the stranger with a sigh; "one really hates to close them. But business is business."

He still had the bandanna in his hand, and Jabez Stone felt sick as he saw the cloth struggle and flutter.

"Are they all as small as that?" he asked hoarsely.

"Small?" said the stranger. "Oh, I see what you mean. Why, they vary." He measured Jabez Stone with his eyes, and his teeth showed. "Don't worry, Mr. Stone," he said. "You'll go with a very good grade. I wouldn't trust you outside the collection box. Now, a man like Dan'l Webster, of course —well, we'd have to build a special box for him, and even at that, I imagine the wing spread would astonish you. He'd certainly be a prize. I wish we could see our way clear to him. But, in your case, as I was saying——"

"Put that handkerchief away!" said Jabez Stone, and he began to beg and to pray. But the best he could get at the end was a three years' extension, with conditions.

But till you make a bargain like that, you've got no idea of how fast four years can run. By the last months of those years Jabez Stone's known all over the state and there's talk of running him for governor—and it's dust and ashes in his mouth. For every day, when he gets up, he thinks, "There's one more night gone," and every night, when he lies down, he thinks of the black pocketbook and the soul of Miser Stevens, and it makes him sick at heart. Till, finally, he can't bear it any longer, and, in the last days of the last year, he hitches up his horse and drives off to seek Dan'l Webster. For Dan'l was born in New Hampshire, only a few miles from Cross Corners, and it's well known that he has a particular soft spot for old neighbors.

It was early in the morning when he got to Marshfield, but

Dan'l was up already, talking Latin to the farm hands and wrestling with the ram, Goliath, and trying out a new trotter and working up speeches to make against John C. Calhoun. But when he heard a New Hampshireman had come to see him, he dropped everything else he was doing, for that was Dan'l's way. He gave Jabez Stone a breakfast that five men couldn't eat, went into the living history of every man and woman in Cross Corners, and finally asked him how he could serve him.

Jabez Stone allowed that it was a kind of mortgage case.

"Well, I haven't pleaded a mortgage case in a long time, and I don't generally plead now, except before the Supreme Court," said Dan'l, "but if I can, I'll help you."

"Then I've got hope for the first time in ten years," said Jabez Stone and told him the details.

Dan'l walked up and down as he listened, hands behind his back, now and then asking a question, now and then plunging his eyes at the floor, as if they'd bore through it like gimlets. When Jabez Stone had finished, Dan'l puffed out his cheeks and blew. Then he turned to Jabez Stone and a smile broke over his face like the sunrise over Monadnock.

"You've certainly given yourself the devil's own row to hoe, Neighbor Stone," he said, "but I'll take your case."

"You'll take it?" said Jabez Stone, hardly daring to believe.

"Yes," said Dan'l Webster. "I've got about seventy-five other things to do and the Missouri Compromise to straighten out, but I'll take your case. For if two New Hampshiremen aren't a match for the devil, we might as well give the country back to the Indians."

Then he shook Jabez Stone by the hand and said, "Did you come down here in a hurry?"

"Well, I admit I made time," said Jabez Stone.

"You'll go back faster," said Dan'l Webster, and he told 'em to hitch up Constitution and Constellation to the carriage. They were matched grays with one white forefoot, and they stepped like greased lightning.

Well, I won't describe how excited and pleased the whole Stone family was to have the great Dan'l Webster for a guest, when they finally got there. Jabez Stone had lost his hat on the way, blown off when they overtook a wind, but he didn't take much account of that. But after supper he sent the family off to bed, for he had most particular business with Mr. Webster. Mrs. Stone wanted him to sit in the front parlor, but

Dan'l Webster knew front parlors and said he preferred the kitchen. So it was there they sat, waiting for the stranger, with a jug on the table between them and a bright fire on the hearth—the stranger being scheduled to show up on the stroke of midnight, according to specification.

Well, most men wouldn't have asked for better company than Dan'l Webster and a jug. But with every tick of the clock Jabez Stone got sadder and sadder. His eyes roved round, and though he sampled the jug you could see he couldn't taste it. Finally, on the stroke of 11:30 he reached over and grabbed Dan'l Webster by the arm.

"Mr. Webster, Mr. Webster!" he said, and his voice was shaking with fear and a desperate courage. "For God's sake, Mr. Webster, harness your horses and get away from this place while you can!"

"You've brought me a long way, neighbor, to tell me you don't like my company," said Dan'l Webster, quite peaceable, pulling at the jug.

"Miserable wretch that I am!" groaned Jabez Stone. "I've brought you a devilish way, and now I see my folly. Let him take me if he wills. I don't hanker after it, I must say, but I can stand it. But you're the Union's stay and New Hampshire's pride! He mustn't get you, Mr. Webster! He mustn't get you!"

Dan'l Webster looked at the distracted man, all gray and shaking in the firelight, and laid a hand on his shoulder.

"I'm obliged to you, Neighbor Stone," he said gently. "It's kindly thought of. But there's a jug on the table and a case in hand. And I never left a jug or a case half finished in my life."

And just at that moment there was a sharp rap on the door.

"Ah," said Dan'l Webster very coolly, "I thought your clock was a trifle slow, Neighbor Stone." He stepped to the door and opened it. "Come in!" he said.

The stranger came in—very dark and tall he looked in the firelight. He was carrying a box under his arm—a black japanned box with little air holes in the lid. At the sight of the box Jabez Stone gave a low cry and shrank into a corner of the room.

"Mr. Webster, I presume," said the stranger, very polite, but with his eyes glowing like a fox's deep in the woods.

"Attorney of record for Jabez Stone," said Dan'l Webster, but his eyes were glowing too. "Might I ask your name?"

"I've gone by a good many," said the stranger carelessly.

"Perhaps Scratch will do for the evening. I'm often called that in these regions."

Then he sat down at the table and poured himself a drink from the jug. The liquor was cold in the jug, but it came steaming into the glass.

"And now," said the stranger, smiling and showing his teeth, "I shall call upon you, as a law-abiding citizen, to assist me in taking possession of my property."

Well, with that the argument began—and it went hot and heavy. At first Jabez Stone had a flicker of hope, but when he saw Dan'l Webster being forced back at point after point, he just sat scrunched in his corner, with his eyes on that japanned box. For there wasn't any doubt as to the deed or the signature—that was the worst of it. Dan'l Webster twisted and turned and thumped his fist on the table, but he couldn't get away from that. He offered to compromise the case; the stranger wouldn't hear of it. He pointed out the property had increased in value, and state senators ought to be worth more; the stranger stuck to the letter of the law. He was a great lawyer, Dan'l Webster, but we know who's the King of Lawyers, as the Good Book tells us, and it seemed as if, for the first time, Dan'l Webster had met his match.

Finally, the stranger yawned a little. "Your spirited efforts on behalf of your client do you credit, Mr. Webster," he said, "but if you have no more arguments to adduce. I'm rather pressed for time . . ." and Jabez Stone shuddered.

Dan'l Webster's brow looked dark as a thundercloud.

"Pressed or not, you shall not have this man!" he thundered. "Mr. Stone is an American citizen, and no American citizen may be forced into the service of a foreign prince. We fought England for that in '12 and we'll fight all hell for it again!"

"Foreign?" said the stranger. "And who calls me a foreigner?"

"Well, I never yet yeard of the dev—of your claiming American citizenship," said Dan'l Webster with surprise.

"And who with better right?" said the stranger with one of his terrible smiles. "When the first wrong was done to the first Indian, I was there. When the first slaver put out for the Congo, I stood on her deck. Am I not in your books and stories and beliefs, from the first settlements on? Am I not spoken of still in every church in New England? 'Tis true the North claims me for a Southerner and the South for a

Northerner, but I am neither. I am merely an honest American like yourself—and of the best descent—for, to tell the truth, Mr. Webster, though I don't like to boast of it, my name is older in this country than yours."

"Aha!" said Dan'l Webster with the veins standing out in his forehead. "Then I stand on the Constitution! I demand a trial for my client!"

"The case is hardly one for an ordinary court," said the stranger, his eyes flickering. "And, indeed, the lateness of the hour—"

"Let it be any court you choose, so it is an American judge and an American jury!" said Dan'l Webster in his pride. "Let it be the quick or the dead; I'll abide the issue!"

"You have said it," said the stranger, and pointed his finger at the door. And with that, and all of a sudden, there was a rushing of wind outside and a noise of footsteps. They came, clear and distinct, through the night. And yet they were not like the footsteps of living men.

"In God's name, who comes by so late?" cried Jabez Stone in an ague of fear.

"The jury Mr. Webster demands," said the stranger, sipping at his boiling glass. "You must pardon the rough appearance of one or two; they will have come a long way."

And with that the fire burned blue and the door blew open and twelve men entered, one by one.

If Jabez Stone had been sick with terror before, he was blind with terror now. For there was Walter Butler, the loyalist, who spread fire and horror through the Mohawk Valley in the times of the Revolution; and there was Simon Girty, the renegade, who saw white men burned at the stake and whooped with the Indians to see them burn. His eyes were green, like a catamount's, and the stains on his hunting shirt did not come from the blood of the deer. King Philip was there, wild and proud as he had been in life, with the great gash in his head that gave him his death wound, and cruel Governor Dale, who broke men on the wheel. There was Morton of Merry Mount, who so vexed the Plymouth Colony, with his flushed, loose, handsome face and his hate of the godly. There was Teach, the bloody pirate, with his black beard curling on his breast. The Reverend John Smeet, with his strangler's hands and his Geneva gown, walked as daintily as he had to the gallows. The red print of the rope was still around his neck, but he carried a perfumed handkerchief in one hand. One and all, they came into the room with the fires of hell still upon them, and the stranger named their names and their deeds as they came, till the tale of twelve was told. Yet the stranger had told the truth—they had all played a part in America.

"Are you satisfied with the jury, Mr. Webster?" said the stranger mockingly, when they had taken their places.

The sweat stood upon Dan'l Webster's brow, but his voice was clear.

"Quite satisfied," he said. "Though I miss General Arnold from the company."

"Benedict Arnold is engaged upon other business," said the stranger with a glower. "Ah, you asked for a justice, I believe."

He pointed his finger once more, and a tall man, soberly clad in Puritan garb, with the burning gaze of the fanatic, stalked into the room and took his judge's place.

"Justice Hathorne is a jurist of experience," said the stranger. "He presided at certain witch trials once held in Salem. There were others who repented of the business later, but not he."

"Repent of such notable wonders and undertakings?" said the stern old justice. "Nay, hang them—hang them all!" And he muttered to himself in a way that struck ice into the soul of Jabez Stone.

Then the trial began, and, as you might expect, it didn't look anyways good for the defense. And Jabez Stone didn't make much of a witness in his own behalf. He took one look at Simon Girty and screeched, and they had to put him back in his corner in a kind of swoon.

It didn't halt the trial though; the trial went on, as trials do. Dan'l Webster had faced some hard juries and hanging judges in his time, but this was the hardest he'd ever faced, and he knew it. They sat there with a kind of glitter in their eyes, and the stranger's smooth voice went on and on. Every time he'd raise an objection, it'd be "Objection sustained," but whenever Dan'l objected, it'd be "Objection denied." Well, you couldn't expect fair play from a fellow like this Mr. Scratch.

It got to Dan'l in the end, and he began to heat, like iron in the forge. When he got up to speak he was going to flay that stranger with every trick known to the law, and the judge and jury too. He didn't care if it was contempt of court or what would happen to him for it. He didn't care any more what happened to Jabez Stone. He just got madder and madder, thinking of what he'd say. And yet, curiously enough, the more he thought about it, the less he was able to arrange his speech in his mind.

Till, finally, it was time for him to get up on his feet, and he did so, all ready to bust out with lightnings and denunciations. But before he started he looked over the judge and jury for a moment, such being his custom. And he noticed the glitter in their eyes was twice as strong as before, and they all leaned forward. Like hounds just before they get the fox, they looked, and the blue mist of evil in the room thickened as he watched them. Then he saw what he'd been about to do, and he wiped his forehead, as a man might who's just escaped falling into a pit in the dark.

For it was him they'd come for, not only Jabez Stone. He read it in the glitter of their eyes and in the way the stranger hid his mouth with one hand. And if he fought them with their own weapons, he'd fall into their power; he knew that, though he couldn't have told you how. It was his own anger and horror that burned in their eyes; and he'd have to wipe that out or the case was lost. He stood there for a moment, his black eyes burning like anthracite. And then he began to speak.

He started off in a low voice, though you could hear every word. They say he could call on the harps of the blessed when he chose. And this was just as simple and easy as a man could talk. But he didn't start out by condemning or reviling. He was talking about the things that make a country a country and a man a man.

And he began with the simple things that everybody's known and felt—the freshness of a fine morning when you're young, and the taste of food when you're hungry, and the new day that's every day when you're a child. He took them up and he turned them in his hands. They were good things for any man. But without freedom they sickened. And when he talked of those enslaved, and the sorrows of slavery, his voice got like a big bell. He talked of the early days of America and the men who had made those days. It wasn't a spread-eagle speech, but he made you see it. He admitted all the wrong that had ever been done. But he showed how, out of the wrong and the right, the suffering and the starvations, something new had come. And everybody had played a part in it, even the traitors.

Then he turned to Jabez Stone and showed him as he was—an ordinary man who'd had hard luck and wanted to change it. And, because he'd wanted to change it, now he was going to be punished for all eternity. And yet there was good in Jabez Stone, and he showed that good. He was hard and mean, in some ways, but he was a man. There was sadness in being a man, but it was a proud thing too. And he showed what the pride of it was till you couldn't help feeling it. Yes, even in hell, if a man was a man, you'd know it. And he wasn't pleading for any one person any more, though his voice rang like an organ. He was telling the story and the failures and the endless journey of mankind. They got tricked and trapped and bamboozled, but it was a great journey. And no demon that was ever foaled could know the inwardness of it—it took a man to do that.

The fire began to die on the hearth and the wind before morning to blow. The light was getting gray in the room when Dan'l Webster finished. And his words came back at the end to New Hampshire ground, and the one spot of land that each man loves and clings to. He painted a picture of that, and to each one of that jury he spoke of things long forgotten. For his voice could search the heart, and that was his gift and his strength. And to one his voice was like the forest and its secrecy, and to another like the sea and the storms of the sea; and one heard the cry of his lost nation in it, and another saw a little harmless scene he hadn't remembered for years. But each saw something. And when Dan'l Webster finished he didn't know whether or not he'd saved Jabez Stone. But he knew he'd done a miracle. For the glitter was gone from the eyes of judge and jury, and, for the moment, they were men again, and knew they were men.

"The defense rests," said Dan'l Webster and stood there like a mountain. His ears were still ringing with his speech, and he didn't hear anything else till he heard Judge Hathorne say, "The jury will retire to consider its verdict."

Walter Butler rose in his place and his face had a dark, gay pride on it. "The jury has considered its verdict," he said and looked the stranger full in the eye. "We find for the defendant, Jabez Stone."

With that, the smile left the stranger's face, but Walter Butler did not flinch. "Perhaps 'tis not strictly in accordance with the evidence," he said, "but even the damned may salute the eloquence of Mr. Webster."

With that, the long crow of a rooster split the gray morning sky, and judge and jury were gone from the room like a puff of smoke and as if they had never been there. The stranger returned to Dan'l Webster, smiling wryly.

"Major Butler was always a bold man," he said. "I had not thought him quite so bold. Nevertheless, my congratulations, as between two gentlemen."

"I'll have that paper first, if you please," said Dan'l Webster, and he took it and tore it into four pieces. It was queerly warm to the touch. "And now," he said, "I'll have you!" and his hand came down like a bear trap on the stranger's arm. For he knew that once you bested anybody like Mr. Scratch in fair fight, his power on you was gone. And he could see that Mr. Scratch knew it too.

The stranger twisted and wriggled, but he couldn't get out of that grip. "Come, come, Mr. Webster," he said, smiling palely. "This sort of thing is ridic—ouch!—is ridiculous. If you're worried about the costs of the case, naturally, I'd be glad to pay——"

"And so you shall!" said Dan'l Webster, shaking him till his teeth rattled. "For you'll sit right down at that table and draw up a document, promising never to bother Jabez Stone nor his heirs or assigns nor any other New Hampshireman till doomsday! For any hades we want to raise in this state, we can raise ourselves, without assistance from strangers."

"Ouch!" said the stranger. "Ouch! Well, they never did run very big to the barrel, but—ouch!—I agree!"

So he sat down and drew up the document. But Dan'l Webster kept his hand on his coat collar all the time.

"And now may I go?" said the stranger, quite humble, when Dan'l'd seen the documents in proper and legal form.

"Go?" said Dan'l, giving him another shake. "I'm still trying to figure out what I'll do with you. For you've settled the costs of the case, but you haven't settled with me. I think I'll take you back to Marshfield," he said, kind of reflective. "I've got a ram there named Goliath that can butt through an iron door. I'd kind of like to turn you loose in his field and see what he'd do."

Well, with that the stranger began to beg and to plead. And he begged and he pled so humble that finally Dan'l, who was naturally kindhearted, agreed to let him go. The stranger seemed terrible grateful for that and said, just to show they were friends, he'd tell Dan'l's fortune before leaving. So Dan'l agreed to that, though he didn't take much stock in fortune-tellers ordinarily. But, naturally, the stranger was a little different.

Well, he pried and he peered at the lines in Dan'l's hands. And he told him one thing and another that was quite remarkable. But they were all in the past.

"Yes, all that's true, and it happened," said Dan'l Webster. "But what's to come in the future?"

The stranger grinned, kind of happily, and shook his head. "The future's not as you think it," he said. "It's dark. You have a great ambition, Mr. Webster."

"I have," said Dan'l firmly, for everybody knew he wanted to be President.

"It seems almost within your grasp," said the stranger, "but you will not attain it. Lesser men will be made President and you will be passed over."

"And, if I am, I'll still be Daniel Webster," said Dan'l. "Say on."

"You have two strong sons," said the stranger, shaking his head. "You look to found a line. But each will die in war and neither reach greatness."

"Live or die, they are still my sons," said Dan'l Webster. "Say on."

"You have made great speeches," said the stranger. "You will make more."

"Ah," said Dan'l Webster.

"But the last great speech you make will turn many of your own against you," said the stranger. "They will call you Ichabod; they will call you by other names. Even in New England some will say you have turned your coat and sold your country, and their voices will be loud against you till you die."

"So it is an honest speech, it does not matter what men say," said Dan'l Webster. Then he looked at the stranger and their glances locked.

"One question," he said. "I have fought for the Union all my life. Will I see that fight won against those who would tear it apart?"

"Not while you live," said the stranger grimly, "but it will be won. And after you are dead, there are thousands who will fight for your cause, because of words that you spoke."

"Why, then, you long-barreled, slab-sided, lantern-jawed, fortune-telling note shaver," said Dan'l Webster with a great roar of laughter, "be off with you to your own place before I put my mark on you! For, by the thirteen original colonies, I'd go to the Pit itself to save the Union!"

And with that he drew back his foot for a kick that would have stunned a horse. It was only the tip of his shoe that caught the stranger, but he went flying out of the door with his collecting box under his arm.

"And now," said Dan'l Webster, seeing Jabez Stone beginning to rouse from his swoon, "let's see what's left in the jug, for it's dry work talking all night. I hope there's pie for breakfast, Neighbor Stone."

But they say that whenever the devil comes near Marshfield, even now, he gives it a wide berth. And he hasn't been seen in the state of New Hampshire from that day to this. I'm not talking about Massachusetts or Vermont.

A ROSE FOR EMILY

William Faulkner

Born in Mississippi in 1897 and descended from a long line of Southern governors and public figures, William Faulkner is the most famous of all contemporary writers of the South. His two best novels are probably The Sound and the Fury *(1929) and* As I Lay Dying *(1930). It is in the field of the short story, however, that his most perfect works are to be found. Among the more well-known of these are "That Evening Sun Go Down," "The Bear," "Barn Burning," and "Dry September." Faulkner depicts the particular psychological stresses associated with the decline of the South from its romantically glorious past. On this theme probably no other story equals the profound analysis and moving horror of "A Rose for Emily."*

When Miss Emily Grierson died, our whole town went to her funeral: the men through a sort of respectful affection for a fallen monument, the women mostly out of curiosity to see the inside of her house, which no one save an old manservant—a combined gardener and cook—had seen in at least ten years.

It was a big, squarish frame house that had once been white, decorated with cupolas and spires and scrolled balconies in the heavily lightsome style of the seventies, set on what had once been our most select street. But garages and cotton gins had encroached and obliterated even the august names of that neighborhood; only Miss Emily's house was left, lifting its stubborn and coquettish decay above the cotton wagons and the gasoline pumps—an eyesore among eyesores. And now Miss Emily had gone to join the representatives of those august names where they lay in the cedar-bemused cemetery among the ranked and anonymous graves of Union and Confederate soldiers who fell at the battle of Jefferson.

Alive, Miss Emily had been a tradition, a duty, and a care; a sort of hereditary obligation upon the town, dating from that day in 1894 when Colonel Sartoris, the mayor—he who fathered the edict that no Negro woman should appear on the streets without an apron—remitted her taxes, the dispensation dating from the death of her father on into perpetuity. Not that Miss Emily would have accepted charity. Colonel Sartoris invented an involved tale to the effect that Miss Emily's father had loaned money to the town, which the town, as a matter of business, preferred this way of repaying. Only a man of Colonel Sartoris' generation and thought could have invented it, and only a woman could have believed it.

When the next generation, with its more modern ideas, became mayors and aldermen, this arrangement created some little dissatisfaction. On the first of the year they mailed her a tax notice. February came, and there was no reply. They wrote her a formal letter, asking her to call at the sheriff's office at her convenience. A week later the mayor wrote her himself, offering to call or to send his car for her, and received in reply a note on paper of an archaic shape, in a thin, flowing calligraphy in faded ink, to the effect that she no longer went out at all. The tax notice was also enclosed, without comment.

They called a special meeting of the Board of Aldermen. A deputation waited upon her, knocked at the door through which no visitor had passed since she ceased giving china-painting lessons eight or ten years earlier. They were admitted by the old Negro into a dim hall from which a stairway mounted into still more shadow. It smelled of dust and disuse—a close, dank smell. The Negro led them into the parlor. It was furnished in heavy, leather-covered furniture. When the Negro opened the blinds of one window, they could see that the leather was cracked; and when they sat down, a faint dust rose sluggishly about their thighs, spinning with slow motes in the single sunray. On a tarnished gilt easel before the fireplace stood a crayon portrait of Miss Emily's father.

They rose when she entered—a small, fat woman in black, with a thin gold chain descending to her waist and vanishing into her belt, leaning on an ebony cane with a tarnished gold head. Her skeleton was small and spare; perhaps that was why what would have been merely plumpness in another was obesity in her. She looked bloated, like a body long submerged in motionless water, and of that pallid hue. Her eyes, lost in the fatty ridges of her face, looked like two small pieces of coal pressed into a lump of dough as they moved from one face to another while the visitors stated their errand.

She did not ask them to sit. She just stood in the door and listened quietly until the spokesman came to a stumbling halt. Then they could hear the invisible watch ticking at the end of the gold chain.

Her voice was dry and cold. "I have no taxes in Jefferson. Colonel Sartoris explained it to me. Perhaps one of you can gain access to the city records and satisfy yourselves."

"But we have. We are the city authorities, Miss Emily. Didn't you get a notice from the sheriff, signed by him?"

"I received a paper, yes," Miss Emily said. "Perhaps he considers himself the sheriff. . . . I have no taxes in Jefferson."

"But there is nothing on the books to show that, you see. We must go by the—"

"See Colonel Sartoris. I have no taxes in Jefferson."

"But, Miss Emily—"

"See Colonel Sartoris." (Colonel Sartoris had been dead almost ten years.) "I have no taxes in Jefferson. Tobe!" The Negro appeared. "Show these gentlemen out."

II

So she vanquished them, horse and foot, just as she had vanquished their fathers thirty years before about the smell. That was two years after her father's death and a short time after her sweetheart—the one we believed would marry her—had deserted her. After her father's death she went out very little; after her sweetheart went away, people hardly saw her at all. A few of the ladies had the temerity to call, but were not received, and the only sign of life about the place was the Negro man—a young man then—going in and out with a market basket.

"Just as if a man—any man—could keep a kitchen properly," the ladies said; so they were not surprised when the smell developed. It was another link between the gross, teeming world and the high and mighty Griersons.

A neighbor, a woman, complained to the mayor, Judge Stevens, eighty years old.

"But what will you have me to do about it, madam?" he said.

"Why send her word to stop it," the woman said. "Isn't there a law?"

"I'm sure that won't be necessary," Judge Stevens said. "It's probably just a snake or a rat that nigger of hers killed in the yard. I'll speak to him about it."

The next day he received two more complaints, one from a man who came in diffident deprecation. "We really must do something about it, Judge. I'd be the last one in the world to bother Miss Emily, but we've got to do something." That night the Board of Aldermen met—three graybeards and one younger man, a member of the rising generation.

"It's simple enough," he said. "Send her word to have her place cleaned up. Give her a certain time to do it in, and if she don't . . ."

"Dammit, sir," Judge Stevens said, "will you accuse a lady to her face of smelling bad?"

So the next night, after midnight, four men crossed Miss Emily's lawn and slunk about the house like burglars, sniffing along the base of the brickwork and at the cellar openings while one of them performed a regular sowing motion with his hand out of a sack slung from his shoulder. They broke open the cellar door and sprinkled lime there, and in all the outbuildings. As they recrossed the lawn, a window that had been dark was lighted and Miss Emily sat in it, the light behind her, and her upright torso motionless as that of an idol. They crept quietly across the lawn and into the shadow of the locusts that lined the street. After a week or two the smell went away.

That was when people had begun to feel really sorry for her. People in our town, remembering how old lady Wyatt, her great-aunt, had gone completely crazy at last, believed that the Griersons held themselves a little too high for what they really were. None of the young men were quite good enough for Miss Emily and such. We had long thought of them as a tableau; Miss Emily a slender figure in white in the background, her father a spraddled silhouette in the foreground, his back to her and clutching a horsewhip, the two of them framed by the back-flung front door. So when she got to be thirty and was still single, we were not pleased exactly, but vindicated; even with insanity in the family she wouldn't have turned down all of her chances if they had really materialized.

When her father died, it got about that the house was all that was left to her; and in a way, people were glad. At last they could pity Miss Emily. Being left alone, and a pauper, she had become humanized. Now she too would know the old thrill and the old despair of a penny more or less.

The day after his death all the ladies prepared to call at the house and offer condolence and aid, as is our custom. Miss Emily met them at the door, dressed as usual and with no trace of grief on her face. She told them that her father was not dead. She did that for three days, with the ministers calling on her, and the doctors, trying to persuade her to let them dispose of the body. Just as they were about to resort to law and force, she broke down, and they buried her father quickly.

We did not say she was crazy then. We believed she had to do that. We remembered all the young men her father had driven away, and we knew that with nothing left, she would have to cling to that which had robbed her, as people will.

III

She was sick for a long time. When we saw her again, her hair was cut short, making her look like a girl, with a vague resemblance to those angels in colored church windows—sort of tragic and serene.

The town had just let the contracts for paving the sidewalks, and in the summer after her father's death they began the work. The construction company came with niggers and mules and machinery, and a foreman named Homer Barron, a Yankee—a big, dark, ready man, with a big voice and eyes lighter than his face. The little boys would follow in groups to hear him cuss the niggers, and the niggers singing in time to the rise and fall of picks. Pretty soon he knew everybody in town. Whenever you heard a lot of laughing anywhere about the square, Homer Barron would be in the center of the group. Presently we began to see him and Miss Emily on Sunday afternoons driving in the yellow-wheeled buggy and the matched team of bays from the livery stable.

At first we were glad that Miss Emily would have an interest, because the ladies all said, "Of course a Grierson would not think seriously of a Northerner, a day laborer." But there were still others, older people, who said that even grief could not cause a real lady to forget *noblesse oblige*—without calling it *noblesse oblige*. They just said, "Poor Emily. Her kinsfolk should come to her." She had some kin in Alabama; but years ago her father had fallen out with them over the estate of old lady Wyatt, the crazy woman, and there was no communication between the two families. They had not even been represented at the funeral.

And as soon as the old people said, "Poor Emily," the whispering began. "Do you suppose it's really so?" they said to one another. "Of course it is. What else could . . ." This behind their hands; rustling of craned silk and satin behind jalousies closed upon the sun of Sunday afternoon as the thin, swift clop-clop-clop of the matched team passed: "Poor Emily."

She carried her head high enough—even when we believed that she was fallen. It was as if she demanded more than ever the recognition of her dignity as the last Grierson; as if it had wanted that touch of earthiness to reaffirm her imperviousness. Like when she bought the rat poison, the arsenic. That was over a year after they had begun to say "Poor Emily," and while the two female cousins were visiting her.

"I want some poison," she said to the druggist. She was over thirty then, still a slight woman, though thinner than usual, with cold, haughty black eyes in a face the flesh of which was strained across the temples and about the eyesockets as you imagine a lighthousekeeper's face ought to look. "I want some poison," she said.

"Yes, Miss Emily. What kind? For rats and such? I'd recom—"

"I want the best you have. I don't care what kind."

The druggist named several. "They'll kill anything up to an elephant. But what you want is—"

"Arsenic," Miss Emily said. "Is that a good one?"

"Is . . . arsenic? Yes, ma'am. But what you want—"

"I want arsenic."

The druggist looked down at her. She looked back at him, erect, her face like a strained flag. "Why, of course," the druggist said. "If that's what you want. But the law requires you to tell what you are going to use it for."

Miss Emily just stared at him, her head tilted back in order to look him eye for eye, until he looked away and went and got the arsenic and wrapped it up. The Negro delivery boy brought her the package; the druggist didn't come back. When she opened the package at home there was written on the box, under the skull and bones: "For rats."

IV

So the next day we all said, "She will kill herself"; and we said it would be the best thing. When she had first begun to be seen with Homer Barron, we had said, "She will marry him." Then we said, "She will persuade him yet," because Homer himself had remarked—he liked men, and it was known that he drank with younger men in the Elk's Club—that he was not a marrying man. Later we said, "Poor Emily," behind the jalousies as they passed on Sunday afternoon in the glittering buggy, Miss Emily with her head high and Homer Barron with his hat cocked and a cigar in his teeth, reins and whip in a yellow glove.

Then some of the ladies began to say that it was a disgrace to the town and a bad example to the young people. The men did not want to interfere, but at last the ladies forced the Baptist minister—Miss Emily's people were Episcopal—to call upon her. He would never divulge what happened during that interview, but he refused to go back again. The next Sunday they again drove about the streets, and the following day the minster's wife wrote to Miss Emily's relations in Alabama.

So she had blood-kin under her roof again and we sat back to watch developments. At first nothing happened. Then we were sure that they were to be married. We learned that Miss Emily had been to the jeweler's and ordered a man's toilet set in silver, with the letters H.B. on each piece. Two days later we learned that she had bought a complete outfit of men's clothing, including a nightshirt, and we said, "They are married." We were really glad. We were glad because the two female cousins were even more Grierson than Miss Emily had ever been.

So we were not surprised when Homer Barron—the streets had been finished some time since—was gone. We were a little disappointed that there was not a public blowing-off, but we believed that he had gone on to prepare for Miss Emily's coming, or to give her a chance to get rid of the cousins. (By that time it was a cabal, and we were all Miss Emily's allies to help circumvent the cousins.) Sure enough, after another week they departed. And, as we had expected all along, within three days Homer Barron was back in town. A neighbor saw her Negro man admit him at the kitchen door at dusk one evening.

And that was the last we saw of Homer Barron. And of Miss Emily for some time. The Negro man went in and out with the market basket, but the front door remained closed. Now and then we would see her at a window for a moment, as the men did that night when they sprinkled the lime, but for almost six months she did not appear on the streets. Then we knew that this was to be expected too; as if that quality of her father which had thwarted her woman's life so many times had been too virulent and too furious to die.

When we next saw Miss Emily, she had grown fat and her hair was turning gray. During the next few years it grew grayer and grayer until it attained an even pepper-and-salt iron-gray, when it ceased turning. Up to the day of her death at seventy-four it was still that vigorous iron-gray, like the hair of an active man.

From that time on her front door remained closed, save for a period of six or seven years, when she was about forty, during which she gave lessons in china-painting. She fitted up a studio in one of the downstairs rooms, where the daughters and granddaughters of Colonel Sartoris' contemporaries were sent to her with the same regularity and in the same spirit that they were sent on Sundays with a twenty-five cent piece for the collection plate. Meanwhile her taxes had been remitted.

Then the newer generation became the backbone and the spirit of the town, and the painting pupils grew up and fell away and did not send their children to her with boxes of color and tedious brushes and pictures cut from the ladies' magazines. The front door closed upon the last one and remained closed for good. When the town got free postal delivery Miss Emily alone refused to let them fasten the metal numbers above her door and attach a mailbox to it. She would not listen to them.

Daily, monthly, yearly we watched the Negro grow grayer and more stooped, going in and out with the market basket. Each December we sent her a tax notice, which would be returned by the post office a week later, unclaimed. Now and then we would see her in one of the downstairs windows—she had evidently shut up the top floor of the house—like the carven torso of an idol in a niche, looking or not looking at us, we could never tell which. Thus she passed from generation to generation—dear, inescapable, impervious, tranquil, and perverse.

And so she died. Fell ill in the house filled with dust and shadows, with only a doddering Negro man to wait on her. We did not even know she was sick; we had long since given up trying to get any information from the Negro. He talked to no one, probably not even to her, for his voice had grown harsh and rusty, as if from disuse.

She died in one of the downstairs rooms, in a heavy walnut bed with a curtain, her gray head propped on a pillow yellow and moldy with age and lack of sunlight.

V

The Negro met the first of the ladies at the front door and let them in, with their hushed, sibilant voices and their quick, curious glances, and then he disappeared. He walked right through the house and out the back and was not seen again.

The two female cousins came at once. They held the funeral on the second day, with the town coming to look at Miss Emily beneath a mass of bought flowers, with the crayon face of her father musing profoundly above the bier and the ladies sibilant and macabre; and the very old men—some in their brushed Confederate uniforms—on the porch and the lawn, talking of Miss Emily as if she had been a contemporary of theirs, believing that they had danced with her and courted her perhaps, confusing time with its mathematical progression, as the old do, to whom all the past is not a diminishing road, but, instead, a huge meadow which no winter ever quite touches, divided from them now by the narrow bottleneck of the most recent decade of years.

Already we knew that there was one room in that region above stairs which no one had seen in forty years, and which would have to be forced. They waited until Miss Emily was decently in the ground before they opened it.

The violence of breaking down the door seemed to fill this room with pervading dust. A thin, acrid pall as of the tomb seemed to lie everywhere upon this room decked and furnished as for a bridal: upon the valance curtains of faded rose color, upon the rose-shaded lights, upon the dressing table, upon the delicate array of crystal and the man's toilet things backed with tarnished silver, silver so tarnished that the monogram was obscured. Among them lay a collar and tie, as if they had just been removed, which, lifted, left upon the surface a pale crescent in the dust. Upon a chair hung the suit, carefully folded; beneath it the two mute shoes and the discarded socks.

The man himself lay in the bed.

For a long while we just stood there, looking down at the profound and fleshless grin. The body had apparently once lain in the attitude of an embrace, but now the long sleep that outlasts love, that conquers even the grimace of love, had cuckolded him. What was left of him, rotted beneath what was left of the nightshirt, had become inextricable from the bed in which he lay; and upon him and upon the pillow beside him lay that even coating of the patient and biding dust.

Then we noticed that in the second pillow was the indentation of a head. One of us lifted something from it, and leaning forward, that faint and invisible dust dry and acrid in the nostrils, we saw a long strand of iron-gray hair.

THE METAMORPHOSIS

Franz Kafka

Franz Kafka was born in Prague in 1883 and died in 1924. His three novels, all published posthumously, are The Trial, The Castle, *and* Amerika. *His best-known stories are "The Metamorphosis" (1937), "The Penal Colony," "A Hunger Artist," and "The Hunter Gracchus." A surrealist and existentialist, Kafka could recreate the emotion-laden atmosphere of the dream with amazing skill. The contrast between his stories and those of Poe reveals how far modern man has come in his exploration of the nightmare world below the threshold of consciousness. Modern man—lost in a maze of bureaucracy, searching for an elusive God, torn by inner guilt and inferiority complexes—is the theme of Kafka's writing. More than any other writer of his time, he is the voice of "the age of anxiety."*

Part 1

As Gregor Samsa awoke one morning from a troubled dream, he found himself changed in his bed to some monstrous kind of vermin.

He lay on his back, which was as hard as armour-plate, and, raising his head a little, he could see the arch of his great brown belly, divided by bowed corrugations. The bed-cover was slipping helplessly off the summit of the curve, and Gregor's legs, pitiably thin compared with their former size, fluttered helplessly before his eyes.

"What has happened?" he thought. It was no dream. His room, a real man's room—though rather small—lay quiet within its four familiar walls. Over the table, where a collection of cloth samples was scattered—Samsa was a commercial traveller—hung the picture that he had recently cut from an illustrated paper and had put in a pretty gilded frame. This picture showed a lady sitting very upright, with a small fur hat, and a fur boa; she offered to the gaze a heavy muff, into which her arm was thrust up to the elbow.

Gregor looked towards the window; rain could be heard falling on the panes; the foggy weather made him sad. "How would it be if I go to sleep again for a while, and forget all this stupidity?" he thought; but it was absolutely impossible, for he was used to sleeping on the right side, and in his present plight, he could not get into that position. However hard he tried to throw himself violently on his side, he always turned over on his back, with a little swinging movement. He tried a hundred times, closing his eyes so that he should not see the trembling of his legs, and he did not give up until he felt in his side a slight but deep pain, never before experienced.

"God!" he thought. "What a job I've chosen. Travelling day in, day out. A much more worrying occupation than working in the office! And apart from business itself, this plague of travelling; the anxieties of changing trains, the irregular, inferior meals, the ever-changing faces, never to be seen again, people with whom one has no chance to be friendly. To hell with it all!" He felt a little itch above his stomach and wriggled nearer to the bedpost, dragging himself slowly on his back, so that he might more easily raise his head, and he saw, just where he was itching, a few little white points, whose purpose he could not guess at; he tried to scratch the place with one of his feet, but he had to draw it back quickly, for the contact made him shudder coldly.

He returned to his former position. He said to himself: "Nothing is more degrading than to have to rise always so early. A man must have his sleep. Other travellers can live like harem women. When I return to the hotel in the morning to enter my orders, I find these gentlemen still at breakfast. I'd like to see what my boss would say if I tried it; I should be sacked immediately. Who knows if that wouldn't be a good thing after all! If I didn't hold back because of my parents, I would have given notice long ago; I would have gone to the boss, and I wouldn't have minced matters. He would have fallen from his desk. That's a funny thing; to sit on a desk so as to speak to one's employees from such a height especially when one is hard of hearing and people must come close! Still, all hope is not lost; once I have got together the money my parents owe him—that will be in about five or six years—I shall certainly do it. Then I'll take the big step! Meanwhile, I must get up, for my train goes at five."

He looked at the alarm-clock which ticked on the chest. "My God!" he thought; it was half-past six; quarter-to-seven was not far off. Hadn't the alarm gone? From the bed it could be seen that the little hand was set at four, right enough; the alarm had sounded. But had he been able to sleep calmly through that furniture-shattering din? Calmly, no, his sleep had not been calm, but he had only slept the sounder for that. What should he do now?

The next train went at seven; to catch it he must hurry madly, and his collection of samples was not packed; besides he himself did not feel at all rested nor inclined to move. And even if he did catch the train his employer's anger was inevitable, since the firm's errand-boy would have been waiting at the five o'clock train, and would have notified the firm of his lapse. He was just a toady to his boss, a stupid and servile boy. Supposing Gregor pretended to be ill? But that would be very tiresome, and suspicious too, for during the four years that he had been with the firm he had never had the slightest illness. The manager would come with the Health Insurance doctor, he would reproach his parents for their son's idleness, and would cut short any objections by giving the doctor's arguments that no people are sick, only idle. And would he be so far wrong, in such a case? Gregor felt in very good fettle, apart from his unnecessary need for more sleep after such a long night; he even had an unusually keen appetite.

Just as he was quickly turning these thoughts over in his mind without being able to decide to leave the bed—while the alarm-clock struck a quarter to seven—he heard a cautious knock on his door, close by his bed's head. "Gregor," someone called—it was his mother—"It is a quarter to seven. Didn't you want to catch the train?" What a soft voice! Gregor trembled as he heard his own voice reply. It was unmistakably his former voice, but with it could be heard, as if from below, a painful whining, which only allowed the words their real shape for a moment, immediately to confuse their sound so that one wondered if one had really heard aright. Gregor would have liked to answer fully and to give an explanation, but in these circumstances, he contented himself by saying, "Yes, yes, thank you mother. I am just getting up." No doubt the door prevented her from judging the change in Gregor's voice, for the explanation reassured his mother, who went away, shuffling in her slippers. But by this little dialogue, the other members of the family had become aware that, contrary to custom, Gregor was still in the house, and his father started to knock on one of the side-doors; softly, but with his fists. "Gregor, Gregor," he cried. "What is the matter?" And after a moment, in a warning tone, "Gregor! Gregor!" At the other side-door, the young man's sister softly called, "Gregor, aren't you well? Do you need anything?" "I am getting ready," said Gregor, answering either side and forcing himself to pronounce carefully and to separate each word with a long pause, to keep a natural voice. His father went back to breakfast, but the sister still whispered, "Gregor, open the door, I beg you." But Gregor had no intention of answering this request; on the contrary, he complimented himself on having learned the habit of always locking his door, as if in a hotel.

He would get up quietly, without being bothered by anyone, he would dress, and above all, he would have breakfast; then would come the time to reflect, for he felt it was not in bed that a reasonable solution could be found. He recalled how often an unusual position adopted in bed had resulted in slight pains which proved imaginary as soon as he arose, and Gregor was curious to see his present hallucination gradually dissolve. As for the change in his voice, his private opinion was that it was the prelude to some serious quinsy, the occupational malady of travellers.

He had no difficulty in turning back the coverlet; he needed only to blow himself up a little and it fell of its own accord. But beyond that, he was impeded by his tremendous girth. To get up, he needed arms and hands, but he had only numerous little legs in perpetual vibration, over which he had no control. Before he could bend one, he had first to stretch it out, and when at last he performed the desired movement, all the others worked uncontrollably, in intensely painful agitation. "I must not stay uselessly in bed," said Gregor to himself.

To get his body out of bed, he first tried with the hind-part. But unfortunately this hind-part which he had not yet seen, and of which he could form no very precise idea, proved to be very difficult to move, it went so slowly; he summoned all his strength to throw himself forward, but ill-calculating his course, he hurled himself violently against one of the bedposts, and the searing pain he felt showed that the lower part of his body was without doubt the most sensitive.

He then tried to start with the fore-part of his body, and cautiously turned his head towards the side of the bed. In this he succeeded quite easily, and the rest of his body, despite its weight and size, followed the direction of his head. But when his head had left the bed and was hanging in mid-air, he was afraid to continue any further; if he were to fall in this position, it would be a miracle if he did not crack his head; and this was no moment to lose his senses; better to stay in bed.

But when, panting after his efforts, he found himself again stretched out just as before, when he saw his little legs struggling together more wildly than ever, despairing of finding any means of bringing peace and order into this chaotic procedure, he once again realised that he absolutely could not stay in bed and that it was perfectly reasonable to sacrifice everything to the slightest chance of getting out. At the same time he did not forget that cool and wise reflection would be far better than desperate resolutions. Ordinarily, at such moments, he turned his eyes to the window to gain encouragement and hope. But this day, the fog prevented him from seeing the other side of the street; it gave him neither confidence nor strength. "Seven o'clock already," he said as he listened once more to the sound of the alarm-clock. "Seven o'clock already, and the fog has got no thinner!" He lay back again for a moment, breathing weakly, as though, in the complete silence, he could calmly await the return to his normal self.

Then he said, "Before a quarter past, it is absolutely essential for me to be up. In any case, someone will be sent from the office to ask for me before then, for the place opens at seven." And he began to rock on his back in order to get his whole body out of bed in one movement. In this manner, he would be able to protect his head by raising it sharply as he fell. His back seemed to be hard, nothing would be risked by falling on it to the floor, his only fear was that the noise of his fall, which must surely resound through the whole house, might arouse terror, or at the very least, uneasiness. However, that would have to be risked.

When Gregor had half his body out of bed—the new method seemed more like a game than a task, he had only to swing himself on his back—he began to think how easily he could have got up if only he had had a little assistance. Two strong people—he thought of his father and the servant-girl—would have been quite enough; they would only have needed to pass their arms under his round back, raise it from the bed, quickly lean forward with their burden, and then wait carefully till he had completed the operation of settling himself on the ground, where he hoped that his feet would at last find a way of working together. But, even if the doors had not been closed, would it have been wise for him to call for help? At this idea, despite his misery, he could not repress a smile.

Now he had so far progressed that, by accentuating sharply his swinging movement, he felt he was nearly losing his balance; he would have to take a serious decision, for in five minutes it would be a quarter to eight—but suddenly there was a knock at the front door. "Someone from the office," he said to himself and he felt his blood run cold, while his little legs quickened their saraband. For a moment all was quiet. "They're not going to the door," thought Gregor in an access of absurd hope. But of course the maid went to the door with a firm tread, and opened it. Gregor only needed to hear the caller's first words of greeting, to know immediately who it was—the manager himself. Why particularly was Gregor condemned to work for a firm where the worst was suspected at the slightest inadvertence of the employees? Were the employees, without exception, all scoundrels? Was there among their number not one devoted, faithful servant, who, if it did so happen that by chance he missed a few hours work one morning, might have found himself so numbed with remorse that he just could not leave his bed? Would it not have been enough to send some apprentice to put things right—if, in any case, it was necessary to make enquiries at all—instead of the manager himself having to come, in order to let the whole innocent family know that the clearing-up of so suspicious an affair could only be entrusted to a person of his importance? These thoughts so irritated Gregor that he swung himself with all his might out of bed. This made a loud thud, but not the terrible crash that he had feared. The carpet somewhat softened the blow, and Gregor's back was more elastic than he had thought, and so his act was not accompanied by any din. Only his head had been slightly hurt. Gregor had not raised it enough, and it had been knocked in the fall. He turned over a little to rub it on the carpet, in pain and anger.

"Something fell in there just then," cried the manager in the room on the left. Gregor tried to imagine his employer's face if such a mishap had occurred to him; for such a thing was possible, he had to admit. But, as if in brutal reply, the manager began pacing up and down in the next room, making his patent-leather boots creak. And in the other room on the right, Gregor's sister whispered to warn her brother, "Gregor, the manager is here." "I know," said Gregor to himself, but he dared not raise his voice enough for his sister to hear.

"Gregor," said his father in the room on the left, "the manager has come to find out why you didn't catch the early train. We don't know what to say. He wants to speak to you personally. So please open the door. I'm sure he will be kind enough, to excuse the untidiness of your room." "Good morning, good morning, Mr. Samsa," interrupted the manager, cordial and brisk. "He is not well," said his mother to the manager, while his father went on shouting through the door. "Believe me, he is not well, sir. How else could Gregor have missed the train? The boy thinks of nothing but his work! It makes me upset to see how he never goes out after supper; do you know, he's just spent a whole week here and been at home every evening! He sits down with us at the table and stays there quietly reading the paper or studying his time-tables. His greatest indulgence is to do a little fretwork. Just lately he made a small picture-frame. It was finished in two or three evenings, and you'd be surprised how pretty it is; it is hanging up in his room. As soon as Gregor opens his door, you will be able to see it. I am so glad you came, sir, because without you we would never have got Gregor to open his door, he is so obstinate; and surely he must be ill, even though he denied it this morning." "I am just coming," said Gregor slowly and carefully, but he continued to lie still, so as not to miss a word of the conversation. "I can offer no other suggestion," declared the manager. "Let us only hope it is nothing serious. However, we business men must often—fortunately or not, as you will—get on with our jobs, and ignore our little indispositions."

"Well, can the manager come in now?" asked his father impatiently, rapping again on the door. "No," said Gregor. In the room on the left there was a painful silence; in that on the right the sister began to sob.

Why did she not go to the others? Possibly she had only just got out of bed and was not yet dressed. And why did she weep? Because he did not get up to let the manager in, because he risked losing his position, and because the boss would once more worry his parents about their old debts? These were misplaced troubles! Gregor was still there, and had not the slightest intention of letting his family down. At this very moment he was stretched out on the carpet, and nobody seeing him in this state could seriously have demanded that he should let the manager enter his room. But it was not on account of this slight impoliteness—for which in normal times he could easily have made his excuses later—that Gregor would be dismissed. And he thought it would be more reasonable just now to leave him alone rather than to upset him with tears and speeches. But it was just the uncertainty which was making the others uneasy and which excused their behaviour.

"Herr Samsa," now cried the manager, raising his voice, "What is the matter? You barricade yourself in your room, you don't answer yes or no, you needlessly upset your parents and you neglect your professional duties in an unheard-of manner. I am speaking in the name of your employer and of your parents, and I beg you seriously to give us a satisfactory explanation immediately. I am astonished, astonished. I took you for a quiet, reasonable young man, and here you suddenly give yourself airs, behaving in an absolutely fantastic manner! The head of the firm, speaking to me this morning in your absence, suggested an explanation which I rejected; he mentioned the samples which were entrusted to you a while ago; I gave him my word of honour that this had nothing to do with the affair, but now that I have been witness to your obstinacy, I can assure you, Herr Samsa, that it deprives me of any wish to defend you. Your job is by no means safe! I had intended to tell you this in private, but since you oblige me to waste my time here for nothing, I see no reason for keeping quiet before your parents. I'd have you know that lately your work has been far from satisfactory; we realise, of course, that the time of the year is not propitious for big business, but you must understand, Herr

Samsa, that a period with no business at all should not and can not be tolerated!"

Gregor was beside himself; in his anxiety he forgot everything else. "But sir," he cried, "I will open the door immediately. I will open it. I felt a little ill, a slight giddiness prevented me from getting up. I am still in bed. But already I feel better. I am just getting up. Only a moment's patience, I am not quite so well as I thought. But I am all right, really. How can it be that illness should take one so quickly? Only yesterday I felt quite well, my parents could tell you; and then last evening I had a slight symptom. They must have noticed it. Why ever didn't I let them know at the office! But then one always thinks one will be able to get rid of an illness without staying at home. Please, sir, spare my parents. The complaints you made just now are really without any foundation. No one has even suggested them before. Perhaps you have not seen the last orders which I sent in. I will leave on the eight o'clock train; these few moments of rest have done me a great deal of good. Please don't stay sir, I shall be at the office immediately; and please inform the director of what has happened, and put in a good word for me."

And while Gregor hastily cried these words, scarcely realising what he said, he had, with an ease due to his previous exertions, approached the chest of drawers, against which he now tried to raise himself. He wanted to open the door, he wanted to be seen, and to speak with the manager. He was curious to know what impression he would make on these people who were so imperiously demanding his presence. If he frightened them, that would be reassuring, for he would stop being cross-questioned, and would be left in peace. If they took everything quietly, then he, too, need not be alarmed. And if he hurried he might still catch the eight o'clock train. The chest was polished, and Gregor slipped on it several times, but by a supreme effort he managed to get upright. He paid no attention to the pains in his stomach, though they were hurting him. He let himself drop forward onto the top of a near-by chair and clung there with his little legs. Then, finding himself master of his body, he stayed very quiet in order to listen to what the manager had to say.

"Did you understand a word of what he said?" the manager asked the parents, "Is he trying to make fools of us?" "Good heavens," cried the mother, already in tears. "Perhaps he is seriously ill, and here we are torturing him all this while! Grete! Grete!" she called. "Mother!" cried the daughter from the other side. They were separated by Gregor's room. "Fetch a doctor immediately. Gregor is ill. A doctor, quickly! Did you hear him speak?" "It was an animal's voice," said the manager; after the cries of the women, his voice seemed curiously gentle. "Anna, Anna!" shouted the father through the hall, into the kitchen, clapping his hands. "Get a locksmith quick!" and already the two young girls—how could his sister have dressed so soon?—ran along the corridor with rustling skirts, and opened the front door. No one heard the door close; no doubt it had been left open as is the custom in houses to which a great misfortune has come.

However, Gregor had become calmer. Doubtless they had not understood his words, though they had seemed clear enough to him, clearer, indeed, than the first time; perhaps his ears were becoming more accustomed. But at least they were obliged to realise that his case was not normal, and they were ready now to help him. The assurance and resourcefulness with which the first steps had been taken comforted him considerably. He felt himself reintegrated into human society once again, and without differentiating between them, he hoped for great and surprising things from the locksmith and the doctor. To clear his throat for the decisive conversation which he would have to hold soon, he coughed a little, but as quietly as possible, for he feared that even his cough might not sound human. Meanwhile, in the next room, it had become quiet. Perhaps his parents were sitting at table in a secret conference with the manager, perhaps everyone was leaning against the door, listening.

Gregor made his way slowly towards it with the chair; then he abandoned the chair and flung himself at the door, holding himself erect against the woodwork—for the bottom of his feet secreted a sticky substance—and he rested a moment from his efforts. After this, he tried to turn the key in the lock with his mouth. Unfortunately it seemed he had no proper teeth. How could he take hold of the key? In compensation, he possessed instead a pair of very strong mandibles, and he succeeded in seizing the key in the lock, regardless of the pain which this caused him; a brownish liquid flowed out of his mouth, spread over the lock and dropped to the floor. "Listen!" said the manager in the next room, "He is just turning the key." This was valuable encouragement for Gregor; he would have liked his father, his mother, everybody to start calling to him, "Courage, Gregor, go on, push hard!" And with the idea that everyone was following his efforts with passionate attention, he clutched the key with all the power of his jaws, until he was nearly unconscious. Following the progress of the turning key, he twisted himself around the lock, hanging on by his mouth, and, clinging to the key, pressed it down again, whenever it slipped, with all the weight of his body. The clear click of the lock as it snapped back awoke Gregor from his momentary coma. "I have dispensed with the locksmith," he thought, and sighed and leaned his head against the handle to open one panel of the double doors completely.

This method, the only possible one, prevented the others from seeing him for some time, even with the door open. Still erect, he had to grope his way round the door with great caution in order not to spoil his entry by falling flat on his back; so he was concentrating towards this end, with all his attention absorbed by the manœuvre, when he heard the manager utter a sonorous "Oh!" such as the roaring of the wind produces, and saw him—he was just by the door—press his hand over his open mouth and slowly stagger back as if some invisible and intensely powerful force was driving him from the spot. His mother—who, despite the presence of the manager, was standing by with her hair in curlers, still disordered by sleep—began to look at the father, clasping her hands, then she made two steps towards Gregor, and fell backwards into the family circle in the midst of a confusion of skirts which spread around her, while her face, falling on her breast, was concealed from sight. The father clenched his fists with a menacing air, as if to beat Gregor back into his room; then he looked around the dining room in perplexity, covered his eyes with his hand, and wept with great sobs which shook his powerful chest.

Gregor did not enter the room, he stood against the closed half of the double doors, allowing only a part of his body to be seen, while above, his head was turned to one side to see what would happen. Meanwhile it had grown much lighter; on either side of the street a part of the long, dark building opposite, could clearly be seen—it was a hospital, with regular windows startlingly pitting its facade; it was still raining, but in great separate drops which fell one by one to the ground. The breakfast crockery was spread all over the table, for breakfast was the most important meal of the day for Gregor's father; he would prolong it for hours while he read various newspapers. On the wall hung a photograph of Gregor in lieutenant's uniform, taken while he was on military service; he was smiling, his hand lay on the hilt of his sword. By his expression, he seemed happy to be alive; by his gesture, he appeared to command respect for his rank. The living-room door was ajar, and as the front door was also open, the balcony and the first steps of the stairway could just be seen.

"Now," said Gregor, and he realised that he was the only one to have kept calm, "Now I will get dressed, collect together my samples, and go. Will you, will you let me go? Surely you can now see, sir, that I am not obstinate, that I do mean to work; commercial travelling is tiresome, I admit, but without it I cannot live. Where are you going, sir? To the office? Yes? Will you give them a faithful account of what has happened? After all, anyone might find for a moment that they were incapable of resuming their work, but that's just a good opportunity to review the work they have been doing, and to bear in mind that, once the obstacle is removed, they will be able to return with twice the heart. I owe so much to the director, as you know very well. I have my parents and my sister to consider. I am in an awkward position, but I shall return to work. Only please do not make things more difficult for me, they are hard enough as it is. Take my part at the office. I know only too well they don't like travellers. They think we earn our money too easily, that we lead too grand a life. I realise that the present situation doesn't encourage the removal of this prejudice; but you sir, the manager, can judge the circumstances better than the rest of the staff, better than the director himself—though this is between ourselves—for in his executive capacity he is often easily misled by an employee's prejudice. You know quite well that the traveller, who is hardly ever in the office the whole year round, is often the victim of scandal, of a chance undeserved complaint against which he is powerless to defend himself, for he does not even know that he is being accused, he only learns of it as he returns, exhausted, at the end of his trip, when the sad consequences of an affair whose circumstances he can no longer recall, painfully confront him. Please sir, don't leave me without a word to show that you think all this at least a little reasonable."

But, at Gregor's first words, the manager had turned away and only glanced back, with snarling lips, over his trembling shoulder. And, during Gregor's speech, he had not stood still for a moment, instead, he had retreated furtively, step by step, towards the door—always keeping Gregor in sight—as if some secret law forbade him to leave the room. He had already reached the hall, and as he took the very last step out of the living-room, one would have thought the floor was burning his shoes, so sharply did he spring. Then he stretched his hand towards the balustrade, as if some unearthly deliverance awaited him at the foot of the stairs.

Gregor realised that on no account must he be allowed to leave in this condition, if he was to keep his job. Unfortunately his parents did not realise the position very clearly; they had for so long held the idea that Gregor was settled in the firm for life and were so taken up with their present troubles, that they had little thought for such a contingency. But Gregor had more foresight. The manager must be stopped, calmed, convinced, and finally won over. The future of Gregor, and of his family, depended on it! If only his sister were there! She had understood, she had actually begun to weep while Gregor still lay quietly on his back. And the manager, who liked women, would have listened to her; he would have let himself be guided by her; she would have closed the door, and would have proved to him, in the hall, how unreasonable his terror was. But she was not there; Gregor himself must manage this affair. And without even considering whether he would ever be able to return to work, nor whether his speech had been understood, he let go of the doorpost to glide through the opening and overtake the manager (who was clutching the balustrade with both hands in a ridiculous manner), vainly sought for a foothold, and uttering a cry, he fell, with his frail little legs crumpled beneath him.

Suddenly, for the first time in the whole morning, he experienced a feeling of physical well-being; his feet were on firm ground, he noticed with joy that his legs obeyed him wonderfully, and were even eager to carry him wherever he might wish. But while he hesitated on the spot, under the nervous influence of his need for haste, not far from his mother, he saw her suddenly jump, fainting though she seemed to be, and throwing her arms about, with outspread fingers, and crying, "Help, for God's sake, help!" she turned her head, the better to see Gregor, then in flagrant contradiction she began to retreat madly, having forgotten that behind her stood the table, still laden with breakfast things. She staggered against it, and sat down suddenly like one distraught, regardless of the fact that at her elbow, the overturned coffeepot was making a pool of coffee on the carpet.

"Mother, mother," whispered Gregor, looking up at her. The manager had quite gone out of his mind; seeing the coffee spilling, Gregor could not prevent himself from snapping his jaws several times in the air, as if he were eating. Thereupon, his mother again began to shriek, quickly jumped up from the table and fell into the arms of the father, who had rushed up behind her. But Gregor had no time to bother about them; the manager was already on the stairs; with his chin on the balustrade, he was looking back for the last time. Gregor summoned all his courage to try to bring him back; the manager must have suspected something of the sort, for he leaped several steps at a single bound, and disappeared with a cry of "Huh!" which resounded in the hollow of the stair-well. This flight had the unfortunate effect of causing Gregor's father—who till now had remained master of himself—to lose his head completely; instead of running after the manager, or at least not interfering with Gregor in his pursuit, he seized in his right hand the manager's walking-stick, which had been left behind on a chair with his overcoat and hat, took up in his left a newspaper from the table, and began stamping his feet and brandishing the newspaper and the cane to drive Gregor back into his room. Gregor's prayers were unavailing, were not even understood; he had turned to his father a supplicating head, but meek though he showed himself, his father merely stamped all the louder. In the dining room, despite the cold, the mother had opened the window wide and was leaning out as far as possible, pressing her face in her hands. A great rush of air swept the space between the room and the stairway, the curtains billowed, the papers rustled, and a few sheets flew over the carpet. But the father pursued Gregor pitilessly, whistling and whooping like a savage, and Gregor, who was not used to walking backwards, progressed but slowly.

Had he been able to turn round, he could have reached his room quickly, but he feared to make his father impatient by the slowness of his turning, and feared also that at any moment he might receive a mortal blow on his head or on his back, from this menacing stick. Soon Gregor had no choice; for he realised with terror that when he was going backwards, he was not master of his direction, and still fearfully watching the attitude of his father out of the corner of his eye, he began his turning movement as quickly as possible, which was really only very slowly. Perhaps his father realised his good intention, for instead of hindering this move, he guided him from a little distance away, helping Gregor with the tip of the stick. If only he had left off that insupportable whistling! Gregor was completely losing his head. He had nearly completed his turn, when, bewildered by the din, he mistook his direction and began to go back to his former position. When at last to his great joy he found himself facing the half-opened double doors he discovered that his body was too big to pass through without hurt. Naturally it never occurred to his father, in his present state, to open the other half of the double doors, in order to allow Gregor to pass. He was dominated by the one fixed idea, that Gregor should be made to return to his room as quickly as possible. He would never have entertained the long-winded performance which Gregor needed to rear up and pass inside. Gregor heard him storming behind him, no doubt to urge him through as though there were no obstacle in his path; the hubbub no longer sounded like the voice of one single father; now was no time to play, and Gregor—come what may—hurled himself into the doorway. There he lay jammed in a slanting position, his body raised up on one side and his flank crushed by the door jamb, whose white paint was now covered with horrible brown stains. He was caught fast and could not free himself unaided; on one side his little legs fluttered in the air, on the other they were painfully pressed under his body; then his father gave him a tremendous blow from behind with the stick. Despite the pain, this was almost a relief; he was lifted bodily into the middle of the room and fell bleeding thickly. The door was slammed by a thrust of the stick, and then at last all was still.

THE WALL

Jean-Paul Sartre

Jean-Paul Sartre, born in 1905, is the chief living exponent of the philosophical system known as "existentialism." A prisoner in Germany during World War II, he escaped and became active in the resistance movement. His plays have been successfully presented in both Europe and America, and recently two of his novels, The Age of Reason *and* The Reprieve, *have been translated into English and published in America. His finest short story is generally agreed to be "The Wall," a story whose stark, probing, unsentimental explicitness illustrates with tremendous impact certain of the basic tenets of existentialism.*

They pushed us into a big white room and I began to blink because the light hurt my eyes. Then I saw a table and four men behind the table, civilians, looking over the papers. They had bunched another group of prisoners in the back and we had to cross the whole room to join them. There were several I knew and some others who must have been foreigners. The two in front of me were blond with round skulls; they looked alike. I supposed they were French. The smaller one kept hitching up his pants; nerves.

It lasted about three hours; I was dizzy and my head was empty; but the room was well heated and I found that pleasant enough: for the past 24 hours we hadn't stopped shivering. The guards brought the prisoners up to the table, one after the other. The four men asked each one his name and occupation. Most of the time they didn't go any further—or they would simply ask a question here and there: "Did you have anything to do with the sabotage of munitions?" Or "Where were you the morning of the 9th and what were you doing?" They didn't listen to the answers or at least didn't seem to. They were quiet for a moment and then looking straight in front of them began to write. They asked Tom if it were true he was in the International Brigade; Tom couldn't tell them otherwise because of the papers they found in his coat. They didn't ask Juan anything but they wrote for a long time after he told them his name.

"My brother José is the anarchist," Juan said, "you know he isn't here any more. I don't belong to any party, I never had anything to do with politics."

They didn't answer. Juan went on, "I haven't done anything. I don't want to pay for somebody else."

His lips trembled. A guard shut him up and took him away. It was my turn.

"Your name is Pablo Ibbieta?"

"Yes."

The man looked at the papers and asked me, "Where's Ramon Gris?"

"I don't know."

"You hid him in your house from the 6th to the 19th."

"No."

They wrote for a minute and then the guards took me out. In the corridor Tom and Juan were waiting between two guards. We started walking. Tom asked one of the guards, "So?"

"So what?" the guard said.

"Was that the cross-examination or the sentence?"

"Sentence," the guard said.

"What are they going to do with us?"

The guard answered dryly, "Sentence will be read in your cell."

As a matter of fact, our cell was one of the hospital cellars. It was terrifically cold there because of these drafts. We shivered all night and it wasn't much better during the day. I had spent the previous five days in a cell in a monastery, a sort of hole in the wall that must have dated from the middle ages: since there were a lot of prisoners and not much room, they locked us up anywhere. I didn't miss my cell; I hadn't suffered too much from the cold but I was alone; after a long time it gets irritating. In the cellar I had company.

Juan hardly ever spoke: he was afraid and he was too young to have anything to say. But Tom was a good talker and he knew Spanish well.

There was a bench in the cellar and four mats. When they took us back we sat and waited in silence. After a long moment, Tom said, "We're screwed."

"I think so too," I said, "but I don't think they'll do anything to the kid."

"They don't have a thing against him," said Tom. "He's the brother of a militiaman and that's all."

I looked at Juan: he didn't seem to hear. Tom went on, "You know what they do in Saragossa? They lay the men down on the road and run over them with trucks. A Moroccan deserter told us that. They said it was to save ammunition."

"It doesn't save gas," I said.

I was annoyed at Tom: he shouldn't have said that.

"Then there's officers walking along the road," he went on, "supervising it all. They stick their hands in their pockets and smoke cigarettes. You think they finish off the guys? Hell no. They let them scream. Sometimes for an hour. The Moroccan said he damned near puked the first time."

"I don't believe they'll do that here," I said. "Unless they're really short on ammunition."

Day was coming in through four airholes and a round opening, they had made in the ceiling on the left, and you could see the sky through it. Through this hole, usually closed by a trap, they unloaded coal into the cellar. Just below the hole there was a big pile of coal dust; it had been used to heat the hospital but since the beginning of the war the patients were evacuated and the coal stayed there, unused; sometimes it even got rained on because they had forgotten to close the trap.

Tom began to shiver. "Good Jesus Christ I'm cold," he said. "Here it goes again."

He got up and began to do exercises. At each movement his shirt opened on his chest, white and hairy. He lay on his back, raised his legs in the air and bicycled. I saw his great rump trembling. Tom was husky but he had too much fat. I thought how rifle bullets or the sharp points of bayonets would soon be sunk into this mass of tender flesh as in a lump of butter. It wouldn't have made me feel like that if he'd been thin.

I wasn't exactly cold, but I couldn't feel my arms and shoulders any more. Sometimes I had the impression I was missing something and began to look around for my coat and then suddenly remembered they hadn't given me a coat. It was rather uncomfortable. They took our clothes and gave them to their soldiers leaving us only our shirts—and those canvas pants that hospital patients wear in the middle of summer. After a while Tom got up and sat next to me, breathing heavily.

"Warmer?"

"Good Christ, no. But I'm out of wind."

Around eight o'clock in the evening a major came in with two *falangistas*. He had a sheet of paper in his hand. He asked the guard, "What are the names of those three?"

"Steinbock, Ibbieta and Mirbal," the guard said.

The major put on his eyeglasses and scanned the list: "Steinbock . . . Steinbock . . . Oh yes . . . You are sentenced to death. You will be shot tomorrow morning." He went on looking. "The other two as well."

"That's not possible," Juan said. "Not me."

The major looked at him amazed. "What's your name?"

"Juan Mirbal," he said.

"Well, your name is there," said the major. "You're sentenced."

"I didn't do anything," Juan said.

The major shrugged his shoulders and turned to Tom and me.

"You're Basque?"

"Nobody is Basque."

He looked annoyed. "They told me there were three Basques. I'm not going to waste my time running after them. Then naturally you don't want a priest?"

We didn't even answer.

He said, "A Belgian doctor is coming shortly. He is authorized to spend the night with you." He made a military salute and left.

"What did I tell you," Tom said. "We get it."

"Yes," I said, "it's a rotten deal for the kid."

I said that to be decent but I didn't like the kid. His face was too thin and fear and suffering had disfigured it, twisting all his features. Three days before he was a smart sort of kid, not too bad; but now he looked like an old fairy and I thought how he'd never be young again, even if they were to let him go. It wouldn't have been too hard to have a little pity for him but pity disgusts me, or rather it horrifies me. He hadn't said anything more but he had turned grey; his face and hands were both grey. He sat down again and looked at the ground with round eyes. Tom was good hearted, he wanted to take his arm, but the kid tore himself away violently and made a face.

"Let him alone," I said in a low voice, "you can see he's going to blubber."

Tom obeyed regretfully; he would have liked to comfort the kid, it would have passed his time and he wouldn't have been tempted to think about himself. But it annoyed me: I'd never thought about death because I never had any reason to, but now the reason was here and there was nothing to do but think about it.

Tom began to talk. "So you think you've knocked guys off, do you?" he asked me. I didn't answer. He began explaining to me that he had knocked off six since the beginning of August; he didn't realize the situation and I could tell he didn't *want* to realize it. I hadn't quite realized it myself, I wondered if it hurt much, I thought of bullets, I imagined their burning hail through my body. All that was beside the real question; but I was calm: we had all night to understand. After a while Tom stopped talking and I watched him out of the corner of my eye; I saw he too had turned grey and he looked rotten; I told myself "Now it starts." It was almost dark, a dim glow filtered through the airholes and the pile of coal and made a big stain beneath the spot of sky; I could already see a star through the hole in the ceiling: the night would be pure and icy.

The door opened and two guards came in, followed by a blond man in a tan uniform. He saluted us. "I am the doctor," he said. "I have authorization to help you in these trying hours."

He had an agreeable and distinguished voice. I said, "What do you want here?"

"I am at your disposal. I shall do all I can to make your last moments less difficult."

"What did you come here for? There are others, the hospital's full of them."

"I was sent here," he answered with a vague look. "Ah! Would you like to smoke?" he added hurriedly, "I have cigarettes and even cigars."

He offered us English cigarettes and *puros,* but we refused. I looked him in the eyes and he seemed irritated. I said to him, "You aren't here on an errand of mercy. Besides, I know you. I saw you with the fascists in the barracks yard the day I was arrested."

I was going to continue, but something surprising suddenly happened to me; the presence of this doctor no longer interested me. Generally when I'm on somebody I don't let go. But the desire to talk left me completely; I shrugged and turned my eyes away. A little later I raised my head; he was watching me curiously. The guards were sitting on a mat. Pedro, the tall thin one, was twiddling his thumbs, the other shook his head from time to time to keep from falling asleep.

"Do you want a light?" Pedro suddenly asked the doctor. The other nodded "Yes": I think he was about as smart as a log, but he surely wasn't bad. Looking in his cold blue eyes it seemed to me that his only sin was lack of imagination. Pedro went out and came back with an oil lamp which he set on the corner of the bench. It gave a bad light but it was better than nothing: they had left us in the dark the night before. For a long time I watched the circle of light the lamp made on the ceiling. I was fascinated. Then suddenly I woke up, the circle of light disappeared and I felt myself crushed under an enormous weight. It was not the thought of death, or fear; it was nameless. My cheeks burned and my head ached.

I shook myself and looked at my two friends. Tom had hidden his face in his hands. I could only see the fat white nape of his neck. Little Juan was the worst, his mouth was open and his nostrils trembled. The doctor went to him and put his hand on his shoulder to comfort him: but his eyes stayed cold. Then I saw the Belgian's hand drop stealthily along Juan's arm, down to the wrist. Juan paid no attention. The Belgian took his wrist between three fingers, distractedly, the same time drawing back a little and turning his back to me. But I leaned backward and saw him take a watch from his pocket and look at it for a moment, never letting go of the wrist. After a minute he let the hand fall inert and went and leaned his back against the wall, then, as if he suddenly remembered something very important which had to be jotted down on the spot, he took a notebook from his pocket and wrote a few lines. "Bastard," I thought angrily, "let him come and take my pulse. I'll shove my fist in his rotten face."

He didn't come but I felt him watching me. I raised my head and returned his look. Impersonally, he said to me, "Doesn't it seem cold to you here?" He looked cold, he was blue.

"I'm not cold," I told him.

He never took his hard eyes off me. Suddenly I understood and my hands went to my face: I was drenched in sweat. In this cellar, in the midst of winter, in the midst of drafts, I was sweating. I ran my hands through my hair, gummed together with perspiration; at the same time I saw my shirt was damp and sticking to my skin: I had been dripping for an hour and hadn't felt it. But that swine of a Belgian hadn't missed a thing; he had seen the drops rolling down my cheeks and thought: this is the manifestation of an almost pathological state of terror; and he had felt normal and proud of being alive because he was cold. I wanted to stand up and smash his face but no sooner had I made the slightest gesture than my rage and shame were wiped out; I fell back on the bench with indifference.

I satisfied myself by rubbing my neck with my handkerchief because now I felt the sweat dropping from my hair onto my neck and it was unpleasant. I soon gave up rubbing, it was useless; my handkerchief was already soaked and I was still sweating. My buttocks were sweating too and my damp trousers were glued to the bench.

Suddenly Juan spoke. "You're a doctor?"

"Yes," the Belgian said.

"Does it hurt . . . very long?"

"Huh? When . . . ? Oh, no," the Belgian said paternally. "Not at all. It's over quickly." He acted as though he were calming a cash customer.

"But I . . . they told me . . . sometimes they had to fire twice."

"Sometimes," the Belgian said, nodding. "It may happen that the first volley reaches no vital organs."

"Then they had to reload their rifles and aim all over again?" He thought for a moment and then added hoarsely, "That takes time!"

He had a terrible fear of suffering, it was all he thought about: it was his age. I never thought much about it and it wasn't fear of suffering that made me sweat.

I got up and walked to the pile of coal dust. Tom jumped up

and threw me a hateful look: I had annoyed him because my shoes squeaked. I wondered if my face looked as frightened as his: I saw he was sweating too. The sky was superb, no light filtered into the dark corner and I had only to raise my head to see the Big Dipper. But it wasn't like it had been: the night before I could see a great piece of sky from my monastery cell and each hour of the day brought me a different memory. Morning, when the sky was a hard, light blue, I thought of beaches on the Atlantic; at noon I saw the sun and I remembered a bar in Seville where I drank *manzanilla* and ate olives and anchovies; afternoons I was in the shade and I thought of the deep shadow which spreads over half a bull-ring leaving the other half shimmering in sunlight; it was really hard to see the whole world reflected in the sky like that. But now I could watch the sky as much as I pleased, it no longer evoked anything in me. I liked that better. I came back and sat near Tom. A long moment passed.

Tom began speaking in a low voice. He had to talk, without that he wouldn't have been able to recognize himself in his own mind. I thought he was talking to me but he wasn't looking at me. He was undoubtedly afraid to see me as I was, grey and sweating: we were alike and worse than mirrors of each other. He watched the Belgian, the living.

"Do you understand?" he said. "I don't understand."

I began to speak in a low voice too. I watched the Belgian. "Why? What's the matter?"

"Something is going to happen to us that I can't understand."

There was a strange smell about Tom. It seemed to me I was more sensitive than usual to odors. I grinned. "You'll understand in a while."

"It isn't clear," he said obstinately. "I want to be brave but first I have to know . . . Listen, they're going to take us into the courtyard. Good. They're going to stand up in front of us. How many?"

"I don't know. Five or eight. Not more."

"All right. There'll be eight. Someone'll holler 'aim!' and I'll see eight rifles looking at me. I'll think how I'd like to get inside the wall, I'll push against it with my back . . . with every ounce of strength I have, but the wall will stay, like in a nightmare. I can imagine all that. If you only knew how well I can imagine it."

"All right, all right!" I said, "I can imagine it too."

"It must hurt like hell. You know, they aim at the eyes and the mouth to disfigure you," he added mechanically. "I can feel the wounds already; I've had pains in my head and in my neck for the past hour. Not real pains. Worse. This is what I'm going to feel tomorrow morning. And then what?"

I well understood what he meant but I didn't want to act as if I did. I had pains too, pains in my body like a crowd of tiny scars. I couldn't get used to it. But I was like him, I attached no importance to it. "After," I said, "you'll be pushing up daisies."

He began to talk to himself: he never stopped watching the Belgian. The Belgian didn't seem to be listening. I knew what he had come to do; he wasn't interested in what we thought; he came to watch our bodies, bodies dying in agony while yet alive.

"It's like a nightmare," Tom was saying. "You want to think something, you always have the impression that it's all right, that you're going to understand and then it slips, it escapes you and fades away. I tell myself there will be nothing afterwards. But I don't understand what it means. Sometimes I almost can . . . and then it fades away and I start thinking about the pains again, bullets, explosions. I'm a materialist, I swear it to you; I'm not going crazy. But something's the matter. I see my corpse; that's not hard but *I'm* the one who sees it, with *my* eyes. I've got to think . . . think that I won't see anything any more and the world will go on for the others. We aren't made to think that, Pablo. Believe me: I've already stayed up a whole night waiting for something. But this isn't the same: this will creep up behind us, Pablo, and we won't be able to prepare for it."

"Shut up," I said. "Do you want me to call a priest?"

He didn't answer. I had already noticed he had the tendency to act like a prophet and call me Pablo, speaking in a toneless voice. I didn't like that: but it seems all the Irish are that way. I had the vague impression he smelled of urine. Fundamentally, I hadn't much sympathy for Tom and I didn't see why, under the pretext of dying together, I should have any more. It would have been different with some others. With Ramon Gris, for example. But I felt alone between Tom and Juan. I liked that better, anyhow: with Ramon I might have been more deeply moved. But I was terribly hard just then and I wanted to stay hard.

He kept on chewing his words, with something like distraction. He certainly talked to keep himself from thinking. He smelled of urine like an old prostate case. Naturally, I agreed with him, I could have said everything he said: it isn't *natural* to die. And since I was going to die, nothing seemed natural to me, not this pile of coal dust, or the bench, or Pedro's ugly face. Only it didn't please me to think the same things as Tom. And I knew that, all through the night, every five minutes, we would keep on thinking things at the same time. I looked at him sideways and for the first time he seemed strange to me: he wore death on his face. My pride was wounded: for the past 24 hours I had lived next to Tom, I had listened to him, I had spoken to him and I knew we had nothing in common. And now we looked as much alike as twin brothers, simply because we were going to die together. Tom took my hand without looking at me.

"Pablo, I wonder . . . I wonder if it's really true that everything ends."

I took my hand away and said, "Look between your feet, you pig."

There was a big puddle between his feet and drops fell from his pants-leg.

"What is it," he asked, frightened.

"You're pissing in your pants," I told him.

"It isn't true," he said furiously. "I'm not pissing. I don't feel anything."

The Belgian approached us. He asked with false solicitude, "Do you feel ill?"

Tom did not answer. The Belgian looked at the puddle and said nothing.

"I don't know what it is," Tom said ferociously. "But I'm not afraid. I swear I'm not afraid."

The Belgian did not answer. Tom got up and went to piss in a corner. He came back buttoning his fly, and sat down without a word. The Belgian was taking notes.

All three of us watched him because he was alive. He had the motions of a living human being, the cares of a living human being; he shivered in the cellar the way the living are supposed to shiver; he had an obedient, well-fed body. The rest of us hardly felt ours—not in the same way anyhow. I wanted to feel my pants between my legs but I didn't dare;

I watched the Belgian, balancing on his legs, master of his muscles, someone who could think about tomorrow. There we were, three bloodless shadows; we watched him and we sucked his life like vampires.

Finally he went over to little Juan. Did he want to feel his neck for some professional motive or was he obeying an impulse of charity? If he was acting by charity it was the only time during the whole night.

He caressed Juan's head and neck. The kid let himself be handled, his eyes never leaving him, then suddenly, he seized the hand and looked at it strangely. He held the Belgian's hand between his own two hands and there was nothing pleasant about them, two grey pincers gripping this fat and reddish hand. I suspected what was going to happen and Tom must have suspected it too: but the Belgian didn't see a thing, he smiled paternally. After a moment the kid brought the fat red hand to his mouth and tried to bite it. The Belgian pulled away quickly and stumbled back against the wall. For a second he looked at us with horror, he must have suddenly understood that we were not men like him. I began to laugh and one of the guards jumped up. The other was asleep, his wide open eyes were blank.

I felt relaxed and over-excited at the same time. I didn't want to think any more about what would happen at dawn, at death. It made no sense. I only found words or emptiness. But as soon as I tried to think of anything else I saw rifle barrels pointing at me. Perhaps I lived through my execution twenty times; once I even thought it was for good: I must have slept a minute. They were dragging me to the wall and I was struggling; I was asking for mercy. I woke up with a start and looked at the Belgian: I was afraid I might have cried out in my sleep. But he was stroking his moustache, he hadn't noticed anything. If I had wanted to, I think I could have slept a while; I had been awake for 48 hours. I was at the end of my rope. But I didn't want to lose two hours of life: they would come to wake me up at dawn, I would follow them, stupefied with sleep and I would have croaked without so much as an "Oof!"; I didn't want that, I didn't want to die like an animal, I wanted to understand. Then I was afraid of having nightmares. I got up, walked back and forth, and, to change my ideas, I began to think about my past life. A crowd of memories came back to me pell-mell. There were good and bad ones—or at least I called them that *before*. There were faces and incidents. I saw the face of a little *novillero* who was gored in Valencia during the *Feria,* the face of one of my uncles, the face of Ramon Gris. I remembered my whole life: how I was out of work for three months in 1926, how I almost starved to death. I remembered a night I spent on a bench in Granada: I hadn't eaten for three days. I was angry, I didn't want to die. That made me smile. How madly I ran after happiness, after women, after liberty. Why? I wanted to free Spain, I admired Pi y Margall, I joined the anarchist movement, I spoke in public meetings: I took everything as seriously as if I were immortal.

At that moment I felt that I had my whole life in front of me and I thought, "It's a damned lie." It was worth nothing because it was finished. I wondered how I'd been able to walk, to laugh with the girls: I wouldn't have moved so much as my little finger if I had only imagined I would die like this. My life was in front of me, shut, closed, like a bag and yet everything inside of it was unfinished. For an instant I tried to judge it. I wanted to tell myself, this is a beautiful life. But I couldn't pass judgment on it; it was only a sketch; I had spent my time counterfeiting eternity, I had understood nothing. I missed nothing: there were so many things I could have missed, the taste of *manzanilla* or the baths I took in summer in a little creek near Cadiz; but death had disenchanted everything.

The Belgian suddenly had a bright idea. "My friends," he told us, "I will undertake—if the military administration will allow it—to send a message for you, a souvenir to those who love you . . ."

Tom mumbled, "I don't have anybody."

I said nothing. Tom waited an instant then looked at me with curiosity. "You don't have anything to say to Concha?"

"No."

I hated this tender complicity: it was my own fault, I had talked about Concha the night before, I should have controlled myself. I was with her for a year. Last night I would have given an arm to see her again for five minutes. That was why I talked about her, it was stronger than I was. Now I had no more desire to see her, I had nothing more to say to her. I would not even have wanted to hold her in my arms: my body filled me with horror because it was grey and sweating—and I wasn't sure that her body didn't fill me with horror. Concha would cry when she found out I was dead, she would have no taste for life for months afterward. But I was still the one who was going to die. I thought of her soft, beautiful eyes. When she looked at me something passed from her to me. But I knew it was over: if she looked at me *now* the look would stay in her eyes, it wouldn't reach me. I was alone.

Tom was alone too but not in the same way. Sitting cross-legged, he had begun to stare at the bench with a sort of smile, he looked amazed. He put out his hand and touched the wood cautiously as if he were afraid of breaking something, then drew back his hand quickly and shuddered. If I had been Tom I wouldn't have amused myself by touching the bench; this was some more Irish nonsense, but I too found that objects had a funny look: they were more obliterated, less dense than usual. It was enough for me to look at the bench, the lamp, the pile of coal dust, to feel that I was going to die. Naturally I couldn't think clearly about my death but I saw it everywhere, on things, in the way things fell back and kept their distance, discreetly, as people who speak quietly at the bedside of a dying man. It was *his* death which Tom had just touched on the bench.

In the state I was in, if someone had come and told me I could go home quietly, that they would leave me my life whole, it would have left me cold: several hours or several years of waiting is all the same when you have lost the illusion of being eternal. I clung to nothing, in a way I was calm. But it was a horrible calm—because of my body; my body, I saw with its eyes, I heard with its ears, but it was no longer me; it sweated and trembled by itself and I didn't recognize it any more. I had to touch it and look at it to find out what was happening, as if it were the body of someone else. At times I could still feel it, I felt sinkings, and fallings, as when you're in a plane taking a nosedive, or I felt my heart beating. But that didn't reassure me. Everything that came from my body was all cockeyed. Most of the time it was quiet and I felt no more than a sort of weight, a filthy presence against me; I had the impression of being tied to an enormous vermin. Once I felt my pants and I felt they were damp; I didn't know whether it was sweat or urine, but I went to piss on the coal pile as a precaution.

The Belgian took out his watch, looked at it. He said, "It is three-thirty."

Bastard! He must have done it on purpose. Tom jumped;

we hadn't noticed time was running out; night surrounded us like a shapeless, somber mass, I couldn't even remember that it had begun.

Little Juan began to cry. He wrung his hands, pleaded, "I don't want to die. I don't want to die."

He ran across the whole cellar waving his arms in the air then fell sobbing on one of the mats. Tom watched him with mournful eyes, without the slightest desire to console him. Because it wasn't worth the trouble: the kid made more noise than we did, but he was less touched: he was like a sick man who defends himself against his illness by fever. It's much more serious when there isn't any fever.

He wept: I could clearly see he was pitying himself; he wasn't thinking about death. For one second, one single second, I wanted to weep myself, to weep with pity for myself. But the opposite happened: I glanced at the kid, I saw his thin sobbing shoulders and I felt inhuman: I could pity neither the others nor myself. I said to myself, "I want to die cleanly."

Tom had gotten up, he placed himself just under the round opening and began to watch for daylight. I was determined to die cleanly and I only thought of that. But ever since the doctor told us the time, I felt time flying, flowing away drop by drop.

It was still dark when I heard Tom's voice: "Do you hear them?"

Men were marching in the courtyard.

"Yes."

"What the hell are they doing? They can't shoot in the dark."

After a while we heard no more. I said to Tom, "It's day."

Pedro got up, yawning, and came to blow out the lamp. He said to his buddy, "Cold as hell."

The cellar was all grey. We heard shots in the distance.

"It's starting," I told Tom. "They must do it in the court in the rear."

Tom asked the doctor for a cigarette. I didn't want one; I didn't want cigarettes or alcohol. From that moment on they didn't stop firing.

"Do you realize what's happening," Tom said.

He wanted to add something but kept quiet, watching the door. The door opened and a lieutenant came in with four soldiers. Tom dropped his cigarette.

"Steinbock?"

Tom didn't answer. Pedro pointed him out.

"Juan Mirbal?"

"On the mat."

"Get up," the lieutenant said.

Juan did not move. Two soldiers took him under the arms and set him on his feet. But he fell as soon as they released him.

The soldiers hesitated.

"He's not the first sick one," said the lieutenant. "You two carry him; they'll fix it up down there."

He turned to Tom. "Let's go."

Tom went out between two soldiers. Two others followed, carrying the kid by the armpits. He hadn't fainted; his eyes were wide open and tears ran down his cheeks. When I wanted to go out the lieutenant stopped me.

"You Ibbieta?"

"Yes."

"You wait here; they'll come for you later."

They left. The Belgian and the two jailers left too, I was alone. I did not understand what was happening to me but I would have liked it better if they had gotten it over with right away. I heard shots at almost regular intervals; I shook with each one of them. I wanted to scream and tear out my hair. But I gritted my teeth and pushed my hands in my pockets because I wanted to stay clean.

After an hour they came to get me and led me to the first floor, to a small room that smelt of cigars and where the heat was stifling. There were two officers sitting smoking in the armchairs, papers on their knees.

"You're Ibbieta?"

"Yes."

"Where is Ramon Gris?"

"I don't know."

The one questioning me was short and fat. His eyes were hard behind his glasses. He said to me, "Come here."

I went to him. He got up and took my arms, staring at me with a look that should have pushed me into the earth. At the same time he pinched my biceps with all his might. It wasn't to hurt me, it was only a game: he wanted to dominate me. He also thought he had to blow his stinking breath square in my face. We stayed for a moment like that, and I almost felt like laughing. It takes a lot to intimidate a man who is going to die; it didn't work. He pushed me back violently and sat down again. He said, "It's his life against yours. You can have yours if you tell us where he is."

These men dolled up with their riding crops and boots were still going to die. A little later than I, but not too much. They busied themselves looking for names in their crumpled papers, they ran after other men to imprison or suppress them; they had opinions on the future of Spain and on other subjects. Their little activities seemed shocking and burlesqued to me; I couldn't put myself in their place, I thought they were insane. The little man was still looking at me, whipping his boots with the riding crop. All his gestures were calculated to give him the look of a live and ferocious beast.

"So? You understand?"

"I don't know where Gris is," I answered. "I thought he was in Madrid."

The other officer raised his pale hand indolently. This indolence was also calculated. I saw through all their little schemes and I was stupefied to find there were men who amused themselves that way.

"You have a quarter of an hour to think it over," he said slowly. "Take him to the laundry, bring him back in fifteen minutes. If he still refuses he will be executed on the spot."

They knew what they were doing: I had passed the night in waiting; then they had made me wait an hour in the cellar while they shot Tom and Juan and now they were locking me up in the laundry; they must have prepared their game the night before. They told themselves that nerves eventually wear out and they hoped to get me that way.

They were badly mistaken. In the laundry I sat on a stool because I felt very weak and I began to think. But not about their proposition. Of course I knew where Gris was; he was hiding with his cousins, four kilometers from the city. I also knew that I would not reveal his hiding place unless they tortured me (but they didn't seem to be thinking about that). All that was perfectly regulated, definite and in no way interested me. Only I would have liked to understand the reasons for my conduct. I would rather die than give up Gris. Why? I didn't like Ramon Gris any more. My friendship for him had died a little while before dawn at the same time as my love for Concha, at the same time as my desire to live. Undoubtedly I thought highly of him: he was tough.

But it was not for this reason that I consented to die in his place; his life had no more value than mine; no life had value. They were going to slap a man up against a wall and shoot at him till he died, whether it was I or Gris or somebody else made no difference. I knew he was more useful than I to the cause of Spain but I thought to hell with Spain and anarchy; nothing was important. Yet I was there, I could save my skin and give up Gris and I refused to do it. I found that somehow comic; it was obstinacy. I thought, "I must be stubborn!" And a droll sort of gaiety spread over me.

They came for me and brought me back to the two officers. A rat ran out from under my feet and that amused me. I turned to one of the *falangistas* and said, "Did you see the rat?"

He didn't answer. He was very sober, he took himself seriously. I wanted to laugh but I held myself back because I was afraid that once I got started I wouldn't be able to stop. The *falangista* had a moustache. I said to him again, "You ought to shave off your moustache, idiot." I thought it funny that he would let the hairs of his living being invade his face. He kicked me without great conviction and I kept quiet.

"Well," said the fat officer, "have you thought about it?"

I looked at them with curiosity, as insects of a very rare species. I told them, "I know where he is. He is hidden in the cemetery. In a vault or in the gravediggers' shack."

It was a farce. I wanted to see them stand up, buckle their belts and give orders busily.

They jumped to their feet. "Let's go. Molés, go get fifteen men from Lieutenant Lopez. You," the fat man said, "I'll let you off if you're telling the truth, but it'll cost you plenty if you're making monkeys out of us."

They left in a great clatter and I waited peacefully under the guard of *falangistas*. From time to time I smiled, thinking about the spectacle they would make. I felt stunned and malicious. I imagined them lifting up tombstones, opening the doors of the vaults one by one. I represented this situation to myself as if I had been someone else: this prisoner obstinately playing the hero, these grim *falangistas* with their moustaches and their men in uniform running among the graves; it was irresistibly funny. After half an hour the little fat man came back alone. I thought he had come to give the orders to execute me. The others must have stayed in the cemetery.

The officer looked at me. He didn't look at all sheepish. "Take him into the big courtyard with the others," he said. "After the military operations a regular court will decide what happens to him."

"Then they're not . . . not going to shoot me? . . ."

"Not now, anyway. What happens afterwards is none of my business."

I still didn't understand. I asked, "But why . . . ?"

He shrugged his shoulders without answering and the soldiers took me away. In the big courtyard there were about a hundred prisoners, women, children and a few old men. I began walking around the central grass-plot, I was stupefied. At noon they let us eat in the mess hall. Two or three people questioned me. I must have known them, but I didn't answer: I didn't even know where I was.

Around evening they pushed about ten new prisoners into the court. I recognized Garcia, the baker. He said, "What damned luck you have! I didn't think I'd see you alive."

"They sentenced me to death," I said, "and then they changed their minds. I don't know why."

"They arrested me at two o'clock," Garcia said.

"Why?" Garcia had nothing to do with politics.

"I don't know," he said. "They arrest everybody who doesn't think the way they do." He lowered his voice. "They got Gris."

I began to tremble. "When?"

"This morning. He messed it up. He left his cousin's on Tuesday because they had an argument. There were plenty of people to hide him but he didn't want to owe anything to anybody. He said, 'I'd go and hide in Ibbieta's place, but they got him, so I'll go hide in the cemetery.' "

"In the cemetery?"

"Yes. What a fool. Of course they went by there this morning, that was sure to happen. They found him in the gravediggers' shack. He shot at them and they got him."

"In the cemetery!"

Everything began to spin and I found myself sitting on the ground: I laughed so hard I cried.

JUDAS

Frank O'Connor

Frank O'Connor, whose true name is Michael O'Donovan, was born of humble parents in Cork, Ireland, in 1903. He fought against the English for Irish independence and was for a time a director of the famous Abbey Theater. Although he has written plays and criticism, it is as a writer of short stories that he has won his greatest fame. He is a frequent contributor to The New Yorker. *In 1952, he published his* Collected Short Stories. *His writing is distinguished by a marvelous warmth and humor.*

I'll forget a lot of things before I forget that night. As I was going out the mother said: "Sure, you won't be late, Jerry?" and I only laughed at her and said: "Am I ever late?" As I went down the road I was thinking it was months since I had taken her to the pictures. You might think that funny, Michael John, but after the father's death we were thrown together a lot. And I knew she hated being alone in the house after dark.

At the same time I had troubles of my own. You see, Michael John, being an only child, I never knocked round with girls the way others did. All the chaps in the office went with girls, or at any rate they let on they did. They said: "Who was the old doll I saw you with last night, Jerry? Aha, Jerry, you'd better mind yourself, boy, or you'll be getting into trouble!" Paddy Kinnane, for instance, talked like that, and he never saw how it upset me. I think he thought it was a great compliment. It wasn't until years after that I began to suspect that Paddy's acquaintance with dolls was about of one kind with my own.

Then I met Kitty Doherty. Kitty was a hospital nurse, and all the chaps in the office said a fellow should never go with hospital nurses—they knew too much. I knew when I met Kitty that that was a lie. She was a well-educated, superior girl; she lived up the river in a posh locality, and her mother was on all sorts of councils and committees. She was small and wiry; a good-looking girl, always in good humor, and when she talked, she hopped from one thing to another like a robin on a frosty morning.

Anyway, she had me dazzled. I used to meet her in the evenings up the river road, as if I was walking there by accident and very surprised to see her. "Fancy meeting you!" I'd say, or "Well, well, isn't this a great surprise?" Then we'd stand talking for half an hour and I'd see her home. Several times she asked me in, but I was too nervous. I knew I'd lose my head, break the china, use some dirty word, and then go home and cut my throat. Of course, I never asked her to come to the pictures or anything like that. I knew she was above that. My only hope was that if I waited long enough I might be able to save her from drowning, the White Slave Traffic, or something of the sort. That would show in a modest, dignified way how I felt about her. Of course, I knew at the same time I ought to stay at home more with the mother, but the very thought that I might be missing an opportunity like that would be enough to spoil a whole evening on me.

This night in particular I was nearly distracted. It was three weeks since I'd seen Kitty. You know what three weeks are at that age. I was sure that at the very least the girl was dying and asking for me and that no one knew my address. A week before, I'd felt I simply couldn't bear it any longer, so I made an excuse and went down to the post-office. I rang up the hospital and asked for her. I fully expected them to say that she was dead, and I got a shock when the girl at the other end asked my name. "I'm afraid," I said, "I'm a stranger to Miss Doherty, but I have an important message for her." Then I got completely panic-stricken. What could a girl like Kitty make of a damned deliberate lie like that? What else was it but a trap laid by an old and cunning hand. I held the receiver out and looked at it. "Moynihan," I said to it, "you're mad. An asylum, Moynihan, is the only place for a fellow like you." Then I heard her voice, not in my ear at all, but in the telephone booth as if she were standing before me, and I nearly dropped the receiver with terror. I put it to my ear and asked in a disguised voice: "Who is that speaking, please?" "This is Kitty Doherty," she said rather impatiently. "Who are you?" "I am Monsieur Betrand," said I, speaking in what I hoped was a French accent. "I am afraid I have de wrong number." Then I put down the receiver carefully and thought how nice it would be if only I had a penknife handy to cut my throat with. It's funny, but from the moment I met Kitty I was always coveting sharp things like razors and penknives.

After that an awful idea dawned on my mind. Of course, I should have thought of it before, but, as you've probably guessed, I wasn't exactly knowledgeable. I began to see that I wasn't meeting Kitty for the very good reason that Kitty didn't want to meet me. That filled me with terror. I examined my conscience to find out what I might have said to her. You know what conscience is at that age. I remembered every remark I'd made and they were all brutal, indecent or disgusting. I had talked of Paddy Kinnane as a fellow who "went with dolls." What could a pure-minded girl think of a chap who naturally used such a phrase except—what, unfortunately, was true—that he had a mind like a cesspit.

It was a lovely summer evening, with views of hillsides and fields between the gaps in the houses, and that raised my spirits a bit. Maybe I was wrong, maybe she hadn't found out the sort I was and wasn't avoiding me, maybe we might meet and walk home together. I walked the full length of the river road and back, and then started off to walk it again. The crowds were thinning out as fellows and girls slipped off up the lanes or down to the river. As the streets went out like lamps about me I grew desperate. I saw clearly that she was avoiding me; that she knew I wasn't the quiet, good-natured chap I let on to be but a volcano of brutality and lust. "Lust, lust, lust!" I hissed to myself, clenching my fists.

Then I glanced up and saw her on a tram. I forgot instantly about the lust and smiled and waved my cap at her, but she was looking ahead and didn't see me. I ran after the car, intending to jump on it, to sit on one of the back seats on top and then say as she was getting off: "Fancy meeting you here!" (Trams were always a bit of a problem. If you sat beside a girl and paid for her, it might be considered forward; if you didn't, it looked mean. I never quite knew.) But as if the driver knew what was in my mind, he put on speed and away went the tram, tossing and screeching down the straight, and I stood panting in the middle of the road, smiling as if missing a tram was the best joke in the world and wishing all the time I had the penknife and the courage to use it. My position was hopeless. Then I must have gone a bit mad, for I started to race the tram. There were still lots of people out walking, and they stared after me, so I lifted my fists to my chest in the attitude of a professional runner and dropped into a comfortable stride which I hoped vaguely would delude them into the belief that I was in training for a big race.

Between the running and the halts I just managed to keep the tram in view all the way through town and out at the other side. When I saw Kitty get off and go up a hilly street I collapsed and was just able to drag myself after her. When she went into a house on a terrace I sat on the curb with my head between my knees till the panting stopped. At any rate I felt safe. I could now walk up and down before the house till she came out, and accost her with an innocent smile and say: "Fancy meeting you!"

But my luck was dead out that night. As I was walking up and down out of range of the house I saw a tall chap come strolling up at the opposite side and my heart sank. It was Paddy Kinnane.

"Hullo, Jerry," he chuckled with that knowing grin he put on whenever he wanted to compliment you on being discovered in a compromising situation, "what are you doing here?"

"Ah, just waiting for a chap I had a date with, Paddy," I said, trying to sound casual.

"Begor," said Paddy, "you look to me more like a man that was waiting for an old doll. Still waters run deep. . . . What time are you supposed to be meeting him?"

"Half eight," I said at random.

"Half eight?" said Paddy in surprise. " 'Tis nearly nine now."

"I know," said I, "but as I waited so long I may as well give him another few minutes."

"Ah, I'll wait along with you," said Paddy, leaning against the wall and taking out a packet of fags. "You might find yourself stuck by the end of the evening. There's people in this town and they have no consideration for anyone."

That was Paddy all out; no trouble too much for him if he could do you a good turn.

"As he kept me so long," I said hastily, "I don't think I'll bother with him. It only struck me this very minute that there's a chap up the Asragh road that I have to see on urgent business. You'll excuse me, Paddy. I'll tell you about it another time."

And away I went hell for leather to the tram. When I reached the tram-stop below Kitty's house I sat on the river wall in the dusk. The moon was rising, and every quarter of an hour the trams came grunting and squeaking over the old bridge and then went black out while the conductors switched the trolleys. I stood on the curb in the moonlight searching for Kitty. Then a bobby came along, and as he seemed to be watching me, I slunk slowly off up the hill and stood against a wall in the shadow. There was a high wall at the other side too, and behind it the roofs of a house shining in the moon. Every now and then a tram would come in and people would pass in the moonlight, and the snatches of conversation I caught were like the warmth from an open door to the heart of a homeless man. It was quite clear now that my position was hopeless. The last tram came and went, and still there was no Kitty and still I hung on.

Then I heard a woman's step. I couldn't even pretend to myself that it might be Kitty till she shuffled past me with that hasty little walk of hers. I started and called out her name; she glanced over her shoulder and, seeing a man emerging from the shadow, look fright and ran. I ran too, but she put on speed and began to outdistance me. At that I despaired. I stood on the pavement and shouted after her at the top of my voice.

"Kitty!" I cried. "Kitty, for God's sake, wait for me!"

She ran a few steps further and then halted, turned, and came back slowly down the path.

"Jerry Moynihan!" she whispered, lifting her two arms to her breasts as if I had found her with nothing on. "What in God's name are you doing here?"

I was summoning up strength to tell her that I just happened to be taking a stroll in that direction and was astonished to see her when I realized the improbability of it and began to cry instead. Then I laughed. I suppose it was nerves. But Kitty had had a bad fright and now that she was getting over it she was as cross as two sticks.

"What's wrong with you, I say," she snapped. "Are you out of your senses or what?"

"Well, you see," I stammered awkwardly, half in dread I was going to cry again, "I didn't see you in town."

"No," she replied with a shrug, "I know you didn't. I wasn't out. What about it?"

"I thought it might be something I said to you," I said desperately.

"No," said Kitty candidly, "it wasn't anything to do with you. It's Mother."

"Why?" I asked almost joyously. "Is there something wrong with her?"

"I don't mean that," said Kitty impatiently. "It's just that she made such a fuss, I felt it wasn't worth it."

"But what did she make a fuss about?" I asked.

"About you, of course," said Kitty in exasperation. "What did you think?"

"But what did I do?" I asked, clutching my head. This was worse than anything I'd ever imagined. This was terrible.

"You didn't do anything," said Kitty, "but people were talking about us. And you wouldn't come in and be introduced to her like anyone else. I know she's a bit of a fool, and her head is stuffed with old nonsense about her family. I could never see that they were different to anyone else, and anyway, she married a commercial herself, so she has nothing much to boast about. Still, you needn't be so superior. There's no obligation to buy, you know."

I didn't. There were cold shivers running through me. I had thought of Kitty as a secret between God, herself, and me and that she only knew the half of it. Now it seemed I didn't even know the half. People were talking about us! I was superior! What next?

"But what has she against me?" I asked despairingly.

"She thinks we're doing a tangle, of course," snapped Kitty as if she was astonished at my stupidity, "and I suppose she imagines you're not grand enough for a great-great-grandniece of Daniel O'Connell. I told her you were a different sort of fellow entirely and above all that sort of thing, but she wouldn't believe me. She said I was a deep, callous, crafty little intriguer and that I hadn't a drop of Daniel

O'Connell's blood in my veins." Kitty began to giggle at the thought of herself as an intriguer.

"That's all she knows," I said bitterly.

"I know," said Kitty with a shrug. "The woman has no sense. And anyway she has no reason to think I'm telling lies. Cissy and I always had fellows, and we spooned with them all over the shop under her very nose, so why should she think I'm lying to her now?"

At that I began to laugh like an idiot. This was worse than appalling. This was a nightmare. Kitty, whom I had thought so angelic, talking in cold blood about "spooning" with fellows all over the house. Even the bad women in the books I'd read didn't talk about love in that cold-blooded way. Madame Bovary herself had at least the decency to pretend that she didn't like it. It was like another door opening on the outside world, but Kitty thought I was laughing at her and started to apologize.

"Of course I had no sense," she said. "You're the first fellow I ever met that treated me properly. The others only wanted to fool around with me, and now because I don't like it, Mother thinks I'm getting stuck-up. I told her I liked you better than any fellow I knew, but that I'd grown out of all that sort of thing."

"And what did she say to that?" I asked fiercely. It was—how can I describe it?—like a man who'd lived all his life in a dungeon getting into the sunlight for the first time and afraid of every shadow.

"Ah, I told you the woman was silly," said Kitty, getting embarrassed.

"Go on!" I shouted. "I want to know everything. I insist on knowing everything."

"Well," said Kitty with a demure little grin, "she said you were a deep, designing guttersnipe who knew exactly how to get round feather-pated little idiots like me. . . . You see," she added with another shrug, "it's quite hopeless. The woman is common. She doesn't understand."

"But I tell you she does understand," I shouted frantically. "She understands better than you do. I only wish to God I was deep and designing so that I'd have some chance with you."

"Do you really?" asked Kitty, opening her eyes wide. "To tell you the truth," she added after a moment, "I thought you were a bit keen the first time, but then I didn't know. When you didn't kiss me or anything, I mean."

"God," I said bitterly, "when I think of what I've been through in the past couple of weeks!"

"I know," said Kitty, biting her lip. "I was the same." And then we said nothing for a few moments.

"You're sure you're serious?" she asked suspiciously.

"I tell you, girl," I shouted, "I was on the point of committing suicide."

"What good would that be?" she asked with another shrug, and then she looked at me and laughed outright—the little jade!

It is all as clear in my mind as if it had happened last night. I told Kitty about my prospects. She didn't care, but I insisted on telling her. It was as if a stone had been lifted off my heart, and I went home in the moonlight singing. Then I heard the clock strike, and the singing stopped. I remembered the mother at home, waiting, and began to run again. This was desperation too, but a different sort.

The door was ajar and the kitchen in darkness. I saw her sitting before the fire by herself, and just as I was going to throw my arms about her, I smelt Kitty's perfume round me and was afraid to go near her. God help us, as if it would have told her anything!

"Hallo, Mum," I said with a laugh, rubbing my hands, "you're all in darkness."

"You'll have a cup of tea?" she said.

"I might as well," said I.

"What time is it?" she said, lighting the gas. "You're very late."

"Ah, I met a fellow from the office," I said, but at the same time I was stung by the complaint in her tone.

"You frightened me," she said with a little whimper. "I didn't know what happened you. What kept you at all?"

"Oh, what do you think?" I said, goaded into retorting. "Drinking and blackguarding as usual."

I could have bitten my tongue off when I'd said it; it sounded so cruel, as if some stranger had said it instead of me. She turned to me for a moment with a frightened stare as if she was seeing the stranger too, and somehow I couldn't bear it.

"God Almighty," I said, "a fellow can have no life in his own house," and away with me upstairs.

I lit the candle, undressed and got into bed. I was wild. A chap could be a drunkard and blackguard and not be made to suffer more reproach than I was for being late one single night. That, I felt, was what you got for being a good son.

"Jerry," she called from the foot of the stairs, "will I bring you up your cup?"

"I don't want it now, thanks," I said.

I heard her give a heavy sigh and turn away. Then she locked the two doors front and back. She didn't wash up, and I knew my cup of tea was standing there on the table with a saucer on top in case I changed my mind. She came slowly up the stairs, and she walked like an old woman. I blew out the candle before she reached the landing in case she came in to ask me if I wanted anything else, and the moonlight came in the attic window and brought me memories of Kitty. But every time I tried to imagine her face while she grinned up at me, waiting for me to kiss her, it was the mother's face that came up with that look like a child's when you strike him the first time—as if he suddenly saw the stranger in you. I remembered all our life together from the night the father—God rest him!—died; our early Mass on Sunday; our visits to the pictures; our plans for the future, and Christ, Michael John, it was as if I was inside her mind and she sitting by the fire, waiting for the blow to fall! And now it had fallen, and I was a stranger to her, and nothing I ever did could make us the same to each other again. There was something like a cannon-ball stuck in my chest, and I lay awake till the cocks started crowing. Then I couldn't bear it any longer. I went out on to the landing and listened.

"Are you awake, Mother?" I asked in a whisper.

"What is it, Jerry?" she said in alarm, and I knew she hadn't slept any more than I had.

"I only came to say I was sorry," I said, opening the room door, and then as I saw her sitting up in bed under the Sacred Heart lamp, the cannon-ball burst inside me and I began to bawl like a kid.

"Oh, child, child," she cried out, "what are you crying for at all, my little boy?" and she spread out her arms to me. I went to her and she hugged me and rocked me just as she did when I was only a nipper. "Oh, oh, oh," she was saying to herself in a whisper, "my storeen bawn, my little man!"

—all the names she hadn't called me since I was a kid. That was all we said. I couldn't bring myself to tell her what I'd done, and she wouldn't confess to me that she was jealous; all she could do was to try and comfort me for the way I'd hurt her, to make up to me for the nature she'd given me. "My storeen bawn," she said. "My little man!"

OF THIS TIME, OF THAT PLACE

Lionel Trilling

Lionel Trilling was born in New York City in 1905. Besides writing stories and criticism for leading magazines and holding editorial positions on The Kenyon Review *and* The Partisan Review, *he has published two critical biographies,* Matthew Arnold *(1939) and* E. M. Forster *(1943); a novel,* The Middle of the Journey *(1949); and a collection of essays,* The Liberal Imagination *(1950). Two of his short stories, "The Other Margaret" and "Of This Time, Of That Place," have received high critical acclaim. The latter is generally considered to be one of the finest stories yet written on college life.*

It was a fine September day. By noon it would be summer again, but now it was true autumn with a touch of chill in the air. As Joseph Howe stood on the porch of the house in which he lodged, ready to leave for his first class of the year, he thought with pleasure of the long indoor days that were coming. It was a moment when he could feel glad of his profession.

On the lawn the peach tree was still in fruit and young Hilda Aiken was taking a picture of it. She held the camera tight against her chest. She wanted the sun behind her, but she did not want her own long morning shadow in the foreground. She raised the camera, but that did not help, and she lowered it, but that made things worse. She twisted her body to the left, then to the right. In the end she had to step out of the direct line of the sun. At last she snapped the shutter and wound the film with intense care.

Howe, watching her from the porch, waited for her to finish and called a good morning. She turned, startled, and almost sullenly lowered her glance. In the year Howe had lived at the Aikens', Hilda had accepted him as one of her family, but since his absence of the summer she had grown shy. Then suddenly she lifted her head and smiled at him, and the humorous smile confirmed the pleasure in the day. She picked up her bookbag and set off for school.

The handsome houses on the streets to the college were not yet fully awake, but they looked very friendly. Howe went by the Bradby house where he would be a guest this evening at the first dinner party of the year. When he had gone the length of the picket fence, the whitest in town, he turned back. Along the path there was a fine row of asters and he went through the gate and picked one for his buttonhole. The Bradbys would be pleased if they happened to see him invading their lawn and the knowledge of this made him even more comfortable.

He reached the campus as the hour was striking. The students were hurrying to their classes. He himself was in no hurry. He stopped at his dime cubicle of an office and lit a cigarette. The prospect of facing his class had suddenly presented itself to him and his hands were cold; the lawful seizure of power he was about to make seemed momentous. Waiting did not help. He put out his cigarette, picked up a pad of theme paper, and went to his classroom.

As he entered, the rattle of voices ceased, and the twenty-odd freshmen settled themselves and looked at him appraisingly. Their faces seemed gross, his heart sank at their massed impassivity, but he spoke briskly.

"My name is Howe," he said, and turned and wrote it on the blackboard. The carelessness of the scrawl confirmed his authority. He went on, "My office is 412 Slemp Hall, and my office-hours are Monday, Wednesday, and Friday from eleven-thirty to twelve-thirty."

He wrote, "M., W., F., 11:30-12:30." He said, "I'll be very glad to see any of you at that time. Or if you can't come then, you can arrange with me for some other time."

He turned again to the blackboard and spoke over his shoulder. "The text for the course is Jarman's *Modern Plays*, revised edition. The Co-op has it in stock." He wrote the name, underlined "revised edition" and waited for it to be taken down in the new notebooks.

When the bent heads were raised again he began his speech of prospectus. "It is hard to explain—" he said, and paused as they composed themselves. "It is hard to explain what a course like this is intended to do. We are going to try to learn something about modern literature and something about prose composition."

As he spoke, his hands warmed and he was able to look directly at the class. Last year on the first day the faces had seemed just as cloddish, but as the term wore on they became gradually alive and quite likable. It did not seem possible that the same thing could happen again.

"I shall not lecture in this course," he continued. "Our work will be carried on by discussion and we will try to learn by an exchange of opinion. But you will soon recognize that my opinion is worth more than anyone else's here."

He remained grave as he said it, but two boys understood and laughed. The rest took permission from them and laughed too. All Howe's private ironies protested the vulgarity of the joke, but the laughter made him feel benign and powerful.

When the little speech was finished, Howe picked up the pad of paper he had brought. He announced that they would write an extemporaneous theme. Its subject was traditional, "Who I am and why I came to Dwight College." By now the class was more at ease and it gave a ritualistic groan of protest. Then there was a stir as fountain pens were brought out and the writing-arms of the chairs were cleared, and the paper was passed about. At last, all the heads bent to work, and the room became still.

Howe sat idly at his desk. The sun shone through the tall clumsy windows. The cool of the morning was already passing. There was a scent of autumn and of varnish and the stillness of the room was deep and oddly touching. Now and then a student's head was raised and scratched in the old, elaborate students' pantomime that calls the teacher to witness honest intellectual effort.

Suddenly a tall boy stood within the frame of the open door. "Is this," he said, and thurst a large nose into a college catalogue, "is this the meeting place of English 1A? The section instructed by Dr. Joseph Howe?"

He stood on the very sill of the door, as if refusing to enter until he was perfectly sure of his rights. The class looked up from work, found him absurd and gave a low mocking cheer.

The teacher and the new student, with equal pointedness, ignored the disturbance. Howe nodded to the boy, who pushed his head forward and then jerked it back in a wide elaborate arc to clear his brow of a heavy lock of hair. He advanced into the room and halted before Howe, almost at attention. In a loud, clear voice he announced, "I am Tertan, Ferdinand R., reporting at the direction of Head of Department Vincent."

The heraldic formality of this statement brought forth another cheer. Howe looked at the class with a sternness he could not really feel, for there was indeed something ridiculous about this boy. Under his displeased regard the rows of heads dropped to work again. Then he touched Tertan's elbow, led him up to the desk and stood so as to shield their conversation from the class.

"We are writing an extemporaneous theme," he said. "The subject is 'Who I am and why I came to Dwight College.' "

He stripped a few sheets from the pad and offered them to the boy. Tertan hesitated and then took the paper, but he held it only tentatively. As if with the effort of making something clear, he gulped and a slow smile fixed itself on his face. It was at once knowing and shy.

"Professor," he said, "to be perfectly fair to my classmates"—he made a large gesture over the room—"and to you"—he inclined his head to Howe—"this would not be for me an extemporaneous subject."

Howe tried to understand. "You mean you've already thought about it—you've heard we always give the same subject? That doesn't matter."

Again the boy ducked his head and gulped. It was the gesture of one who wishes to make a difficult explanation with perfect candor. "Sir," he said, and made the distinction with great care, "the topic I did not expect, but I have given much ratiocination to the subject."

Howe smiled and said, "I don't think that's an unfair advantage. Just go ahead and write."

Tertan narrowed his eyes and glanced sidewise at Howe. His strange mouth smiled. Then in quizzical acceptance, he ducked his head, threw back the heavy, dank lock, dropped into a seat with a great loose noise and began to write rapidly.

The room fell silent again and Howe resumed his idleness. When the bell rang, the students who had groaned when the task had been set now groaned again because they had not finished. Howe took up the papers, and held the class while he made the first assignment. When he dismissed it, Tertan bore down on him, his slack mouth held ready for speech.

"Some professors," he said, "are pedants. They are Dryasdusts. However some professors are free souls and creative spirits. Kant, Hegel, and Nietzsche were all professors." With this pronouncement he paused. "It is my opinion," he continued, "that you occupy the second category."

Howe looked at the boy in surprise and with good-natured irony, "With Kant, Hegel, and Nietzsche?"

Not only Tertan's hand and head, but his whole awkward body waved away the stupidity. "It is the kind and not the quantity of the kind," he said sternly.

Rebuked, Howe said as simply and seriously as he could, "It would be nice to think so." He added, "Of course I am not a professor."

This was clearly a disappointment but Tertan met it. "In the French sense," he said with composure. "Generically, a teacher."

Suddenly he bowed. It was such a bow, Howe fancied, as a stage-director might teach an actor playing a medieval student who takes leave of Abelard—stiff, solemn, with elbows close to the body and feet together. Then, quite as suddenly, he turned and left.

A queer fish, and as soon as Howe reached his office, he sifted through the batch of themes and drew out Tertan's. The boy had filled many sheets with his unformed headlong scrawl. "Who am I?" he had begun. "Here, in a mundane, not to say commercialized academe, is asked the question which from time long immemorably out of mind has accreted doubts and thoughts in the psyche of man to pester him as a nuisance. Whether in St. Augustine (or Austin as sometimes called) or Miss Bashkirtsieff or Frederic Amiel or Empedocles, or in less lights of the intellect than these, this posed question has been ineluctable."

Howe took out his pencil. He circled "academe" and wrote "vocab." in the margin. He underlined "time long immemorably out of mind" and wrote "Diction!" But this seemed inadequate for what was wrong. He put down his pencil and read ahead to discover the principle of error in the theme. "Today as ever, in spite of gloomy prophets of the dismal science (economics) the question is uninvalidated. Out of the starry depths of heaven hurtles this spear of query demanding to be caught on the shield of the mind ere it pierces the skull and the limbs be unstrung."

Baffled but quite caught, Howe read on. "Materialism, by which is meant the philosophic concept and not the moral idea, provides no aegis against the question which lies beyond the tangible (metaphysics). Existence without alloy is the question presented. Environment and heredity relegated aside, the rags and old clothes of practical life discarded, the name and the instrumentality of livelihood do not, as the prophets of the dismal science insist on in this connection, give solution to the interrogation which not from the professor merely but veritably from the cosmos is given. I think, therefore I am (cogito etc.) but who am I? Tertan I am, but what is Tertan? Of this time, of that place, of some parentage, what does it matter?"

Existence without alloy: the phrase established itself. Howe put aside Tertan's paper and at random picked up another. "I am Arthur J. Casebeer, Jr.," he read. "My father is Arthur J. Casebeer and my grandfather was Arthur J. Casebeer before him. My mother is Nina Wimble Casebeer. Both of them are college graduates and my father is in insurance. I was born in St. Louis eighteen years ago and we still make our residence there."

Arthur J. Casebeer, who knew who he was, was less interesting than Tertan, but more coherent. Howe picked up Tertan's paper again. It was clear that none of the routine marginal comments, no "sent. str." or "punct." or "vocab." could cope with this torrential rhetoric. He read ahead, contenting himself with underscoring the errors against the time when he should have the necessary "conference" with Tertan.

It was a busy and official day of cards and sheets, arrangements and small decisions, and it gave Howe pleasure. Even when it was time to attend the first of the weekly Convocations he felt the charm of the beginning of things when intention is still innocent and uncorrupted by effort. He sat among the young instructors on the platform, and joined in their humorous complaints at having to assist at the ceremony, but actually he got a clear satisfaction from the ritual of prayer and prosy speech, and even from wearing his academic gown. And when the Convocation was over the pleasure continued as he crossed the campus, exchanging greetings with men he had not seen since the spring. They were people who did not yet, and perhaps never would, mean much to him, but in a year they had grown amiably to be part of his life. They were his fellow-townsmen.

The day had cooled again at sunset, and there was a bright chill in the September twilight. Howe carried his voluminous gown over his arm, he swung his doctoral hood by its purple neckpiece, and on his head he wore his mortarboard with its heavy gold tassel bobbing just over his eye. These were the weighty and absurd symbols of his new profession and they pleased him. At twenty-six Joseph Howe had discovered that he was neither so well off nor so bohemian as he had once thought. A small income, adequate when supplemented by a sizable cash legacy, was genteel poverty when the cash was all spent. And the literary life—the room at the Lafayette, or the small apartment without a lease, the long summers on the Cape, the long afternoons and the social evenings—began to weary him. His writing filled his mornings and should perhaps have filled his life, yet it did not. To the amusement of his friends, and with a certain sense that he was betraying his own freedom, he had used the last of his legacy for a year at Harvard. The small but respectable reputation of his two volumes of verse had proved useful—he continued at Harvard on a fellowship and when he emerged as Doctor Howe he received an excellent appointment, with prospects, at Dwight.

He had his moments of fear when all that had ever been said of the dangers of the academic life had occurred to him. But after a year in which he had tested every possibility of corruption and seduction he was ready to rest easy. His third volume of verse, most of it written in his first years of teaching, was not only ampler but, he thought, better than its predecessors.

There was a clear hour before the Bradby dinner party, and Howe looked forward to it. But he was not to enjoy it, for lying with his mail on the hall table was a copy of this quarter's issue of *Life and Letters*, to which his landlord subscribed. Its severe cover announced that its editor, Frederic Woolley, had this month contributed an essay called

"Two Poets," and Howe, picking it up, curious to see who the two poets might be, felt his own name start out at him with cabalistic power—Joseph Howe. As he continued to turn the pages his hand trembled.

Standing in the dark hall, holding the neat little magazine, Howe knew that his literary contempt for Frederic Woolley meant nothing, for he suddenly understood how he respected Woolley in the way of the world. He knew this by the trembling of his hand. And of the little world as well as the great, for although the literary groups of New York might dismiss Woolley, his name carried high authority in the academic world. At Dwight it was even a revered name, for it had been here at the college that Frederic Woolley had made the distinguished scholarly career from which he had gone on to literary journalism. In middle life he had been induced to take the editorship of *Life and Letters,* a literary monthly not widely read but heavily endowed, and in its pages he had carried on the defense of what he sometimes called the older values. He was not without wit, he had great knowledge and considerable taste, and even in the full movement of the "new" literature he had won a certain respect for his refusal to accept it. In France, even in England, he would have been connected with a more robust tradition of conservatism, but America gave him an audience not much better than genteel. It was known in the college that to the subsidy of *Life and Letters* the Bradbys contributed a great part.

As Howe read, he saw that he was involved in nothing less than an event. When the Fifth Series of *Studies in Order and Value* came to be collected, this latest of Frederic Woolley's essays would not be merely another step in the old direction. Clearly and unmistakably, it was a turning point. All his literary life Woolley had been concerned with the relation of literature to morality, religion, and the private and delicate pieties, and he had been unalterably opposed to all that he had called "inhuman humanitarianism." But here, suddenly, dramatically late, he had made an about-face, turning to the public life and to the humanitarian politics he had so long despised. This was the kind of incident the histories of literature make much of. Frederic Woolley was opening for himself a new career and winning a kind of new youth. He contrasted the two poets, Thomas Wormser, who was admirable, Joseph Howe, who was almost dangerous. He spoke of the "precious subjectivism" of Howe's verse. "In times like ours," he wrote, "with millions facing penury and want, one feels that the qualities of the *tour d'ivoire* are well-nigh inhuman, nearly insulting. The *tour d'ivoire* becomes the *tour d'ivresse,* and it is not self-intoxicated poets that our people need." The essay said more: "The problem is one of meaning. I am not ignorant that the creed of the esoteric poets declares that a poem does not and should not *mean* anything, that it *is* something. But poetry is what the poet makes, and if he is a true poet he makes what his society needs. And what is needed now is the tradition in which Mr. Wormser writes, the true tradition of poetry. The Howes do no harm, but they do no good when positive good is demanded of all responsible men. Or do the Howes indeed do no harm? Perhaps Plato would have said they do, that in some ways theirs is the Phrygian music that turns men's minds from the struggle. Certainly it is true that Thomas Wormser writes in the lucid Dorian mode which sends men into battle with evil."

It was easy to understand why Woolley had chosen to praise Thomas Wormser. The long, lilting lines of *Corn Under Willows* hymned, as Woolley put it, the struggle for wheat in the Iowa fields, and expressed the real lives of real people. But why out of the dozen more notable examples he had chosen Howe's little volume as the example of "precious subjectivism" was hard to guess. In a way it was funny, this multiplication of himself into "the Howes." And yet this becoming the multiform political symbol by whose creation Frederic Woolley gave the sign of a sudden new life, this use of him as a sacrifice whose blood was necessary for the rites of rejuvenation, made him feel oddly unclean.

Nor could Howe get rid of a certain practical resentment. As a poet he had a special and respectable place in the college life. But it might be another thing to be marked as the poet of a wilful and selfish obscurity.

As he walked to the Bradbys', Howe was a little tense and defensive. It seemed to him that all the world knew of the "attack" and agreed with it. And, indeed, the Bradbys had read the essay but Professor Bradby, a kind and pretentious man, said, "I see my old friend knocked you about a bit, my boy," and his wife Eugenia looked at Howe with her childlike blue eyes and said, "I shall *scold* Frederic for the untrue things he wrote about you. You aren't the least obscure." They beamed at him. In their genial snobbery they seemed to feel that he had distinguished himself. He was the leader of Howeism. He enjoyed the dinner party as much as he had thought he would.

And in the following days, as he was more preoccupied with his duties, the incident was forgotten. His classes had ceased to be mere groups. Student after student detached himself from the mass and required or claimed a place in Howe's awareness. Of them all it was Tertan who first and most violently signaled his separate existence. A week after classes had begun Howe saw his silhouette on the frosted glass of his office door. It was motionless for a long time, perhaps stopped by the problem of whether or not to knock before entering. Howe called, "Come in!" and Tertan entered with his shambling stride.

He stood beside the desk, silent and at attention. When Howe asked him to sit down, he responded with a gesture of head and hand, as if to say that such amenities were beside the point. Nevertheless, he did take the chair. He put his ragged, crammed briefcase between his legs. His face, which Howe now observed fully for the first time, was confusing, for it was made up of florid curves, the nose arched in the bone and voluted in the nostril, the mouth loose and soft and rather moist. Yet the face was so thin and narrow as to seem the very type of asceticism. Lashes of unusual length veiled the eyes and, indeed, it seemed as if there were a veil over the whole countenance. Before the words actually came, the face screwed itself into an attitude of preparation for them.

"You can confer with me now?" Tertan said.

"Yes, I'd be glad to. There are several things in your two themes I want to talk to you about." Howe reached for the packet of themes on his desk and sought for Tertan's. But the boy was waving them away.

"These are done perforce," he said. "Under the pressure of your requirement. They are not significant; mere duties." Again his great hand flapped vaguely to dismiss his themes. He leaned forward and gazed at his teacher.

"You are," he said, "a man of letters? You are a poet?" It was more declaration than question.

"I should like to think so," Howe said.

At first Tertan accepted the answer with a show of appreciation, as though the understatement made a secret between himself and Howe. Then he chose to misunderstand. With his shrewd and disconcerting control of expression, he presented to Howe a puzzled grimace. "What does that mean?" he said.

Howe retracted the irony. "Yes. I am a poet." It sounded strange to say.

"That," Tertan said, "is a wonder." He corrected himself with his ducking head. "I mean that is wonderful."

Suddenly, he dived at the miserable briefcase between his legs, put it on his knees, and began to fumble with the catch, all intent on the difficulty it presented. Howe noted that his suit was worn thin, his shirt almost unclean. He became aware, even, of a vague and musty odor of garments worn too long in unaired rooms. Tertan conquered the lock and began to concentrate upon a search into the interior. At last he held in his hand what he was after, a torn and crumpled copy of *Life and Letters*

"I learned it from here," he said, holding it out.

Howe looked at him sharply, his hackles a little up. But the boy's face was not only perfectly innocent, it even shone with a conscious admiration. Apparently nothing of the import of the essay had touched him except the wonderful fact that his teacher was a "man of letters." Yet this seemed too stupid, and Howe, to test it, said, "The man who wrote that doesn't think it's wonderful."

Tertan made a moist hissing sound as he cleared his throat of saliva. His head, oddly loose on his neck, wove a pattern of contempt in the air. "A critic," he said, "who admits *prima facie* that he does not understand." Then he said grandly, "It is the inevitable fate."

It was absurd, yet Howe was not only aware of the absurdity but of a tension suddenly and wonderfully relaxed. Now that the "attack" was on the table between himself and this strange boy, and subject to the boy's funny and absolutely certain contempt, the hidden force of his feeling was revealed to him in the very moment that it vanished. All unsuspected, there had been a film over the world, a transparent but discoloring haze of danger. But he had no time to stop over the brightened aspect of things. Tertan was going on. "I also am a man of letters. Putative."

"You have written a good deal?" Howe meant to be more than polite, and he was surprised at the tenderness he heard in his words.

Solemnly the boy nodded, threw back the dank lock, and sucked in a deep, anticipatory breath. "First, a work of homiletics, which is a defense of the principles of religious optimism against the pessimism of Schopenhauer and the humanism of Nietzsche."

"Humanism? Why do you call it humanism?"

"It is my nomenclature for making a deity of man," Tertan replied negligently. "Then three fictional works, novels. And numerous essays in science, combating materialism. Is it your duty to read these if I bring them to you?"

Howe answered simply, "No, it isn't exactly my duty, but I shall be happy to read them."

Tertan stood up and remained silent. He rested his bag on the chair. With a certain compunction—for it did not seem entirely proper that, of two men of letters, one should have the right to blue-pencil the other, to grade him or to question the quality of his "sentence structure"—Howe reached for Tertan's papers. But before he could take them up, the boy suddenly made his bow-to-Abelard, the stiff inclination of the body with the hands seeming to emerge from the scholar's gown. Then he was gone.

But after his departure something was still left of him. The timbre of his curious sentences, the downright finality of so quaint a phrase as "It is the inevitable fate" still rang in the air. Howe gave the warmth of his feeling to the new visitor who stood at the door announcing himself with the genteel clearing of the throat.

"Doctor Howe, I believe?" the student said. A large hand advanced into the room and grasped Howe's hand. "Blackburn, sir, Theodore Blackburn, vice-president of the Student Council. A great pleasure, sir."

Out of a pair of ruddy cheeks a pair of small eyes twinkled good-naturedly. The large face, the large body were not so much fat as beefy and suggested something "typical"—monk, politician, or innkeeper.

Blackburn took the seat beside Howe's desk. "I may have seemed to introduce myself in my public capacity, sir," he said. "But it is really as an individual that I came to see you. That is to say, as one of your students to be."

He spoke with an English intonation and went on, "I was once an English major, sir."

For a moment Howe was startled, for the roast-beef look of the boy and the manner of his speech gave a second's credibility to one sense of his statement. Then the collegiate meaning of the phrase asserted itself, but some perversity made Howe say what was really not in good taste even with so forward a student, "Indeed? What regiment?"

Blackburn stared and then gave a little pouf-pouf of laughter. He waved the misapprehension away. "*Very* good, sir. It certainly is an ambiguous term." He chuckled in appreciation of Howe's joke, then cleared his throat to put it aside. "I look forward to taking your course in the romantic poets, sir," he said earnestly. "To me the romantic poets are the very crown of English literature."

Howe made a dry sound, and the boy, catching some meaning in it, said, "Little as I know them, of course. But even Shakespeare, who is so dear to us of the Anglo-Saxon tradition, is in a sense but the preparation for Shelley, Keats, and Byron. And Wadsworth."

Almost sorry for him, Howe dropped his eyes. With some embarrassment, for the boy was not actually his student, he said softly, "Wordsworth."

"Sir?"

"Wordsworth, not Wadsworth. You said Wadsworth."

"Did I, sir?" Gravely he shook his head to rebuke himself for the error. "Wordsworth, of course—slip of the tongue." Then, quite in command again, he went on. "I have a favor to ask of you, Doctor Howe. You see, I began my college course as an English major,"—he smiled—"as I said."

"Yes?"

"But after my first year I shifted. I shifted to the social sciences. Sociology and government—I find them stimulating and very *real*." He paused, out of respect for reality. "But now I find that perhaps I have neglected the other side."

"The other side?" Howe said.

"Imagination, fancy, culture. A well-rounded man." He trailed off as if there were perfect understanding between them. "And so, sir, I have decided to end my senior year with your course in the romantic poets."

His voice was filled with an indulgence which Howe ignored as he said flatly and gravely, "But that course isn't given until the spring term."

"Yes, sir, and that is where the favor comes in. Would you let me take your romantic prose course? I can't take it for credit, sir, my program is full, but just for background it seems to me that I ought to take it. I do hope," he concluded in a manly way "that you will consent."

"Well, it's no great favor, Mr. Blackburn. You can come if you wish, though there's not much point in it if you don't do the reading."

The bell rang for the hour and Howe got up.

"May I begin with this class, sir?" Blackburn's smile was candid and boyish.

Howe nodded carelessly and together, silently, they walked to the classroom down the hall. When they reached the door Howe stood back to let his student enter, but Blackburn moved adroitly behind him and grasped him by the arm to urge him over the threshold. They entered with Blackburn's hand firmly on Howe's biceps, the student inducting the teacher into his own room. Howe felt a surge of temper rise in him and almost violently disengaged his arm and walked to the desk, while Blackburn found a seat in the front row and smiled at him.

II

The question was, At whose door must the tragedy be laid?

All night the snow had fallen heavily and only now was abating in sparse little flurries. The windows were valanced high with white. It was very quiet; something of the quiet of the world had reached the class, and Howe found that everyone was glad to talk or listen. In the room there was a comfortable sense of pleasure in being human.

Casebeer believed that the blame for the tragedy rested with heredity. Picking up the book he read, "The sins of the fathers are visited on their children." This opinion was received with general favor. Nevertheless, Johnson ventured to say that the fault was all Pastor Manders' because the Pastor had made Mrs. Alving go back to her husband and was always hiding the truth. To this Hibbard objected with logic enough, "Well then, it was really all her husband's fault. He *did* all the bad things." De Witt, his face bright with an impatient idea, said that the fault was all society's. "By society I don't mean upper-crust society," he said. He looked around a little defiantly, taking in any members of the class who might be members of upper-crust society. "Not in that sense. I mean the social unit."

Howe nodded and said, "Yes, of course."

"If the society of the time had progressed far enough in science," De Witt went on, "then there would be no problem for Mr. Ibsen to write about. Captain Alving plays around a little, gives way to perfectly natural biological urges, and he gets a social disease, a venereal disease. If the disease is cured, no problem. Invent salvarsan and the disease is cured. The problem of heredity disappears and li'l Oswald just doesn't get paresis. No paresis, no problem—no problem, no play."

This was carrying the ark into battle, and the class looked at De Witt with respectful curiosity. It was his usual way and on the whole they were sympathetic with his struggle to prove to Howe that science was better than literature. Still, there was something in his reckless manner that alienated them a little.

"Or take birth-control, for instance," De Witt went on. "If Mrs. Alving had some knowledge of contraception, she wouldn't have had to have li'l Oswald at all. No li'l Oswald, no play."

The class was suddenly quieter. In the back row Stettenhover swung his great football shoulders in a righteous sulking gesture, first to the right, then to the left. He puckered his mouth ostentatiously. Intellect was always ending up by talking dirty.

Tertan's hand went up, and Howe said, "Mr. Tertan." The boy shambled to his feet and began his long characteristic gulp. Howe made a motion with his fingers, as small as possible, and Tertan ducked his head and smiled in apology. He sat down. The class laughed. With more than half the term gone, Tertan had not been able to remember that one did not rise to speak. He seemed unable to carry on the life of the intellect without this mark of respect for it. To Howe the boy's habit of rising seemed to accord with the formal shabbiness of his dress. He never wore the casual sweaters and jackets of his classmates. Into the free and comfortable air of the college classroom he brought the stuffy sordid strictness of some crowded, metropolitan high school.

"Speaking from one sense," Tertan began slowly, "there is no blame ascribable. From the sense of determinism, who can say where the blame lies? The preordained is the preordained and it cannot be said without rebellion against the universe, a palpable absurdity."

In the back row Stettenhover slumped suddenly in his seat, his heels held out before him, making a loud, dry, disgusted sound. His body sank until his neck rested on the back of his chair. He folded his hands across his belly and looked significantly out of the window, exasperated not only with Tertan, but with Howe, with the class, with the whole system designed to encourage this kind of thing. There seemed a certain insolence in the movement and Howe flushed. As Tertan continued to speak, Howe stalked casually toward the window and placed himself in the line of Stettenhover's vision. He stared at the great fellow, who pretended not to see him. There was so much power in the big body, so much contempt in the Greek-athlete face under the crisp Greek-athlete curls, that Howe felt almost physical fear. But at last Stettenhover admitted him to focus and under his disapproving gaze sat up with slow indifference. His eyebrows raised high in resignation, he began to examine his hands. Howe relaxed and turned his attention back to Tertan.

"Flux of existence," Tertan was saying, "produces all things, so that judgment wavers. Beyond the phenomena, what? But phenomena are adumbrated and to them we are limited."

Howe saw it for a moment as perhaps it existed in the boy's mind—the world of shadows which are cast by a great light upon a sudden reality as in the old myth of the Cave. But the little brush with Stettenhover had tired him, and he said irritably, "But come to the point, Mr. Tertan."

He said it so sharply that some of the class looked at him curiously. For three months he had gently carried Tertan through his verbosities, to the vaguely respectful surprise of the other students, who seemed to conceive that there existed between this strange classmate and their teacher some special understanding from which they were content to be excluded. Tertan looked at him mildly, and at once came brilliantly to the point. "This is the summation of the play," he said and took up his book and read, " 'Your poor father never found any outlet for the overmastering joy of life that was in him. And I brought no holiday into his home, either. Everything seemed to turn upon duty and I am afraid I made your poor father's home unbearable to him, Oswald.' Spoken by Mrs. Alving."

Yes that was surely the "summation" of the play and Tertan had hit it, as he hit, deviously and eventually, the literary point of almost everything. But now, as always, he was wrapping it away from sight. "For most mortals," he said, "there are only joys of biological urgings, gross and crass, such as the sensuous Captain Alving. For certain few there are the transmutations beyond these to a contemplation of the utter whole."

Oh, the boy was mad. And suddenly the word, used in hyperbole, intended almost for the expression of exasperated admiration, became literal. Now that the word was used, it became simply apparent to Howe that Tertan was mad.

It was a monstrous word and stood like a bestial thing in the room. Yet it so completely comprehended everything that had puzzled Howe, it so arranged and explained what for three months had been perplexing him that almost at once its horror became domesticated. With this word Howe was able to understand why he had never been able to communicate to Tertan the value of a single criticism or correction of his wild verbose themes. Their conferences had been frequent and long but had done nothing to reduce to order the splendid confusion of the boy's ideas. Yet, impossible though its expression was, Tertan's incandescent mind could always strike for a moment into some dark corner of thought.

And now it was suddenly apparent that it was not a faulty rhetoric that Howe had to contend with. With his new knowledge he looked at Tertan's face and wondered how he could have so long deceived himself. Tertan was still talking, and the class had lapsed into a kind of patient unconsciousness, a coma of respect for words which, for all that most of them knew, might be profound. Almost with a suffusion of shame, Howe believed that in some dim way the class had long ago had some intimation of Tertan's madness. He reached out as decisively as he could to seize the thread of Tertan's discourse before it should be entangled further.

"Mr. Tertan says that the blame must be put upon whoever kills the joy of living in another. We have been assuming that Captain Alving was a wholly bad man, but what if we assume that he became bad only because Mrs. Alving, when they were first married, acted toward him in the prudish way she says she did?"

It was a ticklish idea to advance to freshmen and perhaps not profitable. Not all of them were following.

"That would put the blame on Mrs. Alving herself, whom most of you admire. And she herself seems to think so." He glanced at his watch. The hour was nearly over. "What do you think, Mr. De Witt?"

De Witt rose to the idea; he wanted to know if society couldn't be blamed for educating Mrs. Alving's temperament in the wrong way. Casebeer was puzzled, Stettenhover continued to look at his hands until the bell rang.

Tertan, his brows louring in thought, was making as always for a private word. Howe gathered his books and papers to leave quickly. At this moment of his discovery and with the knowledge still raw, he could not engage himself with Tertan. Tertan sucked in his breath to prepare for speech and Howe made ready for the pain and confusion. But at that moment Casebeer detached himself from the group with which he had been conferring and which he seemed to represent. His constituency remained at a tactful distance. The mission involved the time of an assigned essay. Casebeer's presentation of the plea—it was based on the freshmen's heavy duties at the fraternities during Carnival Week—cut across Tertan's preparations for speech. "And so some of us fellows thought," Casebeer concluded with heavy solemnity, "that we could do a better job, give our minds to it more, if we had more time."

Tertan regarded Casebeer with mingled curiosity and revulsion. Howe not only said that he would postpone the assignment but went on to talk about the Carnival, and even drew the waiting constituency into the conversation. He was conscious of Tertan's stern and astonished stare, then of his sudden departure.

Now that the fact was clear, Howe knew that he must act on it. His course was simple enough. He must lay the case before the Dean. Yet he hesitated. His feeling for Tertan must now, certainly, be in some way invalidated. Yet could he, because of a word, hurry to assign to official and reasonable solicitude what had been until this moment, so various and warm? He could at least delay and, by moving slowly, lend a poor grace to the necessary, ugly act of making his report.

It was with some notion of keeping the matter in his own hands that he went to the Dean's office to look up Tertan's records. In the outer office the Dean's secretary greeted him brightly, and at his request brought him the manila folder with the small identifying photograph pasted in the corner.

She laughed. "He was looking for the birdie in the wrong place," she said.

Howe leaned over her shoulder to look at the picture. It was as bad as all the Dean's-office photographs were, but it differed from all that Howe had ever seen. Tertan, instead of looking into the camera, as no doubt he had been bidden, had, at the moment of exposure, turned his eyes upward. His mouth, as though conscious of the trick played on the photographer, had the sly superior look that Howe knew.

The secretary was fascinated by the picture. "What a funny boy," she said. "He looks like Tartuffe!"

And so he did, with the absurd piety of the eyes and the conscious slyness of the mouth and the whole face bloated by the bad lens.

"Is he *like* that?" the secretary said.

"Like Tartuffe? No."

From the photograph there was little enough comfort to be had. The records themselves gave no clue to madness, though they suggested sadness enough. Howe read of a father, Stanislaus Tertan, born in Budapest and trained in engineering in Berlin, once employed by the Hercules Chemical Corporation—this was one of the factories that dominated the sound end of the town—but now without employment. He read of a mother Erminie (Youngfellow) Tertan, born in Manchester, educated at a Normal School at Leeds, now housewife by profession. The family lived on Greenbriar Street which Howe knew as a row of once elegant homes near what was now the factory district. The old mansion had long ago been divided into small and primitive apartments. Of Ferdinand himself there was little to learn. He lived with his parents, had attended a Detroit high school and had transferred to the local school in his last year. His rating for intelligence, as expressed in numbers, was high, his scholastic record was remarkable, he held a college scholarship for his tuition.

Howe laid the folder on the secretary's desk. "Did you find what you wanted to know?" she asked.

The phrases from Tertan's momentous first theme came back to him. "Tertan I am, but what is Tertan? Of this time, of that place, of some parentage, what does it matter?"

"No, I didn't find it," he said.

Now that he had consulted the sad, half-meaningless record he knew all the more firmly that he must not give the matter out of his hands. He must not release Tertan to authority. Not that he anticipated from the Dean anything but the greatest kindness for Tertan. The Dean would have the experience and skill which he himself could not have. One way or another the Dean could answer the question, "What is Tertan?" Yet this was precisely what he feared. He alone could keep it still a question. Some sure instinct told him that he must not surrender the question to a clean official desk in a clear official light to be dealt with, settled and closed.

He heard himself saying, "Is the Dean busy at the moment? I'd like to see him."

His request came thus unbidden, even forbidden, and it was one of the surprising and startling incidents of his life. Later when he reviewed the events, so disconnected in themselves, or so merely odd, of the story that unfolded for him that year, it was over this moment, on its face the least notable, that he paused longest. It was frequently to be with fear and never without a certainty of its meaning in his own knowledge of himself that he would recall this simple, routine request, and the feeling of shame and freedom it gave him as he sent everything down the official chute. In the end, of course, no matter what he did to "protect" Tertan, he would have had to make the same request and lay the matter on the Dean's clean desk. But it would always be a landmark of his life that, at the very moment when he was rejecting the official way, he had been, without will or intention, so gladly drawn to it.

After the storm's last delicate flurry, the sun had come out. Reflected by the new snow, it filled the office with a golden light which was almost musical in the way it made all the commonplace objects shine with a sudden sad and noble significance. And the light, now that he noticed it, made the utterance of his perverse and unwanted request even more momentous.

The secretary consulted the engagment pad. "He'll be free any minute. Don't you want to wait in the parlor?"

She threw open the door of the large and pleasant room in which the Dean held his Committee meetings, and in which his visitors waited. It was designed with a homely elegance on the masculine side of the eighteenth-century manner. There was a small coal fire in the grate and the handsome mahogany table was strewn with books and magazines. The large windows gave on the snowy lawn, and there was such a fine width of window that the white casements and walls seemed at this moment but a continuation of the snow, the snow but an extension of casement and walls. The outdoors seemed taken in and made safe, the indoors seemed luxuriously freshened and expanded.

Howe sat down by the fire and lighted a cigarette. The room had its intended effect upon him. He felt comfortable and relaxed, yet nicely organized, some young diplomatic agent of the eighteenth century, the newly fledged Swift carrying out Sir William Temple's business. The rawness of Tertan's case quite vanished. He crossed his legs and reached for a magazine.

It was that famous issue of *Life and Letters* that his idle hand found and his blood raced as he sifted through it, and the shape of his own name, Joseph Howe, sprang out at him, still cabalistic in its power. He tossed the magazine back on the table as the door of the Dean's office opened and the Dean ushered out Theodore Blackburn.

"Ah, Joseph!" the Dean said.

Blackburn said, "Good morning, Doctor." Howe winced at the title and caught the flicker of amusement over the Dean's face. The Dean stood with his hand high on the door-jamb and Blackburn, still in the doorway, remained standing almost under the long arm.

Howe nodded briefly to Blackburn, snubbing his eager deference. "Can you give me a few minutes?" he said to the Dean.

"All the time you want. Come in." Before the two men could enter the office, Blackburn claimed their attention with a long full "er." As they turned to him, Blackburn said, "Can *you* give *me* a few minutes, Doctor Howe?" His eyes sparkled at the little audacity he had committed, the slightly impudent play with hierarchy. Of the three of them Blackburn kept himself the lowest, but he reminded Howe of his subaltern relation to the Dean.

"I mean, of course," Blackburn went on easily, "when you've finished with the Dean."

"I'll be in my office shortly," Howe said, turned his back on the ready "Thank you, sir," and followed the Dean into the inner room.

"Energetic boy," said the Dean. "A bit beyond himself but very energetic. Sit down."

The Dean lighted a cigarette, leaned back in his chair, sat easy and silent for a moment, giving Howe no signal to go ahead with business. He was a young Dean, not much beyond forty, a tall handsome man with sad, ambitious eyes. He had been a Rhodes scholar. His friends looked for great things from him, and it was generally said that he had notions of education which he was not yet ready to try to put into practice.

His relaxed silence was meant as a compliment to Howe. He smiled and said, "What's the business, Joseph?"

"Do you know Tertan—Ferdinand Tertan, a freshman?"

The Dean's cigarette was in his mouth and his hands were clasped behind his head. He did not seem to search his memory for the name. He said, "What about him?"

Clearly the Dean knew something, and he was waiting for Howe to tell him more. Howe moved only tentatively. Now that he was doing what he had resolved not to do, he felt more guilty at having been so long deceived by Tertan and more need to be loyal to his error.

"He's a strange fellow," he ventured. He said stubbornly, "In a strange way he's very brilliant." He concluded, "But very strange."

The springs of the Dean's swivel chair creaked as he came out of his sprawl and leaned forward to Howe. "Do you mean he's so strange that it's something you could give a name to?"

Howe looked at him stupidly. "What do you mean?" he said.

"What's his trouble?" the Dean said more neutrally.

"He's very brilliant, in a way. I looked him up and he has a top intelligence rating. But somehow, and it's hard to explain just how, what he says is always on the edge of sense and doesn't quite make it."

The Dean looked at him and Howe flushed up. The Dean had surely read Woolley on the subject of "the Howes" and the *tour d'ivresse*. Was that quick glance ironical?

The Dean picked up some papers from his desk, and Howe could see that they were in Tertan's impatient scrawl. Perhaps the little gleam in the Dean's glance had come only from putting facts together.

"He sent me this yesterday," the Dean said. "After an interview I had with him. I haven't been able to do more than glance at it. When you said what you did, I realized there was something wrong."

Twisting his mouth, the Dean looked over the letter. "You seem to be involved," he said without looking up. "By the way, what did you give him at mid-term?"

Flushing, setting his shoulders, Howe said firmly, "I gave him A-minus."

The Dean chuckled. "Might be a good idea if some of our nicer boys went crazy—just a little." He said, "Well," to conclude the matter and handed the papers to Howe. "See if this is the same thing you've been finding. Then we can go into the matter again."

Before the fire in the parlor, in the chair that Howe had been occupying, sat Blackburn. He sprang to his feet as Howe entered.

"I said my office, Mr. Blackburn." Howe's voice was sharp. Then he was almost sorry for the rebuke, so clearly and naively did Blackburn seem to relish his stay in the parlor, close to authority.

"I'm in a bit of a hurry, sir," he said, "and I did want to be sure to speak to you, sir."

He was really absurd, yet fifteen years from now he would have grown up to himself, to the assurance and mature beefiness. In banks, in consular offices, in brokerage firms, on the bench, more seriously affable, a little sterner, he would make use of his ability to be administered by his job. It was almost reassuring. Now he was exercising his too-great skill on Howe. "I owe you an apology, sir," he said.

Howe knew that he did, but he showed surprise.

"I mean, Doctor, after your having been so kind about letting me attend your class, I stopped coming." He smiled in deprecation. "Extracurricular activities take up so much of my time. I'm afraid I undertook more than I could perform."

Howe had noticed the absence and had been a little irritated by it after Blackburn's elaborate plea. It was an absence that might be interpreted as a comment on the teacher. But there was only one way for him to answer. "You've no need to apologize," he said. "It's wholly your affair."

Blackburn beamed. "I'm so glad you feel that way about it, sir. I was worried you might think I had stayed away because I was influenced by—" he stopped and lowered his eyes.

Astonished, Howe, said, "Influenced by what?"

"Well, by—" Blackburn hesitated and for answer pointed to the table on which lay the copy of *Life and Letters*. Without looking at it, he knew where to direct his hand. "By the unfavorable publicity, sir." He hurried on. "And that brings me to another point, sir. I am secretary of Quill and Scroll, sir, the student literary society, and I wonder if you would address us. You could read your own poetry, sir, and defend your own point of view. It would be very interesting."

It was truly amazing. Howe looked long and cruelly into Blackburn's face, trying to catch the secret of the mind that could have conceived this way of manipulating him, this way so daring and inept—but not entirely inept—with its malice so without malignity. The face did not yield its secret. Howe smiled broadly and said, "Of course I don't think you were influenced by the unfavorable publicity."

"I'm still going to take—regularly, for credit—your romantic poets course next term," Blackburn said.

"Don't worry, my dear fellow, don't worry about it."

Howe started to leave and Blackburn stopped him with, "But about Quill, sir?"

"Suppose we wait until next term? I'll be less busy then."

And Blackburn said, "Very good, sir, and thank you."

In his office the little encounter seemed less funny to Howe, was even in some indeterminate way disturbing. He made an effort to put it from his mind by turning to what was sure to disturb him more, the Tertan letter read in the new interpretation. He found what he had always found, the same florid leaps beyond fact and meaning, the same headlong certainty. But as his eye passed over the familiar scrawl it caught his own name, and for the second time that hour he felt the race of his blood.

"The Paraclete," Tertan had written to the Dean, "from a Greek word meaning to stand in place of, but going beyond the primitive idea to mean traditionally the helper, the one who comforts and assists, cannot without fundamental loss be jettisoned. Even if taken no longer in the supernatural sense, the concept remains deeply in the human consciousness inevitably. Humanitarianism is no reply, for not every man stands in the place of every other man for this other comrade's comfort. But certain are chosen out of the human race to be the consoler of some other. Of these, for example, is Joseph Barker Howe, Ph.D.—of intellects not the first yet of true intellect and lambent instructions, given to that which is intuitive and irrational, not to what is logical in the strict word, what is judged by him is of the heart and not of the head. Here is one chosen, in that he chooses himself to stand in the place of another for comfort and consolation. To him more than another I give my gratitude, with all respect to our Dean who reads this, a noble man, but merely dedicated, not consecrated. But not in the aspect of the Paraclete only is Dr. Joseph Barker Howe established, for he must be the Paraclete to another aspect of himself, that which is driven and persecuted by the lack of understanding in the world at large, so that he himself embodies the full history of man's tribulations and, overflowing upon others, notably the present writer, is the ultimate end."

This was love. There was no escaping it. Try as Howe might to remember that Tertan was mad and all his emotions invalidated, he could not destroy the effect upon him of his student's stern, affectionate regard. He had betrayed not only a power of mind but a power of love. And however firmly he held before his attention the fact of Tertan's madness, he could do nothing to banish the physical sensation of gratitude he felt. He had never thought of himself as "driven and persecuted" and he did not now. But still he could not make meaningless his sensation of gratitude. The pitiable Tertan sternly pitied him, and comfort came from Tertan's never-to-be-comforted mind.

III

In an academic community, even an efficient one, official matters move slowly. The term drew to a close with no action in the case of Tertan, and Joseph Howe had to confront a curious problem. How should he grade his strange student, Tertan?

Tertan's final examination had been no different from all his writing, and what did one "give" such a student? De Witt must have his A, that was clear. Johnson would get a B. With Casebeer it was a question of a B-minus or a C-plus, and Stettenhover, who had been crammed by the team tutor to fill half a blue-book with his thin feminine scrawl, would have his C-minus which he would accept with mingled indifference and resentment. But with Tertan it was not so easy. The boy was still in the college process and his name could not be omitted from the grade sheet. Yet what should a mind under suspicion of madness be graded? Until the medical verdict was given, it was for Howe to continue as Tertan's teacher and to keep his judgment pedagogical. Impossible to give him an F: he had not failed. B was for Johnson's stolid mediocrity. He could not be put on the edge of passing with Stettenhover, for he exactly did not pass. In energy and richness of intellect he was perhaps even De Witt's superior, and Howe toyed grimly with the notion of giving him an A, but that would lower the value of the A De Witt had won with his beautiful and clear, if still somewhat arrogant, mind. There was a notation which the Registrar recognized—Inc., for Incomplete, and in the horrible comedy of the situation, Howe considered that. But really only a mark of M for Mad would serve.

In his perplexity, Howe sought the Dean, but the Dean was out of town. In the end, he decided to maintain the A-minus he had given Tertan at mid-term. After all, there had been no falling away from that quality. He entered it on the grade sheet with something like bravado.

Academic time moves quickly. A college year is not really a year, lacking as it does three months. And it is endlessly divided into units which, at their beginning, appear larger than they are—terms, half terms, months, weeks. And the ultimate unit, the hour, is not really an hour, lacking as it does ten minutes. And so the new term advanced rapidly, and one day the fields about the town were all brown, cleared of even the few thin patches of snow which had lingered so long.

Howe, as he lectured on the romantic poets, became conscious of Blackburn emanating wrath. Blackburn did it well, did it with enormous dignity. He did not stir in his seat, he kept his eyes fixed on Howe in perfect attention, but he abstained from using his notebook, there was no mistaking what he proposed to himself as an attitude. His elbow on the writing-wing of the chair, his chin on the curled fingers of his hand, he was the embodiment of intellectual indignation. He was thinking his own thoughts, would give no public offense, yet would claim his due, was not to be intimidated. Howe knew that he would present himself at the end of the hour.

Blackburn entered the office without invitation. He did not smile; there was no cajolery about him. Without invitation he sat down beside Howe's desk. He did not speak until he had taken the blue-book from his pocket. He said, "What does this mean, sir?"

It was a sound and conservative student tactic. Said in the usual way it meant, "How could you have so misunderstood me?" or "What does this mean for my future in the course?" But there were none of the humbler tones in Blackburn's way of saying it.

Howe made the established reply, "I think that's for you to tell me."

Blackburn continued icy. "I'm sure I can't, sir."

There was a silence between them. Both dropped their eyes to the blue-book on the desk. On its cover Howe had penciled: "F. This is very poor work."

Howe picked up the blue-book. There was always the possibility of injustice. The teacher may be bored by the mass of papers and not wholly attentive. A phrase, even the student's handwriting, may irritate him unreasonably. "Well," said Howe, "let's go through it."

He opened the first page. "Now here: you write, 'In *The Ancient Mariner*, Coleridge lives in and transports us to a honey-sweet world where all is rich and strange, a world of charm to which we can escape from the humdrum existence of our daily lives, the world of romance. Here, in this warm and honey-sweet land of charming dreams we can relax and enjoy ourselves.' "

Howe lowered the paper and waited with a neutral look for Blackburn to speak. Blackburn returned the look boldly, did not speak, sat stolid and lofty. At last Howe said, speaking gently, "Did you mean that, or were you just at a loss for something to say?"

"You imply that I was just 'bluffing'?" The quotation marks hung palpable in the air about the word.

"I'd like to know. I'd prefer believing that you were bluffing to believing that you really thought this."

Blackburn's eyebrows went up. From the height of a great and firm-based idea he looked at his teacher. He clasped the crags for a moment and then pounced, craftily, suavely. "Do you mean, Doctor Howe, that there aren't two opinions possible?"

It was superbly done in its air of putting all of Howe's

intellectual life into the balance. Howe remained patient and simple. "Yes, many opinions are possible, but not that one. Whatever anyone believes of *The Ancient Mariner,* no one can in reason believe that it represents a—a honey-sweet world in which we can relax."

"But that is what I *feel,* sir."

This was well-done, too. Howe said, "Look, Mr. Blackburn. Do you really relax with hunger and thirst, the heat and the sea-serpents, the dead men with staring eyes, Life in Death and the skeletons? Come now, Mr. Blackburn."

Blackburn made no answer, and Howe pressed forward. "Now, you say of Wordsworth, 'Of peasant stock himself, he turned from the effete life of the salons and found in the peasant the hope of a flaming revolution which would sweep away all the old ideas. This is the subject of his best poems.' "

Beaming at his teacher with youthful eagerness, Blackburn said, "Yes, sir, a rebel, a bringer of light to suffering mankind. I see him as a kind of Prothemeus."

"A kind of what?"

"Prothemeus, sir."

"Think, Mr. Blackburn. We were talking about him only today and I mentioned his name a dozen times. You don't mean Prothemus. You mean—" Howe waited, but there was no response.

"You mean Prometheus."

Blackburn gave no assent and Howe took the reins. "You've done a bad job here, Mr. Blackburn, about as bad as could be done." He saw Blackburn stiffen and his genial face harden again. "It shows either a lack of preparation or a complete lack of understanding." He saw Blackburn's face begin to go to pieces and he stopped.

"Oh, sir," Blackburn burst out, "I've never had a mark like this before, never anything below a B, never. A thing like this has never happened to me before."

It must be true, it was a statement too easily verified. Could it be that other instructors accepted such flaunting nonsense? Howe wanted to end the interview. "I'll set it down to lack of preparation," he said. "I know you're busy. That's not an excuse, but it's an explanation. Now suppose you really prepare, and then take another quiz in two weeks. We'll forget this one and count the other."

Blackburn squirmed with pleasure and gratitude. "Thank you, sir. You're really very kind, very kind."

Howe rose to conclude the visit. "All right, then—in two weeks."

It was that day that the Dean imparted to Howe the conclusion of the case of Tertan. It was simple and a little anticlimactic. A physician had been called in, and had said the word, given the name.

"A classic case, he called it," the Dean said. "Not a doubt in the world," he said. His eyes were full of miserable pity, and he clutched at a word. "A classic case, a classic case." To his aid and to Howe's there came the Parthenon and the form of the Greek drama, the Aristotelian logic, Racine and the Well-Tempered Clavichord, the blueness of the Aegean and its clear sky. Classic—that is to say, without a doubt, perfect in its way, a veritable model, and, as the Dean had been told, sure to take a perfectly predictable and inevitable course to a foreknown conclusion.

It was not only pity that stood in the Dean's eyes. For a moment there was fear too. "Terrible," he said, "it is simply terrible."

Then he went on briskly. "Naturally, we've told the boy nothing. And, naturally, we won't. His tuition's paid by his scholarship, and we'll continue him on the rolls until the end of the year. That will be kindest. After that the matter will be out of our control. We'll see, of course, that he gets into proper hands. I'm told there will be no change, he'll go on like this, be as good as this, for four to six months. And so we'll just go along as usual."

So Tertan continued to sit in Section 5 of English 1A, to his classmates still a figure of curiously dignified fun, symbol to most of them of the respectable but absurd intellectual life. But to his teacher he was now very different. He had not changed—he was still the greyhound casting for the scent of ideas, and Howe could see that he was still the same Tertan, but he could not feel it. What he felt as he looked at the boy sitting in his accustomed place was the hard blank of a fact. The fact itself was formidable and depressing. But what Howe was chiefly aware of was that he had permitted the metamorphosis of Tertan from person to fact.

As much as possible he avoided seeing Tertan's upraised hand and eager eye. But the fact did not know of its mere factuality, it continued its existence as if it were Tertan, hand up and eye questioning, and one day it appeared in Howe's office with a document.

"Even the spirit who lives egregiously, above the herd, must have its relations with the fellowman," Tertan declared. He laid the document on Howe's desk. It was headed "Quill and Scroll Society of Dwight College. Application for Membership."

"In most ways these are crass minds," Tertan said, touching the paper. "Yet as a whole, bound together in their common love of letters, they transcend their intellectual lacks since it is not a paradox that the whole is greater than the sum of its parts."

"When are the elections?" Howe asked.

"They take place tomorrow."

"I certainly hope you will be successful."

"Thank you. Would you wish to implement that hope?" A rather dirty finger pointed to the bottom of the sheet. "A faculty recommender is necessary," Tertan said stiffly and waited.

"And you wish me to recommend you?"

"It would be an honor."

"You may use my name."

Tertan's finger pointed again. "It must be a written sponsorship, signed by the sponsor." There was a large blank space on the form under the heading, "Opinion of Faculty Sponsor."

This was almost another thing and Howe hesitated. Yet there was nothing else to do and he took out his fountain pen. He wrote, "Mr. Ferdinand Tertan is marked by his intense devotion to letters and by his exceptional love of all things of the mind." To this he signed his name, which looked bold and assertive on the white page. It disturbed him, the strange affirming power of a name. With a businesslike air, Tertan whipped up the paper, folding it with decision, and put it in his pocket. He bowed and took his departure, leaving Howe with the sense of having done something oddly momentous.

And so much now seemed odd and momentous to Howe that should not have seemed so. It was odd and momentous, he felt, when he sat with Blackburn's second quiz before him, and wrote in an excessively firm hand the grade of C-minus. The paper was a clear, and undisputable failure. He was carefully and consciously committing a cowardice. Blackburn had told the truth when he had pleaded his past record. Howe had consulted it in the Dean's office. It showed no grade lower than a B-minus. A canvass of some of Blackburn's previous instructors had brought vague attestations to the adequate powers of a student imperfectly remembered, and sometimes surprise that his abilities could be questioned at all.

As he wrote the grade, Howe told himself that his cowardice sprang from an unwillingness to have more dealings with a student he disliked. He knew it was simpler than that. He knew he feared Blackburn: that was the absurd truth. And cowardice did not solve the matter after all. Blackburn, flushed with the first success, attacked at once. The minimal passing grade had not assuaged his feelings and he sat at Howe's desk and again the blue-book lay between them. Blackburn said nothing. With an enormous impudence, he was waiting for Howe to speak and explain himself.

At last Howe said sharply and rudely, "Well?" His throat was tense and the blood was hammering in his head. His mouth was tight with anger at himself for his disturbance.

Blackburn's glance was almost baleful. "This is impossible, sir."

"But there it is," Howe answered.

"Sir?" Blackburn had not caught the meaning but his tone was still haughty.

Impatiently Howe said, "There it is, plain as day. Are you here to complain again?"

"Indeed I am, sir." There was surprise in Blackburn's voice that Howe should ask the question.

"I shouldn't complain if I were you. You did a thoroughly bad job on your first quiz. This one is a little, only a very little better." This was not true. If anything, it was worse.

"That might be a matter of opinion, sir."

"It is a matter of opinion. Of my opinion."

"Another opinion might be different, sir."

"You really believe that?" Howe said.

"Yes." The omission of the "sir" was monumental.

"Whose, for example?"

"The Dean's, for example." Then the fleshy jaw came forward a little. "Or a certain literary critic's, for example."

It was colossal and almost too much for Blackburn himself to handle. The solidity of his face almost crumpled under it. But he withstood his own audacity and went on. "And the

Dean's opinion might be guided by the knowledge that the person who gave me this mark is the man whom a famous critic, the most eminent judge of literature in this country, called a drunken man. The Dean might think twice about whether such a man is fit to teach Dwight students."

Howe said in quiet admonition. "Blackburn, you're mad," meaning no more than to check the boy's extravagance.

But Blackburn paid no heed. He had another shot in the locker. "And the Dean might be guided by the information, of which I have evidence, documentary evidence,"—he slapped his breast pocket twice— "that this same person personally recommended to the college literary society, the oldest in the country, that he personally recommended a student who is crazy, who threw the meeting into an uproar—a psychiatric case. The Dean might take that into account."

Howe was never to learn the details of that "uproar." He had always to content himself with the dim but passionate picture which at that moment sprang into his mind, of Tertan standing on some abstract height and madly denouncing the multitude of Quill and Scroll who howled him down.

He sat quiet a moment and looked at Blackburn. The ferocity had entirely gone from the student's face. He sat regarding his teacher almost benevolently. He had played a good card and now, scarcely at all unfriendly, he was waiting to see the effect. Howe took up the blue-book and negligently sifted through it. He read a page, closed the book, struck out the C-minus and wrote an F.

"Now you may take the paper to the Dean," he said. "You may tell him that after reconsidering it, I lowered the grade."

The gasp was audible. "Oh, sir!" Blackburn cried. "Please!" His face was agonized. "It means my graduation, my livelihood, my future. Don't do this to me."

"It's done already."

Blackburn stood up. "I spoke rashly, sir, hastily. I had no intention, no real intention, of seeing the Dean. It rests with you—entirely, entirely. I *hope* you will restore the first mark."

"Take the matter to the Dean or not, just as you choose. The grade is what you deserve and it stands."

Blackburn's head dropped. "And will I be failed at midterm, sir?"

"Of course."

From deep out of Blackburn's great chest rose a cry of

anguish. "Oh, sir, if you want me to go down on my knees to you, I will, I will."

Howe looked at him in amazement.

"I will, I will. On my knees, sir. This mustn't, mustn't happen."

He spoke so literally, meaning so very truly that his knees and exactly his knees were involved and seeming to think that he was offering something of tangible value to his teacher, that Howe, whose head had become icy clear in the nonsensical drama, thought, "The boy is mad," and began to speculate fantastically whether something in himself attracted or developed aberration. He could see himself standing absurdly before the Dean and saying, "I've found another. This time it's the vice-president of the Council, the manager of the debating team and secretary of Quill and Scroll."

One more such discovery, he thought, and he himself would be discovered! And there, suddenly, Blackburn was on his knees with a thump, his huge thighs straining his trousers, his hand outstretched in a great gesture of supplication.

With a cry, Howe shoved back his swivel chair and it rolled away on its casters half across the little room. Blackburn knelt for a moment to nothing at all, then got to his feet.

Howe rose abruptly. He said, "Blackburn, you will stop acting like an idiot. Dust your knees off, take your paper and get out. You've behaved like a fool and a malicious person. You have half a term to do a decent job. Keep your silly mouth shut and try to do it. Now get out."

Blackburn's head was low. He raised it and there was a pious light in his eyes. "Will you shake hands, sir?" he said. He thrust out his hand.

"I will not," Howe said.

Head and hand sank together. Blackburn picked up his blue-book and walked to the door. He turned and said, "Thank you, sir." His back, as he departed, was heavy with tragedy and stateliness.

IV

After years of bad luck with the weather, the College had a perfect day for Commencement. It was wonderfully bright, the air so transparent, the wind so brisk that no one could resist talking about it.

As Howe set out for the campus, he heard Hilda calling from the back yard. She called, "Professor, professor," and came running to him.

Howe said, "What's this 'professor' business?"

"Mother told me," Hilda said. "You've been promoted. And I want to take your picture."

"Next year," said Howe. "I won't be a professor until next year. And you know better than to call anybody 'professor.' "

"It was just in fun," Hilda said. She seemed disappointed.

"But you can take my picture if you want. I won't look much different next year." Still, it was frightening. It might mean that he was to stay in this town all his life.

Hilda brightened. "Can I take it in this?" she said, and touched the gown he carried over his arm.

Howe laughed. "Yes, you can take it in this."

"I'll get my things and meet you in front of Otis," Hilda said. "I have the background all picked out."

On the campus the Commencement crowd was already large. It stood about in eager, nervous little family groups. As he crossed, Howe was greeted by a student, capped and gowned, glad of the chance to make an event for his parents by introducing one of his teachers. It was while Howe stood there chatting that he saw Tertan.

He had never seen anyone quite so alone, as though a circle had been woven about him to separate him from the gay crowd on the campus. Not that Tertan was not gay, he was the gayest of all. Three weeks had passed since Howe had last seen him, the weeks of examination, the lazy week before Commencement, and this was now a different Tertan. On his head he wore a panama hat, broad brimmed and fine, of the shape associated with South American planters. He wore a suit of raw silk, luxurious, but yellowed with age and much too tight, and he sported a whangee cane. He walked sedately, the hat tilted at a devastating angle, the stick coming up and down in time to his measured tread. He had, Howe guessed, outfitted himself to greet the day in the clothes of that ruined father whose existence was on record in the Dean's office. Gravely and arrogantly he surveyed the scene —in it, his whole bearing seemed to say, but not of it. With his haughty step, with his flashing eye, Tertan was coming nearer. Howe did not wish to be seen. He shifted his position slightly. When he looked again, Tertan was not in sight.

The chapel clock struck the quarter hour. Howe detached himself from his chat and hurried to Otis Hall at the far end of the campus. Hilda had not yet come. He went up into the high portico and, using the glass of the door for a mirror, put on his gown, adjusted the hood on his shoulders and set the mortar board on his head. When he came down the steps, Hilda had arrived.

Nothing could have told him more forcibly that a year had passed than the development of Hilda's photographic possessions from the box camera of the previous fall. By a strap about her neck was hung a leather case, so thick and strong, so carefully stitched and so molded to its contents that it could only hold a costly camera. The appearance was deceptive, Howe knew, for he had been present at the Aikens' pre-Christmas conference about its purchase. It was only a fairly good domestic camera. Still, it looked very impressive. Hilda carried another leather case from which she drew a collapsible tripod. Decisively she extended each of its gleaming legs and set it up on the path. She removed the camera from its case and fixed it to the tripod. In its compact efficiency the camera almost had a life of its own, but Hilda treated it with easy familiarity, looked into its eye, glanced casually at its guages. Then from a pocket she took still another leather case and drew from it a small instrument through which she looked first at Howe, who began to feel inanimate and lost, and then at the sky. She made some adjustment on the instrument, then some adjustment on the camera. She swept the scene with her eye, found a spot and pointed the camera in its direction. She walked to the spot, stood on it and beckoned to Howe. With each new leather case, with each new instrument, and with each new adjustment she had grown in ease and now she said, "Joe, will you stand here?"

Obediently Howe stood where he was bidden. She had yet another instrument. She took out a tape-measure on a mechanical spool. Kneeling down before Howe, she put the little metal ring of the tape under the tip of his shoe. At her request, Howe pressed it with his toe. When she had measured her distance, she nodded to Howe who released the tape. At a touch, it sprang back into the spool. "You have to be careful if you're going to get what you want," Hilda said.

"I don't believe in all this snap-snap-snapping," she remarked loftily. Howe nodded in agreement, although he was beginning to think Hilda's care excessive.

Now at last the moment had come. Hilda squinted into the camera, moved the tripod slightly. She stood to the side, holding the plunger of the shutter-cable. "Ready," she said. "Will you relax, Joseph, please?" Howe realized that he was standing frozen, Hilda stood poised and precise as a setter, one hand holding the little cable, the other extended with curled dainty fingers like a dancer's, as if expressing to her subject the precarious delicacy of the moment. She pressed the plunger and there was a click. At once she stirred to action, got behind the camera, turned a new exposure. "Thank you," she said. "Would you stand under that tree and let me do a character study with light and shade?"

The childish absurdity of the remark restored Howe's ease. He went to the little tree. The pattern the leaves made on his gown was what Hilda was after. He had just taken a satisfactory position when he heard in the unmistakable voice, "Ah, Doctor! Having your picture taken?"

Howe gave up the pose and turned to Blackburn, who stood on the walk, his hands behind his back, a little too large for his bachelor's gown. Annoyed that Blackburn should see him posing for a character study in light and shade, Howe said irritably, "Yes, having my picture taken."

Blackburn beamed at Hilda. "And the little photographer?" he said. Hilda fixed her eyes on the ground and stood closer to her brilliant and aggressive camera. Blackburn, teetering on his heels, his hands behind his back, wholly prelatical and benignly patient, was not abashed at the silence. At last Howe said, "If you'll excuse us, Mr. Blackburn, we'll go on with the picture."

"Go right ahead, sir. I'm running along." But he only came closer. "Doctor Howe," he said fervently, "I want to tell you how glad I am that I was able to satisfy your standards at last."

Howe was surprised at the hard, insulting brightness of his own voice, and even Hilda looked up curiously as he said, "Nothing you have ever done has satisfied me, and nothing you could ever do would satisfy me, Blackburn."

With a glance at Hilda, Blackburn made a gesture as if to hush Howe—as though all his former bold malice had taken for granted a kind of understanding between himself and his teacher, a secret which must not be betrayed to a third person. "I only meant, sir," he said, "that I was able to pass your course after all."

Howe said, "You didn't pass my course. I passed you out of my course. I passed you without even reading your paper. I wanted to be sure the college would be rid of you. And when all the grades were in and I did read your paper, I saw I was right not to have read it first."

Blackburn presented a stricken face. "It was very bad, sir?"

But Howe had turned away. The paper had been fantastic. The paper had been, if he wished to see it so, mad. It was at this moment that the Dean came up behind Howe and caught his arm. "Hello, Joseph," he said. "We'd better be getting along, it's almost late."

He was not a familiar man, but when he saw Blackburn, who approached to greet him, he took Blackburn's arm, too. "Hello, Theodore," he said. Leaning forward on Howe's arm and on Blackburn's, he said, "Hello, Hilda dear." Hilda replied quietly, "Hello, Uncle George."

Still clinging to their arms, still linking Howe and Blackburn, the Dean said, "Another year gone, Joe, and we've turned out another crop. After you've been here a few years, you'll find it reasonably upsetting—you wonder how there can be so many graduating classes while you stay the same. But of course you don't stay the same." Then he said, "Well," sharply, to dismiss the thought. He pulled Blackburn's arm and swung him around to Howe. "Have you heard about Teddy Blackburn?" he asked. "He has a job already, before graduation—the first man of his class to be placed." Expectant of congratulations, Blackburn beamed at Howe. Howe remained silent.

"Isn't that good?" the Dean said. Still Howe did not answer and the Dean, puzzled and put out, turned to Hilda. "That's a very fine-looking camera, Hilda." She touched it with affectionate pride.

"Instruments of precision," said a voice. "Instruments of precision." Of the three with joined arms, Howe was the nearest to Tertan, whose gaze took in all the scene except the smile and the nod which Howe gave him. The boy leaned on his cane. The broad-brimmed hat, canting jauntily over his eye, confused the image of his face that Howe had established, suppressed the rigid lines of the ascetic and brought out the baroque curves. It made an effect of perverse majesty.

"Instruments of precision," said Tertan for the last time, addressing no one, making a casual comment to the universe. And it occurred to Howe that Tertan might not be referring to Hilda's equipment. The sense of the thrice-woven circle of the boy's loneliness smote him fiercely. Tertan stood in majestic jauntiness, superior to all the scene, but his isolation made Howe ache with a pity of which Tertan was more the cause than the object, so general and indiscriminate was it.

Whether in his sorrow he made some unintended movement toward Tertan which the Dean checked, or whether the suddenly tightened grip on his arm was the Dean's own sorrow and fear, he did not know. Tertan watched them in the incurious way people watch a photograph being taken, and suddenly the thought that, to the boy, it must seem that the three were posing for a picture together made Howe detach himself almost rudely from the Dean's grasp.

"I promised Hilda another picture," he announced—needlessly, for Tertan was no longer there, he had vanished in the last sudden flux of visitors who, now that the band had struck up, were rushing nervously to find seats.

"You'd better hurry," the Dean said. "I'll go along, it's getting late for me." He departed and Blackburn walked sedately by his side.

Howe again took his position under the little tree which cast its shadow over his face and gown. "Just hurry, Hilda, won't you?" he said. Hilda held the cable at arm's length, her other arm crooked and her fingers crisped. She rose on her toes and said, "Ready," and pressed the release. "Thank you," she said gravely and began to dismantle her camera as he hurried to join the procession.

THE LOTTERY

Shirley Jackson

Shirley Jackson (1919——) is a native of California, but now lives in the East. She achieved considerable fame some years ago with the appearance of her unusual story, "The Lottery" (1948) in The New Yorker. *Since then she has written several novels and short stories, but nothing has made so immediate and moving an impression upon both critics and the general public as "The Lottery." This is a story that reaches down to expose some deep and terrifying flaw in human nature. The reader will leave it profoundly moved and intensely disturbed. Once read, it is never forgotten.*

The morning of June 27th was clear and sunny, with the fresh warmth of a full-summer day; the flowers were blossoming profusely and the grass was richly green. The people of the village began to gather in the square, between the post office and the bank, around ten o'clock; in some towns there were so many people that the lottery took two days and had to be started on June 26th, but in this village, where there were only about three hundred people, the whole lottery took less than two hours, so it could begin at ten o'clock in the morning and still be through in time to allow the villagers to get home for noon dinner.

The children assembled first, of course. School was recently over for the summer, and the feeling of liberty sat uneasily on most of them; they tended to gather together quietly for a while before they broke into boisterous play, and their talk was still of the classroom and the teacher, of books and reprimands. Bobby Martin had already stuffed his pockets full of stones, and the other boys soon followed his example, selecting the smoothest and roundest stones; Bobby and Harry Jones and Dickie Delacroix—the villagers pronounced this name "Dellacroy"—eventually made a great pile of stones in one corner of the square and guarded it against the raids of the other boys. The girls stood aside, talking among themselves, looking over their shoulders at the boys, and the very small children rolled in the dust or clung to the hands of their older brothers or sisters.

Soon the men began to gather, surveying their own children, speaking of planting and rain, tractors and taxes. They stood together, away from the pile of stones in the corner, and their jokes were quiet and they smiled rather than laughed. The women, wearing faded house dresses and sweaters, came shortly after their menfolk. They greeted one another and exchanged bits of gossip as they went to join their husbands. Soon the women, standing by their husbands, began to call to their children, and the children came reluctantly, having to be called four or five times. Bobby Martin ducked under his mother's grasping hand and ran, laughing, back to the pile of stones. His father spoke up sharply, and Bobby came quickly and took his place between his father and his oldest brother.

The lottery was conducted—as were the square dances, the teen-age club, the Halloween program—by Mr. Summers, who had time and energy to devote to civic activities. He was a round-faced, jovial man and he ran the coal business, and people were sorry for him, because he had no children and his wife was a scold. When he arrived in the square, carrying the black wooden box, there was a murmur of conversation among the villagers, and he waved and called, "Little late today, folks." The postmaster, Mr. Graves, followed him, carrying a three-legged stool, and the stool was put in the center of the square and Mr. Summers set the black box down on it. The villagers kept their distance, leaving a space between themselves and the stool, and when Mr. Summers said, "Some of you fellows want to give me a hand?" there was a hesitation before two men, Mr. Martin and his oldest son, Baxter, came forward to hold the box steady on the stool while Mr. Summers stirred up the papers inside it.

The original paraphernalia for the lottery had been lost

long ago, and the black box now resting on the stool had been put into use even before Old Man Warner, the oldest man in town, was born. Mr. Summers spoke frequently to the villagers about making a new box, but no one liked to upset even as much tradition as was represented by the black box. There was a story that the present box had been made with some pieces of the box that had preceded it, the one that had been constructed when the first people settled down to make a village here. Every year, after the lottery, Mr. Summers began talking again about a new box, but every year the subject was allowed to fade off without anything's being done. The black box grew shabbier each year; by now it was no longer completely black but splintered badly along one side to show the original wood color, and in some places faded or stained.

Mr. Martin and his oldest son, Baxter, held the black box securely on the stool until Mr. Summers had stirred the papers thoroughly with his hand. Because so much of the ritual had been forgotten or discarded, Mr. Summers had been successful in having slips of paper substituted for the chips of wood that had been used for generations. Chips of wood, Mr. Summers had argued, had been all very well when the village was tiny, but now that the population was more than three hundred and likely to keep on growing, it was necessary to use something that would fit more easily into the black box. The night before the lottery, Mr. Summers and Mr. Graves made up the slips of paper and put them in the box, and it was then taken to the safe of Mr. Summers' coal company and locked up until Mr. Summers was ready to take it to the square next morning. The rest of the year, the box was put away, sometimes one place, sometimes another; it had spent one year in Mr. Graves's barn and another year underfoot in the post office, and sometimes it was set on a shelf in the Martin grocery and left there.

There was a great deal of fussing to be done before Mr. Summers declared the lottery open. There were the lists to make up—of heads of families, heads of households in each family, members of each household in each family. There was the proper swearing-in of Mr. Summers by the postmaster, as the official of the lottery; at one time, some people remembered, there had been a recital of some sort, performed by the official of the lottery, a perfunctory, tuneless chant that had been rattled off duly each year; some people believed that the official of the lottery used to stand just so when he said or sang it, others believe that he was supposed to walk among the people, but years and years ago this part of the ritual had been allowed to lapse. There had been, also, a ritual salute, which the official of the lottery had had to use in addressing each person who came up to draw from the box, but this also had changed with time, until now it was felt necessary only for the official to speak to each person approaching. Mr. Summers was very good at all this; in his clean white shirt and blue jeans, with one hand resting carelessly on the black box, he seemed very proper and important as he talked interminably to Mr. Graves and the Martins.

Just as Mr. Summers finally left off talking and turned to the assembled villagers, Mrs. Hutchinson came hurriedly along the path to the square, her sweater thrown over her shoulders, and slid into place in the back of the crowd. "Clean forgot what day it was," she said to Mrs. Delacroix, who stood next to her, and they both laughed softly. "Thought my old man was out back stacking wood," Mrs. Hutchinson went on, "and then I looked out the window and the kids were gone, and then I remembered it was the twenty-seventh and came a-running." She dried her hands on her apron, and Mrs. Delacroix said, "You're in time, though. They're still talking away up there."

Mrs. Hutchinson craned her neck to see through the crowd and found her husband and children standing near the front. She tapped Mrs. Delacroix on the arm as a farewell and began to make her way through the crowd. The people separated good-humoredly to let her through; two or three people said, in voices just loud enough to be heard across the crowd, "Here comes your Missus, Hutchinson," and "Bill, she made it after all." Mrs. Hutchinson reached her husband, and Mr. Summers, who had been waiting, said cheerfully, "Thought we were going to have to get on without you, Tessie." Mrs. Hutchinson said, grinning, "Wouldn't have me leave m'dishes in the sink, now, would you, Joe?" and soft laughter ran through the crowd as the people stirred back into position after Mrs. Hutchinson's arrival.

"Well, now," Mr. Summers said soberly, "guess we better get started, get this over with, so's we can go back to work. Anybody ain't here?"

"Dunbar," several people said. "Dunbar, Dunbar."

Mr. Summers consulted his list. "Clyde Dunbar," he said. "That's right. He's broke his leg, hasn't he? Who's drawing for him?"

"Me, I guess," a woman said, and Mr. Summers turned to look at her. "Wife draws for her husband," Mr. Summers said. "Don't you have a grown boy to do it for you, Janey?" Although Mr. Summers and everyone else in the village knew the answer perfectly well, it was the business of the official of the lottery to ask such questions formally. Mr. Summers waited with an expression of polite interest while Mrs. Dunbar answered.

"Horace's not but sixteen yet," Mrs. Dunbar said regretfully. "Guess I gotta fill in for the old man this year."

"Right," Mr. Summers said. He made a note on the list he was holding. Then he asked, "Watson boy drawing this year?"

A tall boy in the crowd raised his hand. "Here," he said. "I'm drawing for m'mother and me." He blinked his eyes nervously and ducked his head as several voices in the crowd said things like "Good fellow, Jack," and "Glad to see your mother's got a man to do it."

"Well," Mr. Summers said, "guess that's everyone. Old Man Warner make it?"

"Here," a voice said, and Mr. Summers nodded.

A sudden hush fell on the crowd as Mr. Summers cleared his throat and looked at the list. "All ready?" he called. "Now, I'll read the names—heads of families first—and the men come up and take a paper out of the box. Keep the paper folded in your hand without looking at it until everyone has had a turn. Everything clear?"

The people had done it so many times that they only half listened to the directions; most of them were quiet, wetting their lips, not looking around. Then Mr. Summers raised one hand high and said, "Adams." A man disengaged himself from the crowd and came forward. "Hi, Steve," Mr. Summers said, and Mr. Adams said, "Hi, Joe." They grinned at one another humorlessly and nervously. Then Mr. Adams reached into the black box and took out a folded paper. He held it firmly by one corner as he turned and went hastily back to his place in the crowd, where he stood a little apart from his family, not looking down at his hand.

"Allen," Mr. Summers said. "Anderson. . . . Bentham."

"Seems like there's no time at all between lotteries any more," Mrs. Delacroix said to Mrs. Graves in the back row.

"Seems like we got through with the last one only last week."

"Time sure goes fast," Mrs. Graves said.

"Clark. . . . Delacroix."

"There goes my old man," Mrs. Delacroix said. She held her breath while her husband went forward.

"Dunbar," Mr. Summers said, and Mrs. Dunbar went steadily to the box while one of the women said, "Go on, Janey," and another said, "There she goes."

"We're next," Mrs. Graves said. She watched while Mr. Graves came around from the side of the box, greeted Mr. Summers gravely, and selected a slip of paper from the box. By now, all through the crowd there were men holding the small folded papers in their large hands, turning them over and over nervously. Mrs. Dunbar and her two sons stood together, Mrs. Dunbar holding the slip of paper.

"Harburt. . . . Hutchinson."

"Get up there, Bill," Mrs. Hutchinson said, and the people near her laughed.

"Jones."

"They do say," Mr. Adams said to Old Man Warner, who stood next to him, "that over in the north village they're talking of giving up the lottery."

Old Man Warner snorted. "Pack of crazy fools," he said. "Listening to the young folks, nothing's good enough for *them*. Next thing you know, they'll be wanting to go back to living in caves, nobody work any more, live *that* way for a while. Used to be a saying about 'Lottery in June, corn be heavy soon.' First thing you know, we'd all be eating stewed chickweed and acorns. There's *always* been a lottery," he added petulantly. "Bad enough to see young Joe Summers up there joking with everybody."

"Some places have already quit lotteries," Mrs. Adams said.

"Nothing but trouble in *that,*" Old Man Warner said stoutly. "Pack of young fools."

"Martin." And Bobby Martin watched his father go forward. "Overdyke. . . . Percy."

"I wish they'd hurry," Mrs. Dunbar said to her older son. "I wish they'd hurry."

"They're almost through," her son said.

"You get ready to run tell Dad," Mrs. Dunbar said.

Mr. Summers called his own name and then stepped forward precisely and selected a slip from the box. Then he called, "Warner."

"Seventy-seventh year I been in the lottery," Old Man Warner said as he went through the crowd. "Seventy-seventh time."

"Watson." The tall boy came awkwardly through the crowd. Someone said, "Don't be nervous, Jack," and Mr. Summers said, "Take your time, son."

"Zanini."

After that, there was a long pause, a breathless pause, until Mr. Summers, holding his slip of paper in the air, said, "All right, fellows." For a minute, no one moved, and then all the slips of paper were opened. Suddenly, all the women began to speak at once, saying, "Who is it?" "Who's got it?" "Is it the Dunbars?" "Is it the Watsons?" Then the voices began to say, "It's Hutchinson. It's Bill," "Bill Hutchinson's got it."

"Go tell your father," Mrs. Dunbar said to her older son.

People began to look around to see the Hutchinsons. Bill Hutchinson was standing quiet, staring down at the paper in his hand. Suddenly, Tessie Hutchinson shouted to Mr. Summers, "You didn't give him time enough to take any paper he wanted. I saw you. It wasn't fair."

"Be a good sport, Tessie," Mrs. Delacroix called, and Mrs. Graves said, "All of us took the same chance."

"Shut up, Tessie," Bill Hutchinson said.

"Well, everyone," Mr. Summers said, "that was done pretty fast, and now we've got to be hurrying a little more to get done in time." He consulted his next list. "Bill," he said, "you draw for the Hutchinson family. You got any other households in the Hutchinsons."

"There's Don and Eva," Mrs. Hutchinson yelled. "Make *them* take their chance!"

"Daughters draw with their husbands' families, Tessie," Mr. Summers said gently. "You know that as well as anyone else."

"It wasn't *fair*," Tessie said.

"I guess not, Joe," Bill Hutchinson said regretfully. "My daughter draws with her husband's family, that's only fair. And I've got no other family except the kids."

"Then, as far as drawing for families is concerned, it's

you," Mr. Summers said in explanation, "and as far as drawing for households is concerned, that's you, too. Right?"

"Right," Bill Hutchinson said.

"How many kids, Bill?" Mr. Summers asked formally.

"Three," Bill Hutchinson said. "There's Bill, Jr., and Nancy, and little Dave. And Tessie and me."

"All right, then," Mr. Summers said. "Harry, you got their tickets back?"

Mr. Graves nodded and held up the slips of paper. "Put them in the box, then," Mr. Summers directed. "Take Bill's and put it in."

"I think we ought to start over," Mrs. Hutchinson said, as quietly as she could. "I tell you it wasn't *fair*. You didn't give him time enough to choose. *Every*body saw that."

Mr. Graves had selected the five slips and put them in the box, and he dropped all the papers but those onto the ground, where the breeze caught them and lifted them off.

"Listen, everybody," Mrs. Hutchinson was saying to the people around her.

"Ready, Bill?" Mr. Summers asked, and Bill Hutchinson, with one quick glance around at his wife and children, nodded.

"Remember," Mr. Summers said, "take the slips and keep them folded until each person has taken one. Harry, you help little Dave." Mr. Graves took the hand of the little boy, who came willingly with him up to the box. "Take a paper out of the box, Davy," Mr. Summers said. Davy put his hand into the box and laughed. "Take just *one* paper," Mr. Summers said. "Harry, you hold it for him." Mr. Graves took the child's hand and removed the folded paper from the tight fist and held it while little Dave stood next to him and looked up at him wonderingly.

"Nancy next," Mr. Summers said. Nancy was twelve, and her school friends breathed heavily as she went forward, switching her skirt, and took a slip daintily from the box. "Bill, Jr.," Mr. Summers said, and Billy, his face red and his feet over-large, nearly knocked the box over as he got a paper out. "Tessie," Mr. Summers said. She hesitated for a minute, looking around defiantly, and then set her lips and went up to the box. She snatched a paper out and held it behind her.

"Bill," Mr. Summers said, and Bill Hutchinson reached

into the box and felt around, bringing his hand out at last with the slip of paper in it.

The crowd was quiet. A girl whispered, "I hope it's not Nancy," and the sound of the whisper reached the edges of the crowd.

"It's not the way it used to be," Old Man Warner said clearly. "People ain't the way they used to be."

"All right," Mr. Summers said. "Open the papers. Harry, you open little Dave's."

Mr. Graves opened the slip of paper and there was a general sigh through the crowd as he held it up and everyone could see that it was blank. Nancy and Bill, Jr., opened theirs at the same time, and both beamed and laughed, turning around to the crowd and holding their slips of paper above their heads.

"Tessie," Mr. Summers said. There was a pause, and then Mr. Summers looked at Bill Hutchinson, and Bill unfolded his paper and showed it. It was blank.

"It's Tessie," Mr. Summers said, and his voice was hushed. "Show us her paper, Bill."

Bill Hutchinson went over to his wife and forced the slip of paper out of her hand. It had a black spot on it, the black spot Mr. Summers had made the night before with the heavy pencil in the coal-company office. Bill Hutchinson held it up, and there was a stir in the crowd.

"All right, folks," Mr. Summers said. "Let's finish quickly."

Although the villagers had forgotten the ritual and lost the original black box, they still remembered to use stones. The pile of stones the boys had made earlier was ready; there were stones on the ground with the blowing scraps of paper that had come out of the box. Mrs. Delacroix selected a stone so large she had to pick it up with both hands and turned to Mrs. Dunbar. "Come on," she said. "Hurry up."

Mrs. Dunbar had small stones in both hands, and she said, gasping for breath, "I can't run at all. You'll have to go ahead and I'll catch up with you."

The children had stones already, and someone gave little Davy Hutchinson a few pebbles.

Tessie Hutchinson was in the center of a cleared space by now, and she held her hands out desperately as the villagers moved in on her. "It isn't fair," she said. A stone hit her on the side of the head.

Old Man Warner was saying, "Come on, come on, everyone." Steve Adams was in the front of the crowd of villagers, with Mrs. Graves beside him.

"It isn't fair, it isn't right," Mrs. Hutchinson screamed, and then they were upon her.

THE LEDGE

Lawrence Sargent Hall

Lawrence Sargent Hall was born in Haverhill, Massachusetts, in 1915. Educated at Bowdoin and Yale, he served in the Navy during World War II and now teaches English at Bowdoin College, Brunswick, Maine. "The Ledge" won first prize in the O. Henry Memorial Awards for 1960. Wallace Stegner writes of this story about a Maine fisherman who is betrayed by self-reliance, as follows: "This is Conradian, this is Greek, and its sort is rare in 1959." Simplicity and universality in the handling of stark, heroic tragedy sharply set this story off from the prevailing trends in fiction for the past fifty years.

On Christmas morning before sunup the fisherman embraced his warm wife and left his close bed. She did not want him to go. It was Christmas morning. He was a big, raw man, with too much strength, whose delight in winter was to hunt the sea ducks that flew in to feed by the outer ledges, bare at low tide.

As his bare feet touched the cold floor and the frosty air struck his nude flesh, he might have changed his mind in the dark of this special day. It was a home day, which made it seem natural to think of the outer ledges merely as some place he had shot ducks in the past. But he had promised his son, thirteen, and his nephew, fifteen, who came from inland. That was why he had given them his present of an automatic shotgun each the night before, on Christmas Eve. Rough man though he was known to be, and no spoiler of boys, he kept his promises when he understood what they meant. And to the boys, as to him, home meant where you came for rest after you had had your Christmas fill of action and excitement.

His legs astride, his arms raised, the fisherman stretched as high as he could in the dim privacy of his bedroom. Above the snug murmur of his wife's protest he heard the wind in the pines and knew it was easterly as the boys had hoped and he had surmised the night before. Conditions would be ideal, and when they were, anybody ought to take advantage of them. The birds would be flying. The boys would get a man's sport their first time outside on the ledges.

His son at thirteen, small but steady and experienced, was fierce to grow up in hunting, to graduate from sheltered waters and the blinds along the shores of the inner bay. His nephew at fifteen, an overgrown farm boy, had a farm boy's love of the sea, though he could not swim a stroke and was often sick in choppy weather. That was the reason his father, the fisherman's brother, was a farmer and chose to sleep in on the holiday morning at his brother's house. Many of the ones the farmer had grown up with were regularly seasick and could not swim, but they were unafraid of the water. They could not have dreamed of being anything but fishermen. The fisherman himself could swim like a seal and was never sick, and he would sooner die than be anything else.

He dressed in the cold and dark, and woke the boys gruffly. They tumbled out of bed, their instincts instantly awake while their thoughts still fumbled slumbrously. The fisherman's wife in the adjacent bedroom heard them apparently trying to find their clothes, mumbling sleepily and happily to each other, while her husband went down to the hot kitchen to fry eggs —sunny-side up, she knew, because that was how they all liked them.

Always in winter she hated to have them go outside, the weather was so treacherous and there were so few others out in case of trouble. To the fisherman these were no more than woman's fears, to be taken for granted and laughed off. When they were first married, they fought miserably every fall because she was after him constantly to put his boat up until spring. The fishing was all outside in winter, and though prices were high the storms made the rate of attrition high on gear. Nevertheless he did well. So she could do nothing with him.

People thought him a hard man, and gave him the reputation of being all out for himself because he was inclined to brag and be disdainful. If it was true, and his own brother was one of those who strongly felt it was, they lived better than others, and his brother had small right to criticize. There had been times when in her loneliness she had yearned to leave him for another man. But it would have been dangerous. So over the years she had learned to shut her mind to his hard-driving, and take what comfort she might from his unsympathetic competence. Only once or twice, perhaps, had she gone so far as to dwell guiltily on what it would be like to be a widow.

The thought that her boy, possibly because he was small, would not be insensitive like his father, and the rattle of dishes and smell of frying bacon downstairs in the kitchen shut off from the rest of the chilly house, restored the cozy feeling she had had before she was alone in bed. She heard them after a while go out and shut the back door.

Under her window she heard the snow grind drily beneath their boots, and her husband's sharp, exasperated commands to the boys. She shivered slightly in the envelope of her own warmth. She listened to the noise of her son and nephew talking elatedly. Twice she caught the glimmer of their lights on the white ceiling above the window as they went down the path to the shore. There would be frost on the skiff and freezing suds at the water's edge. She herself used to go gunning when she was younger; now, it seemed to her, anyone going out like that on Christmas morning had to be incurably male. They would none of them think about her until they returned and piled the birds they had shot on top of the sink for her to dress.

Ripping into the quiet pre-dawn cold she heard the hot snarl of the outboard taking them out to the boat. It died as abruptly as it had burst into life. Two or three or four or five minutes later the big engine broke into a warm reassuring roar. He had the best of equipment, and he kept it in the best of condition. She closed her eyes. It would not be too long before the others would be up for Christmas. The summer drone of the exhaust deepened. Then gradually it faded in the wind until it was lost at sea, or she slept.

The engine had started immediately in spite of the temperature. This put the fisherman in a good mood. He was proud of his boat. Together he and the two boys heaved the skiff and outboard onto the stern and secured it athwartships. His son went forward along the deck, iridescent in the ray of the light the nephew shone through the windshield, and cast the mooring pennant loose into darkness. The fisherman swung to starboard, glanced at his compass, and headed seaward down the obscure bay.

There would be just enough visibility by the time they reached the headland to navigate the crooked channel between the islands. It was the only nasty stretch of water. The fisherman had done it often in fog or at night—he always swore he could go anywhere in the bay blindfolded—but there was no sense in taking chances if you didn't have to. From the mouth of the channel he could lay a straight course for Brown Cow Island, anchor the boat out of sight behind it, and from the skiff set their tollers off Devil's Hump three hundred yards to seaward. By then the tide would be clearing the ledge and they could land and be ready to shoot around half-tide.

It was early, it was Christmas, and it was farther out than most hunters cared to go in this season of the closing year, so that he felt sure no one would be taking possession ahead of them. He had shot thousands of ducks there in his day. The Hump was by far the best hunting. Only thing was you had to plan for the right conditions because you didn't have too much time. About four hours was all, and you had to get it before three in the afternoon when the birds left and went out to sea ahead of nightfall.

They had it figured exactly right for today. The ledge would not be going under until after the gunning was over, and they would be home for supper in good season. With a little luck the boys would have a skiff-load of birds to show for their first time outside. Well beyond the legal limit, which was no matter. You took what you could get in this life, or the next man made out and you didn't.

The fisherman had never failed to make out gunning from Devil's Hump. And this trip, he had a hunch, would be above the ordinary. The westerly wind would come up just stiff enough, the tide was right, and it was going to storm by tomorrow morning so the birds would be moving. Things were perfect.

The old fierceness was in his bones. Keeping a weather

eye to the murk out front and a hand on the wheel, he reached over and cuffed both boys playfully as they stood together close to the heat of the exhaust pipe running up through the center of the house. They poked back at him and shouted above the drumming engine, making bets as they always did on who would shoot the most birds. This trip they had the thrill of new guns, the best money could buy, and a man's hunting ground. The black retriever wagged at them and barked. He was too old and arthritic to be allowed in December water, but he was jaunty anyway at being brought along.

Groping in his pocket for his pipe, the fisherman suddenly had his high spirits rocked by the discovery that he had left his tobacco at home. He swore. Anticipation of a day out with nothing to smoke made him incredulous. He searched his clothes, and then he searched them again, unable to believe the tobacco was not somewhere. When the boys inquired what was wrong he spoke angrily to them, blaming them for being in some devious way at fault. They were instantly crestfallen and willing to put back after the tobacco, though they could appreciate what it meant only through his irritation. But he bitterly refused. That would throw everything out of phase. He was a man who did things the way he set out to do.

He clamped his pipe between his teeth, and twice more during the next few minutes he ransacked his clothes in disbelief. He was no stoic. For one relaxed moment he considered putting about gunning somewhere nearer home. Instead he held his course and sucked the empty pipe, consoling himself with the reflection that at least he had whiskey enough if it got too uncomfortable on the ledge. Peremptorily he made the boys check to make certain the bottle was really in the knapsack with the lunches where he thought he had taken care to put it. When they reassured him, he despised his fate a little less.

The fisherman's judgment was as usual accurate. By the time they were abreast of the headland there was sufficient light so that he could wind his way among the reefs without slackening speed. At last he turned his bow toward open ocean, and as the winter dawn filtered upward through long layers of smoky cloud on the eastern rim his spirits rose again with it.

He opened the throttle, steadied on his course, and settled down to the two-hour run. The wind was stronger but seemed less cold coming from the sea. The boys had withdrawn from the fisherman and were talking together while they watched the sky through the windows. The boat churned solidly through a light chop, flinging spray off her flaring bow. Astern the headland thinned rapidly till it lay like a blackened sill on the grey water. No other boats were aboard.

The boys fondled their new guns, sighted along the barrels, worked the mechanisms, compared notes, boasted, and gave each other contradictory advice. The fisherman got their attention once and pointed at the horizon. They peered through the windows and saw what looked like a black scum floating on top of gently agitated water. It wheeled and tilted, rippled, curled, then rose, strung itself out and became a huge raft of ducks escaping over the sea. A good sign.

The boys rushed out and leaned over the washboards in the wind and spray to see the flock curl below the horizon. Then they went and hovered around the hot engine, bewailing their lot. If only they had been already out and waiting. Maybe these ducks would be crazy enough to return later and be slaughtered. Ducks were known to be foolish.

In due course and right on schedule they anchored at mid-morning in the lee of Brown Cow Island. They put the skiff overboard and loaded it with guns, knapsacks, and tollers. The boys showed their eagerness by being clumsy. The fisherman showed his in bad temper and abuse which they silently accepted in the absorbed tolerance of being boys. No doubt they laid it to lack of tobacco.

By outboard they rounded the island and pointed due east in the direction of a ridge of foam which could be seen whitening the surface three hundred yards away. They set the decoys in a broad, straddling vee opening wide into the ocean. The fisherman warned them not to get their hands wet, and when they did he made them carry on with red and painful fingers, in order to teach them. Once they got their numbed fingers inside their oilskins and hugged their warm crotches. In the meantime the fisherman had turned the skiff toward the patch of foam where as if by magic, like a black glossy rib of earth, the ledge had broken through the belly of the sea.

Carefully they inhabited their slippery nub of the North American continent, while the unresting Atlantic swelled and swirled as it had for eons round the indomitable edges. They hauled the skiff after them, established themselves as comfortably as they could in a shallow sump on top, lay on their sides a foot or so above the water, and waited, guns in hand.

In time the fisherman took a thermos bottle from the knapsack and they drank steaming coffee, and waited for the nodding decoys to lure in the first flight to the rock. Eventually the boys got hungry and restless. The fisherman let them open the picnic lunch and eat one sandwich apiece, which they both shared with the dog. Having no tobacco the fisherman himself would not eat.

Actually the day was relatively mild, and they were warm enough at present in their woollen clothes and socks underneath oilskins and hip boots. After a while, however, the boys began to feel cramped. Their nerves were agonized by inactivity. The nephew complained and was severely told by the fisherman—who pointed to the dog, crouched unmoving except for his white-rimmed eyes—that part of doing a man's hunting was learning how to wait. But he was beginning to have misgivings of his own. This could be one of those days where all the right conditions masked an incalculable flaw.

If the fisherman had been alone, as he often was, stopping off when the necessary coincidence of tide and time occurred on his way home from hauling trawls, and had plenty of tobacco, he would not have fidgeted. The boys' being nervous made him nervous. He growled at them again. When it came it was likely to come all at once, and then in a few moments be over. He warned them not to slack off, never to slack off, to be always ready. Under his rebuke they kept their tortured peace, though they could not help shifting and twisting until he lost what patience he had left and bullied them into lying still. A duck could see an eyelid twitch. If the dog could go without moving so could they.

"Here it comes!" the fisherman said tersely at last.

The boys quivered with quick relief. The flock came in downwind, quartering slightly, myriad, black, and swift.

"Beautiful—" breathed the fisherman's son.

"All right," said the fisherman, intense and precise. "Aim at singles in the thickest part of the flock. Wait for me to fire and then don't stop shooting till your gun's empty." He rolled up onto his left elbow and spread his legs to brace himself. The flock bore down, arrowy and vibrant, then a hundred yards beyond the decoys it veered off.

"They're going away!" the boys cried, sighting in.

"Not yet!" snapped the fisherman. "They're coming round."

The flock changed shape, folded over itself, and drove into the wind in a tight arc. "Thousands—" the boys hissed through their teeth. All at once a whistling storm of black and white broke over the decoys.

"Now!" the fisherman shouted. "Perfect!" And he opened fire at the flock just as it hung suspended in momentary chaos above the tollers. The three pulled at their triggers and the birds splashed into the water, until the last report went off unheard, the last smoking shell flew unheeded over their shoulders, and the last of the routed flock scattered diminishing, diminishing, diminishing in every direction.

Exultantly the boys dropped their guns, jumped up and scrambled for the skiff.

"I'll handle that skiff!" the fisherman shouted at them. They stopped. Gripping the painter and balancing himself he eased the skiff into the water stern first and held the bow hard against the side of the rock shelf the skiff had rested on. "You stay here," he said to his nephew. "No sense in all three of us going in the boat."

The boy on the reef gazed at the grey water rising and falling hypnotically along the glistening edge. It had dropped about a foot since their arrival. "I want to go with you," he said in a sullen tone, his eyes on the streaming eddies.

"You want to do what I tell you if you want to gun with me," answered the fisherman harshly. The boy couldn't swim, and he wasn't going to have him climbing in and out of the skiff any more than necessary. Besides, he was too big.

The fisherman took his son in the skiff and cruised round and round among the decoys picking up dead birds. Meanwhile the other boy stared unmoving after them from the highest part of the ledge. Before they had quite finished gathering the dead birds, the fisherman cut the outboard and dropped to his knees in the skiff. "Down!" he yelled. "Get down!" About a dozen birds came tolling in. "Shoot—shoot!" his son hollered from the bottom of the boat to the boy on the ledge.

The dog, who had been running back and forth whining, sank to his belly, his muzzle on his forepaws. But the boy on the ledge never stirred. The ducks took late alarm at the skiff, swerved aside and into the air, passing with a whirr no more than fifty feet over the head of the boy, who remained on the ledge like a statue, without his gun, watching the two crouching in the boat.

The fisherman's son climbed onto the ledge and held the painter. The bottom of the skiff was covered with feathery black and white bodies with feet upturned and necks lolling. He was jubilant. "We got twenty-seven!" he told his cousin. "How's that? Nine apiece. Boy—" he added, "what a cool Christmas!"

The fisherman pulled the skiff onto its shelf and all three went and lay down again in anticipation of the next flight. The son, reloading, patted his gun affectionately. "I'm going to get me ten next time," he said. Then he asked his cousin, "Whatsamatter—didn't you see the strays?"

"Yeah," the boy said.

"How come you didn't shoot at 'em?"

"Didn't feel like it," replied the boy, still with a trace of sullenness.

"You stupid or something?" The fisherman's son was astounded. "What a highlander!" But the fisherman, though he said nothing, knew that the older boy had had an attack of ledge fever.

"Cripes!" his son kept at it. "I'd at least of tried."

"Shut up," the fisherman finally told him, "and leave him be."

At slack water three more flocks came in, one right after the other, and when it was over, the skiff was half full of clean, dead birds. During the subsequent lull they broke out the lunch and ate it all and finished the hot coffee. For a while the fisherman sucked away on his cold pipe. Then he had himself a swig of whiskey.

The boys passed the time contentedly jabbering about who shot the most—there were ninety-two all told—which of their friends they would show the biggest ones to, how many each could eat at a meal provided they didn't have to eat any vegetables. Now and then they heard sporadic distant gunfire on the mainland, at its nearest point about two miles to the north. Once far off they saw a fishing boat making in the direction of home.

At length the fisherman got a hand inside his oilskins and produced his watch.

"Do we have to go now?" asked his son.

"Not just yet," he replied. "Pretty soon." Everything had

been perfect. As good as he had ever had it. Because he was getting tired of the boys' chatter he got up, heavily in his hip boots, and stretched. The tide had turned and was coming in, the sky was more ashen, and the wind had freshened enough so that whitecaps were beginning to blossom. It would be a good hour before they had to leave the ledge and pick up the tollers. However, he guessed they would leave a little early. On account of the rising wind he doubted there would be much more shooting. He stepped carefully along the back of the ledge, to work his kinks out. It was also getting a little colder.

The whiskey had begun to warm him, but he was unprepared for the sudden blaze that flashed upward inside him from belly to head. He was standing looking at the shelf where the skiff was. Only the foolish skiff was not there!

For the second time that day the fisherman felt the deep vacuity of disbelief. He gaped, seeing nothing but the flat shelf of rock. He whirled, started toward the boys, slipped, recovered himself, fetched a complete circle, and stared at the unimaginably empty shelf. Its emptiness made him feel as if everything he had done that day so far, his life so far, he had dreamed. What could have happened? The tide was still nearly a foot below. There had been no sea to speak of. The skiff could hardly have slid off by itself. For the life of him, consciously careful as he inveterately was, he could not now remember hauling it up the last time. Perhaps in the heat of hunting, he had left it to the boy. Perhaps he could not remember which was the last time.

"Christ—" he exclaimed loudly, without realizing it because he was so entranced by the invisible event.

"What's wrong, Dad?" asked his son, getting to his feet.

The fisherman went blind with uncontainable rage. "Get back down there where you belong!" he screamed. He scarcely noticed the boy sink back in amazement. In a frenzy he ran along the ledge thinking the skiff might have been drawn up at another place, though he knew better. There was no other place.

He stumbled, half falling, back to the boys who were gawking at him in consternation, as though he had gone insane. "God damn it!" he yelled savagely, grabbing both of them and yanking them to their knees. "Get on your feet!"

"What's wrong?" his son repeated in a stifled voice.

"Never mind what's wrong," he snarled. "Look for the

skiff—it's adrift!" When they peered around he gripped their shoulders, brutally facing them about. "Downwind—" He slammed his fist against his thigh. "Jesus!" he cried, struck to madness by their stupidity.

At last he sighted the skiff himself, magically bobbing along the grim sea like a toller, a quarter of a mile to leeward on a direct course for home. The impulse to strip himself naked was succeeded instantly by a queer calm. He simply sat down on the ledge and forgot everything except the marvellous mystery.

As his awareness partially returned he glanced toward the boys. They were still observing the skiff speechlessly. Then he was gazing into the clear young eyes of his son.

"Dad," asked the boy steadily, "what do we do now?"

That brought the fisherman upright. "The first thing we have to do," he heard himself saying with infinite tenderness as if he were making love, "is think."

"Could you swim it?" asked his son.

He shook his head and smiled at them. They smiled quickly back, too quickly. "A hundred yards maybe, in this water. I wish I could," he added. It was the most intimate and pitiful thing he had ever said. He walked in circles round them, trying to break the stall his mind was left in.

He gauged the level of the water. To the eye it was quite stationary, six inches from the shelf at this second. The fisherman did not have to mark it on the side of the rock against the passing of time to prove to his reason that it was rising, always rising. Already it was over the brink of reason, beyond the margins of thought—a senseless measurement. No sense to it.

All his life the fisherman had tried to lick the element of time, by getting up earlier and going to bed later, owning a faster boat, planning more than the day would hold, and tackling just one other job before the deadline fell. If, as on rare occasions he had the grand illusion, he ever really had beaten the game, he would need to call on all his reserves of practice and cunning now.

He sized up the scant but unforgivable three hundred yards to Brown Cow Island. Another hundred yards behind it his boat rode at anchor, where, had he been aboard, he could have cut in a fathometer to plumb the profound and occult seas, or a ship-to-shore radio on which in an interminably short time he would have heard his wife's voice talking to him over the air about homecoming.

"Couldn't we wave something so somebody would see us?" his nephew suggested.

The fisherman spun round. "Load your guns!" he ordered. They loaded as if the air had suddenly gone frantic with birds. "I'll fire once and count to five. Then you fire. Count to five. That way they won't just think it's only somebody gunning ducks. We'll keep doing that."

"We've only got just two-and-a-half boxes left," said his son.

The fisherman nodded, understanding that from beginning to end their situation was purely mathematical, like the ticking of the alarm clock in his silent bedroom. Then he fired. The dog, who had been keeping watch over the decoys, leaped forward and yelped in confusion. They all counted off, fired the first five rounds by threes, and reloaded. The fisherman scanned first the horizon, then the contracting borders of the ledge, which was the sole place the water appeared to be climbing. Soon it would be over the shelf.

They counted off and fired the second five rounds. "We'll hold off a while on the last one," the fisherman told the boys. He sat down and pondered what a trivial thing was a skiff. This one he and the boy had knocked together in a day. Was a gun, manufactured for killing.

His son tallied up the remaining shells, grouping them symmetrically in threes on the rock when the wet box fell apart. "Two short," he announced. They reloaded and laid the guns on their knees.

Behind thickening clouds they could not see the sun going down. The water, coming up, was growing blacker. The fisherman thought he might have told his wife they would be home before dark since it was Christmas day. He realized he had forgotten about its being any particular day. The tide would not be high until two hours after sunset. When they did not get in by nightfall, and could not be raised by radio, she might send somebody to hunt for them right away. He rejected this arithmetic immediately, with a sickening shock, recollecting it was a two-and-a-half hour run at best. Then it occurred to him that she might send somebody on the mainland who was nearer. She would think he had engine trouble.

He rose and searched the shoreline, barely visible. Then

his glance dropped to the toy shoreline at the edges of the reef. The shrinking ledge, so sinister from a boat, grew dearer minute by minute as though the whole wide world he gazed on from horizon to horizon balanced on its contracting rim. He checked the water level and found the shelf awash.

Some of what went through his mind the fisherman told to the boys. They accepted it without comment. If he caught their eyes they looked away to spare him or because they were not yet old enough to face what they saw. Mostly they watched the rising water. The fisherman was unable to initiate a word of encouragement. He wanted one of them to ask him whether somebody would reach them ahead of the tide. He would have found it possible to say yes. But they did not inquire.

The fisherman was not sure how much, at their age, they were able to imagine. Both of them had seen from the docks drowned bodies put ashore out of boats. Sometimes they grasped things, and sometimes not. He supposed they might be longing for the comfort of their mothers, and was astonished, as much as he was capable of any astonishment except the supreme one, to discover himself wishing he had not left his wife's dark, close, naked bed that morning.

"Is it time to shoot now?" asked his nephew.

"Pretty soon," he said, as if he were putting off making good on a promise. "Not yet."

His own boy cried softly for a brief moment, like a man, his face averted in an effort neither to give nor show pain.

"Before school starts," the fisherman said, wonderfully detached, "we'll go to town and I'll buy you boys anything you want."

With great difficulty, in a dull tone as though he did not in the least desire it, his son said after a pause, "I'd like one of those new thirty-horse outboards."

"All right," said the fisherman. And to his nephew, "How about you?"

The nephew shook his head desolately. "I don't want anything," he said.

After another pause the fisherman's son said, "Yes he does, Dad. He wants one too."

"All right—" the fisherman said again, and said no more.

The dog whined in uncertainty and licked the boys' faces where they sat together. Each threw an arm over his back and hugged him. Three strays flew in and sat companionably down among the stiff-necked decoys. The dog crouched, obedient to his training. The boys observed them listlessly. Presently, sensing something untoward, the ducks took off, splashing the wave tops with feet and wingtips, into the dusky waste.

The sea began to make up in the mountain wind, and the wind bore a new and deathly chill. The fisherman, scouring the somber, dwindling shadow of the mainland for a sign, hoped it would not snow. But it did. First a few flakes, then a flurry, then storming past horizontally. The fisherman took one long, bewildered look at Brown Cow Island three hundred yards dead to leeward, and got to his feet.

Then it shut in, as if what was happening on the ledge was too private even for the last wan light of the expiring day.

"Last round," the fisherman said austerely.

The boys rose and shouldered their tacit guns. The fisherman fired into the flying snow. He counted methodically to five. His son fired and counted. His nephew. All three fired and counted. Four rounds.

"You've got one left, Dad," his son said.

The fisherman hesitated another second, then he fired the final shell. Its pathetic report, like the spat of a popgun, whipped away on the wind and was instantly blanketed in falling snow.

Night fell all in a moment to meet the ascending sea. They were now barely able to make one another out through driving snowflakes, dim as ghosts in their yellow oilskins. The fisherman heard a sea break and glanced down where his feet were. They seemed to be wound in a snowy sheet. Gently he took the boys by the shoulders and pushed them in front of him, feeling with his feet along the shallow sump to the place where it triangulated into a sharp crevice at the highest point of the ledge. "Face ahead," he told them. "Put the guns down."

"I'd like to hold mine, Dad," begged his son.

"Put it down," said the fisherman. "The tide won't hurt it. Now brace your feet against both sides and stay there."

They felt the dog, who was pitch black, running up and down in perplexity between their straddled legs. "Dad," said his son, "what about the pooch?"

If he had called the dog by name it would have been too

personal. The fisherman would have wept. As it was he had all he could do to keep from laughing. He bent his knees, and when he touched the dog hoisted him under one arm. The dog's belly was soaking wet.

So they waited, marooned in their consciousness, surrounded by a monstrous tidal space which was slowly, slowly closing them out. In this space the periwinkle beneath the fisherman's boots was king. While hovering airborne in his mind he had an inward glimpse of his house as curiously separate, like a June mirage.

Snow, rocks, seas, wind the fisherman had lived by all his life. Now he thought he had never comprehended what they were, and he hated them. Though they had not changed. He was deadly chilled. He set out to ask the boys if they were cold. There was no sense. He thought of the whiskey, and sidled backward, still holding the awkward dog, till he located the bottle under water with his toe. He picked it up squeamishly as though afraid of getting his sleeve wet, worked his way forward and bent over his son. "Drink it," he said, holding the bottle against the boy's ribs. The boy tipped his head back, drank, coughed hotly, then vomited.

"I can't," he told his father wretchedly.

"Try—try—" the fisherman pleaded, as if it meant the difference between life and death.

The boy obediently drank, and again he vomited hotly. He shook his head against his father's chest and passed the bottle forward to his cousin, who drank and vomited also. Passing the bottle back, the boys dropped it in the frigid water between them.

When the waves reached his knees the fisherman set the warm dog loose and said to his son, "Turn around and get up on my shoulders." The boy obeyed. The fisherman opened his oilskin jacket and twisted his hands behind him through his suspenders, clamping the boy's booted ankles with his elbows.

"What about the dog?" the boy asked.

"He'll make his own way all right," the fisherman said. "He can take the cold water." His knees were trembling. Every instinct shrieked for gymanastics. He ground his teeth and braced like a colossus against the sides of the submerged crevice.

The dog, having lived faithfully as though one of them for eleven years, swam a few minutes in and out around the fisherman's legs, not knowing what was happening, and left them without a whimper. He would swim and swim at random by himself, round and round in the blinding night, and when he had swum routinely through the paralyzing water all he could, he would simply, in one incomprehensible moment, drown. Almost the fisherman, waiting out infinity, envied him his pattern.

Freezing seas swept by, flooding inexorably up and up as the earth sank away imperceptibly beneath them. The boy called out once to his cousin. There was no answer. The fisherman, marvelling on a terror without voice, was dumbly glad when the boy did not call again. His own boots were long full of water. With no sensation left in his straddling legs he dared not move them. So long as the seas came sidewide against his hips, and then sidewise against his shoulders, he might balance—no telling how long. The upper half of him was what felt frozen. His legs, disengaged from his nerves and his will, he came to regard quite scientifically. They were the absurd, precarious axis around which reeled the surged universal tumult. The waves would come on; he could not visualize how many tossing reinforcements lurked in the night beyond—inexhaustible numbers, and he wept in supernatural fury at each because it was higher, till he transcended hate and took them, swaying like a convert, one by one as they lunged against him and away aimlessly into their own undisputed, wild realm.

From his hips upward the fisherman stretched to his utmost as a man does whose spirit reaches out of dead sleep. The boy's head, none too high, must be at least seven feet above the ledge. Though growing larger every minute, it was a small light life. The fisherman meant to hold it there, if need be, through a thousand tides.

By and by the boy, slumped on the head of his father, asked, "Is it over your boots, Dad?"

"Not yet," the fisherman said. Then through his teeth he added, "If I fall—kick your boots off—swim for it—downwind—to the island. . . ."

"You. . . ?" the boy finally asked.

The fisherman nodded against the boy's belly. "—Won't see each other," he said.

The boy did for the fisherman the greatest thing that can be done. He may have been too young for perfect terror, but he was old enough to know there were things beyond the power of any man. All he could do he did, trusting his father to do all he could, and asking nothing more.

The fisherman, rocked to his soul by a sea, held his eyes shut upon the interminable night.

"Is it time now?" the boy said.

The fisherman could hardly speak. "Not yet," he said. "Not just yet. . . ."

As the land mass pivoted toward sunlight the day after Christmas, a tiny fleet of small craft converged off shore like iron filings to a magnet. At daybreak they found the skiff floating unscathed off the headland, half full of ducks and snow. The shooting *had* been good, as someone hearing on the mainland the previous afternoon had supposed. Two hours afterward they found the unharmed boat adrift five miles at sea. At high noon they found the fisherman at ebb tide, his right foot jammed cruelly into a glacial crevice of the ledge beside three shotguns, his hands tangled behind him in his suspenders, and under his right elbow a rubber boot with a sock and a live starfish in it. After dragging unlit depths all day for the boys, they towed the fisherman home in his own boat at sundown, and in the frost of evening, mute with discovering purgatory, laid him on his wharf for his wife to see.

She, somehow, standing on the dock as in her frequent dream, gazing at the fisherman pure as crystal on the icy boards, a small rubber boot still frozen under one clenched arm, saw him exaggerated beyond remorse or grief, absolved of his mortality.